THE WOLF SHALL DWELL WITH THE LAMB

EMMET HIRSCH

VERMILION
THREAD PRESS

ISBN 978-0-9978430-2-6 (hardcover)
ISBN 978-0-9978430-3-3 (paperback)
ISBN 978-0-9978430-4-0 (ebook)
ISBN 978-0-9978430-5-7 (audiobook)

Cover Design by Miblart
Author photograph by Soohyun Kim. https://www.studiosoo.com/
Library of Congress Cataloging-in-Publication Data has been applied for.

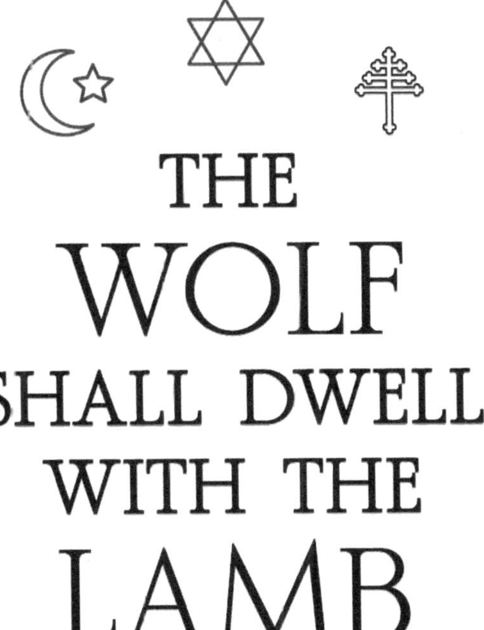

THE WOLF SHALL DWELL WITH THE LAMB

The wolf shall dwell with the lamb, and the leopard shall lie in repose with the young goat, and the calf and the lion and the yearling together; and a small child shall lead them.

Isaiah 11:6

Chapter One

The sun broke over the rolling hills of Bhamdoun, Lebanon, on April 1, 1931, and a fifteen-year-old Jewish girl cried out in terror and pain. Her lamentations mingled with the wails of a muezzin calling the Muslim faithful to prayer from his perch atop the town minaret, and with the soft chanting of lauds from the nearby convent.

The convergence of the three sounds was a common enough occurrence in that region at that time. Yet the weird harmony might have been considered a momentous sign as far as portents go. Most places, and the people who come from them, are the products of such uneasy admixtures. In that respect, the town of Bhamdoun was like most places. That is to say, it was a place from which the dissonance of everyday events might sound chords of blessing or misfortune echoing over a lifetime.

The girl was named Ziva. A house servant had heard her shrieks from his small chamber in the basement and ran upstairs to her bedroom. After knocking uncertainly on the door, he entered to find her screaming, blood pooling in her sheets. He threw a blanket onto the back seat of the Packard convertible, the only one of its kind in the Middle East and his master's prized possession, and loaded Ziva into it. From there, he sped to the infirmary, awakening the nuns with blares of the Packard's horn from outside the gate. The sisters hastened to open the lock.

They rushed Ziva, gasping, panting, a dark stain blooming over the lower part of her nightgown, into a small treatment room. Before allowing himself to be ushered out, the servant assured Ziva that he would wake the telegraph operator and send word to the master that his young bride had been taken to the hospital.

The attendant, a nun of indeterminate age, a white coif covering her hair and a wooden cross dangling from a black cord around her neck, wiped the girl's brow. "Shh, child," she murmured in Arabic as she tucked a wad moistened with some bitter substance between Ziva's cheek and gum. "It is God's decree that you endure this with dignity. Offer your pain up as a sacrifice to Him."

"What are you talking about? What is happening to me?"

"Why, child, do you not know you are having a baby?"

A baby! Ziva wailed and fainted.

As she came to, the room's white walls and metal furnishings blurred, as though layered with honey. Ziva breathed in and sighed, a deep exhalation that dislodged her consciousness and cast it backward in time and space. Gathering speed, she soared eastward over Mount Lebanon and the Beqaa Valley. In her delirium, she spied a prior version of herself far below in the passenger seat of the Packard, wending west on the Beirut-Damascus road, a middle-aged man at the wheel. Ziva flew over the neighborhoods of Damascus and through the open window of her family's estate in the Jewish quarter, alighting in the library of the house of her father, scion of the Hedaya clan. She looked up at the family tree spanning the southern wall of the room, its many branches proliferating from the source of the clan's glorious birthright: the lineage of King David himself.

Ziva had spent many hours sitting cross-legged on the floor contemplating this family tree, its boughs labeled with the names of traders, rabbis, physicians, royal advisers, and scholars of renown. Ziva's name, like those of other female relatives, was not listed. She had imagined it hidden behind those of her brothers, trapped like a dove in the foliage, neither seeing nor seen. The world outside her family and community, she had been told, was a heaving, vulgar, dangerous place, a place where corruption overwhelmed merit. It was the necessary province of her father and brothers but something from which she required protection.

In her dream, Ziva rose and approached her father, who sat scowling in his chair behind the desk, scholarly texts towering over them in shelves stacked to the ceiling. Her mother stood at his side, her face buried in her hands, her stooped frame shaking with sobs. Ziva's father's face was flushed, his beard flecked with gray hairs and spittle. "Thus do you bring shame upon us?" he thundered. "By consorting with a Christian boy?"

"Father!" Ziva cried. "It was nothing! I was only speaking to him!"

"Hush!" he shouted. "I have had business dealings with his father, an honorable man! Had he not come to me at the last moment, your shame would have stained both our families! A Jewish girl, my own daughter, escaping the house at night to meet with a boy? A *Christian* boy? Why not a Muslim? Why not a Kurd or Druze?"

"Father! There was nothing between us! We were only talking!"

"Enough, Ziva! Secret conversations in the middle of the night lead to other activities! His parents have already sent him to an uncle in Cairo."

"No!" cried Ziva. "Father, no!" She wanted to rush toward him, but the massive desk stood between them.

Her father lowered his eyes. "You make it very clear how much of a 'nothing' this boy is to you," he muttered. He rose and turned to face the window. "And as for you . . . as for you, my Ziva, my light, you will be married to a man named Friedmann within the month."

"Father!" Ziva wailed. "Father, hear me!"

"A very fortunate match, given the circumstances," he murmured, his face toward the window, the narrow alleyways of the city crowding in beyond. "Praise God, Friedmann approached the matchmaker not two weeks ago. Were it not for the reputation and fortune of our family, you would have been forsaken."

Ziva learned that her betrothed was a forty-five-year-old Belgian, a childless widower with a mansion in Beirut and a summer home in the village of Bhamdoun. He was an Ashkenazi Jew, she was told in apologetic tones, but no one else was available on such short notice. And Friedmann was very wealthy; he had business interests all over the Far East, Europe, and the Americas. The wedding would take place in three weeks.

Her mother tried to teach her something about "marital relations" before the wedding, and Ziva had nodded without understanding. Then, before she knew what was happening to her, Ziva had immersed in a *mikvah* and stood at the *chuppah*, a ring on her finger, the glass broken at her feet, strangers shouting, "Mazal tov!" Shortly after that, the unimagined horror of being laid on her back, her husband, sweating and groaning, on top of her. And then he was somehow inside her, together with a new, ripping pain and blood between her legs.

The following day, they had driven together in silence in the Packard to Beirut, where he introduced her to the household staff at his mansion. He left the following day on a business trip abroad. Friedmann had spent the majority of the time since then overseas, leaving her in care of the staff and returning from time to time to lay her again on her back and enter her as before. In the morning, they would share awkward conversations on the veranda over coffee and *shakshuka* before the arrival of business associates, to whom she was instructed to serve tea and sweet cakes, and not to speak.

Her mother came once to visit while Ziva was at the summer home in Bhamdoun. She praised the Lord that her daughter lived in more luxury than she had dared hoped for. She did not notice the swelling of Ziva's belly, concealed beneath a loose-fitting dress. And what was Ziva to make of this strange growth, which was but one more in a series of bewilderments, each related somehow to the preceding in ways she did not understand? Everything had happened so quickly, without preparation, without explanation. Having no one to consult, Ziva hid her shame and confusion from herself as well as others. Perhaps a resolution would come with time, or perhaps she might wake to find it all a dream. For all she knew, this change in her body might happen to anyone after being separated from her family, after marriage, after moving from Damascus to Beirut . . .

⸙

The drug began to wear off, and the images in Ziva's mind faded. She began to feel again the hard surface of the delivery table and the excruciating pain in her belly. The rest passed quickly, and Ziva could not be certain of the line between reality and imagination, only that she crossed it repeatedly in either direction. An elderly woman, dressed from head to foot in black, a cross at her neck and another at her hip, spoke kindly to her, introducing herself as "the abbess." A phantom materialized in a corner of the room, and when Ziva called out, "Father!" he turned away, disgust marring his face before he faded into nothingness.

Then, a man stood between her legs, and something about him frightened Ziva. "Stop shrieking, child!" the nurse commanded. "This is your doctor!"

The doctor was nothing like the kindly physician who had made house calls to her childhood home. He had three days of stubble on his chin and reeked of alcohol. He touched her roughly, and a short time later, her agony reached its peak and then abruptly subsided.

Panting and sobbing with her eyes screwed shut, Ziva heard a baby screech and a female voice call out, "*Mabrouk!* God has granted you a son!" Ziva opened her mouth to speak, but the world was again obliterated by a new kind of pain: being stitched together without anesthesia.

And then the nurse placed into her arms a baby swaddled in a blanket, and Ziva wept with this final rupture of everything she had known.

I was the child in that blanket.

Chapter Two

It is now nearly ninety years later. How can I claim my mother's recollections as though they are my own? Over time, I acquired knowledge that etched the events I have described into my consciousness, a falsehood no greater than all the other things I refer to as "memory." As I approach the end of my life, knowledge and memory have begun to blend like paint on a palette, creating something new through their merging and, often enough, blotting out what was once true. Many of my recollections are no longer things remembered so much as things I remember remembering, as though in their origin they belonged to someone else. They are no more and no less real than my reflection in a mirror.

Yesterday my arm was pierced with a needle for a blood test. Yet where is the pain I felt as the needle penetrated my skin? Even in the instant when it was the most prominent thing in my world, the pain was not a physical thing, a space-occupying object, a measurable article of which it might be said: This is real. I have come to understand that only two things are real: what one believes to be true, and love.

What most people fail to recognize, what I failed to recognize until late in life, is that in the absence of the latter, the former has no meaning.

I remember sitting on my mother's lap by the window, not yet four years old. A late-summer breeze sweeps the scent of cedars into the drawing room of our country house in Bhamdoun. I feel her cool forearm on my cheek. She gazes out the window and recites my favorite book from memory, a French version of the fable of the ant and the grasshopper. I turn the pages as she speaks, feeling sorry for the grasshopper, who wasted his summer on frivolous entertainments instead of preparing for winter. She pauses, and I look up to follow my mother's gaze. Terraced houses seem piled one atop another against the hillside, their sides painted bright blue, Levant-style, to ward off evil spirits. A flock of sheep grazes on the side of the mountain. A lorry labors up the winding road. But I cannot see the thing she appears to be focusing on.

There is a crash from somewhere in the house. She puts me down beside the chair, the sound of her bare feet soft on the Persian rug as she leaves the room to see which of the housekeepers has dropped a dish or vase or tureen filled with that afternoon's fruit compote.

I climb onto the armchair and feel my mother's warmth, already fading, on the cushion. I place the book in my lap. The words leap off the page in a burst of meaning, and suddenly, I am reading.

"Vous avez dansé et chanté tout l'été. Maintenant nourrisez-vous en dansant et en chantant pendant l'hiver!" ("You've been dancing and singing all summer long. Now feed yourself on dancing and singing during the winter!")

My early childhood was solitary but not lonely. When we were not at the country house, we lived in a three-story mansion on the north side of Beirut in the Wadi Abou Jamil neighborhood, also known as Wadi al Yahud, the Valley of the Jews. Even though it was a bustling community with schools, families, commerce, and a stately synagogue, I rarely ventured out to play in the streets with other children. My companions were my mother, little more than a melancholy child herself, and my governess, a kindly old Maronite woman named Rahma.

In the early mornings, I would slip out of bed and steal into my mother's room to watch her brush her long, black hair, the rhythm of her thin arms taking my breath away. Her eyes were sad and dark and deep, set above soft brown cheeks like almonds in melted chocolate. Her smile, a quivering, unfinished thing, was sometimes bestowed just upon me when she spied me observing her.

My father sent us postcards from time to time, and the images printed upon them merged in my imagination with the contents of my books, substituting for companions my own age. I created seafaring adventures in the bathtub, pretended that the kitchen and housekeeping staff were South American cannibals, imagined that the columns of books in the library were canyons I was navigating in a raft on the Yangtze River. I would engage in these fantasies for as long as I could before the ache for my mother drew me toward her. I would creep up on her in the drawing room while she read or sewed or sat gazing out the window. Then I would throw my arms around her neck and press my lips upon her sweet cheek, and afterward, I would continue playing on my own for a while. When I was bored, I employed Rahma as Friday to my Robinson Crusoe, or as a damsel in distress I would rescue from train robbers in the American Wild West. Rahma would grumble at the indignity, but she always indulged me.

Every few months, my father, in transit from the Orient to Moscow to Europe and back, would come to stay with us for several days at a time. I retain only a few images of him, each truncated by an unseen censor: a hand gripping the goose-head knob of an ebony cane; a razor-straight hairline above a crisp white collar; manicured fingers bringing a cup of Turkish coffee to bearded lips. And I remember the gifts—ivory figurines, lace napkins, ornate daggers, Venetian chocolate.

But more significant than things remembered are the things not remembered: no football practice in the courtyard, no warm hand on the shoulder, no declarations of affection. And, soon, nothing at all.

I was five years old when he visited us for the last time. I was sent to bed after opening my present, a spyglass he had purchased in London. ("Just like Long John Silver's!" he'd exulted.) I was awakened by the sounds of an argument in my mother's bedroom, indistinct roars and shrieks, and finally, the shattering of glass. My father's heavy footsteps crossed the floor and descended the staircase while he shouted instructions in Arabic to prepare his things. Then the sound of the servants' feet racing up from the basement and bustling in the foyer. He silenced a wailing Rahma, sending her to her room with an order not to emerge until morning. The front door slammed, and my father's motorcar roared off. I sprang out of bed, terrified, and raced toward my mother's room, stopping outside the closed door when I received proof that she was alive: the sound of her weeping. I listened for a while at the threshold, then lay down and fell asleep.

The following morning, I awoke with a start and crept through the open door into her room to discover she was not there. Panicking, I ran down the stairs and found her sitting in the drawing room in front of the open window, her hair disheveled, her eyes swollen, her face lined with the salty residue of tears.

"There is bad news, Joseph," she said.

I climbed into her lap and kissed her below the eyes.

"No, *Maman*," I answered. "I am here."

"Nonetheless, Joseph, there is bad news. Your father and I will no longer be living together. You and I are alone."

This didn't sound like bad news to me at all. On the contrary, it did not seem much different from our former situation, except for the absence of my father's intrusions upon our lives.

"What about Rahma? And Cook and the housekeepers? Will they be staying with us?"

My mother brushed the hair back from my face and bent her head to whisper in my ear, sending a thrill through me.

"Yes, for now, *chéri*. I am not sure about the future."

"Then that is fine, *Maman*," I said. "For now." I leaned back to rest in her arms, and we sat like that together for a long time.

Chapter Three

My physicians tell me that the cancer now filling my pelvis began as a single cell in my colon. It mutated, evading my immune system, and then proliferated. A small mass formed and, still undetected, breached the intestinal wall. The daughter cells, each more bizarrely transformed than its parent, migrated through my lymphatic system, lodged in my spine, overwhelmed my bone marrow and, most recently, crept into my brain.

My doctors estimate it took years for that first mutated cell to create the metastases that manifested as a nagging pain in my lower back. But from there, it was a whirlwind. An X-ray revealed a spine half eaten away by tumor. Another X-ray of my lungs led one physician to wonder aloud how I could breathe. Within three days of my first visit to a doctor in five years, I had become a dying man.

The devastation set in motion by the separation of my parents followed a relentless course. Like the man I was a few months ago, my five-year-old self was unaware that a malignancy had germinated and would eventually manifest in the tissue of his life, redefining him.

At first, our routines changed little. My mother's eyes dried, and we remained in the house in Beirut. The country house in Bhamdoun was forbidden to us. Rahma stayed on as my governess. She and my mother helped me learn to read and write in French and Arabic. I continued to occupy myself with books and self-generated tales of adventure. I did not see my father again, but on every birthday, he sent a gift—one year an electric train set; another, the complete Sherlock Holmes collection. With the arrival of the mid-1930s, we heard echoes of trouble brewing for the Jews of distant Europe, but it seemed of little consequence to us.

In the fall of the year I turned six, I was sent to school at the *Alliance Israélite Universelle*, within walking distance of our house. The knowledge that after school my mother would be waiting for me at home, that she would sit with me while I ate my lunch, teach me to play the piano, and send me out the following morning with the imprint of a kiss from her sweet lips on my forehead—these things sustained me in my hours of separation from her. Somehow, the absence of a father did not mark me as an outcast at school. I became a favorite of the teachers and popular with the other children. I excelled at schoolwork, was chosen first for pickup games of football, was a spirited opponent at backgammon and unbeatable at chess.

One day, at the age of eight, I came home to find not my mother but Rahma standing at the door. After lunch, I was left to read and practice the piano on my own. Another day, I came trotting through the gate in time to see a man in his midtwenties, dressed in a suit, tie, and hat, step into a motorcar parked outside our house and drive away.

And then came the day when I ran into the drawing room and found my mother standing in her usual spot by the window. I stopped short at the sight of her. She wore a green dress with a narrow waist and hemline above the knee. Her hair was braided and folded up in the back, and a red hat swooped fashionably toward her forehead, a feather at its crest. And when she turned to face me, a strange sight: lipstick. We stared at each other, both of us out of breath.

I noticed a man's hat resting on the table beside the window, a hat I now know as a skimmer, with a red band wrapped above the brim.

"*Maman*, what is wrong?" I asked.

"Nothing, *chéri*. Everything is fine. As a matter of fact, everything is *very* fine." She smiled strangely, showing her teeth.

"Something is wrong. What is it?"

She sighed. "Joseph, I have someone I would like to introduce to you. An old friend." She stepped out of the room into the adjacent library and returned with the young man I had spied getting into his car several months earlier. He wore a smart double-breasted suit with a striped tie, a scarf about his neck, and ridiculous two-toned shoes. A lit cigarette jutted out between thin lips. I hated him immediately.

"Who is this man?" I demanded of my mother in Hebrew, a language we used when we did not want the servants to understand us, and which I knew instinctively was foreign to him.

"Do not be rude, Joseph," she snapped in French. Then, more softly: "Come shake hands and say, *enchanté.* This is Pierre. He and I were neighbors when we were your age. He has recently returned from Cairo."

Reluctantly, I stepped forward and offered my hand. I remember trying to hurt him by squeezing hard, a foolish, childish thing to do, the memory of which continues to humiliate me all these years later. His hand dwarfed my own and crushed it. I suppressed a cry of pain. He narrowed his eyes, and a cold smile curled on his lips as he held my gaze in his own. Then he picked up his hat, nodded at my mother, murmured, *"Ma'a salaame,"* and strode from the room.

My mother's absences began to extend to most afternoons and, soon thereafter, to evenings. Within a few weeks, I was eating dinner alone and putting myself to sleep. She would creep into my room late at night, preceded by the creaking of the door and the smell of alcohol and cigarettes. She would kiss me while I, terrified, pretended to sleep.

Soon I discovered the full-grown malignancy that had sprouted in the space vacated by my father. I returned from school one day to find my mother waiting for me in her chair in the drawing room. "Sit down, Joseph," she said. "I have something important to tell you."

Writing these words all these years later, I am powerless to do more than bear witness. The phrase *I have something important to tell you* is the moment from which the life I knew in my childhood flickers, fades, and is extinguished. The shadow cast by these words created a void that neither memory nor imagination had the capacity to fill for many years. It was the black hole at the center of my universe. Not even illusion could escape it.

Decades later, when I finally became immune to both pain and recollection, I acquired the knowledge of things as I relate them in this narrative. But by the time the child and the memory could inhabit the same person and survive, who might determine what was real?

This is what I now know: That my mother had been lonely and unhappy since before her marriage. That after her divorce, she needed a husband and protector. That Pierre, a Christian with whom she had shared the forbidden love that precipitated her hurried union with my father, proposed marriage. That she had accepted. That Pierre refused to raise another man's son in his house. That I was to be sent away. That my father would have nothing to do with us anymore.

That the hatred I felt for all three of them would have annihilated me had I not buried it deep.

Chapter Four

I was deposited outside a tranquil compound in the town of Bhamdoun—I know not by whom—and stood near an iron gate spanning a stone archway. The car from which I had been instructed to emerge with my valise sounded its horn. A chill was in the early morning air. I peered through the bars, my breath dissipating in the courtyard on the other side. A dark figure emerged from the wooden doorway of the building beyond, and the car gunned its engine and sped away.

It was a woman, bent over as though she were burdened with a large sack. She gathered the skirt of her black habit in her fist and shuffled sideways down the steps, her face unseen behind a white coif and wimple. Reaching the bottom of the short flight of stairs, she turned and hobbled toward me. The grim line of a mouth came into focus, wrinkles radiating from it toward the outer reaches of her face and merging with the angles of her eyes.

She scrutinized me while working her way across the gravel courtyard. Finally, she reached the gate where I stood with my suitcase at my feet.

"*Shalom Aleichem*," she said. I was surprised by the youthful voice that emerged from the craggy face, and by her use of the Hebrew formulation of the traditional greeting.

She waited.

"*Aleichem shalom*," I finally responded.

"Ah, it speaks!" she declared in Arabic. "Come in, then, since I now know that you are civilized."

She withdrew an enormous key ring from beneath her habit. Using the backs of her knotted fingers, she found one that unlocked the gate, backing away as she swung it open on squealing hinges. I picked up my bag and took one step forward.

"Well? Don't just stand there. Come all the way in! I can't close the gate with you standing in the middle of it like a frightened cow, can I?"

And when I failed to move: "*Eyes have they but see not; ears have they but hear not.* Are you there, boy? Please come in through the gate so that it may be shut."

I took three steps forward and turned to face her.

Her eyes flashed. "*Hallelujah! Give thanks to the Lord, for He is good. For His mercy endureth forever.*" She raised the key ring and gave it a vigorous shake. "Would you be so good, child, as to shut and lock the gate for me? In my old age, it has become difficult for me to accomplish even so simple a task as keeping the world and its profanity out of our virtuous grounds." As she spoke, the line of her mouth stretched sideways, an expression I eventually came to recognize as a smile.

I took the key ring from her and selected the key I had seen her use from among the fifteen or more it held. She seemed impressed by this achievement and nodded her approval. I swung the gate closed and locked it. She retrieved the keys, which she deposited beneath her habit. Over the course of time, I saw a great many things disappear beneath that habit. For all I knew, it contained a portal to another dimension.

"My name is Mother Maria Theresa. I am the abbess of this convent."

I gaped at her. Though I had seen plenty of nuns in the streets of Beirut, I had never spoken to one, nor had I any notion of the meaning of the words *abbess* and *convent.*

"And you? Do you have a name?" When I did not answer, she asked, "Is your name Joseph Friedmann?"

Still, I gawked at her.

"Are you eight years old?"

I did not answer.

She sighed. "All right, Joseph, have it your way. I suspect, however, that you will find your tongue when it comes time to ask someone to pass you the potatoes. Let us go inside."

She hobbled toward the entrance from which she had emerged and up the stairs. I had to wait at each step until she lumbered up to it. As we crossed the threshold, I could hear chanting from within. It was a rich sound of female voices, otherworldly and harmonious, nothing like the cacophonous wailing I associated with Jewish prayers. We stood for a moment, taking in the building's warmth. The abbess smiled again. Then she turned to the right and slowly led me down the hall.

The passageway was lined with statues and paintings of saints and priests and nuns and biblical scenes. There were long hallways branching left from the one we traversed, and from one of these emanated the sound of children reciting something in unison. At the end of the passageway was her office, and she led me to it, gesturing for me to sit in one of the two chairs in front of her desk while she worked her way around to the other side and heaved herself into her own seat, breathing heavily.

We sat staring at each other for a few minutes. She employed the thumb and forefinger of her right hand to stroke the thin moustache that grew on her upper lip.

Finally, she spoke again: "I know you, Joseph."

You do not, I said to myself. *I have never seen you before.*

"You are wrong, my boy. I witnessed your birth!" And upon seeing my astonishment, she added, "What do you find so surprising, that I remember so vividly the moment of your birth or that I can read your mind? No small measure of both, I suspect.

"Joseph, since you are not inclined to speak, I will continue for both of us, yes? Question one: What am I doing here? Answer: Your mother sent you here to be cared for and educated.

"Question two: What is this place? Answer: This is a convent, an institution where young women spend several years preparing to become nuns in the Maronite Church, a branch of the Catholic Church.

"Question three: What does a convent have to do with me? I have no intention of becoming a nun! Answer: I am glad to hear it. As part of our good works, we have several additional undertakings here. One of these is the infirmary where you were born. A second you will learn about later. The third is a schoolroom for local children ages eight to fifteen. Despite our small size, we are proud to have the finest schoolteacher in all of Lebanon. You will be a student in that school, but unlike the other pupils, after class is done, you will have the good fortune of staying on our grounds as a member of our large family. This"—she swept her arm about her to indicate the compound that lay outside her office—"is your new home. Naturally, you will be expected to contribute your services to our community, as all who dwell here do.

"Question four: But I am a Jewish boy! Why has my mother sent me to a Maronite institution? Answer: Ah, there are some things that even I am unable to answer and have the good sense not to try. But Joseph . . ." Here, her dark eyes narrowed. "I have no intention of turning you into a Catholic boy. We will do our best to provide you with a general education, which in this place includes lessons in Christianity. We will also educate you in what we know of your faith. If you are interested in learning more than we can teach you, you will have to create those opportunities on your own."

She sat peering at me through her clouded eyes and then grasped the armrests of her chair. With effort, she hauled herself to a standing position.

"And now, Joseph, seeing that you have no additional questions . . ." She smiled again and, picking up a small bell, gave it a shake. "I will have one of our novices show you to your quarters."

Before the echo of the bell had died away, a girl a few years older than I appeared at the door. Her head was uncovered, and thick ginger curls, bound in a cord at the nape of the neck, cascaded over her shoulder.

"Isabella," said the abbess, "please take Master Friedmann to his room and then to class." Then, addressing me, the abbess added, "I will see you again at dinner, Joseph, where the potatoes will be just out of your reach."

Again, her mouth stretched sideways.

Isabella smiled and turned on her heels. I followed her down one of the side halls, through several doors and around corners, up three floors of a spiral stone staircase, and to the end of one of several narrow passageways. She attempted to comport herself with the dignity of her elders but was unable to suppress the bounce in her gait, the smile that constantly played on her lips, and the shimmering of her gray eyes.

Isabella pushed open a wooden door to reveal a tiny room containing a cot, a chest, a nightstand with a basin and jug on its surface, and a chamber pot in the space below it. A writing desk and matching wooden chair stood by the southern wall under a small window. There was a candleholder on the desk and a bare shelf above it. The only other furnishing was one I discovered later: a hook on the back of the door, which had no latch or lock. I later learned that mine was the only room in the complex without a crucifix. This kindness, one of hundreds great and small shown me by the abbess, moves me even all these years later.

"This is where you live now!" Isabella said, smiling. Her voice sounded like the bell the abbess had rung to summon her.

I clambered up the chair and stood on the desk. I opened the window latch and swung open the little door to peer outside. Crisp air wafted in. I gazed upon the mountains and heard boys at play in the courtyard just out of my field of view.

"It's quite an agreeable room, don't you think?" Isabella asked eagerly. "It's nicer than the novices' rooms, and a thousand times nicer than my old room at home. And you don't even have to share it!"

"Well, it is nothing like *my* old room at home."

"Did your old room have brothers and sisters in it, and your father's tools, and the dining room table, and aunts and uncles and grandparents, and sometimes goats and chickens?"

"No. It had books and toys and a globe, and it was my room alone. And my mother was in the house."

"Oh, well, then your old room was nothing like my old room, and this room must not seem so fine to you as it does to me."

"I suppose not. But still, I like it." And so I did.

"I will show you the outhouses on our way to the classroom. How were your outhouses?"

"They weren't . . . Our outhouses were inside the house."

"Yuck!" She giggled. "That's disgusting. I have heard about strange things in the city." She shrugged. "Anyway, put down your bag. You can unpack later. The abbess told me to take you directly to class."

She led me back the way we had come, a route so circuitous, it took me two days to learn it on my own. We found the main corridor and turned into the classroom from where I had previously heard the sounds of recitation. We walked through the open door to find the teacher standing with her back to us at the front of an empty classroom. She was writing in beautiful Arabic script on the blackboard.

"*Salaam aleikum*, Madame Farouq," Isabella chirped. "This is Joseph Friedmann."

Madame Farouq turned from the board to examine us. Her face looked like a prune having a bad day. Though she seemed to be about 150 years old, her hair was jet black and her eyes shone. She stood erect, her head topping out at an elevation slightly higher than mine. She gave an energetic grin and put her hands on her hips, the better to survey me.

"*Ahlan wasahlan*, Yusouf!" she declared, using the Arabic pronunciation of my name. My name had always been spoken with the French or Hebrew pronunciation. I didn't mind that she renamed me. I later learned that Madame Farouq renamed all her students. If they preferred the French, she called them by their Arabic names. If they preferred Arabic, she called them by their Latin names. And in some cases, she simply made up a name that was more to her liking than the one given to the student by his parents.

"*Ahlan bi'iki*," I whispered.

"I have prepared a desk for you in the front row, Yusouf." She showed it to me. Like all the others in the classroom, it was a two-seater. A pile of disintegrating books was stacked in front of the left-hand seat. "Did you bring a pencil and paper?"

"No, Madame."

She reached into the top drawer of her desk and withdrew a sharpened pencil and notebook. "These are my first, and least significant, gifts to you, Yusouf. The rest will come in the form of knowledge, for which you will never be able to repay me. The pencil I will want back." She stared at me without a hint of a smile. Then she grinned ferociously, reminding me of a photo of President Roosevelt I had seen in the newspaper, though Madame Farouq didn't have a cigarette holder in the corner of her mouth.

The school bell sounded, and I took my seat. A few moments later, a crowd of about thirty boys of various ages ran through the door, smelling of sweat, dirt, candy, and blood. They each stopped short and fell silent when they saw me.

"Take your seats, please," called Madame Farouq, "and be quick about it!" She turned to write something on the chalkboard. A mousy little boy my age but smaller than I sat beside me.

"I am Émile," he whispered.

"Émile, *débile*! (stupid)" a voice directly behind me whispered. I turned and saw that it belonged to a leering boy of about fifteen with rotting teeth.

The clamor rose again while Madame Farouq finished writing on the board: *Yusouf Friedmann*. Before she could lay down the chalk, a guffaw issued from the back row of the class.

"Charles!" she snapped without turning around. 'Charles,' whose real name was Ibrahim Malik, sat in the back row of the classroom.

The rumor I heard later was that he was either repeating fifth grade for the third time or third grade for the fifth time. His nickname, 'Charlie,' was inspired by the film portrayal of an American gangster of that name, whom the boy admired. Charlie was "chairman" of a gang of hoodlums who called themselves *The Committee* and whose main mission consisted of terrorizing the other children in the class. Madame Farouq infuriated Charlie by calling him *Charles*, which she always uttered derisively.

"Charles!" Madame Farouq repeated. "You will kindly cease your discussion with Master Malouf regarding the merits of English football!"

Madame Farouq's ability to comprehend each of several conversations occurring simultaneously while she was reading or writing never failed to astound me.

"Class," she said, turning around. "This is Yusouf Friedmann. He is new to our school. I am confident you will demonstrate your usual civility in welcoming him."

I heard murmurs. *Friedmann? What kind of name is that?*

"At the end of class, you can ask him all the questions you like. Now, please, open your history books to the section on the Greek conquest."

The afternoon was spent studying history, French, and Arabic literature. The rest of the curriculum included Catholic practice and theology, Latin, geography, mathematics, and science. Madame Farouq, whose expertise seemed limitless, had no trouble maintaining order with a savage smile or clever remark. But her pupils were restless, and it was apparent that most were not interested in scholarship, a departure from what I had been accustomed to at Alliance.

At the end of the school day, the boys gathered their things and ran out to the courtyard. I went along with them, cautiously standing to the side as they kicked around a decaying soccer ball. No one spoke to me. Suddenly, a shoe came flying out of a second-story window and landed at my feet. The youth with rotting teeth ran up, shoved me aside, picked up the shoe, and threw it back at the perpetrator.

I was unaccustomed to being shoved and, without thinking, walked up to the boy who had pushed me and pushed him back.

In an instant, all activity on the playground ceased. There was a moment of silence, and then shouts and ululations from all directions as boys streamed toward me. I discovered that I had become the sole agenda item for an impromptu meeting of The Committee. Two members pinned my arms behind me, as the remainder, led by Charlie, lined up and took turns punching me in the stomach. The boys knew their work. No adults were on the playground to witness what they were doing, and they left no marks on my person. When each had had his turn, they left me on my knees and ran out of the playground, the last of them cursing me with the word "Jew!" and spitting in my hair.

Émile helped me up, whispering fiercely: "Are you crazy? They will never leave you alone now as long as you are here. You will wish that you had a thousand shoes to give them to throw at you. And don't tell the teacher, or it will get even worse for you than you can imagine."

I held back my tears and let Émile lead me to rest under a tree. One by one the boys left the compound, some picked up by sleek cars, and others slinging their bags on their shoulders and exiting through the cast-iron gate to walk down the hill to their homes. I made my way back to the empty classroom, where I sat to do my homework. When that was done, I picked up the first book on the right of the top shelf of the small collection and started to read. It was an Arabic translation of the poetry of Omar Khayyam.

When the dinner bell rang, Isabella appeared and took me to the dining room. I was led to a seat at the end of a bench by a long wooden table. To my side and in front of me, solemn nuns arrayed themselves, their heads bowed until the conclusion of grace. I answered none of their questions and made no requests. They loaded my plate with potatoes anyway. I noted the abbess eyeing me from the head table but did not look at her directly. I sat in silence and picked at my food.

After dinner, Isabella helped me find my room. We did not speak to each other, and she left without a word. I unpacked my things: three sets of underclothes, one pair of pajamas, two sets of school clothes, a toothbrush, a washcloth, a towel, a fountain pen, an inkwell, a pad of paper, stamps, and envelopes. I sat down to write my mother a letter, describing my day but omitting my beating at the hands of The Committee.

I wrote her a letter every day for the first two months, an attempt to prevent the fading of my mind's image of her. I never received a reply, but kept writing until the letters started returning, stamped: *Return to sender. No forwarding address.*

I blew out the candle and lay in bed, making plans for the following day.

In the middle of the night, I was awakened by howls coming from beyond one of the courtyard walls. They emanated from the second of the nunnery's good works, the one Mother Maria Theresa told me I would "learn about later." In the adjacent courtyard was an insane asylum, for which the convent provided staffing and other support. The inmates of the asylum were screaming.

Chapter Five

After a night of fitful sleep, I was awakened by the crowing of a rooster and the bleating of goats. A faint light dawned beyond the small window, and I could feel the chill that seeped through its damp pane. I lay in bed listening to the sounds of my new home—a cowbell ringing dully in the distance, a muezzin's cry, the baying of dogs. It was a peaceful counterpoint to the bustle of Beirut, where at the same time of day there would be lorries rumbling through the streets and peddlers hawking their wares in the alleyways. Sweeping my feet out from under the woolen blanket, I was sitting on the edge of the bed when a knock came on the door. I pulled on my pants and rose to open it. It was Isabella.

"*Sabah al-khair!*" she chirped from the threshold, and I wished her a good morning in return. "Time to get ready! Do you need any help with anything?"

"I will need help finding my way out of here. If you don't want me to be missing for the next month and are willing to wait for me, I can be ready in five minutes."

As Isabella waited for me in the hallway, I washed my hands and face and dressed in my school clothes. Isabella led me downstairs, where I stopped at the outhouses. We made our way to breakfast, and I took my seat while the nuns gathered in silence before saying grace. My sparse dinner from the night before had left me famished. I intercepted the serving dishes as they made their way around, loading generous portions onto my plate and ignoring the nuns' suppressed smiles. One serving bowl was kept from me. When I asked to examine its contents, they refused. *Khinzir*, one of them announced, wagging her finger. And so my first taste of pork had to wait until a future time, when I could pilfer it from the kitchens. The residents of the convent never willingly gave me any—not even once.

When breakfast was done, each of us was required to take our pewter plates and silverware to the washing station, where we were to clean our dishes, dry them, and stack them on the shelves. I waited until everyone was done and did as the others did before tucking the dish inside my shirt and sliding the fork into my pocket.

At that moment, the abbess's voice sounded behind me. "*Sabah al-khair*, Joseph," she announced. The shock of hearing her voice caused me to jump, and I felt the plate slide down my pants. Had she seen me pinch the dish and silverware? Her eyes were so clouded with cataracts, and I had been so careful about disguising my actions, that I dared hope she hadn't noticed. On the other hand, it had already been amply demonstrated that the abbess required no direct line of sight to see all that needed seeing. I turned around and would have been glad to find her ghost there. To my disappointment, it was Mother Maria Theresa in the flesh.

She peered at me. "Did you sleep well?"

"Yes, Mother Maria Theresa."

"How was your first day with us?"

"Very good, Mother."

"I am glad to hear it! How did the psalmist put it? *Let the morning bring me word of Your unfailing love, for I have put my trust in You.*" She scrutinized me some more, and I thought I could feel the plate heating up in my trousers. She seemed to be summoning it. I was grateful the dish was too large to slide down my pants leg and clatter onto the floor.

"You will report to the kitchen after class today."

I swallowed hard.

"You recall that you are expected to contribute to our community, yes? The cook informs me that today your contribution will consist of slicing vegetables."

I nodded.

"May you have a day of affirmation, Joseph."

"The same to you, Mother."

She turned and shuffled away, and I resolved to look up the meaning of the word *affirmation* later.

I made my way to class.

The members of The Committee were already in their seats. It was easy to deduce that punctuality was not a trait these boys cultivated for its academic benefits. The leers on their faces assured me of what I had already guessed: Their eagerness was not to learn a lesson but to teach one, and that I was to be the student. I slid into my chair in front of the boy with rotting teeth and began to unpack my books. Soon whispers began: "Friedmann . . . Friedmann . . ." they sang softly. And when I didn't respond: "*Yahudmann . . .* hey, *Yahudmann!*" I felt something wet hit me in the neck and fall down the back of my shirt. I turned to find the boy with rotting teeth smirking as he balled up another piece of paper, inserted it in his mouth, and started to chew. The murmuring stopped abruptly a few minutes later, when the remaining students and Madame Farouq entered the class.

The rest of the day was filled with insults and humiliations. A foot was extended, tripping me when I was called to the blackboard. My lunch, a cheese and olive sandwich I had prepared at the breakfast table, was dropped onto the floor and stepped upon. I dared not leave the room even to go to the bathroom until an opportunity arose when I finished a quiz before anyone else in the class. I stayed indoors during recess and began reading the second book on the shelf, *The Jewish War* by Flavius Josephus.

When the school day was finally over, all the pupils stood, as was the custom, while Madame Farouq gathered her things. She left the room followed by a rush of students, leaving behind only the members of The Committee and myself.

"*Yahudmann . . . Yahudmann . . .*" came the taunts. "Your mamma is not here . . . Where is your father? It's bad enough to be a Jew, but a Jew bastard? The worst!"

I stood, facing the backboard. "Charles . . ." I crooned, using the same singsong voice as my tormentors.

The room snapped silent.

"Charles," I repeated. "Can you hear me, Charles?"

A chair in the back of the room scraped on its legs and fell as Charlie stepped away from his seat. "What did you call me?" he growled.

"I called you *Charles,*" I said placidly. I strolled into the aisle between the desks and turned to face the rear of the classroom. "That is what your mother told me to call you." I had learned on the streets of Beirut that insulting a mother was considered an even greater offense among the Arabs than among the Jews.

"My *mother*? You speak of my mother?"

"Yes, Charles, I speak of your mother, because your sister is too ugly to speak of."

I saw Charlie's eyes widen and his pupils dilate. He rushed at me and cocked his right arm back.

"Not in the face! Not in the face!" his compatriots yelled.

Charlie walloped me in the belly. I flew backward and collided with Madame Farouq's desk, receiving a vicious blow to my hip. But Charlie let out a roar. He had shattered his fingers on the pewter plate I had hidden under my shirt. He stared at his broken fingers and then, howling, rushed at me, drawing his left arm back to strike me with his fist, this time aiming directly at my face. At the last instant, I pulled the fork out of my pocket and swung it up into the path of his arm. He was impaled on the fork, which I felt scrape against bone. Charlie howled in agony, and with a quick motion, I steadied his wrist and pulled out the fork. He crumpled to the floor.

"Is there anyone else who wishes to call me a name?" I asked, taking a step toward the desks.

I turned to the boy with rotting teeth, who stood rooted to his spot, his hands splayed on the desk in front of him. "How about you?" I asked, and with a swift movement brought the fork down. I had intended to stab him, but Providence provided a better outcome, giving the impression not only of ruthlessness but also of supernatural aim. He recoiled, but not before the fork stood embedded in the wood of his desk where the gap between his second and third fingers had been. "Did you lose a piece of paper in my shirt this morning?" I hissed.

The rest of the boys stared at me in terror and then beat a retreat, leaving everything behind, including their fallen leader and his deputy. I stepped over Charlie and left the room, plucking the fork out of the desk and the Josephus from the bookcase on my way out. I knew that rumors of the fight would spread, but I was fairly certain, based upon what I had learned in the streets of Beirut about the code of honor among Arab hooligans, that they would not share details with the staff or their parents. Charlie would conceal his injuries, and The Committee would leave me out of their future activities.

I made my way to the kitchen. When the cook stepped outside for a cigarette break, I removed the plate from inside my shirt. I flattened the dent from Charlie's fist using a meat mallet, washed it, and returned it to the shelf. I had to discard the fork, as its tines were hopelessly bent.

The rest of the afternoon was spent peeling cucumbers and slicing tomatoes and onions. I ate a hearty dinner, returned to my room, did my homework by the light of my candle, wrote a letter to my mother, and read a few chapters from Josephus.

I slept well.

Chapter Six

I never spoke to anyone of my confrontation with The Committee. No one accosted me ever again, nor did I acquire friends at school, even among those whose vulnerabilities might have drawn them to me. One by one, members of The Committee aged out of our little program—it cannot be said that they graduated—and were replaced by younger pupils. Furtive glances and fingers pointed in my direction confirmed that new students were advised to keep a respectful distance from *al Yahudi* (the Jew).

Five years passed. I read the books on the schoolroom shelf and all the books in the main library, about a thousand volumes. My classroom learning and independent reading provided me with a broad but not all-encompassing education. I became an expert on the history of the Middle East, Rome, and ancient Greece. I was an authority on Catholic theology, the poetry of the Middle Ages, military history through the Russo-Japanese War, and the flora of the Lebanese highlands, among other topics. Were it not for the 1912 edition of the *Encyclopaedia Britannica*—with which the abbess had stocked the library unredacted despite the dubious morals of its editors—I would have known next to nothing of the existence of the Americas, astronomy, the theater, or the Far East. There was a small shelf with works of fiction that somehow had made their way onto the grounds, all classics. I read and reread *The Count of Monte Cristo*, *Oliver Twist*, *War and Peace*, and *The Call of the Wild*.

When I could, I read all these works in their original languages. I had become fluent not only in Arabic and French, but in Latin and English as well. I kept up my Hebrew through reading and rereading the abbey's single Hebrew copy of the Old Testament with French translation. Later, when I arrived in Palestine, I was teased because I spoke Hebrew like a psalmist in my

Arabic accent. It would take me months to learn the vast quantities of modern Hebrew that had been invented to render the ancient tongue suitable for use in the modern world.

My fondness for adventure thrived on Scripture. I thrilled at Noah's seafaring voyage, Joshua's conquest of Canaan, Jonah's adventure in the whale. I pretended I was David, stealing into King Saul's camp at night and cutting off the corner of his garment to demonstrate that I might have killed him. I was Ehud, son of Gera, the left-handed hero, infiltrating the throne room of King Eglon, the Moabite, and slaying him with a blade concealed on my right thigh. After reading that story, I taught myself to do everything with either hand to be prepared for just such an eventuality.

I pretended I was Gideon resisting the call to lead the Israelite rebellion against Midian: "How shall I deliver Israel?" I protested modestly, knowing in my heart that I was up to the task. "My family is the least in Manasseh, and I am the youngest in my father's house." And then I imagined myself at the waters of Ein Harod, selecting from more than thirty thousand volunteers my army of a mere three hundred men, chosen by virtue of the fact that they lapped at the spring like dogs instead of kneeling to cup the water in their hands. And with this meager army, I defeated the hordes of Midian using the only weapons available: trumpets, torches, and empty clay pitchers.

I read and reread Josephus's description of the last stand of the Jews against the Romans at Masada, and I delivered from memory, in the solitude of my room, the impassioned speech of Eleazar, son of Yair, advocating for mutual suicide rather than surrender: "I think it is God who has given us this privilege, to breathe our last nobly and as free men . . . Let our wives die unabused, our children without knowledge of slavery . . . Let us do each other an ungrudging kindness."

My isolation from the outside world led to gaping holes in my knowledge and experience. I knew little of music other than the solemn chants and hymns issuing from the chapel and what I read in the encyclopedia. I had only a rudimentary understanding of art. The world outside our quiet community was convulsing during the world war of the late 1930s and early 1940s, yet I knew almost nothing of current events. There were no newspapers at the compound, and its only radio was rumored to reside in the doctor's office in the infirmary.

I had to invent humor on my own. Residents of the convent seemed to consider amusement a kind of character flaw, despite the abundant quantities of wit possessed by the abbess and Madame Farouq. Everything Madame Farouq said had at least two meanings, and she grinned so much that I was certain I failed to understand half of whatever she was saying. Despite my academic accomplishments, I felt like a village idiot compared to Madam Farouq. In the presence of Mother Maria Theresa, I felt naked and exposed.

Every day I performed a variety of chores and became expert in those also. I invented new methods of washing dishes, such that on the days when I was assigned to clean up, the sisters marveled at the speed and thoroughness with which the job was done. I designed a watering system for the vegetable gardens, securing permission from the abbess to punch tiny holes in the hose, which I laid along the roots of each of the plants, a drip irrigation system of my own invention. I discovered through experimentation that I could perfectly peel dozens of hard-boiled eggs in the time most people peeled one, by shaking the cooled eggs in a container until the shells cracked, then simply lifting out the eggs like snakes shedding their skin. I often accompanied the handyman who was summoned from time to time to tinker with the convent's many decrepit fixtures and machines. I learned how to fix nearly anything and soon exceeded my master in skill. The sisters, seeing that my repairs were more long-lasting than the handyman's, began to call upon me to tend to their squeaky door hinges, bent keys, broken kerosene heaters, and even the 1928 Ford pickup truck, the sole almost-modern convenience on the grounds.

Of sexual attraction, I learned using the method by which boys have learned such things since time immemorial, which is to say that I was swept up and consumed in its fire without understanding what was happening to me. Isabella blossomed, her auburn hair igniting me as I lay alone in bed. Her smile—perpetual, gorgeous, freely shared without shame or embarrassment— filled me with a strange hunger and led me to do things to myself I had not read about in any of my books. I remember feeling no shame for these acts, only curiosity for how they fit into the workings of the world, about which I knew I had only a veiled understanding.

For my thirteenth birthday, the abbess presented me with a key to the front gate, and thereafter I was allowed to come and go as I pleased. Almost every afternoon and on weekends, I would exit the grounds for long walks in the countryside. I knew every trail, every farm, every shop, every factory, and every building in a ten-kilometer radius, including the walled private homes of the wealthy, one of which I now know was my father's summer house on the north edge of the village. If I ever saw him on any of these excursions, I am unaware of it.

One Saturday morning, I borrowed a bicycle from the mail delivery boy, with whom I had become friendly, and rode out of the hills westward from Bhamdoun along the Beirut-Damascus road. Rounding a curve after about fifteen kilometers, I saw the city of Beirut lying like a sleeping alley cat on its peninsula in the Mediterranean blue, the limestone walls of its buildings interlaced with thin strips of pavement, its patchwork surface broken by the occasional minaret, church spire, or government building. I straddled the bicycle, gazing down upon the city, and my eye—or was it my heart?—was drawn to the port at its northern edge. I remembered that our house used to be in the neighborhood just south and west of there, a short distance from the large synagogue, whose hulking form and red tile roof I could easily see. I stepped on the pedal and rode down.

The April sun was hot, and I strolled around the Wadi Abou Jamil neighborhood, rolling the bicycle along beside me. The Jewish men were in the streets, walking home from prayers at the grand synagogue clad in dark pants, white shirts, and black hats, their children trailing behind or holding their hands. The women and their grown daughters were at home preparing the midday Sabbath meal. I remembered being one of those children during the High Holy Days, when, in the early years, my father always returned to Beirut from his travels. The Jewish stores were closed for the Sabbath, but the adjacent Christian and Muslim shops were open for business, and warm greetings were exchanged between the Jews and the shopkeepers. No one spoke to me; I was either invisible or no more than a common guttersnipe to them.

I wound my way to our old home without any difficulty and stood outside its limestone wall for several minutes before a young man walked up, pushing a stroller while a child of about five trotted alongside him. A servant I didn't recognize opened the gate and welcomed them with a solemn "*Marhaban, ya sayyidi.*" Two women wearing aprons stood in the shaded courtyard behind the servant, and I desperately peered past him to catch a glimpse, but neither one of them was my mother or Rahma.

After the man and his two children entered through the gate, the servant spied me standing at my observation post. "*Akhraj min hun!*" he yelled, shooing me away and taking three menacing steps toward me. I turned the bicycle around and pedaled away. I never looked upon that house again.

I rode up the mountain and back to Bhamdoun, arriving at the convent with dusk.

Chapter Seven

When I reached the compound in Bhamdoun, I leaned the bicycle on my hip and fished in my pocket for the key but was surprised to discover the gate ajar. A harsh keening arose from the main building, and dropping the bicycle to rush inside, I collided with Isabella, tears streaming down her face. She threw herself into my arms, and though I knew something was terribly wrong, I felt an unnamed thrill.

"What happened?" I asked.

"It's . . . it's . . . Mother . . . She's . . ." She sobbed and buried her face in my neck.

"What about her?" I demanded. "What happened to the Mother Superior?"

Isabella squeezed me harder. "She's gone!"

I do not know why we were all so shocked that the abbess was suddenly taken from us. She had always seemed to me the oldest thing in existence, possibly the oldest thing that had ever existed. For all I knew, she had taken her vows from Saint Peter himself. We assumed that, since she had apparently been living forever, she would simply continue living forever. Her growing frailty was, in retrospect, an inevitable sign of her—and our—coming doom.

Two days later, Mother Maria Theresa was buried in the center plot of the convent's cemetery, her funeral attended by every member of our community, the families of the children educated in the school, the staffs of the infirmary and the insane asylum, the personal secretary of the Patriarch of Antioch (head of the Maronite Church), and other dignitaries. Once the funeral Mass and burial were over and all the guests had left, the rest of us milled about like abandoned dogs. A pall descended on our community.

The following day, as I sat reading in my room, a soft knock came on the door. It was Isabella, holding in her hand an envelope. Prior to the abbess's death, I had never seen Isabella's face without its radiant smile. And yet, with the vermilion of her lips angling downward, her eyes bloodshot, and wisps of scarlet peeking out from beneath her black coif, she seemed to me the most beautiful thing in the world. I wanted her to cast herself into my arms again. Instead, she extended the hand holding the envelope.

"The Mother Superior asked me to give this to you," she said.

I was bewildered. "The Mother Superior?"

"The new abbess." Isabella was on the verge of tears. "Mother Maria Constanta arrived last night."

"Oh. What is she like?"

"We all gathered in the chapel after vespers to meet her. She seems . . . a little . . . strict."

"Mmm."

"She emphasized the value the Patriarch places on rules and order, and she spoke at length on the link between a lack of discipline and depravity. Apparently, we have earned a reputation for looseness here under the former leadership. The abbess has already ordered a stricter dress code, punctuality for all scheduled events, less frivolous talk, and diminished involvement of outsiders in our sacred lives. She mentioned something about 'consequences.'"

"Uh-oh. I don't like the sound of that. What did she mean by *outsiders*?"

"She didn't specify. I suppose she might mean the students at the school or the patients who come to the infirmary, or perhaps the residents of the insane asylum."

I hesitated. "Are you sure she didn't mean me?"

"*You?*" Isabella laughed, and it thrilled me to see this sign that joy might yet return to her. "Why should she mean you?"

"Who is more of an outsider here than I?"

"What are you talking about, Joseph? You are no more of an outsider than I am. Stop speaking nonsense. I am sure the Reverend Mother will provide more details soon. She seemed very certain that improvements in these domains will increase holiness in our community."

"I don't like the sound of that, either."

"Anyway, this was found among Mother Maria Theresa's effects. It is addressed to you. The abbess asked that I deliver it to you." She thrust the envelope forward.

I grasped it by the corner, and for a moment, we held on to its opposite ends before she relinquished it. "Thank you kindly, Isabella."

"Good night." The corners of her mouth lifted.

She turned and departed, and I shut the door behind her. I brought the envelope to my desk and examined it by the light of my lamp. In a shaky script was the address: *Master Joseph Friedmann*. I turned it over. The flap had been closed with the abbess's wax seal. I broke it and read her message, written in French in an unsteady hand, as though it were an echo of her tremulous speech. It was dated one week before she died.

Dear Joseph:

I suppose you thought I would live forever, but the Lord has other plans. Do not mourn for me, Joseph. I will at last have the reward of joining my predecessors in the company of the Heavenly Father and his Son. I have done my best to increase goodness in the world, and though, truly, my achievements are meager, I hope the sincerity of my efforts merits presenting myself without shame to my Maker.

But enough about me.

And here, I smiled, as I know she did when writing these words.

You may wonder why Joseph Friedmann of all people should occupy the thoughts of an ancient nun as she contemplates the end of her many years among the living. The reason is one to which I have already alluded: There is more good to be done, and I hope to do it with this letter. I wish to tell you some things about yourself, things that may help you weather the storms my heart tells me are gathering in your path.

You have a destiny, Joseph. And though I know not what that destiny is in any of its particulars, I sense that you are marked by the hand of God. This mark may signify great risk (remember that Cain was so marked) or great achievement, and perhaps both. But the paths we take in life are not simply matters of fate. As is the case for most people, the future of Joseph Friedmann will in part be determined by the decisions you make. Where you differ from others lies not in that fact, but rather in the magnitude of the peril and potential that rest upon those decisions. When a man's point of origin in life is as exceptional as yours, there is reason to suppose that the remainder of that life will proceed on the unusual trajectory established at the beginning.

You were born into extraordinary circumstances, circumstances I attended in person, as I alluded to in our first conversation but have never explained. Your mother was no more than a girl when she came to our infirmary, unaware that the agony she was experiencing was the pain of childbirth. It was I who named you, suggesting to your mother the appellation Joseph in memory of your biblical forefather, whose perilous journey into the land of Egypt was blessed by the Lord. Joseph's faith in the face of hopelessness was repeatedly rewarded with good fortune, and he achieved things in life beyond anyone's wildest imagination. This, I told your mother, was what my heart boded for you. After two days in our infirmary, your mother took you back to her villa in Bhamdoun. And though she dwelt in wealth and comfort and was surrounded by servants, she was so alone. I feared for her ability to care for herself, much less for a child. She would write from time to time to give me tidings of her life and to describe the remarkable intelligence and vivacity of the boy born under our roof.

But her circumstances changed. Abandoned by her husband, and before she knew what was happening to her, in love with a man of another faith, then disowned by her family, she was at the edge of despair. She came to our gate one midnight, pleading for an audience with me. I granted it immediately, of course, and discovered to my horror that she had plans to do away with herself and to take you with her. I could not permit such a sin against God and nature. I beseeched her to allow her family or your father to claim you, notions she fervently opposed on the threat of self-destruction. I gave her a room for the night and prayed to the Virgin to show me a path by which I might avert this terrible outcome. It was I who in the morning advised your mother to marry the man with whom she had fallen in love, and since he could not tolerate another man's child in his home, much less a Jewish child, to entrust me personally with your future.

So, we entered upon a secret pact. In exchange for the opportunity to save your life, I promised to protect you, educate you, and set you free in the world when you were ready to wrestle with it. And though your mother insisted that we never lead you to abandon the faith of your ancestors, neither her family nor your father were ever to know what became of you. Shortly after you arrived here, she disappeared. My inquiries went unanswered, and I never heard from her again.

My heart broke anew with each unread letter returned to you. How could your mother have hardened her own heart so? Perhaps she believed that to do otherwise would only weaken you. But it is also possible—it pains me to write this, Joseph, for I know how devoted you were and perhaps still are to her—that your mother chose, for her own reasons, to continue her life as though you were never a part of it. Of all my obligations before the end, the most difficult is the duty of cautioning you that any hope of refuge you may seek from that quarter may go unfulfilled.

Surely, this is almost too much to ask a boy of thirteen to bear, but I believe in your heart you must already suspect this. You have coped with almost intolerable pain using the resources available to you. But take care, Joseph: Eventually, we must confront the truths within us. You cannot survive forever by suppressing your emotions.

Your residence in our institution was unprecedented. Indeed, it was considered dangerous to the extreme. To have a young man of a different faith dwelling among the novitiates . . . I had to obtain permission from the Patriarch of Antioch himself—may his soul repose in peace—for the arrangement, and he only granted it on my personal assurances. I instructed our residents to suppress their curiosity and instead to treat you with respectful distance—only I and your teachers were to have anything other than the most formal of relationships with you. This was difficult for all, as from your very first moment among us you were revealed as an extraordinary and delightful child. It was only natural that the residents of our community would desire to participate in your upbringing.

I am sorry that you have not had a typical childhood; I have done my best to provide whatever might approximate normalcy under abnormal constraints. I believed and continue to believe that God will reward my faith in Him by not punishing you for any errors I may have committed. I confess to a moment of doubt when I observed you taking without permission—I dare not say "stealing"—the plate and fork from our kitchen after your first breakfast in the convent. (I trust that you honor me, Joseph, by not underestimating my powers of observation.) But upon perceiving the just use to which these borrowed objects were put, I interpreted it as a sign that we were doing God's will. From that point on, you have brought nothing but honor upon yourself and upon our community.

Nonetheless, Joseph, there is danger ahead. As you have blossomed, my foreboding has increased. You are unaware of how extraordinary you are. Your intelligence is too keen, your understanding too profound, your boldness too unbridled, your physical beauty too alluring for life in a place such as this. When I am no longer here to protect you from us and us from you, what might become of you and of the institution to which I have devoted my life? I have contemplated sending you, while there is still time, to your mother's family, if I might find them, or to some other institution, but my promise not to do the former and my fear of harming you through the latter stay my hand.

Joseph, I am sorry that my strength gave out before I was able to finish the task. I fear that leaving you now without the safeguards of which you have been the unwitting beneficiary will jeopardize all that I hope and wish for you in life. As with all things, however, I must trust the Lord. May He watch over you, and if such things are possible, may He grant me the privilege of watching over you from heaven. It is my only wish.

Fondly and forever,
Mother Maria Theresa

Chapter Eight

The next morning, I awoke to find that a piece of paper had been slipped under my door. It was a summons to present myself to the Mother Superior's office after breakfast. I dressed in my school clothes and went to the dining hall. The new abbess was not there. Mother Maria Theresa had always circulated during breakfast, wishing each person a day of affirmation and inquiring as to their well-being. On this occasion, there was none of the usual chatter, and even the scraping of forks on plates seemed carefully muted, as though such sounds had become as reprehensible as idle conversation. Isabella hurried from table to table serving tea and would not stop to speak to me.

I washed my dishes, placed them on the rack, and walked to the office. A thin, middle-aged woman I did not recognize was stationed at a desk in the center of the anteroom. She did not look up from writing on her papers when I approached, so I strode past her and was about to knock on the door to the inner office when she arrested me with a harsh, "What are you doing, young sir?"

"I am going to visit the abbess. I received a note to see her after breakfast."

"And do you believe it is proper to walk right by the secretary and knock on the abbess's door whenever it pleases you to do so?"

That was precisely what I believed, except for the part about the secretary, as there had never been a secretary before. "Yes, Sister."

"I am not your or anybody else's sister," she said curtly. "And allow me to inform you that, despite what you may have been taught, that most certainly is *not* proper."

I gaped at her, waiting to be informed of what *was* proper.

"In case you are wondering what *is* proper, it is for you to sit over there"— she pointed to a straight-backed chair in a corner of the room—"and wait to be called upon."

We stared at each other a little more, and because I didn't know what else to say, I muttered, "As you say, Sister," and took a seat.

"Still not your sister!" she snapped. She returned to her work. "Sit there quietly until you are called."

I sat. When it began to appear there would be a significant delay, I got off the chair to retrieve a book entitled *Notions of Divinity in Medieval France* from the bookcase. A sudden glower from the secretary sent me back to my place without reading material.

A few minutes elapsed before I tried a different tactic toward dispelling boredom. I cleared my throat. "My name is Joseph Friedmann, Madame. What is your name?"

She did not look up from her papers but raised an eyebrow. After a moment, she answered, "You may call me Madame Aoun."

"*Enchanté*, Madame Aoun. I hope you find affirmation in your job here." The corner of her mouth turned up. "Have you been to our institution before? Did you know the former abbess of blessed memory?"

Again, the corner of her mouth rose. Again, she did not lift her head. "I am flattered by your interest, Monsieur Friedmann, but I ask that you wait in silence until the abbess is ready for you."

After about twenty minutes, a bell jingled from within the abbess's chamber, and the secretary rose to enter it. "Stay where you are, and don't touch anything!" she admonished before disappearing behind the door. A moment later, she returned. "You may enter the Reverend Mother's office, Master Friedmann."

I got down from my perch, nodded at Madame Aoun, and strode into the abbess's chamber, where I beheld a figure bent over some papers. *What a great deal of paperwork is suddenly being done here!* I observed to myself, wondering whether Mother Maria Theresa had been exempted from such obligations. I had received exemptions many times from homework demanded of my classmates, and I was certain Maria Theresa was at least as accomplished an abbess as I was a student. I could see only the top of the new abbess's head, covered in a long black wimple that cascaded over her shoulders and onto the desk's surface. Hanging from her neck was a large silver cross.

I stood in silence two meters away and waited.

After a few minutes, the abbess raised her head from the papers, still grasping the pen in her left hand. We examined each other. I was surprised by the smoothness and pallor of her skin, so reminiscent of the marble statue of the Virgin that stood in the sanctuary. Her complexion was an utter contrast to the prior abbess's furrowed, olive-hued visage. The new abbess had pale blue eyes, their almond outlines deeply sunk in sockets lined by long lashes and dark, thin brows. The effect of those eyes was striking. They were pristine and piercing, and called to mind the glacial lakes I had imagined while reading *The Call of the Wild*. Her nose was small and upturned at its tip, and her lips were neat and thin. Had these features been accompanied by a generous smile rather than the severe line of her mouth, or had her eyes sparkled with eagerness rather than examined me so deprecatingly, she might have been mistaken for Isabella's elder sister.

She laid down her pen.

"Monsieur Joseph Friedmann," she said after a long while, her voice surprisingly raspy. The utterance of my name seemed repugnant to her, like a regrettable diagnosis.

"Yes, Mother Maria Constanta," I replied.

"I am not your mother, child. You will refer to me as the *Reverend Abbess*."

"As you wish, The Reverend Abbess."

This elicited no upturning of the corner of her mouth. "Not *The* Reverend Abbess. Only *Reverend Abbess*, if you please."

"As you wish, Reverend Abbess."

She continued to stare at me. "Extraordinary," she murmured. "It emanates."

"Excuse me?"

The abbess shook her head. "Do you like living here?"

"Yes, Reverend Abbess."

"Why?"

I contemplated the question. "I suppose it is because I feel welcome. I have my own room. I have been granted access to the library and freedom to explore the area. I feel liked and respected by the sisters and my teachers. And it is the only place I have in the world."

She scrutinized me some more, and then muttered, "*For there is nothing concealed that shall not be revealed; neither hid that shall not be known.*"

"Luke, chapter two, verse twelve," I responded.

She raised an eyebrow. "You have learned our Scripture, boy? And what does the verse mean to you?"

"That the truth will emerge in the end, even if you try to conceal it."

"Quite right, Master Friedmann. Do you love the Gospel?"

I did not answer.

"Yes, child? I asked you a simple question, did I not?"

"Do I love the Gospel?"

"Yes, and do you love Jesus? Do you accept him as your Savior?"

"I have not been baptized, if that is what you mean."

Her eyes flashed. "That is not what I mean, and it is also precisely what I mean. First: Do you love the Gospel?" Her voice, uniquely raspy in regular conversation, became harsher as it rose in agitation.

I paused before answering. "No, Reverend Abbess, I do not love the Gospel. I have studied it and find much wisdom in it, but I love it no more than I do others of my favorite literary works."

Her features hardened. How strange, I mused, that there was so much more suppleness in the gouged lips of Mother Maria Theresa than in these youthful ones. "And therefore, one might deduce that you do not love Jesus. That you do not accept him as your Savior."

"That has never been a requirement of my being here, Reverend Abbess. Is it now a requirement?"

"It is a requirement of every person who lives here *except* for you, Master Friedmann, an unusual fact I discovered just prior to my arrival. Apparently, you are exempt from the most basic expectation of every other member of the community."

"There are many other expectations I fulfill, and many things I do to benefit the community that are not expectations, Reverend Abbess. I am happy to have the opportunity to do them. I hope the community does not see me as a parasite."

"Parasite . . ." she murmured. "What an unusual word. I find many of the words emerging from your young mouth unusual. You are thirteen years old, yes?"

"Yes."

"And yet your words seem to do your bidding, in the fashion of a much older person."

"Isn't that what words were invented for, Reverend Abbess? To do our bidding?"

"No. They were invented to do the Lord's bidding in creating all the goodness in the world. And occasionally, they are usurped to do Satan's bidding. How is it that you have learned to use them so effectively?"

"Because of my education, here at the convent. I am grateful for it."

She paused, and her eyes narrowed. "The Devil sweetens mischief and corruption using words, evil words that to the innocent are indistinguishable from holy ones. Your Theodor Herzl and Chaim Weizmann have used such words to poison the minds of the British, and your brethren use similar words to seize the homes and lands of our Arab brothers in Palestine."

I had no idea what she was talking about, but her hostility was unmistakable. I remained silent.

"Let us return to the original line of our conversation, Master Friedmann," she said. "A community is defined by its shared beliefs. An outlier such as yourself, who shares not in the most fundamental of those beliefs, threatens the integrity of the whole. This kind of threat must be dealt with."

"Would you like me to be baptized, Reverend Abbess?"

"Not if you propose to do so with such little thought and such great insincerity. And even baptism is not sufficient to turn a wicked person into a righteous one."

"Wicked?"

"I understand that on your very first day here, you assaulted another child."

"That is untrue. It was my second day."

She scoffed.

"So, what would you have me do, Reverend Abbess?"

"The question is not what *you* should do, but rather what *I* must do to preserve the purity and holiness of this place. I must protect our community from corruption. And since apparently I may not transfer you against your will, I must do what I can to diminish the harm you might cause."

"I would never do harm to this place that has shown me such kindness!"

She laughed, a single, harsh syllable, and then added, *"For such people serve not our Lord Jesus Christ, but their own belly; and by good words and fair speeches deceive the hearts of the simple."*

I recognized the quotation from Romans 16:18 and had read enough of the history of anti-Semitism to recognize that over the course of the previous three days, my world had been upended. Yet the virulence of her hostility was beyond anything I had ever experienced, even at the hands of The Committee. She must have known, I pondered, that I had been insulated from the ancient animosities. Was it possible that my being born a Jew was sufficient cause for the threat she saw in me, or was there something else she feared?

"Since you will not be participating in the pious and devotional life of the convent," the abbess continued, "and since you have obvious abilities beyond your years, your time outside of class will be spent in tasks more suited to your natural talents than peeling potatoes and washing dishes. You will return here after school to receive a new assignment from Madame Aoun."

She lowered her eyes to the paperwork on her desk, picked up the pen with her left hand, and with a backward wave of her right dismissed me. I turned and retreated toward the exit.

Just as I touched the handle, she called out, "Master Friedmann. One more thing."

Again, I was struck by the contrast between the new abbess's harsh rasp and her predecessor's sweet singsong. I hesitated at the door.

"What was written in the letter the former abbess left for you?"

"A prophecy," I replied, and left the room.

Chapter Nine

I returned to the office after school and found Madame Aoun sitting, just as before, with her head bowed toward paperwork. She did not look up when I knocked on the door to the anteroom and approached her desk. I waited, determined not to be the one to break the silence.

She lasted about three minutes.

"Monsieur Friedmann," she said, finally raising her head.

"Bonjour, Madame Aoun," I replied. "*Comment allez-vous cet après-midi? It is so nice to see you once more.*"

Again, the upturned corner of her mouth. "I have a letter here for you." She picked up an envelope from the edge of her desk and handed it to me. It was addressed to *Dr. al-Moualem*, and turning it over, I saw the abbess's wax seal over the flap. "You are to go to the infirmary and give the doctor this letter. He will tell you what to do next."

I had seen the doctor, nurses, and orderlies who worked at the clinic and adjacent insane asylum many times. Some of them resided on the convent's grounds in a small structure next to the infirmary fence, and they occasionally appeared in our midst during off-hours for meals and conversation. Yet I had been inside the infirmary only three times in my life. The first was the occasion of my birth. The second was for a physical exam about a year after arriving at the convent.

My third visit to the infirmary was for a bout of dysentery. I was admitted with fever and dehydration and was the sole occupant of the ward where I was hospitalized for two days. The room was scrubbed by orderlies three times daily by commandment of the chief nurse, a steely-eyed nun who made it clear from the first that she would brook no nonsense from either patients or staff. The doctor saw me only once, inquiring as to my name and chief symptoms, and pressing on my belly roughly.

If it is possible for a person to be the opposite of a facility, the doctor was the opposite of his clinic. The spotless floors found their counterpart in his soiled white coat; the neatly organized shelves in his mop of greasy black hair; the perfectly made bedsheets in a perpetual five-day growth of beard; and the crisp smell of antiseptic solution in the sour odor of cigarettes and arak. The residents of the convent were almost all young and healthy, but even in illness, they preferred not to visit the doctor if they could avoid it. He was just as likely to be called upon to minister to our two milk cows and three guard dogs as to the human denizens of the community. Most of his attention was occupied with the needs of the inmates of the insane asylum, though what those needs were and what his duties consisted of were unknown to me at that time.

The infirmary was a one-story whitewashed building situated on the northeast corner of the compound, abutting a three-meter limestone wall that separated the convent from the asylum. Concertina wire was mounted atop both the wall and a fence that surrounded the infirmary on the three sides facing the convent. The infirmary's yellow front door, which was emblazoned with a red cross, could be accessed from the convent only through a padlocked gate in the fence. I was aware that a similar door on the rear side led through the barrier wall into the asylum, the only direct connection between the two institutions.

As for the insane asylum, the high limestone wall surrounded it on all four sides. On its eastern flank, the asylum grounds were accessible from the street via solid wooden doors mounted on massive hinges, through which vehicles passed carrying workers, inmates, supplies, or refuse in one direction or the other several times a day. It was impossible to look through the gate into the grounds of the asylum, as the vehicular entryway was always guarded when opened, and the only view from the street was of an internal two-meter barrier that vehicles had to circumvent in order to gain access.

I was well acquainted with insanity before arriving at the compound in Bhamdoun. On my way to school or synagogue in Beirut, I had often encountered crazies and false prophets on the streets. There were perpetual rumors among my classmates that one forbidding building or another housed a group of lunatics. The fact that such a community was situated adjacent to my new place of residence at the convent did not so much frighten as intrigue me.

The fortresslike sequestration of the asylum had excited my curiosity since my first day at the convent five years earlier. The howls and shrieks breaching the wall on that first night might have been, to the imagination of an eight-year-old for whom the world's truths had been ripped away, the cries of ghosts. But on that night, as on similar nights thereafter, those sounds were soon joined by more earthly ones: scuffling and shouts in Arabic to "hold him down!" or "shut up, you dog!" The desperate cries would fade and die away, to be replaced by slamming doors and muffled voices. I concluded that not ghosts but flesh-and-blood beings inhabited that unseen domain behind the barrier.

Within two weeks of arriving at the convent, I could suppress my curiosity about the goings-on beyond the wall no longer. There were no windows with vantage points overlooking the asylum, and the metal door at the top of the stairs leading to the roof of the main building was locked. One late afternoon, while most of the residents were at vespers, I climbed onto the desk in my room and unlatched my small window. I lifted myself up to the sill, slid my head out the gap, and worked my body through, crouching and then standing upright along the narrow ledge while pressing the tips of my fingers against the top of the window frame for support. A downspout was located about thirty centimeters from the left edge of my window, and I spied an irregularity in the stonework that could serve as a toehold on my way to grasping it. I rested the tip of my left shoe against the small outcropping of stone and stretched out my left hand to grip the downspout while cupping the window frame with my right for support. Then, with a small leap, I brought my legs and hands around to hug the pipe's sides. I shimmied up to a low perimeter wall, over which I hoisted myself to land on the tiles of the roof.

One of the sisters spied me and ran to report to Mother Maria Theresa that the Jewish child who had been deposited in their midst was climbing pipes and scaling walls three stories off the ground. When she questioned me later about this recklessness, I had no explanation other than that I was curious to see the roof and to look beyond the wall into the asylum. Also, that the possibility of falling had not occurred to me.

"And what did you discover, Joseph?" she asked.

"The roof is very dirty," I said.

She guffawed, a noise that lay somewhere between the braying of a donkey and the rumble of a lorry downshifting gears. I was astonished to hear that sound and could be certain it represented amusement only after hearing it a second time, about a month later, when one of the novices fell headfirst into an enormous pot she was scouring at the dishwashing station.

After recovering her breath, Mother Maria Theresa said, "Here is what I meant, Joseph: What did you discover about our neighbors in the asylum?"

"Well, the grounds consist of several shacks spread all over, and one main building where the residents come and go. All the people wear white, and some move about on their own, but others go in pairs, with one person supporting the other. They have scattered trees and a shaded area with some benches, and I saw what looked like a class being conducted there. I also saw some people entering the infirmary from the asylum."

She nodded solemnly.

"And another thing."

"Yes?"

"I saw only men, no women. It was as if they were balancing us out here, where all the people are female except for me and the doctor and the laborers who work but do not live here."

"Anything else?"

"It does not seem like a very happy place."

"You are right about that last point, Joseph. The inmates of the asylum are afflicted with madness, and most have not been happy for a very long time, if they ever were."

"Do they have hope of getting better?"

"Only seldom. The doctor tells me their insanity tends to the incurable, although sometimes it can be controlled using . . ." She hesitated. "Certain procedures."

I opened my mouth to ask more questions, but Mother Maria Theresa cut me off. "That is sufficient for now, Master Friedmann. And now, I am afraid I must extract from you a promise never to climb the pipes again, nor to go to the roof using any other means you are capable of devising, but which I am certainly incapable of conceiving. The roof is not a place you are permitted to go. Will you promise me not to do that again?"

I nodded.

"Come now, Joseph. Let us find inspiration in the Book of Proverbs: *To make an apt answer is a joy to a man, and a word in season, how good it is!*"

"Yes, Mother, I promise." And I never again went to the roof. As my pledge did not extend to learning about the asylum by other means, I considered infiltrating it fair game. On one occasion, I tried to sneak onto the grounds behind a lorry lumbering through the gate from the road. I was dispatched by the sentry, who failed in his attempt to land his boot on my rear end but connected with an Arabic curse impugning my mother's honor.

⸺◉⸺

And now, five years later, I stood outside the locked infirmary gate carrying the new abbess's letter. I called out, "Hello? Is anybody there?"

After a minute, one of the nurses emerged to ask what I desired.

"I have a letter for the doctor," I answered.

She approached the fence and motioned for me to pass the envelope through the narrow gap between the gate's support poles. I did so, and she carried it back to the building, where she disappeared behind the yellow door.

After a few minutes, the doctor himself shuffled out, a spent cigarette hanging from the corner of his mouth. He eyed me from behind the latticework. "Friedmann?" he inquired.

"Yes."

"Do you know why you are here?"

"I am to be given some work."

The doctor spat out his cigarette butt. "That's right. Come back at nine o'clock tonight." And with that, he turned and sauntered back to the door.

I was left standing for a while, and when nothing further happened, I returned to the convent. I finished my homework, ate dinner with the community, read a chapter of *The Count of Monte Cristo*, and at ten minutes to nine dressed in my work clothes and presented myself at the gate in the infirmary fence. A rolled sheet of paper was lodged in the gap between the posts. I unfurled it, and by the light of the moon read a scrawled message: *Enter, and lock the gate behind you.*

The padlock had been opened. I removed the chain, passed through the gate, threaded the chain into its usual position, and snapped the padlock shut. After testing the lock, I turned and walked to the yellow door, using the large knocker that was placed in the center of the red cross to sound three deep clangs.

A heavy slide lock was opened on the inside, and the door swung wide, revealing an orderly of about fifty years clad in a blue uniform. He scowled while surveying me.

"*Masa' al-khair*," I said.

"Good evening to you too," he responded.

"I am Joseph Friedmann."

"So I have been told. I am Mahmoud."

"Should I come in?"

He thought a while. "I have been instructed to let you in." He stepped aside to clear the passage for me. "The doctor is in his office. Down the hall and to the left."

A central corridor led from the door I had entered to its counterpart at the rear. As I traversed this corridor, I passed rooms on either side: first, on the left, the room where I had been hospitalized. It housed three unoccupied beds and was as immaculate as I recalled it. On the right was a closed door labeled "Procedure Room." Other closed doors were labeled "Supplies," "Equipment," "Medications," and the like. In time, I also became familiar with the staff room; the cleaning room, with its large autoclave; the custodial closet; and all the other resources required for running a small clinic.

At the end of the hallway on the left was an open door through which billowed cigarette smoke: the doctor's office. I passed by a plaque labeled "Dr. Ismail al-Moualem" and stood in the open doorway. There was the doctor, absorbed in making smoke rings, his stocking feet on the table, his chair leaning back on its hind legs.

I stared at the beautiful floaters the doctor exhaled as if by magic. Fantastic annular wisps that danced and trembled before dissipating suddenly. Tight loops zooming through larger ones, and others he was somehow able to link together as they made their way toward the door where I was standing. He seemed to enjoy entertaining me for a few minutes. Finally, he brought his feet off the table, and the chair fell onto its front legs. "*Ahlan wasahlan*," he said.

"*Ahlan bik*," I replied.

"How do you feel this evening? Strong? Healthy? Ready to put in some honest work?"

"Yes, Dr. al-Moualem."

"That's a good boy. Perhaps by the time you graduate from my little medical school here, you will be ready to open up a clinic of your own."

From what I had observed thus far, I considered myself less likely to qualify as a medical doctor under his tutelage than as a veterinarian or street cart vendor, but I nodded.

He beckoned me forward with his hand and pointed to a chair opposite his desk. I approached and sat down. "Why don't you tell me about yourself, Friedmann?"

This was the first time I had ever been asked such a question. Everyone I had ever spoken to knew who I was. "Well, I was born here."

"What do you mean, *born here*? Where is *here*? Bhamdoun? I thought you came from Beirut."

"I was born right here in the infirmary."

"*What?* When?"

I paused. "On my birthday."

He stared at me. "But we have had only one birth here in the last . . ." His eyes narrowed and then lit up. "I remember you . . . and your mother. She was young. Nothing more than a child herself. What an extraordinary sequence of events that night . . ." He shook his head, like a person attempting to dispel an unpleasant memory. "Well, never mind that." He eyed me some more. "I have often wondered what became of the two of you. And here you have been under my nose for the last . . . what . . . four years?"

"A little more than five years."

"*Ya haram*," he murmured. It was a phrase meaning "*what a pity*," and was frequently whispered in my presence. I had grown so accustomed to it that I had a stock response, acquired from the hymns chanted in the chapel.

"God moves in a mysterious way," I muttered.

The doctor stared at me, withdrew the cigarette from the corner of his mouth, and blew out a long stream of smoke. "Nothing ever said was truer than that, boy."

He mashed the cigarette in the full ashtray before him. "So, what mysterious way has brought you back here, to the place of your birth, if you don't mind my asking?"

I did mind him asking, but knew it would be impolite to say so. I looked down at my hands while he waited for a response. "I am an orphan," I answered. It was an approximation I frequently employed for its efficiency.

"Ah . . . an orphan . . ." he murmured, raising his eyebrows and pursing his lips. He cocked one corner of his mouth in half a grin and reached for his cigarette box. "I, too, am an orphan," he said, tapping the box against the back of his hand to eject a cigarette. "My wife left me a few years ago."

"You are orphaned of your wife?"

"Hmmm."

"I didn't know one could be orphaned of one's wife."

"And I didn't know one could be orphaned when one's parents are still alive." He smirked. "But, as you have yourself experienced, there are many ways of being abandoned."

The doctor pulled a cigarette from the box with his lips, struck a match, and brought it toward his face. I had never seen a cigarette being lit before and was fascinated by the way its tip drew the flame and flared as he inhaled. "Do you want to know what you will be doing here in the infirmary?"

"Yes."

"Every evening at nine o'clock except for Fridays and Saturdays, you are to come here to the clinic, where you will work for a couple of hours. Mopping floors, cleaning and sterilizing instruments, putting items back in their places. Things like that. Do you think you can do that?"

"Yes."

"Mahmoud will assign your tasks every evening. Good?"

"Good."

"After receiving your assignments from Mahmoud and before beginning to perform them, I will want you to sit with me for a few minutes. We will talk about various things. How does all this sound to you?"

"It sounds all right."

"Good," he said. "Go find Mahmoud. And good night."

"Good night," I answered. I got up from my chair and exited the office, turning briefly to see a smoke ring chase me out the door.

Chapter Ten

Over the next two years, beginning in April 1944, I spent five nights a week, from nine to eleven o'clock, at the infirmary. Those evenings always began with a conversation in Dr. al-Moualem's office, the topics ranging from medicine to science to philosophy to history to world affairs. He took great pride in my fund of knowledge and was genuinely happy when he was able to contribute to it. These contributions were frequent, as I was ignorant of current events and recent history, including the brewing storm in Palestine, which he referred to as "labor pains." He was certain of the coming birth of the Jewish state over the objections of the Palestinian Arabs. "The Arabs, through their obstinacy, will deliver to the Jews their state on a silver platter," he declared. "You, my boy, will be part of it. I doubt it not for an instant."

He taught me about the recent history of the Middle East. He related that, as World War I drew to a close, the British and French divided the region between them. Britain's sphere of influence was in the south, spanning Egypt, Palestine, Transjordan, and Iraq. France took control of Lebanon and Syria. He explained how these imperial powers fabricated countries out of the remnants of the Ottoman Empire using straight rulers without regard to culture, religion, or topography. They seated monarchs as though they were chess pieces they could control. The result was chaos and animosity in the decades since and as far into the future as one could see.

"But the future of Palestine is not in question. The British petitioned the League of Nations for the mandate over Palestine, believing with characteristic arrogance that the inhabitants would rejoice at the mere notion of being subjects of their benevolent empire. In return for flying their flag over Jaffa and Acre and Jerusalem, they expected only gratitude and peace. The gratitude immediately turned to anger, and the peace was never more than wishful thinking. The British couldn't see what was obvious to everyone else: They were lighting the fuse of a bomb that will explode in their faces. Mark my words, Yusouf: the British Mandate in Palestine will disintegrate within three years of the end of the war in Europe. The world will not be able to resist the clamoring of the Jews for a homeland after their near-destruction at the hands of the Nazis. The Arab nations, with all their tens of millions of people, will do nothing more than collapse and give way before a few hundred thousand of your brothers and sisters."

He always referred to the Jews of the world and of Palestine, both of which he held in almost reverential esteem, as *your brethren* or *your people*, ignoring the fact that I felt neither knowledgeable about their interests nor particularly attached to them. What I knew about "my people" had been retained from the recollections of my childhood or acquired from my readings in the convent library: the Hebrew copy of the Old Testament, the *Encyclopaedia Britannica*, and various books of history and philosophy. Most of the latter works were not sympathetic toward the Jews, and few extended their scope beyond the Age of Enlightenment.

I had never forgotten that I was a member of the Jewish people (nor would I be allowed to forget even had I wished to), but I regarded my ancestry more a matter of genetics than of culture or religion. During my childhood in Beirut, I learned the ancient supplications, recited three times daily by the observant, for restoration of the Jews to Zion. But this wish had always seemed a messianic dream, not a prescription for the real world. Occasionally, members of our synagogue would return to great acclaim from pilgrimages to the holy places and tombs of the prophets and mystics. But the Jews of Beirut considered themselves Lebanese patriots of the Jewish religion, and few spoke of relocating, especially not to the Holy Land. Jews in other places suffered persecution at the hands of their neighbors, but my father and his associates considered that fact irrelevant for cosmopolitan, liberal, enlightened Beirut. I had never heard of anyone leaving Lebanon in order to transfer permanently to Palestine, unless it was to be buried there.

The doctor continued, "The Jews, industrious, innovative, educated, and with nowhere else to turn, will get their state while the Arabs bicker among themselves and stab each other in the back. Already your people are growing oranges and alfalfa where, for a thousand years, there was nothing but desert and swamps. They have raised vibrant industries in a region that has lain dormant since the Crusades.

"The war in Europe is ending, Yusouf, and rumors of the destruction the Nazis have wreaked upon your people are too ghastly not to be true. A million displaced Jews will make their way to Palestine within a decade of the end of the war, and you will be one of them. There has never been a better time or place to be an orphan." The doctor knew I was not technically an orphan, but he accepted the equivalency of my situation.

"It is a wonderful thing that the Jews will again have a homeland," I retorted, "but that does not obligate me to join them." I was thinking of Isabella, with whom I hoped to somehow find a future. "My life is here in Lebanon."

"You are wrong, my boy. You have no prospects here at all. The creation of a Jewish state in Palestine will spell the end of all Jewish communities in Arab lands."

This last statement seemed misinformed. "My mother once told me that her family has lived in Syria since the time of King David, three thousand years. There was only one story she ever related about her father. Whenever there was a crisis, she said, he would gather the Jewish community around him and give the same speech: 'We survived the Assyrians, the Babylonians, the Persians, the Greeks, the Romans, the Byzantine Empire, the Muslim invasion, the Crusaders, the Mamluks, the Ottomans, the French, and all the other upheavals of history. We shall survive this too.'"

"A stirring speech," the doctor muttered, blowing cigarette smoke out of the corner of his mouth. "And completely wrong for our time."

"You don't think the Jews will survive their own return to Zion?"

"They will survive and thrive—but not in Arab lands. And it will not be because they choose to leave. Like you, they would prefer to stay. No, it will be because the Arabs, who have never been fond of Jews living among them, will suddenly discover after three thousand years that the continued presence of the Jews is insufferable. It is one thing to abide a productive yet oppressed minority in one's midst. It is another to tolerate thousands of spies and sympathizers for a sovereign state that seeks to subjugate you, as the Arabs will undoubtedly come to see their Jewish citizens."

Thus, the doctor was revealed in short order to be more than he seemed—a scholar, a historian, an educator, a perceptive observer of human nature, and, I discovered, an astute diagnostician and naturalist. He had spent several years in sub-Saharan Africa and Indochina, where he acquired expertise in tropical medicine and infectious disease. He was a master of herbal remedies. He regaled me with tales of rare diagnoses and effective cures he made among the asylum inmates: scrofula, which he treated with incision and drainage; syphilis, which he treated with the bark of a cedar tree growing on a hilltop ten kilometers north of Bhamdoun; fish tank granuloma, which an inmate had acquired from a goldfish bowl prior to his admission to the asylum and for which he had gone from physician to physician before Dr. al-Moualem cured him with an emulsion of turmeric. The doctor would haul his ancient anatomy and physiology texts down from the shelves and, the ash of his cigarette lengthening, instruct me in the structure and function of the human body.

I accompanied Dr. al-Moualem on his annual springtime expedition to northern Lebanon to collect the *Digitalis ferruginea* plant, from which he would boil an extract to treat congestive heart failure. He confided in me that Mother Maria Theresa had been a recipient of this extract, and that he attributed to it the prolongation of her life by a few years.

I grew to cherish my work in the infirmary, and our daily discussions in particular. There was only one topic the doctor refused to speak about: the nighttime commotions that by then were occurring in the asylum nearly every other month, and which always began with shrieking at about two in the morning. "I decline to discuss it," was the closest he ever came to addressing my questions. Neither Mahmoud nor the nurses nor any of the sisters responded to my queries, and never, during my nightly visits to the infirmary, did I find evidence that anything unusual had taken place since I had last been there. Every instrument and piece of linen was in its place; the floors were as spotless as ever, the beds unoccupied.

One evening, the doctor reached into his desk drawer and pulled out a heavy volume. "It is for your fifteenth birthday." He smiled.

"But my birthday isn't for another three months," I protested.

"I know," he answered. "But I saw this in a bookstore in Beirut and knew I had to get it for you. An education should never be postponed."

I examined the gift. It was a French medical dictionary. "Thank you," I said. "This is perfect. I will start reading it tonight after work."

He nodded, smiling again.

About a week later, I found the infirmary gate locked, the chain in place and the padlock secure. From inside the infirmary, I heard the doctor roaring incoherently, slamming doors and banging heavy implements. I called out to Mahmoud, and after several such cries, he lumbered out to the gate.

"Go away," Mahmoud said. "The doctor doesn't need you tonight."

"But he told me yesterday that today we would discuss headache."

"You are the headache, Yusouf! I said go away! The doctor is not available tonight, and the infirmary is closed! Come back tomorrow!"

I went back to my room and fell asleep. At two o'clock, I was awakened by fearsome shrieking from beyond the wall. It seemed that the entire asylum had been awakened, and the grounds convulsed with the clanging of metal cups and unintelligible roars and screams. After about half an hour of bedlam, a singular high-pitched wailing sounded. Finally, Mahmoud's bellow rose above the din: "Will you hold still, you dog!" After that, the wails became feebler, and the sounds eventually died away.

In the morning, I asked the sisters whether they had heard a disturbance from beyond the wall. These inquiries were met with furtive glances and evasive responses. When I returned to the infirmary in the evening, again the gate was locked, and again Mahmoud emerged to inform me that my services were not required. "Tomorrow, Yusouf. Come back tomorrow." He said it like a man whose last strength was seeping away.

That night, all was quiet beyond the wall.

The following evening, I purposely jangled the chain as I threaded it through the gap in the gate and locked it behind me. I thought that by thus announcing my arrival I might not startle the doctor. Treading the long corridor, it was reassuring to see wisps of smoke swirling through the doorway of his office. As I approached, I noticed that the smoke did not emanate from one of the vile cigarettes he rolled by himself from tumbak. Rather, he had a pipe in the corner of his mouth, and he was cupping it contemplatively as I entered the room. It gave off a sweet perfume.

"Yusouf, my boy!" he exclaimed, swinging his feet off the table. "*Marhaban! Marhaban!* So good to see you! Come in and sit down, if you please!"

I took a few steps into the room and stared at him from the front of his desk. His eyes were bloodshot, and the left one was twitching. He looked as though he hadn't slept since I last saw him. He smiled tremulously as he stretched his hand toward the chair.

"What has been going on here for the last two nights?" I demanded, astonishing myself that I felt entitled to demand anything of him.

"What do you mean, Yusouf?"

"You know, what I mean. The locked gate, the screams, the scuffling . . ."

He took the pipe out of his mouth and looked down into its bowl. "Yusouf," he began, stopped, and tried again. "Yusouf, do you know who it is that lives on the other side of this wall?" He gestured to his left with the pipe to indicate the asylum.

I waited.

"These people suffer from delusions, mania, depression, schizophrenia, catatonia . . . Do you know what all these terms mean?"

I nodded. I had read much of the medical dictionary.

"The entire spectrum of mental illness is represented among the inmates here. We do what we can to help them, but . . . most of the cases are hopeless. They will spend the rest of their lives here. And to help make those endless stays more manageable for us, we slowly, in stages, rob these men of their humanity. We deprive them of physical and intellectual stimuli. We give them medicines that, in truth, do nothing more than dull their faculties. We drain away their hope, and when they become docile and stop complaining, we tell ourselves that the therapy is working. Do you understand what I am saying?"

I stepped forward and sat in the chair. "Yes," I replied.

"And from time to time, even these dehumanizing measures are not enough. Sometimes a particularly violent, a particularly dangerous, a particularly obsessive or perverted person must be pacified. That pacification is what we were doing here the night before last, and what we are obliged to do from time to time." He sighed. "And as of last night, I had not yet sufficiently recovered from that effort to meet with you as I had promised. Forgive me."

"What do you do to pacify such people?"

He paused. I waited.

"We castrate them."

"*What?*"

"We castrate them. Do you know what that means?"

I knew what castration was. I had seen it performed on livestock and dogs.

Dr. al-Moualem lit another match to rekindle the pipe. He puffed out a cloud of blue smoke. "I tell you, Yusouf, that among all the things I do, that task is the worst."

We spent a few minutes in silence. He stared down into his pipe and would not look me in the eye.

"Why?" I finally asked.

"What, why?"

"Why do you do it?"

He sighed. "We do it because it has the predictable effect of rendering these violent and sexually obsessed inmates—Yusouf, forgive me, but I believe your understanding is sufficiently mature for me to be frank with you—less so."

"Less violent?"

"Yes."

"Less sexually obsessed?"

"Yes. But it is a terrible, irreversible thing to do to a man."

"How do you determine which inmates need this treatment?"

He examined me intensely, as if weighing in his mind how much he should reveal. "The abbess is the leader of both the convent and the asylum, Yusouf. Once a week, I report to her on the status of each of the inmates. She decides who needs the treatment."

I was astounded. "The abbess?"

He nodded.

"But she is not a medical person! How can she take upon herself to decide such things?"

"The institution is her responsibility. And her decisions are the final law here. I tried to defer the treatment of the patient from two nights ago as long as I could. I even falsified his progress reports, but in the end, I had to give in."

He rekindled the pipe. "*Kus amak,*" he muttered. It was the vilest of oaths, and one that would have been shocking even had it not been uttered in reference to the Mother Superior. "The prior abbess approved the procedure only once in over a dozen years, and it was *I* who had to pressure *her* into it as the only method by which we could give the other inmates peace. That patient was profoundly ill. But this . . . this . . ." He was visibly struggling to control himself. "This *sharmuta* . . ." Again, I was shocked. "She has a perverted view of reality, a fixation. It started less than two months after she assumed her position. She views the sex drive as the source of all the world's ills, and castration as the remedy to all its problems."

He picked up the garbage can that stood by his desk and spat into it. Then he threw his pipe in it also. "I'm sorry, Yusouf. I am still not prepared to have a conversation with you. Go back to your room." He stood and turned to his bookshelf, pulling down a volume in English entitled *Neurological Diseases*. "Take this, Yusouf. There is an excellent chapter here on headache. Go, now. And close the door behind you."

I stood and left the room. Standing outside the door, I listened to the sounds of a drawer opening and shutting, a cork being removed from a bottle, and a thirsty man taking several deep swallows.

After that night, the doctor dwindled steadily. His appearance deteriorated even beyond his usual slovenliness, and his consumption of liquor increased. The sequence of cries, struggle, and silence from beyond the wall accelerated to nearly three times a month. I continued my evening shifts at the clinic, but the doctor became increasingly detached until one night I found his office door closed. The only answers to my knocking were his slurred accompaniments to the songs of Umm Kulthum playing on the phonograph.

One night after I had gone to bed, there was a knock on my door. It was one of the elder nuns. "Joseph," she said, "you are wanted at the infirmary."

"What? When?"

"Now."

"Why? Has something happened to the doctor?"

"I was not informed. But you are needed there."

I dressed quickly and ran down the stairs and onto the grounds. Finding the gate unlocked, I let myself in, slid the chain into position, and secured the padlock. I ran toward the yellow door, flung it open, and raced inside. I heard Dr. al-Moualem bellowing from behind the closed entrance to the operating room. "Mahmoud, you donkey, you choose this night of all nights to leave me?" I rushed through the swinging door and into the operating room area, and saw the doctor standing with his back to me. Using his gloved right hand, he was transferring instruments from a metal sterilization box onto a drape he had laid over a large rolling table. Between the fourth and fifth fingers and thumb of his left hand, he clutched a flask. Each time he completed the transfer of several instruments, he would remove the cigarette from the corner of his mouth using the index and third finger of his left hand and take a swig from the flask.

"Ah, Yusouf! *Alhamdulillah!*" he exclaimed over his shoulder, thanking God when he spied me. "I am in need of your help. Mahmoud has quit his job, and I require a second pair of hands for a procedure tonight." He forced himself to smile, a frightening leer. "How would you like to be my medical assistant?"

"What sort of procedure?" I asked.

Dr. al-Moualem turned to face me. He dragged on the cigarette and let out a long stream of smoke. "The kind we discussed earlier."

"A castration?"

"Yes. The abbess has insisted that it be done tonight, and I cannot do it on my own. I will teach you how to set up the operating room table and administer anesthesia, and you will also learn some surgical techniques."

"While helping to castrate a man."

"Yes, Yusouf. While helping to castrate a man. But I assure you that this time, even I share the opinion that there is no alternative to the procedure. This is a man who in the past has raped more than one woman and who last night nearly succeeded in raping one of the male asylum inmates. Under no circumstances will he ever leave this institution alive."

I hesitated.

"Come, Yusouf. I need you. I will teach you new skills."

And finally, I relented. It was the first and last time in a life replete with questionable decisions that I ever willingly participated in something I knew for certain was wrong.

Chapter Eleven

Dr. al-Moualem, who had been trying to line up his instruments, seemed inebriated nearly to the point of collapse, but suddenly became calm when I gave my assent to assisting him in surgery. His hands were steady and his speech only slightly slurred as he showed me how to take the sterile implements out of the box, how to array them on the table, how to select and prepare the sutures and cautery device. "I will show you my technique," he said. "It is a method of my own invention, the most humane possible, and I don't think anyone else in the world uses it."

He went on to explain that everywhere else, castration was performed by removing the testes. One day about a year earlier, while trying to steel his nerves in preparation for the procedure, and while reviewing the relevant anatomy, he realized that the blood vessels and nerves supplying the testes on each side were all contained within the spermatic cord. Rather than excise the whole testicle, he asked himself, why not simply obliterate the spermatic cord and let the organ die as a result? It was every bit as effective but much less complicated. The testes always atrophied without infection, and there was an additional benefit: because the nerve was taken with the vessels, the patient experienced no pain. "I will show you how I intend to do it."

"I don't want to see how you do it," I replied. "I will assist you, but teach me nothing about it."

"As you wish, Yusouf. But this is the first time I have ever seen you decline to acquire new knowledge."

"I have no need for this kind of knowledge."

We finished setting up the table. He took a final toke from his cigarette, extinguished it on the side of a trash can in the corner of the room, removed the flask from the pocket of his white coat, then uncorked and drained it. "And now for the most difficult part."

I followed the doctor as, for the first time, I exited the infirmary through the door in the back. We shut it behind us, and I saw that, like its fellow on the convent side, it was painted yellow and bore a red cross. We wound our way without a word through the asylum grounds, pushing a gurney along the paved path through a maze of single-story shacks. The quiet seemed unnatural. I suppressed my old childish notion that behind each dormitory door were corpses arrayed in open caskets. Arriving at our destination, the doctor pulled a metal box from a small shelf installed under the head of the gurney and opened it. Inside were two pieces of cloth, two dark glass bottles, and two pairs of thick, black rubber gloves. He motioned me to don one pair of gloves while he did the same with the other.

He withdrew one of the bottles and rags. "Methylbenzene," he whispered. "You must be quiet now, Yusouf. We are about to enter the dormitory." He jerked his head in the direction of the closed door. "If all goes well, I will be able to creep up on the inmate and cover his mouth and nose with the methylbenzene without waking him. Then, all I will ask of you is to pin his arms down until he passes out. If, however, he wakes before I have a chance to approach him, we will reverse roles, as you are not strong enough to hold him down. I will immobilize him, and you will cover his face with the cloth. Make sure you keep the cloth tightly in position over both his mouth and nose until he ceases to move. Don't worry. You will not be harming him. Be careful not to breathe in the fumes, or you will faint. Keep your head away from the rag. Do you understand?"

I nodded.

He opened the bottle and saturated the cloth, screwed the cap back on, and reinserted the bottle into the metal box. "The other inmates will wake up and cause a commotion. Do not be alarmed. They will not leave their beds. We must act quickly. This substance will evaporate completely within three minutes."

I nodded once more.

"*Yallah*," he whispered. "Let's go."

He swung open the door to the dormitory rapidly, no doubt having learned that a quick movement was less likely to cause noise than a slow one.

I followed him inside, being careful to make as light a footfall as possible. In the gloom I saw eight cots arrayed in the room, four on either side. Atop each of the cots was the mound of a sleeping man. Dr. al-Moualem silently pointed to the second on the left, indicating our patient.

The doctor advanced a few more steps, and as he did so, one of the floorboards groaned under his weight. Immediately, the man directly opposite the designated inmate sat bolt upright in his bed and started shrieking.

"Yusouf!" the doctor cried. "The cloth!" He placed the rag, heavy with liquid, into my gloved left hand, and ran toward the patient, casting himself on top of the man, who had started to rise just as the doctor landed on him. At the same moment, all the patients in the dormitory began to scream.

The doctor yelled again. "Now! Now! Now!"

I was disoriented by the eruption of bedlam: ululations, wooden spoons banging on mess kit bowls, shoes pounding on walls and floors, and even a drum one of the men had extracted from somewhere. Within seconds, pandemonium echoed from every other dormitory in the asylum as well.

The doctor struggled to immobilize the thin lunatic on the bed, all the while yelling out my name to spur me to action. The inmate repeatedly snapped his jaws along the side of the doctor's head, and the thought occurred to me that I had not yet been taught how to sew an ear back into position.

"Yusouf!" the doctor cried.

I raced toward the bed and covered the mouth and nose of the patient with the rag in my left hand, placing my right on the back of his head and compressing my two hands toward each other as hard as I could. I turned my own head to the left to avoid the fumes, which had already started to make me feel woozy. The inmate gagged and coughed and issued muffled screams, which died away within a few seconds as his body went limp. The chaos around us persisted.

The doctor gradually relaxed his hold on the patient and rose to face me. "Yusouf," he said. "Yusouf. *Yusouf!*"

I started.

"You may loosen your grip. Let him breathe."

I had continued to press the rag onto the man's face as hard as I could, even after he stopped moving. Horrified that I might have smothered him, I released my hold and raised my gloved hands toward my face. I was trembling.

"It's OK," the doctor said, gently lowering my arms. "You did well. He is only asleep. Go get the cart."

I ran toward the door between the beds, each containing a shrieking and cursing man, and returned with the gurney.

"Quickly, Yusouf, help me get him onto the trolley." The doctor lifted the inmate under the arms. I hoisted his feet, and we laid him in the cart. "Good. Now, we take him back to the clinic."

We left the dormitory and wheeled the gurney in the direction of the infirmary. To my surprise, the cacophony died down almost as suddenly as it had started. Within thirty seconds, the compound was as quiet as it had been when we first set out on our mission.

Dr. al-Moualem withdrew the metal box from the shelf under the man's head and opened it, producing the second bottle and rag. He saturated the cloth. "It is important to not let him breathe too much of this," he said, "or it could harm him. This is chloroform. It produces a deeper anesthesia that is easier to control." He replaced the first cloth with the second and stowed the first in the box. "We must always keep the cloth moist with chloroform. We position it close to his nose to provide him with a steady dosage. If he starts breathing more rapidly or begins to stir, we move it closer. If he takes more than twelve seconds between breaths, we move it farther away. That is how we keep him anesthetized while avoiding toxicity."

Arriving at the threshold of the infirmary, the doctor cocked his head to indicate that I should open the yellow door. I sprinted ahead to do so. As we entered the building, Dr. al-Moualem said, "You will control the anesthetic. Do you understand the instructions I just gave you?"

"Yes," I answered.

"Very good. We go. Straight to the operating room."

We wheeled the gurney down the hall, and I ran ahead to open the operating room door. The doctor rolled in the cart, and I assisted him in transferring the patient onto the operating table. The man groaned. Dr. al-Moualem poured iodine into a metal cup, then placed a gauze pad inside.

"Yusouf, you must keep the cloth wet and move it closer to his nose. Do you see how he stirs?"

I did as I was instructed. "What is his name?" I inquired.

The doctor looked at me intently. "Marwan," he answered. "Marwan Haddad. Help me remove his pants."

We loosened his britches and lowered them along with his underwear. I was embarrassed by the sight of fully mature male genitals, which I had never seen before, and which astonished me in their hairy disorderliness. His scrotum seemed deflated and wrinkly, and his uncircumcised penis was somehow menacing. *Indeed, there is something wrong with this man*, I thought. *Obviously, his organs are diseased.*

The doctor doffed his thick rubber gloves and placed them back in the metal box under the cart. He went to the sink to wash his hands and then bathed them in an antiseptic solution. He picked up the gauze pad soaked in iodine. "Pay attention, Yusouf," the doctor instructed. "He hasn't breathed in the last thirty seconds."

I quickly moved the cloth a short distance away from Marwan Haddad's nostrils and then poured a few more drops of chloroform on it.

"Very good," the doctor said. "You must keep the rag wet even while you are reducing the dose." He bathed the man's scrotum with the iodine, picked up a scalpel and forceps, and went to work. I was amazed at how bloodless, neat, and efficient the procedure was. In less than fifteen minutes, the doctor had placed and tied sutures to close the small incisions he had made into the scrotum above the testicles on both sides, and we were done.

We wheeled the sleeping man back to the dormitory and transferred him to his cot. This time, although most of the inmates awakened at our entry, they did not utter a sound.

We returned to the infirmary and washed and sterilized the instruments. Dr. al-Moualem instructed me to clean the operating room. After I was done, I approached him in his office. He extinguished his cigarette in the overflowing ashtray when he saw me at his doorway. He looked worse than ever, as though, like the patient we had transferred back to the asylum, the drug with which the doctor had anesthetized himself was dissipating. He repeatedly passed tremulous hands through his hair and could not take his eyes off the top drawer of his desk.

"You may go now, Yusouf," he said. "I want you to know you were an excellent assistant today. You have superb instincts and would make a fine physician if you chose that path."

Without responding, I turned and headed out the door. I had seen enough to know that I could never choose that path.

Chapter Twelve

A few months later, and two years after Mother Maria Theresa's death, I finally left the convent, in the middle of the night, without telling anyone in advance, with only the vaguest of notions where I was going, and having first set fire to the abbess's office.

The transformation precipitating that violent departure had required neither two years, nor two months, nor two weeks, but rather two days: the two days between Mother Maria Theresa's ceasing to draw breath at the convent and Maria Constanta's commencing to do so. What lasted two years was the process of understanding that there was nothing left for me other than despair and dehumanization in the place I had called home for seven years. If Mother Maria Theresa indeed watched over me from heaven, as was her dying wish, it must have been hard for her; the new abbess seemed as dedicated to my degradation as the former had been to my preservation.

Countless means were employed to achieve this degradation. The reassignment of my chores to the infirmary, removing me from spaces frequented by the sisters, was merely the first dissonant chord in a symphony of persecution. My classmates had always kept their distance, but soon they shunned me altogether. The teacher, a retired headmaster from Beirut who had taken Madame Farouq's place, never called on me or gave me special assignments. Eventually, he stopped grading my papers and exams. My privilege of roaming away from the convent was rescinded. The sisters ceased sitting next to me at meals. The wide smiles with which I had always been greeted became furtive, shared only after their owners assured themselves that the abbess was not nearby.

But the thing that hit the mark with cruelest precision was the installation of a lock on the library door. The abbess knew I could survive isolation—I had already thrived despite years of it—but my life depended on accessing the library.

"She has an unusually deep hatred for you," the doctor confided in me one evening while we sat in his office.

"What have I done to earn this hatred?"

"As far as I can tell, you earn it by flourishing under circumstances in which you ought to have withered. You are a boy abandoned by his family, a male residing in a women's institution, and a Jew living alone among Christian Arabs. She is a great believer in reward and punishment. The rewards you have received—security, intelligence, education, and the love of your community— seem to her unmerited, and thus a violation of justice and order. I think she believes—forgive me for saying it, Yusouf—that your good fortune can only have been the outcome of some great mischief. She intends to root out that mischief."

"I am grateful for whatever good fortune I have had," I answered, "but my own opinion is that my life has included no small measure of ill fortune."

"I agree with you. That is one of the reasons it seems to me there is something more . . ."

I waited.

He fidgeted in his chair. "You are perhaps unaware, Yusouf, that though you are only fifteen years old, you are an extraordinarily attractive young man, both in physical appearance and in character and temperament."

I lowered my eyes.

"I have already shared with you," the doctor continued, "that I believe the abbess views sexual desire as a source of evil. I think what she fears most in you is your potential to engender lust."

"Even if that is true, what can I do about it, other than ceasing to exist?"

"I think a day will come when you will indeed have to cease to exist—by which I mean you will need to cease existing here and begin existing somewhere else. Meanwhile, I am doing what I can to postpone that day. In our weekly meetings, I report to the abbess how miserable I make you. You should try to confirm that impression whenever you have the opportunity."

That becomes easier with each passing day, I observed to myself.

"But in truth, I have no advice for you, other than to leave. Soon."

"Where will I go?"

"I have told you already: to Palestine."

———————⋙◉⋘———————

I could not have tolerated things as long as I did were it not for Isabella, from whom warmth, innocence, and enthusiasm emanated at all times. In prior years, we had spent hours together on those happy occasions when we were paired for chores, speaking of our former lives and current interests while peeling potatoes, preparing the dining room for meals, or sweeping the grounds. Since the arrival of the new abbess and my forced isolation from the community, such interactions had ceased.

I dared not jeopardize Isabella's status by seeking her company outside of public settings. But the opportunities we found, standing together in the courtyard or sitting side by side on a garden bench when the abbess was away, were sufficient to sustain a kind of sunlight that illuminated even my gloomiest hours. Isabella marveled at the breadth and depth of knowledge I had acquired through my studies. She loved listening to the plots of works of fiction I had read and ones I invented on my own, but the tale she found most fascinating of all was my life story. She is the only person with whom I ever shared it in all its details. In turn, she told me of her own life—of her strict father and pious mother, of what she learned in class, and of her dream of serving as a bride of Christ. Such unadulterated goodness residing within the soul of a single person seemed to me a unique phenomenon—a trait shared not even by the former abbess.

Isabella's sparkling eyes and smile were sufficient to render me, if not oblivious to my wretchedness, at least immune to it for a while. Every time she looked at me, I experienced both exhilaration and fear, for it seemed to me that everyone must read on her face what I saw there: an irrepressible affection for all things, including me. That this cheerful worldview blossomed amid the grimness that had overtaken the convent and, furthermore, that it had room in it for Joseph Friedmann, must have made the abbess livid. She rarely passed by Isabella without admonishing her to tuck her curls under her head-covering or to adjust her habit and, often enough, to wipe the "bovine" smile off her face. The abbess's discourses at mealtime, on topics such as ungodliness, immodesty, and temptation, were often delivered with a glare directed at Isabella alone.

On the evening of my fifteenth birthday, Isabella came to my room. She was dressed in her black novice's habit, her crimson hair erupting, as usual, from beneath a white headdress, and the ruby smile playing on her lips. "Happy birthday, Joseph," she whispered after I opened the door in response to her tapping. "I brought you a gift." She withdrew from beneath her habit the library's copy of *The Count of Monte Cristo*, which she knew to be one of my favorites.

She beamed as I took it from her hand and leafed through the pages. "How did you get this?" I asked.

"I stole it!" She laughed. "Isn't it marvelous? I felt like David cutting the fringe off King Saul's robe! I was so rebellious!"

"But how did you get into the library? I thought the abbess trusts no one to go in there."

"Normally, she doesn't. But she was too busy to go there herself, so she gave me the key and asked me to fetch her a volume . . . some ancient text having to do with sin and redemption. While I was there, I pinched this."

"You could have just given her this book instead of the one she sent you for. *Monte Cristo* is all about sin and redemption. But it is better that you brought it to me. The Mother Superior would never read such a work, and even if she did, she lacks the insight to recognize herself among the villains."

I looked up from my perusal of the pages, and found my eyes trapped within Isabella's gaze. "Why don't I come into your room, Joseph, and you can tell me the story of *The Count of Monte Cristo*?"

These words jolted me like an electric current. "I . . . I . . . have already told you that story."

"I would like to hear it again."

Isabella advanced, crossing the threshold into my room, and I stepped backward. "I am not sure the abbess would approve of that," I stammered.

"Why would the abbess object? You will simply tell me a story of sin and redemption, the most prominent topic in the convent since her first day here. She might applaud you for contributing to the curriculum!"

"Applause seems unlikely, unless by *applause* you mean *spanking*."

"You're right." She laughed again. "I have seen how she looks at you."

"I can feel those looks even when my back is turned," I answered. "What is she thinking, I wonder, when the abbess looks at you?"

Isabella shrugged. "The two looks are not dissimilar," she murmured.

"I hope that is not true," I responded. "The look she reserves for me can only be described as hatred. The one she has for you is more like . . . disapproval."

"The first is nothing more than an amplification of the second."

I looked at the floor. "I can understand where her hatred of me comes from. But she can't possibly find anything objectionable in you."

"Are you sure of that, Joseph? What is so objectionable in you? What is so unobjectionable in me?"

"I am a Jew, a male, an outsider. All things she despises. You . . ." I swallowed. "Are the most beautiful thing on this hilltop."

The smile that always rested on Isabella's lips broadened. "Yet none of the things you are, whether Jew, male, or outsider, is wrong or hateful, while much of what you are should be praised. The fact that she is blinded to your truths is a loss to all of us. And as for me"—her gaze was so tender, it went through me like a shiver—"she sees truths in me to which *you* are blind."

"I don't care what she sees," I snapped. "Instead of criticizing every loose strand of hair or piece of fabric, she should hold you as an example of what this community aspires to be."

Isabella reached up to tuck in her curls. "So many years with us, and such limited understanding of what this community aspires to, Joseph! As perceptive as you are, you remain incapable of perceiving the true nature of our mission or of my role in the church."

Isabella took another step forward, and I backed farther into the small room. She turned to shut the door behind her, then faced me. In the dim light, her eyes darkened, and tears glinted over her lower eyelashes. "I will be eighteen years old in five months, and ready to take my final vows. But I cannot. Not before finding out what I might be giving up with those vows. I have not been able to focus on chastity because you are constantly in my head." Her arms were at her sides, palms slightly raised. Her gaze was unwavering, a posture of such unmitigated frankness that I felt completely exposed. "I know those thoughts are supposed to make me feel guilty and sinful," she continued, "but they do not. Instead, I feel generous and charitable and loving and honest—all the things I have been told are the marks of a good person." She paused and examined me. "Do you understand?"

"What I understand is that I have felt the same about you since my first day here," I answered. "What I understand is that I want nothing more than to be yours and for you to be mine, just like in the Song of Songs. What I do *not* understand is why such feelings should make *anyone* feel guilty or sinful."

Isabella closed her eyes, and the tears that hung there spilled down her cheeks. She wrung her hands. "I have committed myself to a life in which you have no place. To make room for you, I must abandon my calling. Try to understand, if not for yourself, then for me."

"Abandon your calling, then. If not for yourself, then for me." My heart hammered in my chest. "Together we will create a life worthy of you, and I will take on a commitment of my own: to do whatever I can to make you happy. Let's leave this cheerless place."

Isabella reached out and cupped my face with her palm. Her hand was soft and cool and smelled of the scented candles of the chapel. "Perhaps I shall leave with you, Joseph. Perhaps I shall. But not right now." She stepped right up against me and whispered, her lips brushing against my ear and sending a thrill through me: "There is something else first." I could feel her trembling smile against my cheek.

"Isabella," I murmured.

Her breasts grazed my chest. Her thighs pressed against mine, and against my erection. I felt I might burst and pulled back out of shame, though what I wanted most was to embrace her.

She looked down at the swelling in my pants. Her face lit up, and she clasped my shirt by the neck to pull me toward her. "I know what that is!" she whispered. "Don't be embarrassed. I take it as a sign of your . . . fondness for me."

I drew farther back. "Fondness? Don't call it fondness."

"What shall I call it, then? Not love, Joseph. Too much remains unproven for that word."

I thought a moment. "Perhaps passion, then, if you fear that my feelings are not noble enough for love. I think about you all the time. And if you prefer me not to say, *I love you*, then I will say that I love everything about you."

"Hmmm. That is better. I accept your passion in the spirit in which it is intended." She released her grasp on my collar and began to unbutton my shirt, a determined smile on her lips.

When the backs of her fingers began brushing against the skin of my chest, I could control myself no longer and climaxed. "Isabella!" I grunted, seizing her tightly in my arms, pulsating against her until I regained my self-possession.

"I'm sorry, Isabella, I . . ."

"You didn't wait for me."

"I know. I'm sorry."

She drew her head back and straightened her arms to look at me, and smiled. "I shall give you another chance, Joseph. You do believe in second chances, I hope?"

"I do, but it might take a little time." I was aware of this fact through experiments conducted in the privacy of my room, experiments during which Isabella had always been the object of my fantasies.

"We have time, Joseph. Let us spend it together." She finished unbuttoning my shirt and slipped it off my chest. Then she began to undo her white head-covering, the novice's veil. It was a contraption much more complex than I had imagined. When she was done, her hair cascaded down her shoulders in a cataract of crimson curls. She unfastened the buttons and loops of her habit. "Blow out the candles, Joseph," she instructed, and after she was cast into darkness, she let her raiment drop to the floor. She stepped out of the clothes pooled at her feet, her alabaster skin shimmering in the shadows. I was astounded to see the outline of her naked body, the curves I had no idea existed, the breasts that were so unlike my own and so perfect in their formation. She made her way toward my bed and slipped under the covers. "Come join me," she whispered, her voice nearly indistinguishable from the rustling of the sheets.

I finished undressing and slid next to her, drinking in her impossible softness with my hands and body and lips, squeezing her as if by doing so I might bind her to me forever. I was not aware that people kissed each other with open mouths, and when she placed her lips on mine and caressed my tongue with her own, I thought that Isabella and I were as close to becoming one entity as it was possible for two people to be. I was soon to learn of an even greater closeness. When she perceived that I was ready, she instructed me on how to make love to her. My instincts, though mostly sound, required direction, which she provided patiently.

With her hand guiding me, I entered her, and she cried out. I panicked. "Have I hurt you?" I asked urgently, raising my head to look at her.

"No! More . . ." she panted, her eyes shut tight, her hands clasped behind my back to return me to her. I did what came naturally. And when she lost herself, it was with an exhilaration so unbridled, it seemed to me that all of life and creation were channeling directly through her. Isabella's elation crashed over me, and I followed her over an abyss, my body and soul for a second time transformed into something new.

Isabella's heart pounded against my chest, and over a few minutes, its beat subsided. I buried my face in the crook of her neck, inhaling the soft smell of her skin. When we recovered our breath, I pulled my head back to face her. "That was . . . I cannot even describe it." I exhaled, then embraced her with all my strength. "I love—" I began "—everything about you."

Her lips were joined in a sweet smile. "*How great are thy works, Lord!*" she whispered. I think she meant the quotation only for herself. Then she added, aloud, "It really was as wonderful as I was led to believe . . ."

"Isabella, how did you know all this? They can't possibly teach you these things in class, and I have read every book in the library. There are hints everywhere and some entries in the encyclopedia, but nothing comes close to describing what we just did and how it made me feel. How did you know?"

"One of the novitiates led a very . . . rich life before committing herself to the Lord. She explained things to me."

"Did I do a good job?"

"What do you mean?"

"Without your guidance, I would have had no idea what I was supposed to do. I made a lot of it up."

"Hmmm. Well, in answer to your question: Yes, Joseph. You did a good job. You are a wonderful lover."

I was unaccustomed to being complimented, and I felt myself smiling so broadly, I thought my face might crack. "Really? What is it that makes me a wonderful lover?"

"You are generous and true," she answered. "That, I think, is all you will ever need. Of course, I am speaking as a novice in these matters."

"A *former* novice, you mean," I said. "After we leave this place, we will learn more from each other and grow together. I will remain generous and true to you, and we will find new and even more wonderful ways of loving each other."

Isabella closed her eyes and sighed through smiling lips, and as I think back upon that smile, I am reminded of the sadness of some miracles. She eased me off her, and we rolled onto our sides to face each other. She raised her head and rested it in the palm of her hand, bending her arm at the elbow. "I told you I needed to understand what I would give up to become a nun, and now, thanks to you, I have my answer. How exalted will my sacrifice be, to relinquish this great marvel of life!"

"What sacrifice are you talking about?"

"I am now certain I have chosen the correct path. Because of you."

I embraced her. "And my path is yours. *Wheresoever thou goest, I shall go,*" I said, quoting the Book of Ruth.

"Joseph, our paths must diverge."

"Of course. You can pursue your interests, and I will pursue mine. But we will always walk together."

"You misunderstand me. I intend to become a nun."

"That's fine with me. I, too, will find a job, and we can support ourselves that way until we are ready to have children."

She leaned in to kiss me on the lips. "Joseph, listen: I intend to become a bride of Christ."

"But how can you be a bride of Christ if you are married to me?"

She nodded. It was only then I understood what she had been trying to tell me, and it sent a bolt of fear through me. "I don't believe you! How can you have experienced what we just created together and arrive at the exact wrong conclusion about it?"

She sighed. "Do you believe that what is correct for you is correct for everyone?"

"No, but—"

"This isn't a matter of science."

"I know, but—"

"Try to understand me, Joseph. You may believe you love me, and perhaps you do love me. And I tell you frankly that I love you. But there are different kinds of love, and the highest form of my love exists in a realm to which you have no access. I dedicate myself to Jesus."

"Jesus is not of this world, and you are! You should live in the world in which you exist—the same world in which I exist—not the one you go to after you die."

She quoted Colossians to me: "*Set your mind on things above, not on earthly things . . . Put to death whatever belongs to your earthly nature . . .*"

"That is such nonsense!" I rebutted with Ecclesiastes: "*Whatever thy hand findeth to do, do it with all thy might . . .* God doesn't want us to abandon life!"

"Perhaps not according to *your* interpretation of what God wants, Joseph. But Jesus wishes to use me as a conduit for people to discover the divine within themselves. Some will not be able to do that without me. I will make it possible for them to achieve a higher level of holiness. That is a very great thing, and it will last a lifetime and beyond."

My eyes filled with tears. "But what am I to do without you?"

"You? You will do great things. Of that, I am certain." She kissed me again. "And you must leave the convent. There is nothing for you here, including me. Make your plans and go. The time is coming for both of us." She rose from the bed to dress, and I watched in despair as, for the first and last time, I witnessed Isabella transform herself from a woman into a nun.

All words abandoned me but one, her name, and I pleaded it over and over. In response to each utterance of *Isabella*, she granted me a sad look or bent down to kiss me as I sat on the edge of the bed. She turned to leave, and I rose, calling out her name one last time. She crossed the threshold and closed the door, leaving me to wonder how it was possible to have both gained and lost the greatest hope of my life in an instant.

⬤

I spent the next three months in a daze. I barely perceived the passage of time, until one afternoon, after leaving the classroom, I found a commotion in the courtyard. Isabella was dressed not in her usual habit but in work clothes. She was in tears, and all the novices and nuns were arrayed about her in a semicircle, with the abbess at their head. Next to Isabella was a valise. A taxicab stood outside the gate, its engine running.

"I denounce you in the name of his holiness, the Patriarch of Antioch, and all the faithful of this church!" shrieked the abbess. "Oh, cursed wretch! Fornicator! Pretender, professing to dedicate her body and soul to the Lord, all the while whoring! *The body is not meant for fornication*, First Corinthians tells us, *but for the Lord, and the Lord for the body!* You are condemned and banished!"

Isabella fell to her knees in the dust of the courtyard. "Mother Superior!" she pleaded. "I confess willingly! But I have rededicated myself to Jesus. I am committed to serving Him in chastity for the rest of my life!"

"These protestations of modesty come too late! What arrogance! What deceit! Instead of coming to me, in shame and humility, to confess your sin, you boast of it to your sisters!" The abbess thrust her finger at an older novice, who stood sobbing on the edge of the group with her face in her hands. "You poison their minds with your wickedness!"

"I wasn't boasting! I consulted my colleague only to understand what was happening to me! And I was about to come to you!"

"Liar! Speak no more!"

None of the weeping sisters who stood behind the abbess raised their heads to look at Isabella.

"And in your *chastity*," screeched the abbess, "why do you persist in refusing to name the person with whom you have committed this abomination? Why do you not say who has placed this child, conceived in sin, into your belly?"

I rushed toward Isabella, raised her to her feet, picked up the valise, and guided her toward the waiting taxi. She could not catch her breath, so deep was her anguish.

"There is no need for you to name your seducer," shouted the abbess after us. "It is now proven beyond doubt."

I led Isabella to the car, my hand on the small of her back. "It's all right," I said. "Where is this taxi taking you?"

"To . . . to . . . my . . . parents in . . . S . . . in Sidon," she sobbed.

"I will come for you there. Wait for me."

"Joseph, no! Do not even think about doing that. My father would kill you if you came. Besides, I meant what I said: There is nothing for you and me! My path in life does not include you and never will. Promise that you will never come for me!"

I was stunned. "But . . . a baby!"

"Yes, there is a child, but it is not yours."

I reeled. "What do you mean? Has there been . . . someone else?"

She looked away. "Yes, there is someone else."

"I don't believe you! Look at me as you say that."

She turned to face me. Her bright eyes bored into mine, and she thrust out her chin in determination. "There is someone else, and he is the father of the child."

"You are lying."

The chauffer placed her valise into the trunk. He opened the rear door, and Isabella slipped into the seat while the driver rounded the car. I held on to the doorframe. "I do not ask you to forget me, Joseph." She sobbed, wiping away tears with the palm of her hand. "I know that is not in your power, and I do not wish for it, anyway. But promise that you will never contact me again. That is my wish."

The driver put the car in gear, and Isabella reached out to close the door. I released my hold upon it. She lowered her window. The car began to move.

"You're lying!" I muttered.

"Promise!" she cried. "Promise me!"

"I promise," I whispered, as the taxi rolled down the hill.

I stood outside the gate for a long while, watching the car drive away, a cloud of dust marking its motion for several kilometers. When I could no longer follow its path, I turned and reentered the convent. The abbess was still there with a dwindling crowd.

"Accursed Jew!" she hissed at me. "Why did I let you remain here against my better judgment? You have brought disgrace and sin upon this institution! Prepare your things. You have two days to leave this place forever."

I halted a few meters from her. "Where shall I go?" I inquired. I had no idea where my mother and father were, and didn't even know my mother's new last name. The doctor's suggestion to go to Palestine had seemed as practical as relocating to the moon.

"Where you go interests me not in the least!" the abbess rasped. "But the day after tomorrow, that gate will shut upon you for the very last time." She turned on her heel and strode into the main building.

I retreated to my room and took stock of it. The small bag in which my mother had packed my belongings the day I arrived at the convent was stowed under my bed, and almost all my worldly possessions still fit into it. It would take me about half an hour to gather everything I owned and pack it.

I took the copy of *The Count of Monte Cristo* Isabella had stolen from the library. I leafed through it, ripped out a page, carefully folded it, and put it into my pocket. I felt an exhaustion so deep it was all I could do to get into bed, still wearing my day clothes. Making plans for the future would have to wait until morning. Within minutes, I was in a deep sleep.

I was awakened by a wet, sweet-smelling rag pressed firmly against my face.

I struggled. Then the world went black.

Chapter Thirteen

I extend myself, attempting to rise from a great depth, desperate to open my eyes. A heaviness on my thighs weighs me down. I reach out to push the burden aside, but my strength dissipates. I sink again and ascend again, over and over, like a drowning man submerged by an unseen hand whenever he approaches the surface. Blows pound either side of my face. A rasping voice in my left ear: "I turn thy lust against thee . . . I draw from thee thy last drop of evil . . ." The weight pulses against my pelvis. Something scratches my chest, like the claws of a beast. And through the fog, a painful release, like mist, a sickening climax, and rhythmic grunting issuing from my own throat. I go under again, into an even deeper void.

And then, a baritone, "Do not be afraid." My consciousness rises. I swim upward through honey so thick, it threatens to suffocate me. A wave of nausea. Pressure on my cheek turning my face sideways. A light throbbing behind closed eyelids. And then, two fingers on my wrist, assessing my pulse.

I had no trouble recognizing where I was, even with my eyes closed. The smell of antiseptic solution admixed with cigarette smoke existed in only one place in the compound. I pried open an eyelid, and the ceiling lamps and whitewashed walls confirmed that I was in the clinic.

I became aware of a dull ache in my scrotum. Hearing the rush of water, I turned my head to find the doctor, his back to me, at the sink. He was scrubbing instruments, the rapid rhythm of his torso and arms accompanied by the metallic clacking with which I was so familiar from my own turns at the washing station. I groaned, and he rushed to my side, wiping his hands with a towel.

"Ah, Yusouf!" the doctor said. "Do you recognize me?"

I nodded.

"Do you know where you are?"

I nodded again. Under the sheets, I moved my hand in the direction of my groin. "It hurts. How . . . what . . ." I knew what I wanted to ask but couldn't bring myself to utter it.

Dr. al-Moualem looked about himself uneasily. He bent toward me and whispered in my ear. The smoke and whiskey were heavy on his breath. "The abbess herself came to supervise the procedure. She left me no choice. I am sorry, Yusouf."

My eyes teared up. The doctor hurried to dab them with the towel. "Shh," he breathed. "Listen to me. The abbess insisted, and I operated on you. But . . ." He paused.

"What?"

"I made my usual incisions, but instead of obliterating your spermatic cords, I only transected your *vasa deferentia*. Do you understand?"

I understood. The doctor had sterilized me, but I had not been castrated.

"She had observed my technique before and knew my castration procedure leaves the testes in place. She was unable to distinguish between the two operations. You will still be a man, Yusouf. And you can even be a father, though it would take special procedures to make it so."

He continued dabbing at my eyes.

"I am sorry, Yusouf. Tonight I committed an unforgiveable offense against the Hippocratic oath. In a career that, may Allah forgive me, has not otherwise been free of offenses against my calling, I now add betrayal. I am sorry," he murmured again. "Perhaps it was merely self-justification, but I told myself that if I didn't operate on you, she would find someone else who would." He took a deep breath and sighed. "I will be leaving this place. But first, I need to see you safely from here. You first, then me."

"Where . . . where . . . ?"

"You must go, and quickly. I told the abbess you would be unable to move for at least thirty-six hours, and though that is usually advisable, you will have to suffice with twenty-four. If you are still here tomorrow afternoon, she plans a send-off for you that will make Isabella's departure seem like a ladies' tea party. It is now four in the morning. You will leave here tonight. A taxicab will meet you outside the gate two hours after midnight."

I again moved my hand toward my groin. "It hurts."

"Yes, it does, but you must leave, anyway."

"Where . . . will I go? I have no one . . ." I started to doze off.

The doctor jostled me by the shoulder. "I have told you already. Many times. You will go south."

"Why . . . ?"

"To Palestine. You will join the Zionists and be present at the founding of the Jewish state."

"Jewish state . . ." I muttered, and fell asleep.

⸺⸺●⸺⸺

I awoke again to find the abbess looking down at me, the corners of her mouth upturned, her eyes sparkling, the skin of her cheeks as smooth as porcelain. When she was certain she had my attention, she grasped the sheet at my neck and in one motion swept it down to uncover me. I gasped at the sudden movement. Casting her gaze toward my genitals, her lips formed a quick, hard smile, and she departed, leaving me exposed.

I reached down to draw the sheet back over my body and passed out again.

When I awoke the third time, I felt well. The pain had dulled, and I was completely alert, as though nothing had occurred to cloud my senses. It was broad daylight, and a nurse entered the room carrying a tray of food from the convent's kitchen: a bowl of thin soup, some cucumbers, a hard-boiled egg, a pat of the delicious butter churned by the sisters, and two slices of the fresh bread that was delivered to the convent every morning from Beirut. I devoured it all, an urgent hunger having overtaken me.

"I have to pee," I informed the nurse when I was done. She brought me a handheld urinal and instructed me how to use it. After trying without success, I asked her whether I might urinate the old-fashioned way, and she helped me get to the toilet. I was pleased to discover that though I still ached, I was able to empty my bladder without difficulty. It felt nearly normal.

The nurse helped me back into bed. I felt completely awake and vital, yet I was asleep again as soon as I laid my head back. I had witnessed the sedation induced by methylbenzene combined with chloroform several times before, but I had never lingered long enough after the doctor's procedures to observe their potent aftereffects, which lasted nearly a full day. I was next awakened by an attendant who brought me dinner. When I finished eating, the nurse returned and informed me that she was leaving. "Since you are familiar with the infirmary, and Dr. al-Moualem intends to spend the night here," she said, "he has allowed me to go home. *Ma'a salaame*, Yusouf."

"*Ma'a salaame*."

As soon as I heard her shut and lock the yellow front door, Dr. al-Moualem appeared at my bedside. "Yusouf," he said, "it is time to prepare for your journey. Come with me to my office." I wrapped myself in a hospital gown and followed him to the familiar desk, on which was spread a large topographical map of southern Lebanon. "The taxi will take you to the town of Marj 'Ayoun, about ninety kilometers south of here." He pointed with his index finger. "You will stay at the home of a Greek Orthodox colleague of mine named Dr. Barakat. And here"—he took a pencil out of his drawer and drew a circle around a nearby hilltop—"is a small settlement the Jews call Metula, a distance of about nine kilometers across relatively easy terrain, with a climb up a hill at the end. The southern border of Lebanon has been guarded since our independence two years ago, but Dr. Barakat knows all the passages, and he will show you the one to use. You need to rest at Dr. Barakat's home for a day or two because I fear that even an easy nine-kilometer walk will lead to edema. Do you understand?"

"Yes," I said.

"I have informed Dr. Barakat all about you, and he is more than happy to be your host until you are ready to cross the border. He knows how to send a message to inform me that all has gone well."

Bending over the map and drawing a line with his pencil, the doctor continued. "You remember the navigation techniques I taught you, yes? How to line up the map with the landmarks in front of you and to plot your route in the open country using the elevation lines? You can navigate as well as I, so you will have no problem going this short distance."

"Doctor . . ." I interrupted. "Why did you do this to me?"

He laid down the pencil. Then he raised his head, and his eyes met mine. His lips quivered. "Yusouf..."

"I am not a rapist. Not insane. Not a danger to society."

A smile lifted the corner of his mouth, causing his eye to squint, and a tear fell onto the map. He brushed it off. "You are the opposite of those things, my son."

"Do not call me your son!" I snapped. "If you were my father, then you would be the second father to take from me more than he has given."

"I acknowledge that I dreamed of being a father to you," he whispered. "I should have led you away from here two years ago. But you are correct. I am unworthy of the term *father*, just as I am unworthy of the title *healer*. Another failing to add to a long list of failings." He sighed. "This 'holy community' over the years came close to draining me of everything that can be called honor. Last night, I finished the job myself."

I gazed at the broken man in front of me, who had nothing left to him but remorse. Yet I found no compassion for him in my heart. Anger occupied all the spaces where pity might have found purchase.

"And now, Yusouf, I once more beg your forgiveness, though I am not entitled to it, and bid you farewell. At four in the morning, my own taxicab will come to the gate."

"Where will you go?"

"Back to Africa, I think, where the piety is less ungodly." He drew a key from his pocket and unlocked the cabinet beneath his desk. He took out two items: an alarm clock and a nearly full bottle of scotch whiskey. "What an inglorious end to a mediocre career," he muttered. He wound the clock, set it by his watch, and activated the alarm. "I have set this for one thirty in the morning. Go to sleep in the infirmary bed and take this with you. When the alarm rings, you press this button here to silence it." He reached under his desk and withdrew a roll of clothes. "Here are the clothes and shoes you were wearing last night when you fell asleep. Get dressed and exit the compound by the front gate. It will be unlocked. Walk one hundred meters down the road, where it bends to the northeast, and wait for the taxi. The driver knows you will be there. When he arrives, get right in and drive off without delay." The doctor eyed me a moment longer.

"I understand," I said.

"And now, leave me, Yusouf. Shut the door on your way out, please."

I turned and walked out of the office, and as I swung the door closed, he called out to me.

"One more thing. Do not bother going back to your room in the convent. All your things have already been destroyed."

"Everything has been destroyed? My books? My letters?"

"Everything was thrown into the incinerator at dawn. A lock has been set on the door."

I glared at him, and he looked away.

"I see," I said. "May I use your pencil?"

"What? My pencil?"

"Yes, please. And two sheets of paper. If you are inclined to send me on my way with a gift, these are what I ask for. I shall return the pencil."

"What a unique person you are . . ." He opened the drawer and withdrew two sheets of paper, laying them on the desk alongside the pencil.

"Can you sharpen it, please?"

He shrugged and pulled out a small sharpener, with which he honed the point of the pencil.

I approached the desk and took the items.

The doctor uncorked the bottle and took a long gulp. He wiped his mouth with his sleeve. I left and shut the door.

I returned to the bed in the recovery room as the strains of Umm Kulthum's ballads—Dr. al-Moualem's preferred supplement to whiskey for treating sorrow—began issuing from the phonograph in his office.

After an hour, the songs yielded to the rhythmic scratching of the needle on the record's run-out groove. The infirmary was otherwise silent.

I rose from the bed, disengaged the alarm clock, and turned on the small electric light by the desk in the nurse's station. I retrieved the pile of clothes the doctor had given me from under the bed, on which lay the topographical map. Shedding the infirmary gown, I noticed several linear scratches along my chest and flanks, and I recalled the sensation in my delirium of being attacked by a wild animal. I dressed and laid the map on the desk. Taking up the pencil, I drew a route through the backcountry from Bhamdoun to Metula, down dry riverbeds and up hillsides, staying off the roads and only using trails marked as dotted lines. I spent the next hour memorizing the first twelve kilometers of the route, noting the topographical features that would serve as landmarks. At that time of year, the night sky in Lebanon would be cloudless, and the moon was waxing. I would use the stars to navigate.

Next, I sat down with the pencil and paper. On the first sheet, I wrote this note:

Dr. al-Moualem:

You have taught me much over the years, knowledge that will last me a lifetime. That gift of knowledge and your friendship were conferred willingly, and for that, I thank you. Though I would gladly have given you in return almost anything among my small number of possessions, you have taken from me without permission something of great value, and furthermore a thing of no use to you. You have attempted to compensate for this by arranging my escape from here, a former refuge now become a place of torment. But as I see it, the balance between us remains in my favor. I hope you see the justice of what I now do.

I wish you peace.

You said everything I own has been destroyed. But I still have memories, and some of those require destruction also.

Yusouf Friedmann

Next, I fished in my pants pocket. It was still there. The page I had ripped out of *The Count of Monte Cristo* before falling asleep in my room the night before. I smoothed out the folds in the paper on the desk's surface with the palms of my hands. Picking up the pencil, I drew an oval around the passage in which Edmond Dantès names himself the avenger of those who unjustly condemned him to imprisonment and death: *Farewell kindness, humanity, and gratitude! . . . now the God of Vengeance yields to me his power to punish the wicked!*

On the second sheet of paper I wrote this list:
Backpack
Sleeping mat
Blanket
Two canteens

Toothbrush
Soap
Walking shoes
Woolen socks
Sweater
Hat
Money
Food
Map
Compass
Swiss army knife
Electric torch

When the list was done, I stood up, but quickly sat down again to add four more items, not because I needed to be reminded, but because they were an expression of my resolve:

String
Rock
Kerosene
Match

In my stocking feet, I stole into the doctor's office and found him passed out, his head on the table, his arms sprawled in front of him, the empty bottle of whiskey lying on its side on the table. I removed the phonograph needle from the record and turned the player off, laying the letter I had written him on a clean area of the desk alongside the pencil. Then, knowing where the doctor kept his trekking supplies, I collected the items on my list and placed them in his backpack. I pulled open the drawer where he kept his money and cigarettes and withdrew a box of matches and eighty-five Lebanese pounds in various denominations, splitting them between my pockets, the backpack, and a flap on the inside of the hat. Holding his hiking boots in my hand, I padded out and headed back toward the recovery room, where I organized the items in the backpack, donned the woolen socks, which allowed my feet to fit snugly into the doctor's boots, slung the backpack onto my shoulders, and walked out.

Exiting through the yellow door into the convent grounds I headed toward the kitchen, where I packed a half loaf of bread, cucumbers, an apple, hard-boiled eggs, nuts, dried fruit, and cheese. I filled the canteens, attaching them to the doctor's hiking belt at my hips.

My next stop was the equipment shed, where I picked up a twenty-liter jerrican of kerosene. Striding to the darkened main building, I opened the door to Madame Aoun's anteroom and retrieved the key to the abbess's office, which I knew was stored under some papers in the top drawer of her desk. I entered the inner office and splashed a third of the kerosene over every flammable surface. I opened the windows wide, stood at the door, lit the match, and tossed it onto the chair upon which I had sat the day I met the new abbess. It immediately rose up in flames. I shut the door, calculating that the remainder of the convent, whose walls were made of solid limestone, would be unharmed. The abbess's office would be completely consumed in the fire.

I exited the building, setting down the jerrican about thirty meters from the entrance, a safe distance from the flames, and near a hefty rock around which I had tied the page from *Monte Cristo*. I ran toward the building and heaved the rock through the glass window of the abbess's bedroom on the second floor. The pane shattered, and a startled cry issued from the darkness beyond. I waited for her pale face to appear through the jagged opening in the glass, making sure she got a good look at me.

"You!" she screeched. "You!"

"Read the message I have just delivered to you," I called. She retreated into the room, and a few seconds later, I saw the flare of a match and flicker of a candle. She shrieked once more and returned to the window, her face contorted.

"You might be interested to learn that your office is on fire," I shouted. I turned and ambled through the front gate, shutting it behind me. Observing my own fingers resetting the latch conjured the memory of the gnarled hands of Maria Theresa, the old abbess, unlocking that same barrier when I'd first arrived at the compound seven years earlier.

"*Ma'a salaame*, Mother Maria Theresa," I whispered. *Peace be with you.* "*Ma'a salaame*, Isabella. *Ma'a salaame*, Yusouf." I spun around and began to walk down the road. After a few hundred meters, I turned to gaze at the red halo rising from the hilltop. The headlamps of the taxicab the doctor had ordered wound their way up the hill, and when they were about two hundred meters away, I hid behind some shrubbery until the car passed.

Three hundred meters farther down the road, I turned south along a goat path I had hiked many times before, in the direction of Palestine.

It was June 10, 1946. I was fifteen years old.

Chapter Fourteen

My banishment from the convent might have sufficed for the abbess had she been permitted to usher me out on her own terms. But the mode of my leave-taking made it a certainty that nothing short of arrest and imprisonment would satisfy her. My destination, the hilltop town of Metula in Palestine, was about ninety kilometers by foot due south of Bhamdoun. The route I plotted for that first night began in a southerly direction for three kilometers. I planned to leave obvious tracks that would suddenly disappear at a rocky pass. Then I would veer sharply, leaving no traces, and end up several kilometers north and west of Bhamdoun, exactly the opposite direction anyone would have anticipated. It was a twelve-kilometer hike.

In a postscript scribbled on the note I had left on the doctor's desk, I stated my intention to walk south to Marj 'Ayoun and begged him not to share the information with anyone other than Dr. Barakat, who should expect me in three to four days rather than that same morning. Dr. al-Moualem would assume I had used the map to plot a direct southern route either on the roads or, more likely, via off-road trails. I had not doubted Dr. al-Moualem's intent to shield me from harm, but I could not risk the chance of his resolve collapsing in the face of the abbess's fury. He would crack, informing her that I could walk no more than a short distance in my diminished state, and that she would find me in the morning within a few kilometers due south of the convent. Search parties would be dispatched at dawn, with the expectation of returning me to the convent, then to the police station to face justice.

Over the years I had hiked all the trails surrounding Bhamdoun in a radius of ten kilometers and had become familiar with many more spanning a greater distance. I was able to navigate that first night without referring to the map. After heading south down a dry riverbed, known in Arabic as a wadi, and purposely leaving footprints in the dust, trampling upon the brush, and discarding eggshells and an apple core in full view of the path, I scrabbled up a rocky hillside to a paved road. I hid in the bushes while a fire truck and an ambulance raced past, sirens wailing, then walked west on the pavement for about two kilometers before descending into another rock-strewn wadi heading due north. My goal was to reach a small cave I knew, hollowed out of the limestone about five kilometers north of the Beirut-Damascus road and used as a shelter by shepherd boys during the hot summer months. At that time of year, the cave would be unoccupied, and I would be able to hide from view in the cool shade for the entire following day.

My scrotum had begun aching as soon as I'd set out. I cupped my genitals in my hand, but the swelling increased with every step until it seemed like I was cradling an object the size and consistency of an orange. I reached my destination at dawn, the ache so profound, I believed it would have been impossible for me to take even a single additional step. Within minutes of removing my backpack and laying out the mat with a rolled-up sweater as a pillow, I was asleep.

I remained in place the entire day, the following night, and the next day, leaving plenty of time for recuperation and reflection. It made perfect sense to me that a life begun as the offspring of a melancholy teenage mother and a detached older father should come to hiding out in a cave as a fugitive. My expectations from life had been modeled on the examples of Oliver Twist, Edmond Dantès, Jephthah the Gileadite, and others like them. As far as I knew, every boy or young man encountered an inflection point, and I was happy to think that mine was finally upon me. Though I would have chosen none of the milestones on my life's journey to that point, I accepted as a matter of course that my path would lead, if not to happiness, then at least to adventure. I felt no fear, only resolve and confidence.

The sun set into my eyes and roused me from sleep on my second evening in the cave, casting a spotlight on the convergence of time and space in my life. It seemed to me that everything I had experienced was part of a grand plan propelling me toward my destination, the nascent Jewish state in Palestine. Yet that destination remained mostly indefinable. The city of Jerusalem, whose destroyed temple had been the beating heart of Jewish souls for nearly three thousand years, was less than 250 kilometers from Beirut. But it had always seemed to belong to a different dimension, one that would manifest in the physical world only after the coming of the Messiah.

During my childhood, even the most irreligious Jewish home had a box on the mantel into which loose change would be deposited before the Sabbath for the benefit of Jews settling the Holy Land. To a child's ears, the exploits of those pioneers seemed like mythological tales. Young men and women draining swamps, braving malaria, fending off Arab marauders . . . These accounts seemed like echoes of the report delivered by the spies Moses had sent to scout the country after the Exodus from Egypt: *That land . . . devours its inhabitants.* And yet hadn't the generation born in the wilderness after forty years of wandering risen to achieve the impossible? The Bible stories that had always resonated most with me were from the Book of Judges—tales of the adventures of Israelite heroes struggling to establish sovereignty in the Land of Israel. Was it really possible that history could repeat itself, and that I might play a role in the modern-day version of those grand events?

What was I to expect, I wondered, in this land to which I was headed? According to the Hebrew Bible, it was the province of kings and prophets, shepherds and poets. According to my reading of Christian works, it was the forfeited inheritance of a faithless people who refused to accept Jesus as their savior. According to Dr. al-Moualem, it was the plaything of geopolitical superpowers and a seething pot of religious, ethnic, and political upheaval.

I later learned that all these characterizations were true. But there was one overriding truth, imparted to me by the Muslim doctor of a Maronite mission. What made me feel that the Land of Israel had been my unknown home all along was this: For me, and for the majority of the Jewish people, it had become the last and only place on Earth where we might feel we belonged. And thus, I directed my thoughts and steps toward Palestine, eager to join the great Zionist project and consign the vestiges of my former life to the flames with which I had torched the abbess's office.

On the third evening, I was finally ready to continue my journey. The swelling and pain had subsided. I had eaten all the food I'd taken from the convent's kitchen, and for the moment was content. I took out my map to review the twenty kilometers I intended to cover that night, skirting Bhamdoun on its north side, recrossing the road ten kilometers east of town, and heading south. I memorized the entire route and all the landmarks, hoping by doing so to avoid needing to use the torch to examine the map.

I soon passed a farm, where I filled my canteens from an irrigation spout and picked some cucumbers and grapes. The moon, nearly full, had risen over the eastern horizon, dimming the haze of the Milky Way. I made good time and, with the tip of Orion's sword pointing south and the North Star at my back, easily kept track of my bearings without referring to the compass. During my orienteering training with the doctor, I had learned how many paces were required to cover one hundred meters on flat ground, a number I adjusted upward depending on the terrain. With accuracy within a few dozen meters, I could keep track of my progress even over a distance of many kilometers.

As dawn approached, I clambered out of the ravine in which I was walking and reached the outskirts of a village. My nose led me to a bakery, where rows of bread rolls were cooling on outdoor racks alongside tables stacked with supplies for the day's business. A chained dog began to bay. I raced to the shelves, pocketed three rolls, a block of hard cheese, and a small jar of olives in oil, leaving a couple of Lebanese pounds under a rock on a nearby table. I sped back into the wadi just as the sky began to lighten, walked an additional thousand meters, and found a resting spot between two large boulders that would provide shade throughout the day and that I hoped was not popular with scorpions.

Thus I passed three additional days sleeping and nights trekking, and before dawn on the final day camped about two kilometers south of Marj 'Ayoun. I had never intended to present myself to Dr. Barakat, who could not be trusted to keep me safe. Awakening in the afternoon, I scoped out the town and its surroundings from a hilltop, seeing nothing unusual. No search parties. No uproar. Just a quiet Lebanese village on a hot day. To the west, the nine-hundred-year-old Crusader castle of Beaufort stood sentry over the deep gorge of the Litani River. I had read about Beaufort in history books and was thrilled to be standing in sight of the spot where Saladin besieged the Crusader garrison in 1189. To the east, Mount Hermon soared above the Golan Heights, snow still coating its crest. Thinking of Isabella, I recited to myself Hebrew lines from the fourth chapter of the Song of Songs: *With me from Lebanon, my bride, with me from Lebanon, come! Look from the top of Amana, from the peaks of Senir and Hermon, from the lions' dens, from the mountain haunts of leopards.*

That night I would make the crossing into Palestine.

Darkness fell, and I laced up the doctor's shoes, checked my pack, and set out. Though the distance to Metula was less than seven kilometers, I would wait until daylight to enter the settlement. The danger of capture by the abbess might be behind me, but there were plenty of other ways of encountering disaster. The doctor's teaching of current events had included newspaper accounts illustrating the hair-trigger tensions in the border region. The British were desperately trying to maintain control over Palestine while the Arabs and Jews jockeyed for primacy in the preliminaries to the conflict everyone knew was coming. Stealing into any community along the frontier under the cover of darkness was a reliable method of getting shot by a sentry. I intended to camp overnight a few hundred meters outside Metula and present myself at daybreak at its front gate, a white undershirt held high above my head with both hands.

My path led me to the bridge traversing the stream Nahr Bareighit, known in Hebrew as Nahal 'Ayoun. From there, it was a short walk on the road to Metula. There was a small British encampment on the Lebanese side of the bridge and a guard booth along the road. In the three hours I spent scouting the crossing, I learned that once every hour, a British soldier ventured out for a brief patrol before retreating to the booth.

After the third such foray, I entered the ditch on the far side of the road, passed the British camp, and stole up the embankment, pausing at the foot of the bridge. Crossing over would be a metamorphosis for me. I would shed my former life on its north side and, on its south, emerge as a participant in the rebirth of the Jewish nation after nearly two thousand years of exile. The notion that the biblical history I so treasured would be recapitulated in my own lifetime was thrilling beyond expression. There was no need to look back. I adjusted my pack and strode from Lebanon into Palestine, fancying myself a Joshua crossing the Jordan.

As my heel touched the Land of Israel for the very first time, I heard the crunch of gravel, and before I could react, a hood was thrown over my head. A heavy body barreled into me, hurling me off the road and down the incline. A pair of strong arms encircled me and rushed me onward, simultaneously propelling and supporting me while I stumbled across the rocky terrain. About fifteen seconds later, there was a huge explosion as the bridge I had just crossed blew up.

Still enveloped in the iron embrace, my unknown companion and I staggered at the blast but kept our footing. I was driven onward, quaking under the hood. After a few meters, a strong hand was placed on my shoulder, and we came to a stop.

"Who the hell is that?" a whisper demanded in Hebrew.

"I have no idea. Some fucking Arab kid," came the reply.

"Is he a spy, an idiot, or just the luckiest person in the world?"

"No idea, Gidi."

"We don't have time for this shit. Take the sack off him, Avi." And then, raising his voice slightly so it could be heard, the voice who had been addressed as Gidi called out: "Yossi, get over here, and bring your Arabic with you. We have thirty seconds to figure out who this kid is and what to do with him before the shooting starts."

The sack was ripped off my head, and I found myself facing a man in his early twenties, dressed in military fatigues, shirtsleeves rolled up above the elbow. His curly locks cascaded onto his forehead, his eyes glinting red in the light of the fire coming from the bridge. A scowl was set on his lips, and his rifle pointed at my chest.

"Yossi, come on, get over here!" he ordered.

A heavyset, red-faced youth raced forward and panted in Arabic. "Who are you? What are you doing here?"

"I can answer in Arabic," I responded, "but I can also speak Hebrew, if you like."

Yossi's mouth fell open.

"What'd he say?" demanded Gidi.

"He said he speaks Hebrew."

"*What?*" Addressing me, Gidi asked, "Where did you learn Hebrew?"

"At first in my father's house, then in school, and then from reading the Bible."

"Are you Jewish?"

"Of course."

"What is this," Gidi exclaimed, "some kind of movie?" The sound of gunning car engines erupted from over the ridge, and a searchlight began sweeping the area. Machine gun and rifle fire began ringing out. "Damn it, damn it!" He took about three seconds to make up his mind. "He's coming with us!"

Gidi turned to the circle of young men who surrounded us clad in various shades of khaki (I later learned that two of the men were women) and gave orders. "We're moving out! I am in the lead. Avi, you are in the rear. This little cockroach of an I-don't-know-what-he-is stays in the middle of the column with Yossi's hand on his shoulder or his belt or his ass or his balls. I don't care how you do it, Yossi, but he makes it to the gathering point with the rest of us. And you!" he whispered fiercely, jabbing me in the chest with his forefinger. "You don't make a sound, and you keep up with the platoon or you will be shot and left in the field! Do you understand?"

Had I not already good reason to escape the scene of the bridge bombing, the prospect of Yossi grabbing me by my still-sensitive balls would have sufficed to keep me quiet and moving. I nodded.

"And Yossi, take the backpack off him, won't you? For all I know, he has explosives of his own in there."

We double-timed it for about two and a half hours to Kibbutz Gan Miriam, where we arrived a couple of hours before dawn. Gidi stood waiting just inside the gate, eyeing each of the soldiers as they passed. When Yossi and I came up, he grabbed me by the shirt. "You're staying with me," he said. "Yossi, search his pack, remove anything suspicious, and bring the rest back. We will be in the office. Bring sandwiches, a thermos of tea, and a couple of glasses, please."

I stood by Gidi until all the men and women passed, and he addressed each of them by name, complimenting them on a good job and thanking them for their work. When Avi brought up the rear, Gidi raised his hand, and Avi clapped it and gave him a bear hug. "We did it!" Avi exclaimed.

Gidi turned to me. "Let's go. After me."

He led me to a shack that contained a makeshift office. A naked electric bulb hung from a wire in the middle of the ceiling, and in the back of the room was a desk with three chairs around it, one behind and two in front. Gidi rounded the desk to sit behind it and motioned me into one of the chairs in front.

"What is your name?" he asked.

"Yosef," I answered, using the Hebrew pronunciation of my name.

"Yosef what?"

"Yosef Friedmann."

"What were you doing on the bridge?"

I searched for an explanation that might sound credible.

"Yes?" Gidi pressed.

"I was immigrating."

He laughed out loud, a sound so startlingly uninhibited, I dared hope it might signify my own liberation. His green eyes sparkled. "Ah, that explains it. You were immigrating!"

"Yes."

"Where from, and where to?"

"From Bhamdoun, a town on the Beirut-Damascus road about ninety kilometers from here, to Palestine." I pronounced the name the Arabic way: *Falesteen.*

Gidi suddenly became serious. "Not *Falesteen*. *Eretz Yisrael*. The Land of Israel. Our past and future sovereign state."

"*Eretz Yisrael*," I said, nodding. I liked the sound of it. And this young soldier, this dashing, courageous, decisive, caring, and intelligent commander, who reminded me so much of the biblical Gideon, was exactly what I had imagined the youth of this country to be. Within seconds of the sack being torn off my head by the bridge, I had felt like my place was among them.

Yossi entered with my pack and the sandwiches and tea Gidi had requested. Gidi poured two cups and gestured toward the refreshments. He grabbed a sandwich and started chewing.

"You sound like an Arab and speak like you learned Hebrew from a book. Why?"

"Because I grew up among the Arabs and learned Hebrew from a book— the Bible."

"How old are you?"

"Fifteen and three months."

Gidi ran his hand through his hair. "You look at least fifteen and a half." He smiled. "Where is your family?"

"I have no family."

"You are an orphan?"

I hesitated. "Yes."

"How did you come here?"

"I was raised in a . . ." I didn't know the Hebrew word for *convent*, and used the French. "In a *couvent*, and—"

"What's a *couvent*?"

"A *couvent* is a place where women learn to become . . . uh . . . *moniales*, and—"

"What's a *moniales*?"

I searched for words. "It is like a Christian female Nazirite," I answered, using the term applied in the Bible to individuals consecrated to serve God.

Gidi threw up his arms. "So, you were raised in some kind of Christian yeshiva for Nazirite girls. Is that what you are telling me?"

It was a useful characterization. "Yes. A Christian yeshiva for Nazirite girls," I answered.

"Are you a Christian?"

"I told you. I am Jewish."

"A Nazirite?"

"No."

"A girl?" The corner of his mouth turned up.

I did not answer.

Gidi swallowed the last of his sandwich and wiped his mouth with his sleeve. He downed the tea and poured himself another glass. "OK. For the moment, let's pretend this is not the most unbelievable thing I have ever heard. That rather than being an Arab spy trained to speak Hebrew, you are a Jewish orphan raised in a Christian yeshiva for Nazirite girls. How is it that you were at my bridge precisely at the moment I was assigned to blow it up?"

I paused. "It was a good time for me to immigrate."

"Again with the immigration? Why did you need to immigrate precisely tonight? Why not the night before or the night after?"

"This was the first opportunity I had to make it here on foot after setting fire to the office of the *couvent*'s leader."

Gidi nodded thoughtfully. "Of course. Before leaving the yeshiva, it was only natural for you to set fire to the rabbi's office, and that delayed your 'immigration' over the bridge."

"Yes, but not a rabbi. She is a woman and—" I shrugged, despairing of my ability to explain the concept of "abbess" in biblical Hebrew. The Old Testament, the source of almost all my Hebrew, was completed centuries before the birth of Jesus. "All right. She is like a rabbi. But she deserved it."

"No doubt, no doubt. Of course she deserved it. I am only glad that I am not your religious studies teacher." He slapped his hands on the table and stood. "Yosef, we are not making a lot of progress in this conversation. The British will be raiding this kibbutz in less than two hours. My unit needs to disappear into thin air within the next thirty minutes. You will have to continue this tale from *One Thousand and One Nights* some other time. After me." He led me out of the office.

"By the way," Gidi added, as we made our way to a bus idling in the courtyard of the kibbutz, "I hope you realize I saved your life today. It was lucky I saw you approaching the bridge just before the charge was set to go off. I had to send Avi racing up to stop the engineer. And then I wanted to strangle someone while you dragged your tuchus across the bridge like some sort of general on parade. A different commander might not have risked the mission to figure out whether you were friend or foe, reckoning that either way, you weren't worth the trouble." He frowned. "They would have been right to do so."

"Thank you," I said.

"You're welcome," he replied, and climbed into the bus, beckoning me to sit beside him on the front bench.

Chapter Fifteen

And thus, by crossing the creek at Nahal 'Ayoun, I cast myself into one of the most extraordinary torrents of modern history. After nearly two thousand years in exile, the Jews were streaming toward Zion, their ancient new homeland. Their purpose was to restore a kind of normalcy to a nation withered by centuries of dependence and alienation in the Diaspora. Zionism, the movement to reestablish a Jewish state in the Land of Israel, had been a fantasy fifty years earlier. By the end of World War II, idealistic youth had transformed countless clichés into reality—draining swamps, making the desert bloom, raising industry in a land that in many ways had been frozen in time since the days of Jesus.

The Jewish community in Palestine was desperate to acquire as many citizens as possible, regardless of their background, education, culture, language, wealth, and religious observance. These were thrown into the most diverse and cacophonous melting pot the world has ever seen. The gathering of exiles from every inhabited corner of the earth led to a doubling of the Jewish population of Palestine between 1931 and 1936, from 175,000 to 370,000 people. This trend accelerated in the aftermath of the Holocaust, as tens of thousands fled devastation in search of refuge. And in this place where almost everyone was from somewhere else, I permitted myself to feel that I had finally found a home.

It was a home perched atop an active volcano. I pursued my education in regional history and politics, which Dr. al-Moualem had initiated, by reading every newspaper, essay, and history book I could find. I learned about early attempts to create internal governance in Palestine through collaboration between Jews and Arabs. These efforts had failed, sealing the fate of the region to ethnic turmoil. Hostility between the two peoples swelled over the years, and in 1936, the Arabs of Palestine adopted a new tactic. The Arab Revolt began, a three-year uprising against the British colonial administration of the region, known as the Mandate. The revolt's goals were Arab independence and curtailment of Jewish immigration and land purchases. When it morphed into a terror campaign, the Jewish community in Palestine (known as the *Yishuv*) formed an underground army called the *Haganah* (*defense* in Hebrew). There was a tacit understanding, through which the Yishuv supported the British in suppressing the rebellion, and later on in the struggle to defeat Nazi Germany, and the British turned a blind eye toward the Haganah's mostly defensive military actions.

By the time the Arab Revolt ebbed in 1939, thousands were dead, the large majority of them Arabs. The Yishuv emerged strengthened in arms, territory, and political and military organization while the Arabs suffered further disunity, political turmoil, and marginalization, along with economic hardship due to their disengagement from the financially thriving Jewish community.

Good relations between the Yishuv and the British eventually soured, in part when the British, in order to stem the tilt of the Arab world's sympathies toward the Nazis, reneged on promises made earlier to support the establishment of a Jewish homeland in Palestine. By the end of World War II, hostilities between Jews and Arabs had escalated beyond the point of repair, and the Haganah was in active conflict with the Mandatory government. It sank British patrol boats, bombed British outposts, raided British prisons to free Jewish prisoners, and finally destroyed ten strategic bridges controlled by the British on the night of June 16, 1946. One of those ten bridges spanned Nahal 'Ayoun, the stream I'd crossed on my way into Palestine.

Gidi took me under his wing, presenting me to his commanding officer and introducing me to his family. He arranged for me to be absorbed into Kibbutz Gan Miriam, the settlement to which we had retreated after blowing up the bridge at Nahal 'Ayoun. I melded into kibbutz life effortlessly, harmonizing with its ideals of physical labor and practical socialism. All children and youth on the kibbutz, starting as early as six months of age and up to eighteen years, lived in "children's houses," self-governing, bonding, and caring for one another. It was just as Dr. al-Moualem had said it would be: There was no better time or place in the world to be an orphan. Thousands of solitary youths had been absorbed into the Yishuv from the devastated remnants of the Holocaust, joining other young people from around the world who either willingly or by necessity left their homelands to play their part in fulfilling the Zionist dream.

Every morning began before dawn. We were awakened by the night sentries and donned our work clothes to plough, pick, prune, sow, gather, milk, or collect. Breakfast was brought to us in the fields, after which we would work some more and return to the settlement for a few hours of school. I learned as much outside the classroom as in it, including Hebrew literature, Jewish history, mathematics, agriculture, and other topics to round out my education. In contrast to the cloistered life of the convent, in the kibbutz, political philosophy and current events were considered the most important topics.

I quickly learned modern Hebrew and adopted wholesale the Zionist ethic of work, sacrifice, mutual responsibility, and personal and national redemption through working the land. I memorized the words to all the popular songs, even the ones in Yiddish, the language of the European Diaspora. I joined every hiking trip and bonfire. Within ten months, I was elected leader of the kibbutz youth group, and my friends were astounded to be reminded that I had joined their ranks less than a year earlier.

At the end of every workday, we entertained ourselves with discussions of Marxist and Zionist texts. We fantasized about the egalitarian society we would create after the war was over. We danced and sang songs around campfires while potatoes and onions roasted under the embers. And often, the excitement of being on the threshold of realizing ancient dreams brimmed over into sexual release. I remember each of the women with whom I made love, with whom even a brief connection presented the illusion of a true bond. In those encounters, I was reminded again and again of Isabella, whose openness and enthusiasm she refused to label as love. And though there was nothing in the world that thrilled me more than the union of my body with that of a woman, I never again felt the same intensity of my single encounter with Isabella.

Meanwhile, the tide of history surged toward the inevitable flood. The British Mandate for Palestine was set to expire on May 14, 1948. In anticipation of that date and the inevitable fighting to follow, the Yishuv had for years been developing military and civilian infrastructures. Several of the kibbutzim had underground munitions factories. The lathes and powder-packing equipment were constantly failing, and my facility with machine repair, honed by learning to fix every broken piece of machinery at the convent, quickly became known. I was sent all over the Galilee to install and maintain equipment vital for the growing supply chain.

But my main interest was to become a soldier in the mold of my biblical and literary heroes, and that of my new role model, Gidi. I was sixteen years old when I enlisted in the Haganah, whose elite units formed the *Palmach* ("strike companies"). It was a unit of the Palmach that had carried out the bridge bombing by which I was ushered into my new life. And it was into the Palmach that I desperately longed to be admitted.

Everyone had a nickname in the Haganah, and mine was *al Arabi* ("The Arab" in Arabic). After nearly a lifetime of being *al Yahudi* ("The Jew"), I bore the new moniker with ironic pride, despite the knowledge that most Israelis, who were either European immigrants or their descendants, had nearly as much disdain for Jews from Arab countries as they had for Arabs themselves.

Twice a week, we trained in paramilitary activities using broomsticks instead of rifles, and later, barely functional World War I carbines. When arms imports increased, a few modern weapons began to appear: British Stens, Czech rifles, surplus weapons recovered from the Nazis, and even mortars and grenades. Because of the British embargo on munitions, these were smuggled in the holds of fishing vessels, in the bottoms of cargo crates, and under women's skirts. The smugglers learned to operate at night and to use diversion and distraction to escape detection. Later, when the British imposed a similar embargo on Jewish immigration, techniques perfected trafficking arms were used by the Haganah and Palmach to smuggle human refugees.

By most accounts, the Yishuv would be outnumbered, outgunned, and out-supplied in the coming war. The seven nations comprising the Arab League were poised to invade the day after British withdrawal, with the support of a dozen other Arab states. These armies, which possessed tanks, artillery, air forces, and other heavy weaponry, would be mobilized for the purpose of destroying a nation that barely had the resources to absorb the thousands of immigrants arriving daily. In 1947, the secretary general of the Arab League warned that if the Jews attempted to establish a state in Palestine, the result would be "a war of extermination and momentous massacre."

But the young men and women of the Haganah had no doubts regarding their ultimate victory. On the rare occasion when soldiers complained about insufficient or malfunctioning equipment, the answer was uniform: "This is what we have, and with this we will win." And like the biblical Gideon, who defeated the Midianites using nothing more than trumpets, torches, and clay pitchers, these warriors relied upon stratagem, courage, and sacrifice to claim victory from superior, though disorganized and poorly trained, forces.

I finally belonged, after being the outsider for nearly as long as I could remember. And yet, as I think back on that time all those decades ago, the warmth with which I was welcomed to my country, my kibbutz, and my peer group leaves me feeling like an impostor. I had planted myself in a new land, but where were the roots that would bind me to it? I had no mother at whose kitchen table I could sit while making her both proud and fearful over my exploits as a farmer and soldier. And what was I to do with my tender recollections of Mother Maria Theresa crossing herself before beginning any new venture, even one as unambitious as getting out of her chair? Was I to forsake the memory of tranquility carried into my little room by the voices of the sisters chanting vespers while I read the *Encyclopaedia Britannica* at my desk?

These vital chords of consciousness found no resonance in my new life. And what of the wounds, still festering, inflicted by my father, my mother, my classmates, the new abbess, the doctor, and even sweet Isabella? What of those injuries, which were both the cause and effect of a yearning I could never satisfy, either through society or solitude?

I suppressed these reservations as best I could, persuading myself that what I had acquired was more than I was entitled to expect from a world on the precipice of upheaval.

Chapter Sixteen

"It's time you saw some action," Gidi told me one Saturday afternoon. He was visiting Kibbutz Gan Miriam for my seventeenth birthday. We sat under the shade of a eucalyptus tree while families strolled along the settlement's dirt paths and children played football on the lawn.

"Your training has been going well. Six weeks from now, the British will leave, and the real war will start. The enemy will no longer be bands of Arab villagers doing what comes naturally and half-hearted British troops whose only wish is to return home on their own two legs. The enemy will be seven organized armies bent upon driving us into the sea. We need you, Yosef," he said, using the Hebrew pronunciation of my name. "My commander has approved your induction into the Palmach."

He tousled my hair. "I hope you don't object."

I looked down at my bare feet. "You know this is what I want," I whispered.

He paused, fishing in the breast pocket of his jacket for a cigarette box. "Be careful about wanting things . . . and about getting the things you want."

Good advice to give a person who has never in their life received anything they want, I thought. But I forgave Gidi his remark, as I had not shared my full story, even with him. "What happens next?" I asked.

"You leave with me this afternoon for Rosh Pina. I borrowed the commander's jeep with the promise that you would be in it when I return to camp. Tomorrow morning we have a twenty-kilometer loaded march to the top of Jebel Jarmak—the highest peak in the Land of Israel, twelve hundred meters above sea level. This climb is the hardest thing you will have ever done, I promise you, exceeding even the challenges of your 'immigration.' Don't embarrass me by weeping like a child before you reach the top of the mountain.

Once we summit, there will be an induction ceremony for new recruits. Only then may you weep like a child. Bring your hiking boots and some good socks."

"And after that?"

"I have asked that you be assigned to my unit. We will camp on the mountaintop and set out in the morning for a new mission."

"What is the mission?"

"Later, *habibi*," he said, using the Arabic term for dear one. "One assignment at a time. Go get your things."

I trotted over to my bunk in the youth dwelling. I had acquired a few new possessions since arriving in Palestine, yet everything I could call my own fit into a trunk stored under my bed. The trunk itself was not mine but borrowed. The things I deemed necessary for a month away from the kibbutz easily fit into the backpack I had brought with me from Bhamdoun.

I next ran to the kibbutz foreman, whom I found on his knees weeding the small garden outside his shack. "I'm leaving, Yoram," I announced. "I won't be available for my work assignments."

"Really? Where are you going?"

"To join the Palmach."

He stood and brushed off his pants. "The Palmach? Well, well. That's really something, Yosef." His brow furrowed, and I imagined he was doing some calculations in his head. "All right. The Yishuv needs you in uniform more than we here in Gan Miriam need you in work clothes. I will take you out of the rotation for now." He smiled sadly. "The Palmach will grant you leave from time to time, and when they do, you will return, and I will find a job for you."

"That sounds good."

His eyes grew moist. "Just make sure," he said, "that you come back to us." He drew me toward him and squeezed. "Don't forget. That work assignment will be waiting."

I ran back to Gidi, who stood smoking under the eucalyptus. "I'm ready," I said.

Gidi extinguished the cigarette on the sole of his boot and placed the butt back into the cigarette box. "Let's go." We climbed into the jeep and drove off.

In less than an hour, we were at Rosh Pina. Gidi pulled the jeep into a clearing. A cloud of dust engulfed us as we stepped out of the vehicle. To our left were several neat rows of two-man pup tents. Many had pairs of legs sticking out their openings, and the absurd thought occurred to me that at any moment, the tents might stand up and walk away.

Gidi strode into the open area next to a command tent in the center of the encampment. "That's our Operations department," he said. "We sleep in the small tents. Hey, Aviva!" he called out to a young woman exiting the Operations tent wearing a khaki shirt and shorts. "Can you find Yossi and send him over here? Tell him I have some fresh meat!"

"Fresh meat?" she exclaimed. "Great!" She ran off.

A few moments later, Yossi, the heavyset soldier assigned to keep me in the column on our retreat from the bridge at Nahal 'Ayoun, appeared from behind the tents.

"Yossi," Gidi said. "This is Yosef, also known as *al Arabi*. You may remember him."

"*Remember him?*" Yossi cried. "I was present the moment he emerged from the mists! My comrades in the proletariat have often called me a liar for telling the outlandish tale of his 'immigration.' Why, I know Yosef as well as I know my own ass, having spent plenty of time fondling both." And here, Yossi quoted from the Book of Jeremiah: "*My beloved son . . . playful child! For whenever I speak of him, so do I remember him fondly.*" Like almost everyone else in the Palmach, Yossi was an atheist, but he had extensive familiarity with the Bible.

"Yossi," Gidi interrupted, "I have to see the commander. Yosef will be joining our unit. Will you please set him up with gear and a tent mate, introduce him to the group, and make sure he's ready for tomorrow?"

"Of course!" Yossi replied. "I will welcome him as though he were a member of my own family. After all, we share the same name." I looked at him, puzzled. He pointed to himself: "Yossi. Does that seem familiar, Yosef?" The fact that my name and his were the same had been lost upon me.

Gidi walked up to the large tent, raised the flap, and ducked inside. Yossi turned to me. "First stop: supplies," he announced. He led me to a tent where a young man smirked behind a waist-high plank, wooden crates stacked all about him and a cigarette parked in the angle of his mouth.

Yossi asked for "the basic package," and the young man raised his thumb and scrutinized me with a squinting eye. He clicked his tongue on the roof of his mouth, as though questioning the Palmach's expectation of winning a war with the likes of me in its ranks. Sighing and rolling his eyes, he reached into the crates to pull out two pairs of khaki pants, two shirts, two canteens, a canvas belt with two empty rifle magazine holders, a helmet, a mess kit, a wide-brimmed canvas hat, and a kit bag.

"This is all you get," the supply man said. "If anything gets dirty, wash it. If anything is damaged, fix it. If anything is lost or breaks, make a new one out of stones." This latter directive, to manufacture things out of stones, was commonly used to signify that everything was in short supply except rocks and ingenuity.

I gathered the items and was about to turn to leave when Yossi interrupted: "Better try on the helmet, Yosef. You have an extraordinarily large head. What are you storing in there, I wonder?"

"My extraordinarily large brain," I answered, and contemplating Yossi's ample backside, murmured, "I think I know where *your* extra brains are stored." I immediately regretted the remark and felt my cheeks start to burn.

Yossi stared at me in astonishment and, after a moment, roared in laughter. "Ha, ha, he tells jokes too!" he cried, clapping me on the shoulder. "Good one, Yosef! Do it again, and I will slay you, but if you had to choose only one offensive joke, that was a good choice!" He turned to the equipment clerk. "In addition to all the other supplies, mark off that he has used up his one offensive joke! He will have to manufacture the next one out of stones!"

With relief, I tried on the helmet. As Yossi had predicted, it was too small. "A bigger one, please," Yossi said, handing the helmet back. With a scowl, the clerk surrendered a larger helmet. I signed the ledger, and we set off.

"Next stop: your villa." Yossi led me past the rows of pup tents. "This section belongs to our company. The other companies are there and there," he said, pointing to his right. "Our platoon is in the third row, and your tent is fourth from the right side of the line. You will be sleeping on the left."

"Who is on the right?"

"Me, of course," he replied. "Gidi has not yet rescinded his order for me to keep my hand on your balls."

Yossi spent a couple of hours showing me how to pack and use my gear and giving me tips for the following morning's march. "I know you are fit, Yosef, but you have no idea how difficult this will be. One thing is most important of all: Make sure your socks are thick and your boots snug. Otherwise, this will be pure agony for you."

As I began to array my gear, other members of the platoon began to congregate around us. "Say hello to Yosef, everyone!" Yossi announced. "Some of you may remember him from the Night of the Bridges."

I discovered that about half the unit's members had been present at Nahal 'Ayoun. Cries of amazement rang out:

"I remember him!"

"It's the Arab kid!"

"What, now he's *Palmachnik*?"

"Indeed, he is a Palmachnik," Yossi answered, "and he has just come off the assembly line. But in contrast to the reception you usually give rookies, in this instance you will need to be polite. Yosef is the personal protégé of Gidi."

"Ooh, a protégé!" one soldier teased.

Another added, "I hope he doesn't injure himself licking Gidi's tuchus."

"Still looks too skinny," one of the women proclaimed.

"That will do, everyone! Back to work! We have a big day tomorrow!"

The Palmach was run informally. Everyone was known by his or her first name or nickname, including the highest-ranking officers. Commanders were promoted from among the ranks of regular soldiers only after first demonstrating their field savvy and leadership skills. Discipline was loose except during operations. Even the lowliest soldier was expected to understand the mission and be creative in contributing to its successful execution. Women were present in the fighting units, though they usually did not go on missions where face-to-face combat was anticipated.

The unit's dedication to Gidi was obvious. "He is the finest platoon commander in the Palmach," Yossi informed me. "It won't be long before he is promoted to company commander."

"Who will take his place?" I asked.

"Avi, for sure," Yossi answered. "You remember Avi from the bridge? The strong, quiet giant who never encountered a task he could not accomplish, who volunteers for every mission, who brings up the rear if he can't be in the lead, like a shepherd making sure none of the flock loses its way. Gidi trusts Avi with his life, and we all entrust our lives to both of them. If either of them told me to storm an enemy fort with nothing but my grandmother's umbrella, I would say to myself, 'Well, that seems odd . . .' And then I would pick up the umbrella and charge, confident they would bring me home safely."

When it was time for dinner, the platoon took its position in line, mess kits in hand. We shuffled alongside a series of tables, behind which soldiers manned massive pots, dipping in their ladles and dropping the contents onto our bowls. At the end of the line were piles of cucumbers and stacks of stale rye bread.

"What, again no fresh bread?" one of the soldiers complained.

The cook overheard and walked toward the soldier. "Would you like today's bread?" he asked the soldier kindly.

"Yes, please," the latter said.

"Come tomorrow," the cook snapped to howls of laughter from the ranks.

After dinner, we washed our kits and gathered for a huge bonfire, where we danced and sang patriotic songs, and soldiers told tales of past operations. As the flames died down, some couples stood and walked away from the circle, holding hands. Yossi yawned and rose. "We have the two to three a.m. guard shift, Yosef. Let's get to bed. We have a big day tomorrow."

And so I rose and walked with him to our tent, scarcely believing my good fortune. I was a Jewish soldier in the struggle for independence after what seemed to me a lifetime of running in place.

⎯⎯⎯⎯⎯◉⎯⎯⎯⎯⎯

We were awakened at dawn. Groans sounded as everyone struggled to regain consciousness and stretch their sore limbs. Gidi strolled down the row of tents, tapping feet with his boot, lifting flaps to poke his head inside. "Let's go, let's go!" he cried. "What does the Book of Psalms teach us? *Behold, the Guardian of Israel neither slumbers nor sleeps!* Aren't you the guardians of Israel? So why are your lazy bones still in your tents? We have a mountain to climb! Up, up, let's go! Tents down, hearts aloft, breakfast in fifteen minutes!"

Avi, Gidi's second-in-command, also appeared. "Come on, people! The mountain awaits! Glory will be ours at the top!"

We got moving. The tents came down and were rolled up and carried to a covered supply truck, where we tossed them to soldiers who stacked them neatly in the back. We brushed our teeth and washed our faces with water from the canteens. Then we packed our belongings in kit bags and threw them into the truck as well, refilling the canteens from a mobile water container hitched to the back of a second vehicle. The gear for the march had been laid out the afternoon before: backpacks adapted for five- or ten-liter jerricans filled with water, ammunition boxes, and heavy loads of sand to simulate explosives. In addition, many of the soldiers had rifles, and there was one portable machine gun. Avi handed out the gear as each soldier approached the stacks.

"What am I carrying?" I asked Avi.

He held out a five-liter jerrican in a backpack. I had seen some of the women pick up similar loads. I shook my head. "Too light. Give me something heavier."

"Not a chance, little Yosef. There'll be five liters of fluid in your blisters before you're halfway up the mountain. I'm not adding ten kilos of water onto your back."

"Avi, I can carry more."

"Perhaps you can, but what is certain right now is that these are my orders. Five liters it is. Besides, do you see those items over there?" He gestured with his head toward two stretchers laid out on the dirt. "Those are coming with us also. We will need some people to carry them, and others to lie on them. I would rather you be under a stretcher than on top of it when we reach the mountaintop. Trust me. This is going to be hard, *habibi*."

I picked up the pack with the jerrican and slung it over my shoulder.

We ate a prepared breakfast of pita halves stuffed with slices of cheese, cucumber, and tomato, and drank tea in tin cups while milling about the staging area. Finally, the commanders of each unit waded into the ranks and began calling out: "Line up! Everyone into position!"

Nine platoons had gathered at the camp, each comprising approximately thirty men and women. Three platoons formed a company, and the three companies together constituted the third battalion of the Palmach. The units took their positions, arranged according to their designated numbers. Ours was the ninth platoon, and therefore we were the last unit in the last company, bringing up the rear of the battalion.

The sun broke over the top of the Golan Heights in the east. Gidi strolled up and down the line, checking gear, tightening straps, patting shoulders. As the units ahead of us started moving, he spoke: "All right, comrades, we are about to set out. This is not a race but a training exercise. The purpose is to demonstrate to ourselves that no task that can be considered humanly possible is out of our reach, and that some tasks are within our reach even if they seem impossible. Remember that we are a unit. We succeed only as a unit. If one of us fails to make it to the top, we have failed as a unit."

And then he cried out, "Who are we?"

"The Palmach!" came the full-throated reply.

"Who are we?"

"The Palmach!"

"Who are we?"

"The Palmach!"

"Correct. I am in front. Avi is in the rear. After me." And he led us onto the path and into the column.

We proceeded at an energetic pace up a steep incline within a dry riverbed for a few kilometers. The banks of the wadi were covered in brush and dotted with Galilee oaks and olive trees. Spirits were high, with soldiers breaking out in song and telling jokes along the way. After about ninety minutes, we joined the rest of the battalion at a rest stop in a clearing by an oak thicket. A truck stood by with a water tank and crates of oranges and buns. Soon the signal went up for everyone to gather close and be seated, and a man in his early thirties positioned himself in front of the group.

"Boys and girls of the Palmach!" he called out. "Behind me, at the top of the hill, is the city of Safed."

Yossi, who sat cross-legged next to me, whispered in my ear, "That is the battalion commander. In his normal life, he is an archaeologist and university professor. He knows every centimeter of this country. He believes he has a secret weapon to overpower the Arab armies: that the love of his soldiers for the land they are fighting for will imbue them with supernatural strength. He says that love of the land comes from knowing its history and walking it on one's own two legs."

The commander continued, "When the Israelites conquered Canaan after the Exodus three thousand years ago, Safed, the city on the hilltop behind me, was situated in the territory of the tribe of Naphtali. There has been a Jewish presence here throughout recorded history. The town has been shared with Arabs since they occupied Palestine in the mid-seventh century and, after the Crusades, with a small number of Christians. The Mamluks captured it in the thirteenth century. After the expulsion of the Jews from Spain in 1492, Jewish mystics congregated in Safed. Some of the greatest works of Jewish law and ritual, and of kabbalah, Jewish mysticism, were composed here. The Ottomans took over in the sixteenth century, and there was relative peace until the massacre of 1929, in which twenty Jews were murdered by their Arab neighbors. Since that time, the Jewish population of Safed has dwindled, and it now consists of a small number of extremely religious and elderly persons who await the arrival of the Messiah and the redemption to follow. According to the best information I have, the arrival of the Messiah will be delayed a while longer, and redemption will spring from alternative sources."

There were snickers in the ranks.

"The sources of that redemption are the Haganah and the Palmach." A roar arose from the battalion, with scattered chants of "We are the Palmach!" accompanied by rhythmic clapping.

The commander waited for the din to subside. "In about a month, the British will leave this town, and many of you will be back to fight over it, as it is situated on a crucial hilltop overlooking the Sea of Galilee and the eastern frontier. You will take Safed and secure it for our future state, thus ensuring that this place, inhabited by Jews since the beginning of the historical record, and the site of some of our people's greatest intellectual achievements, will never again fall out of our hands. Do not say 'goodbye' to Safed, soldiers; say, 'Until we meet again.'"

Shouts and whistles sounded from the assembly. After surveying the troops a while longer from where he stood, the commander announced, "Unit leaders, prepare your teams. We are moving out. Next stop: the top of Jebel Jarmak."

We stood, filled our canteens, and pressed on.

By midmorning, the sun was high and hot in the cloudless sky. We descended from the crest of the hill into a valley, the mountain towering above us. After passing the lowest point, we began a steep ascent on a barely discernible path of dirt, loose rocks, prickly shrubs, and tree roots. Gidi increased the pace to match that of the units ahead of us, and soon it seemed that we were sprinting up the incline. Everyone was sweating and panting, and grim faces focused on the ground in front of us. It was all we could do to keep moving.

A few hundred meters up the mountain, the column came to an abrupt halt. I was relieved to have a rest, but the soldiers around me groaned. They knew what the stop meant. It was no respite. A cry descended from higher up the mountain: "Open stretchers!"

The female soldiers who had carried the stretchers unslung them and began to untie the straps. Avi came up from the rear and strolled into the breathless platoon. "Volunteers? Volunteers, anyone? Anyone want a ride on a stretcher?" He stood directly in front of me. "How about you, *al Arabi*? It's much easier than continuing to run up this mountain . . ."

"Not a chance," I panted.

Gidi soon joined us, descending from higher up the column. "Let's go, let's go, people! Time to move! Someone needs to get on the stretchers." No one volunteered. Finally, Gidi announced, "Well, I suppose I can appoint some volunteers. Yossi, you first."

Yossi, with his bulk, was the last person anyone would want to carry up a mountain unless it was absolutely necessary. The two women came forward, and one of them spoke up: "Oh, come on, Gidi. Why did you waste our time asking for volunteers? You know very well that if the only alternative is to lug this hippopotamus up the hill, you leave Tamar and me no choice but to sacrifice ourselves for the benefit of the platoon."

Yossi, who had been wiping his brow with his sleeve, called out, "Hey, let's not get personal! As Yosef has already pointed out, I need this body type to store all my extra intellect. There is no need for zoological comparisons."

"Yossi, take your zoological comparisons and deposit them where you store your extra intellect," Gidi declared. "OK, girls, up you go. We are out of time for this discussion. Move out!"

The two women, both thankfully slender, lay down on the stretchers, and four soldiers each raised them to their shoulders.

Yossi was at my side. "The stretchers stay in front of the platoon, directly behind Gidi," he said. "We follow in two packs, one behind each stretcher. When one of the stretcher-bearers raises his hand, the next in line rushes up to relieve him. When you need to be relieved, you raise your hand, and after passing off to the next person, go to the end of the line. When your turn comes up, the sequence repeats itself. Understood?"

I nodded.

The column resumed its ascent up the mountain. Within a few hundred meters, I was first in the pack when one of the soldiers raised his hand. I rushed forward, positioned myself behind him on the right side of the stretcher, matching his pace, and placed my left hand on the support pole. "Ready," I announced. The soldier stepped away, and I assumed the load. I was shocked by the weight of the pole digging into the soft flesh between my shoulder and neck. Within seconds, the burning was nearly unbearable, and keeping the pace proved impossible. I stumbled, and the stretcher nearly fell. I regained my balance and carried the load a few meters more before I stumbled again, and the stretcher almost fell a second time.

A voice behind me said, "Go," and I realized that one of the soldiers had come forward to relieve me even though I had not given the signal. I didn't want to be replaced and kept walking. "Go!" the soldier yelled. "You're slowing us down! Go to the back of the line!" I relinquished my position.

I summoned the strength to keep walking, and when my turn again came to replace one of the soldiers, I ran forward to assume my position, this time on the left side of the stretcher, hoping that I would be stronger on that side. Again, within seconds, the pain felt like a hot knife being passed through my flesh, and the weight became too great to bear. I raised my hand, heard a groan from the column behind, and after a moment received the ready signal to let go of the stretcher. I relinquished my hold on the pole and sank back.

After a few meters more, it seemed to me that the mountain began to sway above us. The five-liter pack on my back might as well have weighed fifty kilograms. My thighs were burning. My heart pounded in my chest. I started weaving on the path and feared I might topple over. I began to lose my place in the column, as those behind began to pass me by. Yossi saw my distress, forcibly removed my backpack and slung it over his shoulder to the side of his own pack, and grabbed me by my canvas belt, pulling me up the mountain behind him. I became aware of Avi hovering nearby, and I forced myself to keep walking. Staggering forward, I knew Avi was about to give the order to have me take a place on one of the stretchers. In a few seconds, I would fall far behind without hope of recovery. Leaving me in the field was out of the question, and so was slowing down.

"Halt!" Avi cried, and the order was relayed to the front in shameful waves: "*Halt! Halt!*"

The two stretchers were slung off shoulders and brought to the ground, and the bearers began to massage and stretch their necks. Gidi appeared from up the hill, assessed the situation in a single glance and gave a command: "Tamar: off the stretcher. Yosef: on." I didn't protest, for I could see there was no choice. My mates would have to carry me, but that would be a lesser burden to them than any attempt to remain on my own two feet. With shame, I lay in the spot vacated by Tamar, covered my eyes with my arm, and was hoisted into the air.

From my position atop the stretcher, I could hear the grunts and gasps of the bearers and felt the fear of being dropped whenever one of them stumbled. They had to raise and tilt the stretcher in the final push to the summit, and I gripped the poles at my sides with all my strength to keep from sliding off. When we finally cleared the crest, I saw the battalion lined up by platoons, and a cheer rose skyward.

"Stretchers, down!" Avi ordered. I was lowered to the ground and rose to my feet. I couldn't bear to look at anything but the tops of my boots. Yossi was suddenly at my side. "Here is your pack," he said.

I took the pack but didn't answer him.

"You did a great job. It's no shame to have faltered on your first march."

I shook my head.

Avi approached us and put a hand on my shoulder. "Nice work, Yosef. Sincerely. I expected you to fall before the first rest stop. You did a really good job."

Suddenly, Gidi was there also. "I will speak to you later. Meanwhile, welcome to the Palmach."

The afternoon sky was clear, and a breeze blew in from the west. Mount Hermon loomed in the northeast, the Golan Heights sprawling down its flank. The Jordan Rift Valley hid the Sea of Galilee and the city of Tiberias from view. The town of Safed lay below us on a hilltop to the southeast at a distance it was hard to believe we had passed in a few short hours on foot. To the far west were the blue waters of the Mediterranean. To the south, the hills of the lower Galilee rolled away toward the fertile fields of the Jezreel Valley. All around were scattered villages and ploughed fields, olive groves, orchards, and the greenery of junipers, oaks, and terebinths.

The commander took his position facing the battalion. "Welcome to Jebel Jarmak, the Arabic name for this mountain. A group of historians of which I am a member has submitted a request to the geographical naming commission to change its name formally to Mount Meron, for the ancient village situated at its feet. This is a place of historical significance for the Jewish people. It is first mentioned in the Book of Joshua as the site of a great victory over the combined armies of the northern Canaanite kingdoms. The tomb of the renowned Talmudic sage Rabbi Shimon bar Yochai is located here, as are those of his son, Rabbi Elazar, and the heads of the scholarly houses of Hillel and Shamai. For hundreds of years, religious pilgrims have gathered in this place on special days to pray for rain and other blessings through the merit of these holy men. Here the prophet Elijah walked, and here, according to tradition, he will return to blow the shofar heralding the coming of the Messiah. In this instance, too, we intend to supplement the efforts of the Almighty with those of the Palmach."

Scattered shouts sounded from the exhausted battalion.

The commander continued, "New recruits: Come forward and face your comrades!"

Yossi shoved me in the back, and I hobbled up to the front of the battalion with ten other men and women from the different platoons, each seeming to be struggling as much as I to put one foot in front of the other. We turned to face the battalion, which was arrayed before us in nine sections, each forming three neat rows.

A sergeant major marched to the commander's side and bellowed, "Attention!" Nearly three hundred men and women snapped to attention. "Present arms!" Soldiers who bore rifles raised them crisply and thrust them forward, their barrels pointing skyward.

"Recruits," the commander announced. "You will now receive weapons. These are the tools with which you will kill and maim the enemy. Remember that each of those men upon whom you train deadly force is someone's son. Many are fathers. Each has a home they want to keep safe. Each has a cause they fight for, just as you do. Each is endowed with human dignity.

"We have no doubts about the justice of our cause, and we will do what is necessary to win our independence. But remember: You are a Jewish army. Your ancient texts and traditions have shown the entire world how to behave ethically, both in peace and in war. We will not turn our backs on those traditions. Nor will we violate the human rights of our enemy, even though ours have been so viciously violated by this very same enemy. You must not loot and pillage, as so many armies have done before you. You will use the weapons we give you now to fight the adversary rising against you, but you will bury his dead and bind his wounds when the battle is over. You will not kill noncombatants, which is murder. You will win our freedom. But if that freedom is purchased through immorality, it will be a wound to our own persons, from which we and our descendants should never recover. This is the sacred trust with which our people bind you."

Turning to the platoon commanders, he issued an order: "Commanders: Distribute rifles!"

Gidi walked toward me, smiling. In his hands he held a surplus World War II Czech rifle.

"Attention!" Gidi and the other platoon commanders stood at attention before their new recruits. "Present arms!" Gidi snapped the rifle toward me, its barrel pointing skyward. "Recruits: Present arms!" I took the rifle from Gidi and presented it toward him as he had done with me. "Join your units!" We limped back to the ranks.

The commander continued, facing the troops:

"This, the Land of Israel, is our tiny corner of the world. It is so small that from this point, you can view its entire width from west to east, a distance of about fifty kilometers. This is our refuge from the discrimination, persecution, and annihilation that have been our lot since the destruction of the second temple and dispersion of our people around the globe in the seventieth year of the Common Era. In the nearly two thousand years since, either willingly or by force, we relinquished our right to self-determination. That period of history has ended. This is the homeland of the Jewish people, to which we have finally returned from the lands of our exile, and from which we will never again be turned away. The lands we have developed, cultivated, and settled since the end of the last century were purchased with the pocket change of Jews from around the world. We are prepared to live in peace and share this land with our Arab neighbors, but all signs point to their unwillingness to share it with us.

"It now seems inevitable that in a short time, we will find ourselves in a full-scale war for survival. If we lose this war, the Jewish remnant in Palestine will again be destroyed. The great Zionist experiment of the modern age would end before it had barely begun. But that will never happen, and you are the reason why. Each of you has a critical role to play in bringing about a miracle nearly two thousand years in the making."

He drew in his breath and roared, "Who are you?"

"The Palmach!"

"Who are you?"

"The Palmach!"

Never before had I such a sense of purpose, nor the feeling that the hand of destiny had led me to a specific time and place. I vowed that I would play my part in bringing about the establishment of the Jewish state and devote my life to its preservation, or die doing so.

I vowed that I would never again lie on a stretcher as long as I was conscious. The following morning, I would begin a self-administered training program to make me the most fit soldier in the Palmach.

And I wept like a child.

Chapter Seventeen

Avi was on his knees, excavating furrows in the earth and heaping the dirt into piles. He placed a rock atop of one of the mounds and stood, brushing the dust off his pants. He turned toward a large topographical map perched on an easel and stuck a colored pin in it. The rest of the platoon sat on the ground in front of the display in three semicircular rows.

When Avi was done, Gidi, holding a ruler in his right hand, pointed to the pin on the map. "This is the police station known as Nabi Idris. It was erected by the British to prevent the infiltration into Palestine of terrorist gangs from Syria and Lebanon during the Arab Revolt of 1936 to 1939. The station holds a commanding position over the Hula Valley"—he indicated the valley and the small lake in its center—"and is an outpost from which infantry units can mobilize to reach most of the Upper Galilee. The side that controls Nabi Idris controls the road from Rosh Pina to Metula, whose retention is critical for our defense of the north.

"Unfortunately, the British, who have begun withdrawing from the region as they prepare for their full departure in mid-May, have already bequeathed Nabi Idris to the Arabs. The enemy used the opportunity to cut off our supply route to Metula. That is why capture of the station is essential. Five days ago, a joint attack by forces from the Haganah and Palmach failed. Four of our boys were killed."

Gidi slapped the map with the ruler. "Tonight, we take Nabi Idris." He turned his attention to the earth model. "The plan is for a two-pronged attack. The first arm will be staffed by our friends in Platoon B, approaching from the south." He drew the ruler across the model. "They will make a noisy advance, drawing the Arabs toward the southern side of the fort. Once engaged, the enemy will be pinned down by fire. We are the second arm: the strike force.

"We will approach from the northeast." Gidi stooped and drew a line with the ruler up a furrow in the model leading toward the rock Avi had planted at the top of the mound. "We will advance under the cover of darkness. Five of you will carry ten kilograms of TNT each. When we arrive at the perimeter fence, the explosives will be pooled and fitted with a wire detonator by Moishe, the sapper on loan to us from the Palmach's demolition unit." Gidi nodded at Moishe, a wiry lad of about twenty who bore a perpetual smile. Moishe stood and doffed his cap, sweeping it across his midriff while executing a deep bow. The men snickered, and some clapped their hands in mock applause.

"Explosion first, praise after," Gidi admonished. "But I appreciate your optimism. While Moishe is rigging the explosive, Yosef and Alon"—he shifted his gaze to us; Alon was a Palmachnik from Jerusalem about two years older than I—"will use wire cutters to create a gap in the fence two meters wide and one and a half meters high. Then Yossi, whose intellect is matched only by his courage, and who has volunteered for this task together with Avi—of course, Avi—will pass through the gap and lay the charge along the north wall of the fort, a distance of about thirty meters from the fence."

Moishe spoke up: "Take care to string the detonator wire behind yourselves without dislodging it from the package!"

Avi took a step forward and glared at Moishe, who hushed. Gidi continued, "Once they have placed the charge by the wall with the wire still attached to it"—Gidi nodded at Moishe—"Avi and Yossi will retreat to our line. After their safe return, I will give the order, and the sapper will set off the explosive. Everyone then follows me through the gaps in the fence and the wall to take the fort. Remember: No one jumps ahead of me! We charge only after the smoke clears and I have verified that the explosion has blasted a hole in the building.

"Once inside, we neutralize the enemy, as we have practiced. Sergeant Doron leads the ground-floor squad, Avi is in charge of the second level, and I lead the force that takes the top floor and tower. You will kill who you have to and take as prisoners only those who lay down their arms or who are wounded too severely to cause harm. Yosef, speaking his native Arabic, together with Alon, are in charge of prisoners. Once we control the fort, we radio the diversionary team to cease fire and help us set up a perimeter."

Gidi paused and surveyed the platoon. "Any questions?" No one spoke. "Chain of command: me, then Avi, then Sergeant Doron, followed by each of the squad commanders. If someone falls, the next in line carries on the mission, improvising as necessary. Each of you knows enough to step up and complete the assignment. As always, we succeed or fail as a unit, and tonight, as always, we shall succeed. Get ready. In two hours, we move out."

Two hours later, we stood in three grim rows in the darkness, each of us laden with packs. Gidi and Avi passed through the ranks, tightening buckles and checking gear. When Gidi reached me, he put his hand on the back of my neck and drew my face forward, kissing me on both cheeks. "Good luck, Yosef," he whispered. "Your first military action! The first, I hope, of many by which you will help establish a Jewish state in the Land of Israel. Are you nervous?"

"Yes," I said.

"Good." He smiled. "Tuck that dog tag into your shirt, will you? It would be a shame if your tag gave us all away by glinting in the moonlight." I quickly did as he instructed. He stepped back and surveyed me once more. "You're ready. After tonight, we will be brothers in battle."

When he finished the inspection, Gidi stood in front of the platoon. "All right, everyone, you may take off your packs and keep them close while we await the transport. They should be here in a few minutes." He examined his watch. "Ten o'clock," he murmured. "Where are they?"

"A few minutes" became two hours. Some of the soldiers lay down and fell asleep, amazing me with their equanimity before the mission. Avi sat on a boulder, calmly lighting and smoking a cigarette about every half hour. Gidi passed the time pacing. After a while, I rose to ask him whether we could radio someone who might explain the delay. "We're out of range," he answered. "There's only one thing to do: wait."

Finally, we heard the growl of a medium-size lorry and saw a dust cloud forming against the black horizon. The transport rumbled into view, its lights doused.

"Everybody up!" Avi cried. "We're moving out!"

The soldiers roused themselves, grabbed their packs, and huddled together. The lorry pulled into the clearing and swung a wide arc, stopping next to the group and facing the way it had come. Gidi hurried toward the driver. "Where the hell have you been?" he demanded.

"I'm sorry, Gidi. We had a flat and got lost on the way."

"Dammit, dammit!" Gidi exclaimed. And then, turning to us: "Everybody in, quickly!"

We gathered at the rear of the lorry and scrambled into the covered hold, the first men inside reaching down to hoist the others inside. After Gidi verified that all the men were seated on the benches bolted to the sides of the compartment, he shut and secured the tailgate and jogged to the front to sit with the driver. The lorry shuddered as it shifted into gear and rumbled out.

In the back, we were thrown side to side and up and down with every movement of the truck as it raced toward the starting point for our march to the fort. One of the soldiers tried to get the group to sing patriotic songs, but the general mood was too bleak, and his cheery voice died away. Another soldier made his way to the tailgate so he could lean out and vomit over the side. The asphalt sped away behind us and was soon replaced by a dirt road, and our speed lessened.

After about forty-five minutes, the lorry came to a stop, and Gidi appeared at the rear. "Everybody out!" he said. "Line up!"

We clambered down and formed our ranks. "Count off!" Avi commanded, and we did so. Twenty-one men, not including Gidi and Avi.

"Communications set!" Gidi ordered.

"Here!" replied the man who carried the radio on his back, coming forward.

Gidi checked the settings and spoke into the receiver. "This is Spear. Two-hour delay in transport. I am at the starting point. Over."

After about twenty seconds the set squawked, "Chieftain here. There was a delay on the other end also. Proceed. Make up time. Out."

"All right, people," Gidi announced. He pointed at the lorry and then motioned briskly with two fingers in the direction from which we had come. The driver, who sat behind the wheel with the motor idling, put the truck into gear and drove off. Gidi turned to us. "It's almost one o'clock. According to the plan, we were supposed to be at the target about now. We will make up some of the delay by double-timing it to the station. After me." And we set out.

It was three kilometers at a near trot down a smooth incline to the mouth of a dry riverbed, a half-moon lighting the way. From there, we climbed. Up and up, two kilometers, as fast as we could go, panting and sweating from exertion.

Finally, we saw the square silhouettes of a building and tower rising at the top of the hill against a starlit sky. Gidi slowed the pace and stopped. He motioned for us to gather round him.

"The station is two hundred fifty meters ahead," he whispered. "It is nearly two thirty in the morning. We are ninety minutes behind schedule, but there is still enough time to complete the mission. No change in the plan. Is that clear to everyone?"

"Yes," we murmured in reply.

"Where is the radio?" Gidi asked.

"Here," responded the soldier carrying the communication set, coming forward. Gidi pulled out the handset, adjusted the volume on the speaker to low, and whispered, "This is Spear. I will be in position in fifteen minutes. Over."

Ten seconds later came the reply. "Confirmed. Burma is still delayed. Wait for the signal. Out."

We moved forward, crouching and then crawling to the perimeter fence. Gidi nodded at Avi, who pointed at Alon and then to the spot on the fence where he was to position himself. Avi did the same for me. We pulled the wire cutters from our packs and lay on the ground at our positions. The soldiers carrying the explosives swung the packs from their shoulders, piling them next to Moishe, who began assembling them into a single large bundle. And then we waited.

According to the plan, we should have heard gunfire from the south within a few minutes of our arrival at the fence. Instead, there was a delay of about an hour, which we later learned was due to a transportation mishap for the diversionary force. The sky had already begun to brighten behind us when a shout issued from the fort, soon joined by other urgent calls and, shortly thereafter, gunfire. Sporadic shots turned to the *pop-pop-pop* of continuous firing in the south.

We looked toward Gidi, who jabbed his finger at the fence—the signal to begin cutting the wire. Alon and I, crouching two meters apart, worked the cutters, making good progress. When we reached a level above our shoulders, we began to cut crossways and met in the middle. We eased out the section we had severed and brought it to the side, leaning it upright against the barrier. By then, we could see each other clearly, as the gloom had given way to morning light.

Gidi pointed at Avi and Yossi, who crouched next to the fifty-kilogram bundle of TNT, each holding one of the rope handles the sapper had rigged on its sides.

They hoisted it off the ground, crouched through the gap in the fence, and staggered toward the building, the wire unspooling behind them.

When they were about ten meters from the wall, a volley of automatic fire sounded from the parapet of the fort directly facing us. I looked toward the roof of the building and saw a line of enemy soldiers peering over their gunsights. By the time I returned my gaze to Avi and Yossi, they lay motionless by the package, dozens of bullets raining into them, each spraying small bits of clothing, gear, and flesh.

Gidi became a whirlwind. "Return fire!" he ordered. "Everyone shoot, with everything you have!" Some of us knelt, and others cast themselves flat on the earth, propping up their rifles and firing at the parapet, such a fierce volley that all shooting ceased from that quarter, and chunks of the building began to careen into the air. Before I knew what he was doing, Gidi took off, running in the open field toward the fort. I watched in horror as he seized the explosive by both handles and, with his back toward the building, heaved repeatedly to drag the package the rest of the way toward the wall.

"Keep firing!" Doron, the sergeant, yelled. We knew that our cover was Gidi's only hope of making it back.

Somehow Gidi managed to prop the heavy package against the fort, after which he compressed his body to the wall, where the defending riflemen could see him only if they leaned over the roof. Two did so, and after spying his location, held out their rifles, pointing them downward and firing blindly along the wall below. One of them shot Gidi in the foot. I picked that man off and Alon shot the other. The intensity of the fire rose, and bullets whizzed through the air and thudded into the earth all around us as the Arabs reinforced the north wall with troops dispatched from the fort's southern wing.

Gidi was shouting at us from his position against the wall. He had edged away from the explosive as far as the building would allow. We could not discern his words over the sound of our own fire, but what he wanted was clear. He mimed the action of pushing down the plunger on the detonator box.

I glanced at Moishe, who was peering at the action from behind a boulder, his hands on the plunger. I could see from his eyes that he understood the order but was paralyzed with indecision.

I stood, motioning to Gidi to run back to us across the field, the only way he might survive. He balanced himself on his one good leg, the other lightly touching the ground, and continued yelling and signaling that he wanted the charge blown. A bullet hissed by my left ear, but I kept crying out and swinging my right arm, as if by that motion I could sweep Gidi to safety. It was then that a grenade dropped from a second-story window. It hit the ground one meter from Gidi and bounced in his direction, coming to rest at his feet. He stooped to pick it up, and it exploded.

I watched Gidi collapse, knowing that he was dead before his body hit the ground.

"Blow the fucking charge!" the sergeant yelled at the sapper. "Blow it!" With one swift motion, Moishe pushed the plunger down, and I prepared to storm the building. The only thing of which I was aware was my wish to rush into the fort and kill everyone in it.

Nothing happened. The hand of fate, which had already put its thumb on the scale of our operation, was not yet done. By dragging the package the last ten meters to the wall, Gidi had dislodged the wire.

"Communications set!" the sergeant yelled. The soldier carrying the set crawled toward him, and Doron spoke rapidly into the handset. "This is Spear. Three have fallen, including the commander and deputy. The charge has failed to go off. We are taking heavy fire. No option but to retreat. Over."

"No!" I cried.

There was a brief pause before the radio came to life. "Retreat. We will provide as much cover as we can. Out."

The shooting from the diversionary force on the south side of the police station intensified, a firestorm hammering Nabi Idris.

"Is anybody wounded?" the sergeant asked. No one answered. He took quick stock of the platoon. "Take only your rifles and ammunition, the communication set, and the stretchers. Save your bullets! We will need them later, I promise you. When I give the order, we will retreat." He pointed at two soldiers and commanded, "The two of you will stay behind and maintain fire. After thirty meters, the two of you"—he pointed at Alon and me—"will turn around and provide cover so that these two can join us. Leave them"—he jerked his head toward the bodies in the field—"but no one else behind. We shall return, and when we do, we will recover Gidi, Avi, and Yossi, and we will take twenty Arabs for every one of our boys."

I wanted to object, to stay and gather the bodies, but even in that moment, I understood there was nothing but death in that plan. I loaded a fresh magazine, my last, into my rifle.

The sergeant gave the order, and we ran from the fence. The sun was well over the horizon and shone directly in our faces during the retreat. That was the sole element of good fortune during the operation. The sun blinded the fortress's defenders, preventing them from killing most of us where we stood. After thirty meters, Alon and I turned and began firing toward the fort. The two men we had left at the fence rose and raced in our direction, bullets dancing all around them. One of them suddenly yelled and fell headfirst, clutching the back of his thigh. I raced forward and hoisted him across my shoulders, his blood pouring down the side of my face. I ran screaming toward the platoon while Alon kept firing.

We found our way back to the wadi we had traversed during the night and began descending toward the extraction point. I was hardly aware that I was carrying the full load of a man on my back as we raced down. After about two hundred meters, heavy fire was directed at us from the ridge to our left. Inhabitants of the nearby Arab village had been roused by the gunfire and emerged with their weapons. They hid themselves behind boulders and bushes along the upper edge of the wadi. With their advantages of concealment and higher ground, we were easy targets in easy range. There was nowhere to shelter from the onslaught. I felt a bullet enter the body of the soldier I carried. Another bullet passed through the head of the soldier in front of me, and he crumpled to the ground. I couldn't stop myself in time and tripped over him, dropping the soldier I was carrying. He landed on his side with a thud and didn't move. He bled no more.

"Spread out, return fire, and attack!" the sergeant ordered. We were hopelessly outnumbered, but not a single Palmachnik considered laying down his arms. We arrayed ourselves for an assault, teams of three men each, two providing cover while the third advanced a short distance before hurling himself to the ground and shooting until his fellows could move forward. In this way we began clambering up the incline. I remember thinking that we were as good as dead when a bullet struck a rock in front of me, sending a large piece of shrapnel at my head, and the world around me suddenly ceased to exist.

—◦—

For the second time, I came to consciousness in an infirmary, the knot of a hospital gown resting against the nape of my neck, and the odor of antiseptic solution sharp in my nostrils. I kept my eyes shut. Though I wished desperately to linger a while in the delusion that I was in my bed at the convent, Isabella soft at my side, my throbbing head and aching heart granted me no such kindness.

A gentle whisper in Hebrew: "I can tell you are awake."

I said nothing in return and pretended to continue sleeping. After a long while, during which I perceived that the woman standing at the foot of my bed had not moved, I asked, "Where am I?"

"Haifa."

"Haifa? How did I get here?"

"You were brought in the back of a pickup truck, almost completely—but not entirely—dead. We didn't have any blood to give you, so we just infused you with saline and hoped for the best. Your youth did the rest."

"How long has it been?" I asked.

"Three days."

Three days might as well have been three hours or three decades. It made no difference to me. What meaning had loss of time to a person who had lost everything else of value in his life? First his father, then his mother, then his home, his protector, his love, his mentor, his past, his hero, his comrades, and finally, the innocence he thought had been lost at the very beginning. I opened my eyes.

I was lying on my back in a hospital bed, my head propped on a pillow, and a clean white sheet resting on me. I glanced right and left. Guardrails were raised on either side, and beyond the rails about a dozen wounded men were arrayed in similar beds in a ward about the size of the dining room at Kibbutz Gan Miriam. All the men were bandaged in various parts of their bodies, some oozing blood, some seeping other fluids, some with limbs suspended, some with limbs absent. After a while, I realized I was looking out on this scene through my left eye only. I lifted my hand toward the right side of my face and felt a thick bandage there.

Panicking, I raised both hands to confirm they were accounted for, as were all the fingers. Though it caused a spasm of pain in my upper abdomen and sent a wave of nausea through me, I raised my head off the pillow and looked down to see two elevations in the sheet where I expected my feet to be. When the sheet moved on both sides in response to wiggling my toes, I felt a surge of relief and breathed an Arabic phrase of thanks: "*Alhamdulillah!*"

"I agree," responded the nurse standing at the foot of the bed, the owner of the voice I had heard earlier. "I would have said it in Hebrew, however: *Baruch Hashem.*"

I looked up to face her. She was a few years older than I and wore a white uniform and cap. She smiled and jotted something down on a clipboard she held in her right hand. As she bowed and turned her head toward the paper, a dark braid came into view, extending from the base of her cap to her lower back.

"Are there any other body parts you wish to inspect?" she asked. "You may discover an additional cause for gratitude."

"Turn your head."

She did as I asked. "It's all there," she said, a smile in her voice. "It was my duty to check."

I verified her report with my left hand and looked up at her. A patch was sewn over the right breast of her uniform, reading, *British Government Hospital.* "British Government Hospital?" I asked. "Am I a prisoner?"

She turned to face me and laughed. "Not even a little bit. It's just a name that will change as soon as we get around to it. We have some other things to tend to first."

I swallowed. My throat was so dry. "What about my platoon?"

She averted her eyes. "I don't know the details, but I heard it was bad. You were the only one who made it to our hospital. Some of the wounded were taken to Tiberias. How many others were cared for in field units, I can't say."

She handed me a washcloth, and I dabbed my eye. "You have a deep laceration by your right eye and a skull fracture, but both your eyes are unharmed. You lost some blood from that injury, but far worse damage was done by a bullet that entered your back, passed a centimeter from your spleen, and exited through your side. How you survived long enough to make it into surgery is a miracle the doctors have discussed but cannot explain. They will be here on rounds soon to try to explain it to you anyway."

I peered at the name tag pinned over her left breast. "Yael," I murmured.

"That is my name," she responded.

"Are you like your name?" I asked. The word *yael* means *mountain goat* in Hebrew.

She smiled. "My mother says I am as graceful as a mountain goat."

"Will you give me water, please, Yael?"

She reached for a glass that was sitting on a table next to my bed and handed it to me. I took a sip, and when it proved to be the best thing I had ever tasted, drained the cup.

"Be careful!" Yael exclaimed. "You have to take it slow! You are sicker than you may realize."

I felt refreshed and drew my sleeve across my mouth to dry it. "You may be like a *yael*, Yael, but I see that you are not like the biblical Yael." I quoted the Book of Judges to her: "*He asked for water. She gave him milk.* I asked you for water, and all you gave me was water."

"You should be grateful for that," she responded. "The biblical Yael gave him milk, and after he drank it, she hammered a tent peg through his skull."

"Ah, yes, I remember that now. Thanks for the water. May I have some more?"

"No. I will bring you some soup, and you will have that, lucky boy."

"Yes, I am very lucky," I muttered, my own voice tasting like sand to me.

"Don't be so bitter, Yosef. It is not your fault that you survived while your friends didn't make it. The transporters who brought you here said you did everything you could to get yourself killed in the field."

She left to get me the soup.

And I thought, *Mission not accomplished. Comrades not saved. Failure purchased at an immeasurable cost.* My world was made up of a single element: grief.

I spent a week in the hospital and three weeks in a rehabilitation facility. Every few days, delegations from the kibbutz or the Palmach came to visit me. I learned that of the twenty-three soldiers in our unit who set out for Nabi Idris, sixteen were dead and the remainder wounded. Three men had been killed while defending injured soldiers they refused to abandon. The men they had stayed behind to protect were also dead. As if all this were not too much to bear, there was also the fact that, in contrast to the ethos of the Palmach, there had been no choice but to leave the dead in the field. Only when they returned a few weeks later and captured the fort, this time with overwhelming force, was the Palmach able to recover the bodies and lay them to rest in a communal grave on the grounds of Nabi Idris. Gidi was among them.

I was finally discharged from the rehabilitation facility, and the Palmach arranged for a car to drive me back to Kibbutz Gan Miriam. On the way, I asked the driver to take me to the battlefield, where I stood before the plaque that had been posted at the mass burial site. Scanning the names and ranks of the twenty-eight soldiers who had fallen in the three battles for the fort, I saw those of Avi, Yossi, my other comrades and, most painful of all, Gidi. He had been promoted posthumously to the rank of first lieutenant.

I felt drained of everything. When the driver pulled into the kibbutz courtyard, I found the entire community waiting for me. I stepped out of the car and stood to face them. No one uttered a word, but Yoram, the foreman, advanced and embraced me, gingerly at first, and then more forcefully in response to my squeezing him. For the second time since I was a young child, I wept with my entire soul. I shut my eyes, and tears poured down my cheeks and onto the shoulder of the foreman's work shirt, moistening and then drenching the cotton while I quaked in his arms. The kibbutz members crowded around in tears, embracing me and each other, and a keening arose, the likes of which I never heard again in my life. What we were weeping for was the terrible cost of realizing our dreams. And yet, had there been no other choice but to go through the experience again in order to bring about a Jewish state in Palestine, I and everyone there would have done it. I pledged to myself that I would reenter the fight. And if a conflict came in which I was unable to retain a final, decisive advantage, I would die fighting to the end.

Chapter Eighteen

I was in the cucumber patch at Kibbutz Gan Miriam, weeding. I loved the work, a solitary task that allowed me to feel I was contributing to a larger cause. The State of Israel needed cucumbers, too, I reassured myself. Yoram, the foreman, had initially denied my request to go out alone, but later relented. He understood my need to feel both useful and detached, at least for a few hours every day. But he could not refrain from providing detailed instructions, disregarding the fact that, due to my experience at the convent, I was already a skilled cucumberist.

"You must pull up all the weeds, but don't use a hoe, or you will damage the roots," he instructed. I nodded. "And make sure to be on the lookout for aphids, mildew, and infection. Let me know if you see any yellowed leaves or white patches."

I nodded again, gladly participating in the conceit that I required guidance. "Sure, Yoram."

"And Arabs. Watch out for Arabs."

It was the middle of June, 1948. The last British soldier had departed the port of Haifa on May 14, the date I'd left the rehabilitation hospital, which was also the date the leaders of the Yishuv declared the new State of Israel. The formal phase of Israel's War of Independence began the very next day, with attacks on all fronts by the armed forces of Egypt, Jordan, Syria, and Iraq, fortified by thousands of volunteers from other Arab lands. During the preceding six months, the Jews had already achieved substantial gains against Palestinian militias, of which the capture of Nabi Idris was one example. But invasion by multiple organized armies was a very different challenge. Many around the world feared that the life of the new state would be snuffed out as soon as it had begun, and that the Jewish remnant had escaped annihilation in the Diaspora only to be slaughtered in their ancient homeland.

Instead, the momentum of the previous six months was maintained, and our forces continued to conquer territory. Within four weeks of the Arab invasion, the United Nations organized a monthlong ceasefire. The Arabs agreed to a cessation of hostilities—a fateful blunder, as the respite allowed Israel to absorb thousands of immigrants, organize its new army, import arms, and prepare for the inevitable continuation.

It was at the beginning of this ceasefire that I ventured out to tend the cucumber patch. Like most of our fields, cucumbers were planted outside the fence. Despite the official pause in hostilities, a solitary man in the open was an easy target for Arab gangs.

"OK, Yoram. I will watch out for aphids and Arabs."

"Don't joke with me. And take this," he said, handing me a loaded carbine and an extra magazine. "You know the rules. Keep it near you at all times. If anyone you don't recognize approaches, you shoot in the air. If they don't stop, you shoot at their legs, and then, if necessary, to kill. Hold your ground, and we will come running."

After receiving my lesson in cucumber patch management and self-defense, I filled a canteen with water, shouldered the rifle, and trudged out the settlement gate, saluting the sentry on my way.

The hills of Naphtali rose above the valley in front of me, and beyond them and to the north, the mountains of Lebanon from which I had emerged just two years earlier. I cast a glance behind me, where the Golan Heights soared, Mount Hermon reigning at their summit. The air was thick with the fertile smell of turned soil and ripening crops, and flocks of pelicans and cranes traversed the sky on their northward migration from Africa.

Arriving at my destination, I cast off my shirt and bent over the cucumbers. On my head was the conical "dunce cap" that was part of the unofficial uniform of the Israeli laborer. The plants were growing beautifully, a gorgeous spice emanating from their stalks, their orderliness spellbinding. The cucumber skins were darkening green. Harvest time, always a cause for celebration, would come little more than a week later. I returned every couple of meters to reposition the rifle as I advanced through the field, keeping the weapon within reach.

I finished tending the last row at about ten o'clock. The sun was already high, and I could smell the singeing of my own skin. It was time to return to the settlement. I rose to stretch my back and gulped from the canteen while scanning the western horizon. All was clear. But turning toward the housing area, I spied a solitary figure exiting the gate and heading my way on the dirt path. It was a man in Israeli army fatigues, favoring his left leg as he limped forward.

I gathered the shirt and canteen in my right hand, the rifle in my left, and started walking. As we neared each other, I made out a colonel's insignia on the man's epaulets. He appeared about thirty years old. His black hair was close-cropped, not much longer than the three-day growth of beard that carpeted his swarthy complexion. But it was chiefly his street-swagger, unmistakable despite his limp, that marked him as a Jewish native of an Arab country.

"*Ahlan wasahlan, Yusouf,*" he greeted me in Arabic, smiling.

I paused. "*Ahlan bik.*"

"My name is Shmuel Mizrahi."

"*Salaam aleikum,* Shmuel." We eyed each other a while longer, and then I added in Arabic, "How do you know my name?"

"Many people learned your name after the battle at Nabi Idris. I came to Gan Miriam looking for you. They told me I would find you by the cucumbers."

"They gave you good information. You have found both me and the cucumbers," I said, pointing to the plants. He smiled pleasantly, and I added, "When did you emigrate from Baghdad?"

Colonel Mizrahi raised an eyebrow. "Ah. You have a good ear. Fifteen years ago. With my family." He switched to French. "*Et tu? Quand as-tous immigré du Liban?*"

"A little over two years ago," I replied in French. "But I suspect that, along with my name, you already knew that."

"Indeed I did, Joseph, as do I also know the extraordinary circumstances of your arrival in Israel. What I have heard about you either is fiction or ought to be fiction, and perhaps it is a bit of both. Even for a country that is accustomed to taking the impossible for granted, you have an exceptional personal history. We have a file on you that reads like a story from the *One Thousand and One Nights.*"

I smirked. "Who is *we?*"

He switched languages yet again, this time to English. "I am the commander of a special unit," he answered. "Let us leave it at that for the moment. If there is mutual interest, I can provide you with details later." He paused. "Shall we go back to the settlement for some refreshment and conversation? It is getting too hot out here."

"As you wish," I replied in English. I lay down the canteen and rifle and swung my arms into the shirt, wincing as I did so. The movement stretched the scar on my abdomen, and I had not yet become accustomed to the sensation.

"How are your injuries?" he asked, again in English.

"Tolerable and getting better, thank you," I answered.

We began walking toward the kibbutz. I slowed my pace to match his. "*Latine loqueris?*" I inquired.

Colonel Mizrahi laughed out loud. "No," he answered in Hebrew. "I do not speak Latin."

We passed the guard at the gate and made our way to the dining room. The kibbutzniks were lining up for midmorning snack. "I prefer not to wait in line," Colonel Mizrahi said in Arabic, the language least likely to be understood by the other members of the settlement. As Jews of European origins, they ascribed more value to Yiddish, German, French, and English than to the native tongue of the region. "Do you mind if we just get something to drink and sit over there?" He thrust his chin toward a small table in the corner.

"*Marhaban,*" I answered.

We each selected a sturdy Bakelite cup from the stacks on the serving platform and opened the spigots to pour sweet lemonade from metal canisters. I led him to the secluded table. He took the bench against the wall, and I sat opposite him, with my back toward the room.

"How have you been feeling since the battle at Nabi Idris?" the colonel asked, smiling, his voice just loud enough for me to hear over the other conversations and clattering of dishes.

"I told you. Some pain in my scar, but otherwise pretty good."

"That is not what I am asking about, Yusouf. I am asking about your feelings."

"And I answered that I am feeling pretty good."

There was no smile now. "You feel 'pretty good' about an operation that nearly cost you your life?"

I felt my face flush.

The colonel continued, "You feel 'pretty good' about losing Gidi and Avi? Pretty good that most of the members of your unit are gone?"

I stared at him. It was all I could do to not strike him in the face.

"Well?" he demanded.

"We knew the risks," I whispered through clenched teeth.

"Did you? Did Gidi? Did he know the mission would fail? That he would lose his life and the lives of most of his men?"

"Of course he didn't know that. But in war, some missions fail. Some men die. He was prepared to give his life. As was everyone in the unit. As was I. As I am still."

He had raised his cup to his lips but had not drunk from it. He set it down. "After all you have lost, you are still prepared to give more?"

I glared at him. "I have lost more than you know. More than is in your files. And, yes, I am ready to give more." I looked down at my hands, which I had pressed hard against the table to prevent them from shaking.

We sat in silence. When I raised my head, he asked, "Why?"

"Because I have nothing else in the world," I snapped. "Because, like you, and like most of the rest of the Jewish people, I have nowhere else to go."

"I understand you, but—"

"We are like the ancient Israelites," I interrupted. "We have left the lands of our bondage. To return is unthinkable. There is only going forward."

"Yes, Yusouf, but Israel must be more than a refuge for people with no other options. If we summon the vision and the audacity, there are successes around the corner, events of such significance and improbability, they will make the parting of the Red Sea appear commonplace. And yet . . ." Mizrahi paused. "Gidi was one of our finest men, without question. We can't afford to lose many more like him. His courage will inspire hundreds of young men. But the wiser decision would have been to abort the operation when the cover of darkness was lost. Neither the mission commander nor Gidi should have taken the risk at a time when our country needed them so desperately. Can you see that?"

I slammed my fist on the table, and all conversation ceased in the dining hall. I glowered at the colonel. "What would you have us do?" I hissed. "Retreat at every obstacle? Is that how you propose to win a war?"

The foreman sauntered over. "*Shalom*, Shmuel," he said, smiling, to the officer in uniform.

Colonel Mizrahi nodded at him. "*Shalom*, Yoram."

"Yosef," the foreman continued, turning to me, "am I needed here?"

I took a breath. "No." I continued to glare at the colonel. "Everything is all right."

"OK. Let me know if I can help. I will be over there." He pointed in the direction of the benches in the center of the room.

"I want to make something clear," Shmuel Mizrahi continued in a soft voice after Yoram departed. "There was no finer officer in the Palmach than Gidi. No one bolder. No one more adept at improvising in the field. No commander more able to inspire sacrifice in his men. They will sing songs about him. As a matter of fact, there is already a song about him. I heard it on the radio on my way up here."

My mouth fell open.

"I am serious. A song about Gidi. It mentions him by name. It's precisely the kind of Palmach song designed to make you weep," he added, noting that my eyes brimmed with tears. "The words describe him as the Palmachnik who always sang the loudest at bonfires, danced with the greatest abandon, was most popular with the girls, and the first to volunteer for any task. That he ran toward enemy fire and died a hero."

"All true," I whispered. We sat without speaking, the sounds of laughter and conversation swelling from the tables on the other side of the dining hall. I wiped my eyes with my sleeve.

The colonel's mouth formed a grim line. "We have enough songs about our heroes. It may be the only thing this country has in abundance. We are outnumbered, out-armed, out-financed, and surrounded on all sides but the Mediterranean Sea. We need more than daring to win this conflict."

I sighed. "You are telling me things I already know."

"I am trying to tell you things you do not yet know. Why do you think we failed at Nabi Idris? The real reason."

"You said it yourself. We lost the advantages of a nighttime assault."

"That is only partly true. Mostly it was because of bad intelligence."

"Intelligence? What do you mean?"

"We had an informant in the nearby village—the village whose residents came out to massacre you from the high ground as you made your retreat. The informant was a clerk who worked for the sheikh. He had debts he couldn't repay, and we bribed him to provide information on the garrison at Nabi Idris. He underreported the forces defending the station by two thirds, leading us to underman our operation. And someone—maybe the same informant—tipped the Arabs off to our plans. Those bastards were waiting for you. Even had the charge blown a hole in the wall as planned, your unit would have been slaughtered. The mission would have failed."

"Son of a whore!"

"Who, the informant? We don't know if he deceived us or was fed misinformation to pass on to us. He might have been tortured and forced to reveal what he knew about our assault." Colonel Mizrahi drained his cup and set it upon the table. "Either way, the villagers took care of him. In the reprisal raid we conducted after the battle, we found him hanging from a cypress tree with his cock in his mouth."

I ground my teeth.

"Yusouf, one of the things I am trying to tell you that you don't already know is this: You can play a decisive role in securing the State of Israel."

"I *do* know that. I will return to the army as soon as I am able. Maybe in a couple of weeks."

"That is not what I mean. The impact you might have as a soldier can be amplified a thousandfold under the right circumstances."

"What? How?"

"We have many brave men. Intelligent men who can design a tactical military operation and execute it. Men who can improvise in response to changing conditions, who will sacrifice if necessary, and who will inspire others to sacrifice. You yourself are such a man." I opened my mouth to say something, but Mizrahi kept speaking. "But we need more than that. We need subterfuge and deception. We need a far-reaching intelligence apparatus to win, not only this war—for we will surely win this war—but to preserve what will be called 'peace' in the times that follow. You say you are ready to give even more than you have already lost?"

"I am."

He lowered his voice. "What is required of you is to go back from where you came."

I paused. "I don't understand you."

"I am here to recruit you to my unit of *mista'arabin*."

I recognized the word, which in Arabic means *those who become as Arabs*. It was a term used by Jews of Arab lands to describe themselves, by virtue of their adoption of the local language, dress, and customs. These "Arab Jews" were doing what Jews throughout the Diaspora had done since the earliest days of the Dispersion: blending in as best they could while remaining faithful to their traditions.

In Colonel Mizrahi's unit, the word meant something else. The *mista'arvim*, as they were known in Hebrew, were spies. They had begun as the Arab Section, a unit of the Palmach. After establishment of the State of Israel, the Palmach was dissolved and incorporated into the new Israel Defense Forces. The *mista'arabin* were dispatched throughout the Arab world to establish the subterfuge, deception, and intelligence apparatus Colonel Mizrahi believed were so essential to the preservation of the state. They were the nidus of the Shin Bet and Mossad, among the most effective domestic and foreign intelligence services in the world.

"We need to understand what is being said on the Arab street," Shmuel Mizrahi continued. "We need scouts who can blend in behind enemy lines. We need to infiltrate Arab political parties and military units. We need to sabotage Arab arms shipments and operations. For all of that, we need *mista'arabin*. We cannot purchase the kind of loyalty the task demands, not at any price. We need people of extraordinary abilities who are true believers in the cause. We need you, Yusouf."

I swallowed. "My name is Yosef. I left Yusouf in Lebanon—nothing remains of him but ashes."

The colonel looked into my eyes. "We both know that is not true. Yosef is who and what he is because of where he came from and what he experienced there. That is the way of things. You cannot escape your past any more than could your namesake, Joseph from the Book of Genesis. Had his brothers not sold him into slavery, he would never have become a prince of Egypt."

"Joseph did what was necessary to survive. And he never returned to his point of origin."

"True. But at any rate, we will ask you to be neither the old Yusouf nor the new Yosef. The job will require you to be someone else entirely."

"Someone who might wind up hanging from a tree with his cock in his mouth," I muttered.

Mizrahi nodded. "There is no mercy among the Arabs for spies or traitors. We will do what we can to keep you safe. There will be extensive training. And in many circumstances, we have watchers who can help in time of need. But in truth, when you are in the field, you are mostly on your own. The risks are great, the rewards even greater."

"It seems the risks are all mine, and the rewards are all yours."

"Mine? Not mine. The rewards belong to the State of Israel. A single man in the right position could be worth a full battalion. The risks, indeed, are yours. That is why the basis of this conversation is your readiness to sacrifice beyond what we have a right to ask of you. But we would not put you in a situation you were not trained for, nor one in which we felt there was not a reasonable likelihood of both success and safety."

He eyed me while I pursed my lips and gazed off into space, imagining what it would be like to return to the Arab world, once again an outsider. But wasn't that my natural state? I longed to believe I was no longer an impostor, that I had transformed, like a molting caterpillar, into something new. I looked past Colonel Mizrahi at the members of my community—young, lean, sunbaked, unshackled, intoxicated with the attainment of two-thousand-year-old dreams. They were so unlike their forefathers, they might as well be members of a different species. I had come close to achieving my own metamorphosis. Why would I risk my future by returning to the past, a butterfly refusing to emerge from its chrysalis?

I leaned into my hands, pressing the palms against my eyes. An image of the Mother Maria Theresa came to me, the ancient fissures of her smile arcing from the corners of her lips to her eyes. She placed her gnarled hands over mine, and I could feel the tension in my neck and limbs give way. "The past can no longer harm you," she said. "If you have the courage to face us, you will find not only abandonment but also strength in your memories."

My shoulders shook as I sobbed into my hands. "I'm sorry," I whispered. "I am afraid."

Colonel Mizrahi sighed. "I understand, Yosef. It would be a great sacrifice. Harder, perhaps, than giving up your life in battle."

I raised my head and shook it from side to side, and the phantom began to fade. "No, no, I was not speaking to you, Colonel." At last, my mind cleared. I looked into his eyes. "What are you asking me to do?"

"I want you to return with me to our training camp south of Haifa. You can meet other members of the squad and learn more about us. If you choose not to join, you will be free to go. All we ask is that you not speak of our unit to anyone."

Once again, I drew my sleeve across my eyes to wipe away the tears. I nodded and drained my cup. "I will be right back." I stood and strode toward the exit. Yoram intercepted me at the door. He took hold of my elbow and pulled me outside.

"What's happening, Yosef?" he asked.

"I see that you know Shmuel Mizrahi," I answered.

"I do. We met each other smuggling immigrants off boats when the British blockaded the ports in '45. That was before he was shot in the chest and leg capturing an Arab command post single-handedly after his team had been killed all around him."

"Hmm. He now seems to think that kind of behavior is a mistake. Do you know what Colonel Mizrahi does now?"

"Yes. I am aware of his unit. What does he want from you?"

I paused. "He wants me to meet some people."

"Of course he does." Yoram nodded thoughtfully. "But that doesn't obligate you. You have given enough, Yosef. No one has a right to demand any more of you."

"I know. He makes no demands."

"Besides, we can use you here," he continued. "After the cucumbers, there will be grapes, and then dates and figs. The State of Israel—"

"I know, Yoram. The State of Israel requires figs too."

"Why should you do this?"

"I am needed."

"There are other places you are needed. One of them is here."

"Colonel Mizrahi came well prepared for our conversation. Like any good tactician, he assaulted me with overwhelming force."

"What are you talking about?"

"He knew exactly what would move me. He told me I could have saved Gidi and Avi and the rest of our platoon."

"Yosef! How could he say that to you? You know that isn't true!"

"On the contrary, it is very much true. *A man in the right position could be worth a battalion*," I murmured. I made to walk past Yoram.

The foreman, who was still holding me by the elbow, reached up with his other hand to squeeze my shoulder. "So you have made up your mind?"

"Yes. I am going to get my things."

"Do you not know that you are already a hero, to me and to everyone else on this kibbutz?"

"Thank you. The truth is that I have dreamed of being a hero for as long as I can remember. But now what I want is . . . to not feel incomplete anymore. My life has been spent going from 'almost' to 'almost.' I want to achieve something tangible."

The foreman closed his eyes and opened them, and I read a new sorrow there. "Are you certain you can achieve wholeness by uprooting yourself once again? Perhaps your place is with us. There is much you might achieve right here."

"I was once very close with a man," I continued, "a broken man, a doctor, who wanted most in life something other than himself he could believe in. He forsook his calling and in the end could not redeem himself. I don't want to end up like that man."

The foreman sighed. "All right. Perhaps I understand you. But remember: It can be difficult to find yourself while you are pretending to be someone else. Deep within you is a soul belonging to Yosef Friedmann." He smiled. "That soul will always have a safe haven here at Kibbutz Gan Miriam, a place where it can shed its mask and be free, even for a little while. When you feel the need, come back to us. I will find something for you to do."

We hugged, and I walked slowly toward the dormitory, breathing in the pungent odors of the kibbutz, its cowshed and chicken coop, its ploughed soil and baking hay bales. Once again, I placed most of my belongings into my old backpack. I left everything else in the trunk under my bed, including the medal for valor I had received from the Palmach brigade commander. I trotted toward the cafeteria building and found Colonel Mizrahi waiting for me by his jeep.

"*Yallah,*" I said. "Let's go."

We drove the 130 kilometers from Gan Miriam to the training camp of Colonel Mizrahi's unit in the foothills of the Carmel mountain range, farther than the distance between Gan Miriam and Bhamdoun. The three-hour journey was a summary of the signposts of my life in Israel. We passed a few kilometers south of the bridge at Nahal 'Ayoun, where I had entered the land two years earlier. Heading down the Rift Valley toward Rosh Pina, I glimpsed in the west the tower of the police station at Nabi Idris, now in Israel's hands. We skirted south of Safed, the site of my first march in the Palmach, and drove through Haifa, where I was hospitalized while recovering from my injuries. At each of these milestones, it seemed to me that my new life was uncoiling from a reel onto which it had spooled just a short time before. When and how, I wondered, would it start winding itself anew?

I fell asleep in the passenger seat of Colonel Mizrahi's jeep. When we arrived at our destination, he shook me by the shoulder, and I wiped the drool from the side of my mouth with my sleeve. "Come," he said. "I will introduce you to the others." He exited from his side of the vehicle and began limping toward a group of shacks clustered in a fenced compound. I grabbed my pack and ran after him.

Dusk was gathering. Mizrahi led me to a large tent where benches and tables were arrayed, and about twenty men were lining up with plates to be served dinner from large pots resting atop propane-fueled field stoves. He motioned me to throw my pack into a corner of the tent and to stand with him at the back of the line. To my amazement, nearly everyone was speaking Arabic in various accents. As Mizrahi's presence became known, the men came by to greet him.

"Who's the fresh meat?" someone asked, thrusting a chin at me.

Mizrahi raised his voice to be heard above the din. "*Ashabun,*" he called out, using the Arabic word for *friends*, "this is Yosef, who is considering joining our little family."

Greetings rang from the crowd:

"*Ahlan wasahlan, Yosef!*"

"Be careful! In this 'little family,' the youngest member cleans out the latrines!"

"Are you sure this is a *mista'arab*, Shmuel? He is the most Ashkenazi-looking Arab I have ever seen!"

"Yes, completely Ashkenazi-looking!" someone mocked. "Say something in Yiddish, Yosef!"

I obliged them: "*Gey kaken oyfen yam!*" I called out, to roars of laughter. It was a retort meaning *Go take a shit in the sea.*

"It doesn't matter where we shit," another person answered. "Either way, you're cleaning out the latrine!"

A few of the men moved aside to make room for me on their bench. I set my plate down and joined them, and when a woven basket with pita made its way around the table, I grabbed a couple of pieces and set them to wiping the hummus off my plate. I hadn't eaten since dawn.

When the meal was over, we made our way to a bonfire that was already blazing in the far corner of the compound. A few men were wrapping potatoes and onions in aluminum foil and piling them onto a table to place under the embers later, when the fire died down. In the meantime, several men sat in front of *finjanim*, small tin pots with long handles placed in the flames atop metal stands, in which finely ground Turkish coffee mixed with water would be brought to a boil and cooled seven times, tapped once to ward off the evil eye, and only then served. The men gathered around to sing in Arabic, mostly ballads of love and longing and loss. Two played recorders, one stroked a mandolin, and most could not restrain themselves for long. They got up, stretched their arms wide, and danced in slow circles around the fire.

At about midnight, I found Colonel Mizrahi at my shoulder. "Better get to bed," he said. "Your schooling begins at seven tomorrow morning."

Chapter Nineteen

I joined a class of four recruits to the unit of *mista'arabin* code-named *The Dawn*. We spent the next month in relentless training, at least fourteen hours each day. About half our education occurred in the field. We learned sharpshooting, explosives skills, wilderness survival, and martial arts. Driving lessons were part of the curriculum, as none of the recruits had previously driven a car. The sounds of clutches popping, gears grinding, tires squealing, and engines stalling sounded up and down the coastal road.

I learned to disassemble and assemble five kinds of rifles blindfolded. I was sent on solitary nighttime treks without a map or compass or communication set, for which I had to memorize twenty-kilometer off-trail routes, picking up half a dozen tokens along the way to prove I had been at each way station. I was dispatched into the Tel Aviv streets to shadow experienced operatives until I was able to do so without being detected. I learned to identify and lose a tail of my own. As an exercise, I broke into an import-export business to photograph some files. I joined a crew of Arab day laborers unloading a merchant ship at the Tel Aviv Port.

The rest of our learning took place in mind-numbing classroom work: Morse code; encryption; assembling and operating a radio transmitter; techniques of memorization; recognition of vehicles, aircraft, and weapons; the history, culture, literature, art, and religion of Christian and Muslim communities in Arab countries; and many other topics.

We soon became physically and mentally drained from these exertions. On the frequent occasions when a head started to bob in class, the instructor would cease talking and point his finger at the offender, who would awaken to the sudden silence and immediately protest that he wasn't asleep. The finger would gesture in the direction of a bucket of water situated in the back of the classroom. The dozer would stagger toward the bucket, dunk his head, and proclaim, "Thank you, Matilda" (for that was the bucket's name) before returning to his seat.

At night, we somehow found new energy. The men gathered around the bonfire with *finjanim* of Turkish coffee, singing songs of the Orient accompanied by the mandolin and recorder, and telling tales of faraway places. The Dawn unit included a small number of native-born Israelis raised in communities with close ties to their Arab neighbors, but most were immigrants. The accounts of their arrival in Palestine included long treks and perilous journeys, and I told and retold my tale of crossing the bridge at Nahal 'Ayoun. The men howled their appreciation as I described striding into Palestine like a Caesar, only to have a sack thrown over my head, my body hurled down an embankment, and the earth shake beneath my feet when the bridge exploded. They nodded in sympathy when I spoke of losing my comrades in the battle of Nabi Idris. But when they asked about my former life in Lebanon I always demurred, and eventually the questions ceased.

After completing basic training, a new phase began: preparing me for infiltration. "We will make no attempt to turn you into a Muslim," Colonel Mizrahi informed me, referring to the false identities of everyone else in The Dawn. "To do that would require you to unlearn too much. But a Christian? You are perfect for that! When you are done with your career in the field, I hope you come back to our little university as a professor. There will be no one like you to impart knowledge to the next generation.

"The only disadvantage I can see is that, as a Christian, you may have limited access to targets," Colonel Mizrahi continued. "But Muslim and Christian Arabs are sufficiently united in their hatred of the Jews that most doors will be open to you. And perhaps the enemy will be less likely to suspect a professed Christian than a Muslim of being a spy."

Integrating into Palestinian Arab society was not a challenging proposition. Arab populations were migrating all across the contested land, providing the commanders of The Dawn plenty of opportunities to insinuate agents among them. In some instances, these migrations occurred at the request of Arab leaders, who encouraged their people to get out of the way, the better to facilitate their armies' annihilation of the Jews. Arab residents were assured that once victory was in hand, they would regain their homes, as well as the dispossessed property of their enemies. Israel did little to dispel these notions and occasionally actively transferred Arabs out of areas intended for Jewish settlement.

In rare instances, atrocities were committed by Jewish forces. The most infamous of these occurred in Deir Yassin in April 1948, where extremist Jewish militias killed over one hundred people, including women and children. The vast majority of the Jewish community was horrified by the massacre, but the spasms of fear it sent through the Arab population triggered an exodus.

My planned area of activity was in the north. Therefore, I would pose as an Arab native of the central region of Palestine, diminishing the likelihood of encountering someone familiar enough with the elements of my cover story to expose me. Just as the final phase of my training commenced, a fortuitous event occurred: In July 1948, the ceasefire collapsed and fighting resumed for ten days before the UN imposed a second suspension of hostilities. During those ten days the city of Lydda, a mixed Muslim and Christian town of about twenty thousand in central Palestine, was captured by the Israeli army. Almost all the inhabitants of Lydda and the neighboring town of Ramleh either fled or were escorted by Israeli troops across the battle lines and transferred to the Arab Legion on the eastern frontier.

This backdrop provided an opportunity to create my false identity as a refugee. My assumed name was Khalil Haddad, the fictitious son of a laborer from a depressed neighborhood in Lydda. According to my cover story, Khalil's brother was killed during the Israeli operation to take the town, and Khalil was radicalized. Rather than evacuating to the east along with the other townsfolk, he escaped in the chaos to join the campaign against the Zionists.

A private tutor who called himself Bashir arrived at the training camp. Bashir possessed seemingly limitless knowledge of life in Palestinian Arab Christian communities. He taught me everything I needed to know about the differences between the Maronite and Greek Orthodox churches, the Melkite branch of the latter being the strain of Christianity prevalent in Lydda. He spent hours engaging me in conversation, alert to catching me in the slightest inconsistency or inappropriate use of regional slang: "Where can you buy the best hummus in Ramleh?" he would demand. "What are your sisters' names?

What was the nickname the boys called the priest in your church? In which cemetery is your father buried? Where is his plot? What is the name of the grocer on the street corner near your home?" I learned to provide credible answers to these questions.

But then Bashir began asking about matters that hadn't been prefabricated in my cover story. When I stumbled on the responses, he would fly into a rage: "*Bang-bang*, you're dead!" he cried, pointing his index finger at me as though it were the barrel of a pistol. "No! No! No! Anyone can tell you are lying!"

"But I *am* lying. I am making up the answers."

"That's a problem, Khalil!" Bashir shouted, pounding his fist on the table. "You must understand that when you are in the field, *everything* is a lie, both the things you know to be false and the things you know to be true! There is no moral or practical distinction between them. All that matters is what you require to achieve your objectives. Truths and falsehoods are tools, mere pickaxes and drills with which you mine for intelligence. They are the armor with which you protect yourself."

I shook my head. "I understand you, but it works best when I can convince myself that I believe what I am saying. That is hard to do when I am making something up on the spot."

"It is not merely hard. It is deadly. Even the most intelligent person cannot hide behind a screen of flimsy lies."

I threw my hands into the air. "So what am I to do when confronted with a question to which I have no prepared response?"

Bashir ticked the answers off on the fingers of his left hand. "First: That is why we have taken such care with your cover story. We have in fact addressed most questions, and for most of the rest, believable answers should be readily available. Second: When you make any statement of any kind, you do so not because it is true, but because it suits your purposes. That is the reality you must call upon to sound convincing."

I nodded.

Bashir continued, "Third: You do not always have to have an answer. Regular people don't have answers for everything! Stop trying to prove how smart you are, Khalil! You are the uneducated son of an uneducated man. Everything you know, you learned on the street or while accompanying your father on the day jobs he stood for each morning in the town square."

"All right, Bashir. I will try—"

Bashir slammed the table with the palm of his hand. "And fourth: Khalil Haddad has one consuming reality—the hope of achieving through violence what would never be accessible to him by any other route. You crave vengeance—for the loss of your home, your land, your brother, your dignity. That truth needs to boil to the surface in everything you do and everything you say. It will overwhelm any other inconsistencies."

With time, when transforming myself into Khalil and back again, I developed the ability to step in and out of the truth as though it were a comfortable pair of slippers. Of all the sacrifices I made during my life as a spy, perfecting this skill of deception was the most corrosive. I write these words over seventy years after my conversations with Bashir. At the apex of my career, falsehood seemed the defining feature of my world, and I doubted whether I might ever salvage the truth from its wreckage. Now, as I rush to complete one final task, the distillation of Joseph Friedmann's essence from the raw materials of his life, I feel like an outsider peeking in. Even the veracity of my own recollection seems suspect. Decades of duplicity, compounded by the shroud of chemotherapy and the effect of aging on my brain, threaten to turn matter that once was real into smoke as soon as my mind reaches out to grasp it.

I perfected my narrative until it erupted forth on its own, my voice seething and my tears genuine. "It was July eleventh. There were white flags on every building in Lydda, and still the Zionists came in shooting. The Arab Legion, those sons of whores, abandoned the town, leaving the citizens to fend for themselves. When the Jews came, hundreds of our people left their homes in a panic to run like madmen in the street. They were gunned down. Using loudspeakers, the soldiers called everyone else to come out. They slapped the women and shot the men in cold blood if they spoke without being asked to speak. They threw grenades into any building they suspected might have fighters in it, without bothering to check who was actually there. Within hours, bodies and loot lay all over the city. My brother lost his mind and charged at them with a kitchen knife. They shot him in the head and left him in the dirt, refusing to allow any of us to go to him.

"The Zionists gave us two days to leave 'voluntarily,' making it clear that if we didn't volunteer, they would shoot us. They herded the people—men, women, children, and the elderly—on a seventeen-kilometer trek in the summer heat with no food or water to push us over the battle lines into the hands of the Arab Legion. I could not bear to go like a sheep to the slaughter, so in the middle of the night, I escaped through a gap in the fence of the compound where they guarded us and ran across a field. The soldiers shot me, but I managed to hide under a cactus hedge. When the shooting stopped, I balled up my shirt to stop the bleeding and ran to a house on the outskirts of town. The family who lived there hid me under the floorboards until the search party that came looking for me left. A doctor came to clean and sew up my wounds"—here, I could display my scars to substantiate the authenticity of my tale—"and a truck took me north under a shipment of prickly pears."

The purposes of this account were several. First, it was a credible version told from the Arab perspective of actual events. Second, it established how a Palestinian Christian Arab from the central region had found his way north, and why he might be trusted. Third, it helped reinforce popular notions on the Arab street regarding the brutality of Israeli soldiers. If such notions of ruthlessness encouraged local populations to pick up and leave of their own accord, Israel would not dissuade them from it.

At last, I completed my training. "We have an assignment for you, Yosef," Colonel Mizrahi told me one evening in mid-August as I sat opposite his desk in the command hut. "It's a nice demonstration project to try out your new identity and skills on a small stage. Do you feel ready?"

"Yes."

"The second ceasefire is holding, but just barely. In the next phase of the war, we intend to take the entire Upper Galilee. We want to plant you in the town of Al-Hamdan. It lies on the high ground, four kilometers south of the Lebanese border. The residents are fiercely opposed to the State of Israel, encouraged by the local imam, who attracts hundreds to his Friday sermons. And every Friday he goads his flock relentlessly to drive the Jews into the sea, through their own martyrdom if necessary.

"A large part of the Arab resistance in the Galilee emanates from this one town. The Arab Liberation Army holds some of its strategy meetings in the village mosque. Militias based there go out to harass our settlements and snipe onto the adjacent roads. We're having trouble running supplies. The capture of Al-Hamdan is one of the keys to seizing the land all the way to the border with Lebanon. When the war resumes, we will have one brief window of opportunity to take the region before the UN shuts us down again—a window as narrow as sixty hours. Is all this clear?"

"Yes."

"You will infiltrate this community of zealots, transmit to us all the information you can gather about their identities, their numbers, their plans, and their vulnerabilities. If you find an opportunity, you will disrupt their operations so that our capture of the town is as quick and bloodless as possible."

I nodded.

"Is there anyone to whom you wish to write a letter?"

I stared at him, not understanding.

"In case you do not return," he added.

I closed my eyes and breathed. The specters of Isabella and her child shimmered in the darkness behind my lids and faded away.

"We would not deliver the letter unless you are confirmed dead. You may tell the person to whom you write that it is a final message, but you must not provide any details of the mission."

"I intend to come back."

"I am confident you will." He reached into his pocket and extended a small envelope. "This contains a cyanide capsule. You bite down on it, and the end comes quickly. As you know, Yosef, the Arabs do not treat spies kindly. If you are captured, they will torture and then kill you."

"I intend to return."

"You should use it only if you are certain you have no opportunity for escape. For any other circumstance, do not use the capsule."

"Take it back. I will find some other way. I shall return."

Mizrahi sighed and returned the envelope to his pocket. "All right, Yosef. As you wish." He paused. "And the letter?"

"I will give you a letter."

I took the pen and paper he handed me and stepped aside to sit at one of the nearby benches:

Dear Yael:

If you receive this letter, it is because I am dead. I don't mind telling you I hope you never read it.

You have nursed dozens of wounded soldiers, and perhaps you do not remember me. There is no need to differentiate me from the others, and if you cannot exactly recall which of your patients was Yosef Friedmann, that is all right with me. It is sufficient that I remember you.

You are wondering why someone with whom you are barely acquainted would choose to address his final letter to you. The simple explanation is that I have no one else. But do not feel sorry for me. My solitude is both what and why I am.

Your sweet voice smiled at me before I first opened my eyes in the hospital. And when I opened my eyes, the long, beautiful braid running down your back seemed like a lifeline out of my heartache.

Thank you for helping me return to life. But the truth is that I am still in need of resurrection. Perhaps you understand me when I say that you are the resurrection of our people. I come from somewhere else, and I am headed to yet a different place. I will never truly be of this land. But you, Yael, sprouted directly from the earth, like an olive tree. When I think of my hopes for our people, and of why I love this ancient new homeland, I think of you—proud, beautiful, confident, ironical, nurturing, and as graceful as a mountain goat, as your mother might say.

You will be unaware that I carry your smile and braid as placeholders for the things I consider most important in this world. I may call upon these images for comfort in difficult times. If I return, you will never have been aware of this letter. If I do not come back, you will have no cause to worry about me. I am gone. But you will know that once, you saved a stranger and were his inspiration at the end.

Yosef Friedmann

I folded the letter and placed it into the envelope Colonel Mizrahi had proffered. I licked the seal, turned it over and wrote on the front: *Nurse Yael, British Government Hospital, Haifa.* Mizrahi took the envelope and dropped it into his briefcase without looking at the address.

"I will trade that for this," he said. He reached into the briefcase and extracted a thick file. "Here is all the information we have on Al-Hamdan. Study it over the next two days. On Monday night, Khalil Haddad will answer the call to join the holy war against the Jews."

Chapter Twenty

The pickup truck slowed, its headlamps doused, as it approached the drop-off point two kilometers south of the ceasefire line. The driver slapped the side of the vehicle twice through his open window, the signal for me to emerge from my hiding place under some canvas tarps and hop onto the asphalt.

In my hand I clasped the neck of a burlap sack containing a few scraps of clothing, a small Melkite prayer book, a corked fruit juice concentrate bottle I had filled with water, an old toothbrush, some wedges of cheese, and a half-eaten cucumber. A few coins jangled in my pocket. A pewter crucifix hung from a leather cord around my neck. The clothes I wore and the extra shirt and pair of underwear in my sack had been scavenged from the items left behind in Lydda after the city's capture. Care was taken that nothing in my possession could be traced to the Jewish side.

I trotted off the road and down the embankment, turning north through a brush-filled wadi and some abandoned olive groves along a route previously plotted through our lines. Our troops had been alerted to ignore any northward movement of a solitary figure along the narrow path. The midnight half-moon was directly overhead, and by its light I spied my destination—a makeshift camp of about one hundred men sleeping in the open beside an intersection. This was the group of Arab refugees into which I was to insinuate myself. The population of this camp had been renewing itself every few days for months through the ongoing migrations of people displaced by the conflict. The overnight addition of one more impoverished youth would raise no suspicions. I found an unoccupied patch of dirt about two-thirds of the way into the encampment, lay down with my sack as a pillow, and went to sleep.

At dawn, I was awakened by a man stumbling over my feet. I sat up. All about me, men were groaning and stretching, rising from their resting places and dusting off the clothing in which they had slept. Many faced southeast toward Mecca, whispering prayers, bowing and prostrating themselves in the Muslim fashion. Others shuffled a couple of hundred meters away from the group to relieve themselves. There were no women in the camp.

I picked up my sack and joined a lengthening queue at the edge of the encampment behind a canvas-covered truck emblazoned with a large red cross. When I reached the front of the line, I looked up to find a pretty blonde nurse in a white uniform with a red cross over her breast pocket and another on her cap.

"*Sabah al-khair!*" she chirruped in an American accent, handing me a paper bag.

"*Sabah an-nour,*" I replied, taking the bag from her, and stepped away. Unslinging the sack from my shoulder, I extracted my bottle, drained it in two gulps, and refilled it with water from a vat perched on the edge of a table to the side of the truck. I walked several meters away to see what was for breakfast. In the bag were a hard-boiled egg, two stale pita halves, and some hard cheese.

The meal was surprisingly tasty.

After eating, I strolled about the camp catching snippets of conversation:

"My family has owned our land for six generations . . ."

"*Inshallah*, we will be back in time for the olive harvest . . ."

"Damn the Arab nations! They do nothing but boast and lie . . ."

"They say the war is going badly . . ."

"My father says that within three months, the last of the Jews will be driven into the sea . . ."

"Yes, yes, but first I need them to rehire me to finish building the apartment house I was working on in Tiberias . . ."

No one took interest in me or asked me to join them. I sat where I had slept to read from my prayer book, moving my lips in silence.

A short time later, a man strode to the center of the camp carrying two wooden milk crates, one in each hand. A keffiyeh was draped over his head and neck, and a week's growth of beard covered the pockmarks on his face. He set the crates next to each other and stepped up. The man seemed very powerful, his chest, arms, and thighs swelling through military fatigues. "Brothers!

Fighters!" he boomed. "Come and hear the words of the servant of Allah, his holiness, the imam Amr Abu Khadr al Hamdani!"

A murmur rose from the men sitting or lying on the earth:

"There he goes again . . ."

"Another invitation to sacrifice ourselves for a sheikh sitting nice and cozy in his fortress . . ."

"Brothers!" the man called again. "Come and hear!"

I rose, picked up my sack, and moved forward, joining about twenty men who gathered around the speaker.

"My name is Abu Musa," he declared, "and I come to you as an emissary of the holy imam. This is his message: The Jewish dogs want nothing less than to seize your lands and make slaves of you! They will not be satisfied until they have used their wealth—soiled with your sweat—to bring about the moral and physical corruption of every Arab in Palestine! We have routed them on every front—" And here, I heard confirmation of what I scarcely believed from my training: that despite all the evidence to the contrary, Arab leaders persisted in representing to their people the fiction that they were winning the war.

"We have routed them on every front," Abu Musa repeated, pumping the air with his fist, "but like demons, they rise anew. All that is needed now are young men to finish them off. We need you to fight! We need you to defend our land and property and people, to finish the job of slaying the Zionist pigs or driving them into the sea!"

The men reacted to the speaker in the keffiyeh with a range of emotions, from indifference—many had their backs turned—to guarded attention to rapture. I made myself out to belong to the latter group. As the orator progressed through his remarks, I edged closer and closer, an eager look on my face, my body at attention.

"Come with me now to Al-Hamdan, brothers, the center of our resistance in the Galilee! Come join our holy war against the invaders! Come claim what is rightfully ours: our land, our property, and our honor! We will feed and train you. Who will join me now?"

"I will!" cried one youth, raising his hand high, followed by another, then me, and then two more.

"Good." The man nodded. "I see there is virtue yet, and courage, among our people. Follow me." He stepped down, signaling to one of the young men to pick up the crates on which he had stood. He led us to an open pickup in the corner of the field. We piled into the bed of the truck and drove off.

We traversed dirt paths before merging onto an asphalt road. I knew the route thoroughly, not because I had been there before, but because I had memorized the map. My companions were mostly silent but for one, who persisted in asking questions to which only I knew the answers: "How far away is Al-Hamdan? . . . How many people live there? . . . Is the imam really as powerful as Abu Musa claims? . . . Do you think they will let us join the resistance?"

After glaring at him without speaking for ten minutes, the oldest among us, a tough-looking man in his midtwenties with a missing tooth on the side of his mouth, shouted, "Shut up, or I will shut you up!"

We passed the remainder of the trip in silence.

After about ninety minutes, we turned left off the main road. Al-Hamdan was a typical Galilean Muslim village. The pickup passed into a narrow paved street with brightly painted stone houses arrayed on either side like children's blocks cast haphazardly one atop another. The road sloped toward the top of a hill, where a minaret rose over the town. The vehicle pulled into a square in front of the mosque and came to a halt.

We alit onto the paving stones as a man, who appeared to be in his forties, descended the steps. He wore a traditional ankle-length white garment with long sleeves, known as a *thawb*, beneath which his lean frame moved with uncommon grace. A black-and-white-checkered keffiyeh was secured with a black band atop his head. He wore a dark, neatly trimmed beard and smiled, his sharp nose rising and his lips retracting to reveal two perfect rows of white teeth. Without being told to do so, we lined up in silence in front of the vehicle. I was closest to him, and he moved to stand directly in front of me, his disciplined bearing reminding me of a dancer. His green eyes looked down into mine from his slightly taller height.

"I am Abu Khadr," he said in a soft voice, barely louder than a whisper. "What is your name?"

I gulped. "I am Khalil Haddad."

"And what is your father's name?"

"His name was Fadi, Imam."

"Was? Where is your father now, Khalil ibn Fadi?"

"He is buried in Lydda, Imam."

He continued staring, smiling with the angles of his eyes and mouth. "Why are you not in Lydda near your father, Khalil?"

I swallowed and looked about at the others. "I was forced to leave by the Jews after they captured the town and murdered my brother. My sisters and mother allowed themselves to be led across the lines to the Arab Legion, but I escaped."

"And how do you come to be in Al-Hamdan?"

I glanced sideways at Abu Musa. "Abu Musa said I could avenge my brother by joining you."

"You wish to fight?"

"Yes, Imam."

"Do you have any experience? Any special skills?"

I looked down. "No, Imam. But I can learn."

"Are you a good student?"

I shook my head, my eyes on my shoes. "No."

He nodded gravely, raising my chin with the index finger of his left hand, and showed me the open palm of his right. He reached inside my shirt and withdrew my crucifix. "Isa ibn Maryam," he whispered, using the Quranic name for Jesus, son of Mary. "You are a *Nasrani*." It was a declaration, not a question.

"Yes. I am"—I wet my lips—"a Christian."

He searched my face. Never had I felt so penetrated by a person's gaze. I matched it for a few seconds, then looked down again. It was the right thing for me to do; there could be no doubt he expected people to be either unwilling or unable to stare him down, and in truth, it would have been difficult for me to do so had I tried.

He reached out a forefinger again to raise my chin, forcing me to look at him. My eyes began to water.

"You are more than you appear," he murmured.

I did not answer.

The imam looked sideways at Abu Musa and nodded once, which I interpreted as a signal that I had passed an initial inspection. Then he grasped me by the shoulders and kissed my cheeks three times in alternation. He cupped my face in his hands. "Welcome, brother," he whispered, and moved to the youth standing next to me.

I stood at attention as the imam passed down the line, addressing each of the other four men in similar fashion. None received the sideways nod to Abu Musa.

I soon learned that the initial meeting with the imam was only the first of several barriers that must fall before being entrusted with more than the most trivial of roles in the jihad. The men who had joined me in the pickup truck, and almost all the others who followed them day by day, were sent to a barracks near the town's periphery. There, they were employed in various menial tasks and received basic military training. I was brought into the mosque to reside near the headquarters.

Only about one in twenty men passed the imam's intuitive test of character. The examinations carried out by the imam's assistants were of a more practical nature. This interrogation proceeded almost exactly according to the sequence my tutor, Bashir, had anticipated. The questions were couched in curiosity, as though my new companions were merely trying to be friendly, but their purpose of verifying my bona fides was obvious. At dinner, I was asked to tell the story of my escape from Lydda. The audience reacted with curses to my recitation of the brutal conquest of the town by the Israelis and their inhumane treatment of its citizens. I described how I had avoided capture and displayed the scars by my right eye and on my back and abdomen. Other questions followed. Where, exactly, did I live in Lydda? What was the name of the driver who had ferried me to the north, and where was he from? Even the question about the location of my father's burial place was posed.

There were also dozens of unanticipated questions. I was able to answer them all as Khalil Haddad, not as a person pretending to be Khalil Haddad. My two identities no longer existed side by side. Yosef Friedmann was sequestered in a corner of my consciousness, on the far side of the boundary between my real and false selves.

Having performed satisfactorily in this second layer of testing, I was assigned as a servant to the militants stationed in the mosque. I performed kitchen work—setting and clearing tables, washing dishes, helping the cook make meals for the fighting men and their commanders.

Each day I arose before dawn to prepare breakfast and pack lunches. At seven o'clock, approximately thirty men would burst into the communal dining room, boasting and laughing, rifles slung over their shoulders. After eating, they piled into pickup trucks and rode out of town, ululating and shouting slogans. In the evening, they would return to hot meals the kitchen staff prepared.

I threw myself into the work, calling upon old skills learned in the convent. The other kitchen workers washed forks, knives, and spoons piece by piece. I cleaned more silverware in a fraction of the time and with far less water by stirring the pieces in large pots, which I filled with scalding water. I astonished the cook when I showed him my method of peeling hard-boiled eggs more efficiently than he had ever imagined.

By listening to conversations and observing the movements of the fighters, I began to develop an understanding of the strength and layout of the Arab forces in the area. And because of the efficiency of my work, I was soon entrusted with serving tea and sweet cakes to the regional leadership, who convened every week for closed-door conferences in the mosque's meeting room. This room was located in a corner of the building accessible through serpentine corridors. It contained rows of desks and chairs arrayed to face a head table, at which the top commanders sat. I eavesdropped as much as I could, but the attendees avoided talking about military matters when waiters were in the room. A large rectangular board was propped on two easels to the side of the head table. The board was draped with a sheet whenever I was present, and I presumed it was an operations map. I began making plans to break into the room at night to examine it.

On Fridays, I would slip into the prayer hall to attend the imam's sermons from the rear of the room. Worshipers on prayer mats packed every centimeter of the floor, and others lined the walls. The imam would rain condemnation on the enemy. No member of the congregation was more inflamed than I, interjecting "Death to the Zionist pigs!" and "For the sake of Jerusalem!" at the appropriate pauses, and pumping my fist in anger.

After a couple of weeks, Abu Musa approached me while I was peeling potatoes. "Khalil, Abu Khadr has asked to meet with you in his study."

"Me? Why?"

"He will tell you himself."

"When?"

"Now."

I washed and dried my hands and hurried to follow Abu Musa, who had already begun to lead the way. I had never been to the imam's study before.

We passed through the empty prayer hall into a short corridor and came to a stop outside an unmarked white office door. Abu Musa knocked two times.

"Come," issued the imam's voice from within.

Abu Musa reached in front of me to open the door. As I made my way to pass, he stopped me with a heavy hand on the shoulder, turned me sideways to face him, and passed his massive palms over every inch of my body. He then rotated me back to face the office, and I stepped over the threshold. The imam was seated, his head bent over a text, a pencil poised in his right hand over a sheet of paper. The room smelled of cardamom. The door shut behind me.

The imam raised the forefinger of his left hand to acknowledge my presence, then he spent the next few seconds writing something down on the page.

He lifted his head, a warm smile adorning his face.

"Khalil," he said. "Please, Khalil, come in." With his right palm, he gestured toward one of the two chairs in front of his desk. I came forward, bowed my head slightly, and sat.

He paused. "How has your stay with us been?"

"Very good, Imam."

"Yes? You find the food to your liking?"

"Yes. Of course."

"As good as your mother's cooking?" His eyes twinkled.

I was silent.

"Hmmm?"

"No."

He guffawed. "Very good, Khalil! Had you answered otherwise, I would have concluded you were not being completely honest with me!" His eyes narrowed. "We must be completely honest with each other. Without honesty, there can be no trust. Without trust, there can be no unity. Without unity, there can be no victory."

"Yes, Imam."

"How are my men treating you? With respect?"

"Yes. Certainly."

"They respect your religion?"

"Yes, Imam."

"They tell me you rise early every morning to pray."

"I try to honor the memory of my father."

"Our struggle is not only for Muslims, Khalil. There is room for both Christians and Muslims to work together against the enemy. We must collaborate, or we will fail."

"When the Jews pillaged Lydda and murdered its citizens," I responded, my voice trembling, "they did not distinguish between Christians and Muslims."

"Yes. I know. That is why I have instructed my men to avert their eyes if they observe any Christian boys stealing into the prayer hall to hear the weekly sermon." He smiled and winked at me, and I looked down into my lap.

"Of all the weapons the Jews might deploy against us, their unity may prove the most dangerous."

He waited. Finally, I said, "I don't understand you."

"What do you not understand?"

"I would have thought their most dangerous weapon is their guns. Or their explosives. And if you mean to refer to things that are not actual weapons, their money or their wickedness."

"Ah. For the young, it is hard to imagine that a quality like unity could do more harm than guns and bombs. I assure you: Unity is a force that enhances tenfold the deadliness of those other tools." He sighed. "Alas, we Arabs lack the unity that, with few exceptions, characterizes the Jews. Every man thinks he deserves to be a sheikh, and every sheikh believes he knows better than all the others how to conduct the campaign. Every Arab leader pretends to cooperate with the rest while secretly plotting to control them. And the less unified we are, the more unified the Jews become."

The imam drew a breath. "It is common among our leaders to paint the Jews as a people entirely corrupt, demons with no redeeming qualities. I do it myself every Friday, and on other days also. And yet," he said, smiling sadly, "in truth, we say these things so that our people do not get confused. The Jews are clever, educated, innovative . . . They thrive in the most oppressive circumstances. We have much to learn from them."

The imam tapped his fingers on the desk, as though he were contemplating the solution to a vexing problem. "But the Arab populace requires a guiding hand," he continued. "Our common folk see things in black and white. And when they see the Zionists prospering, their plans succeeding, their numbers growing, they might think the Jews deserve to be their masters, and they the Jews' slaves. Were we to acknowledge aloud that the enemy has virtues, we could never mobilize the common man to fight."

He stared at me, adding, "You say nothing."

"Imam, I don't know what to say. Your words are the opposite of everything I have been taught and seen with my own eyes. They viciously attacked our town and murdered my brother right in front of me. If they succeed, it is by taking unfair advantage. If they thrive, it is through theft. Being clever is not enough of a reason to admire someone. I hate them for what they are and what they are doing to our homeland."

"You are a loyal Arab, Khalil. Loyalty is a good quality. But if you want to rise above the common people, you must learn to think with subtlety."

"Imam . . ." I looked down at the hands clasped in my lap.

"You are asking yourself why I would choose to tell you these things, yes? Why I would bother spending time with a poor, uneducated Christian boy from Lydda, and why I would reveal to him that I have internal thoughts that differ from what I say aloud?"

"Yes."

"Did any of your teachers ever take a special interest in you?"

"After I completed the sixth grade, the principal met with my father, begging to keep me in school. But my parents needed help supporting our family, and Father said no one learns anything in a classroom that can't be learned better through working."

"Ah. Muslim tradition teaches that one who wakes in the morning obedient to his parents is like one who finds two doors open for him in heaven. And does not your holy book testify that honoring one's parents is among Allah's greatest commandments? You did well to obey your father's wishes."

"Yes, Imam."

"And now that you are a young man and your father is gone, you have no choice but to make decisions without his guidance."

"Yes, Imam."

"If you allow me to advise you, I will say that I believe there is untapped potential in you. I do not wish to embarrass you, Khalil, but I see in your eyes a great intelligence, and in your silences, I perceive a profound capacity for understanding."

I raised my head and looked into his bright green eyes. "Thank you, Imam," I whispered.

His lips formed a determined smile. "Our people will need this kind of intelligence and understanding in the Palestine that emerges after our victory in this conflict."

"Yes, Imam."

The imam continued interrogating me with his eyes. "If you allow me, Khalil, I will help you educate yourself about the world. The Prophet, peace be upon him, teaches us that seeking knowledge is an obligation of every person. A deep thinker does not merely accept what he is told. He comes to his conclusions based on knowledge and understanding. To acquire knowledge and understanding one must read, listen, think, and above all, be humble." He removed his glasses and rubbed his eyes. "Do you read, Khalil?"

"Some."

The imam rose from his chair and faced the bookcase that rose to the ceiling along the wall to the left of his desk. He ran his finger along the titles on the shelf at eye level, then stopped and withdrew a volume in Arabic, handing it to me. I turned it to examine the title printed on the spine: *The History of Jewish Colonization in Palestine, 1860–1939.* "I ask you to study this over the next few days. I know you are not accustomed to reading this kind of material, but are you willing to try?"

I nodded.

"In addition, I will have my men bring you the daily newspaper when I am done with it. I ask you to read that also. And I would like to meet with you weekly to discuss what you have learned. Can you do these things?"

I looked down at my lap. "Thank you, Imam."

"You are welcome, my son."

"May I ask you a question?"

"Yes."

"If you believe those things about the Zionists, why make war with them? Why not work together for the benefit of everyone?"

His eyes sparkled. "A very good question, and one we can discuss after you have completed your reading assignments. The brief answer is that our leaders are either too selfish or too stupid for that to happen."

"Imam!"

"The Arab nations only pretend to support us, Khalil. In truth, they are rivals seeking to dominate each other. They use us as pawns, and their game requires the appearance of absolute resistance to the Zionists. And our national leadership here in Palestine has failed us. They allied us with Hitler . . . a terrible error, and now the whole world supports the Jews in their quest to establish a state in our homeland."

He sighed. "This is the difference between the world as it is and the world as I wish it to be: In the actual world, collaboration with the Jews is out of the question. And so, I am left without a choice. I must wage war, a ruthless, uncompromising war, when in my heart I know that cooperation is the wiser approach. And yet, I assure you that I am committed to this war, and I will not rest until the Jews are utterly defeated. The only way for our people to survive is to eliminate the force that has invaded us."

"So, in the end, there is no difference between you and me. We both wish to destroy the enemy."

"Yes, Khalil. In that sense, you are correct." He cleared his throat. "And I have a small request of you."

"Anything!"

"Will you keep our conversation a private matter between the two of us? I am afraid people might come to the wrong conclusions if my views came out into the open. But let us see if you and I, in future conversations, might together fertilize the seeds we have planted."

"Yes, Imam. Certainly, Imam. Thank you."

We sat in silence for a while, and he spoke again: "Do you wish to avenge your brother, your family, and your townsfolk?"

"Yes."

"Each of us can play a role in defeating the enemy, Khalil. Some small, some larger. I have a small role for you. If you succeed, perhaps larger roles will follow."

"Imam, I hope you consider what I am already doing here in Al-Hamdan a contribution."

"I do, Khalil. And you have conducted yourself admirably." He paused. "Are you prepared to make an even more meaningful contribution? Perhaps a riskier one?"

"Yes. My life will mean nothing to me until the Jews pay in blood for what they have done to my family, a payment I intend to collect with my own hands."

"You wish to become a fighter?"

"Yes. That is my only wish."

"And yet, you have no training."

"True, but I can learn."

He smiled. "When I first met you, you said that you are not a good student, Khalil."

I raised my head to look at him, only briefly. "There has never been a subject I am as eager to learn." And then I quickly added, "Except for the reading you have assigned to me."

"Hah!" he cried. "I knew you were clever! Let us delay the military training a bit longer and start with something small. Abu Musa awaits in the hallway. He will give you some instructions."

The imam bent his head back to his text and grasped the pencil in his right hand.

I rose, turned toward the exit, and left the office, shutting the door behind me.

Chapter Twenty-One

After closing the door to the imam's study, I turned to find Abu Musa standing uncomfortably close, his breath filling the space between us with the sour smell of cigarettes and coffee.

"The imam seems to have an unusual affection for you, Khalil." His lips were smiling, but not his eyes.

I nodded.

"Do you know why the imam has developed this affection for you?"

"No, but I hope it is because he believes I am worthy."

"I am surprised he has not found a Muslim youth as worthy as you."

"If I understood him correctly, he believes cooperation between Muslims and Christians is essential for our struggle."

"Since that is precisely what he told me a short time ago, I think you understood him correctly. But," Abu Musa added, sucking his teeth, "the holy imam is a theorist and idealist. He is inclined to see things as they ought to be rather than as they are. I am the operations person. He has entrusted me more than once with verifying his instincts."

"Are his instincts usually correct?" I asked.

Abu Musa looked me up and down, and scowled. "I have never known him to be wrong. Follow me."

He led me through the winding passageways toward the meeting room, where I regularly served refreshments at the weekly conferences of the area commanders. The large space was illuminated by about a dozen bare bulbs suspended from the ceiling. The chairs were unoccupied but for two of Abu Musa's lieutenants, whom I knew as Abu Jibril and Muhammad. They sat at the head table on the side facing the large rectangle I had noted before, and which, to my astonishment, lay undraped on its easels. For the first time, I saw confirmation of my suspicion that it was a map of the Galilee, southern Lebanon, and south Syria. Many colored pins adorned it, and I recognized immediately that it displayed the configuration of Arab forces throughout the region—precisely the kind of information I had come to Al-Hamdan to collect. I could not risk giving it more than a brief glance.

Abu Jibril and Muhammad turned to face us as we entered the room. These two were leaders of the companies of men who every day left the village after breakfast in pickup trucks, returning dusty and hungry in the evening. Abu Jibril, the more senior of the two, played with a toothpick in the corner of his mouth.

"Sit down, Khalil," instructed Abu Musa.

I rounded the table and lowered myself into the solitary chair opposite the two seated men, my back to the map. Abu Musa stood behind the empty chair between them.

He pulled a small metal cylinder out of his front pocket before sitting down. "This," he said, placing the cylinder on its base on the tabletop, "is a secret communication from the imam."

I eyed the cylinder without touching it. It was about six centimeters high and made of scuffed and pockmarked tin. Its screw cap had been covered with rice paper and dipped in wax to create a tamper-revealing seal.

Abu Musa resumed, "The cylinder is to be delivered in person into the hands of the sheikh of the town of Sarrach, five kilometers down the road from here."

Muhammad rose, rounded the table, and pointed with a ruler to Sarrach on the map, pausing to make sure I rotated in my chair and paid attention. I used the opportunity to begin memorizing the locations of the colored pins. Muhammad resumed his seat, and I turned back to face the three men. Abu Jibril, who seemed bored by the conversation, began probing his teeth with the toothpick while Abu Musa eyed me narrowly, waiting for me to reengage after diverting my attention from the map.

"For reasons I do not understand and against my advice," Abu Musa continued, "the holy imam has decided to entrust you with the task of delivering this cylinder to the sheikh of that town. The cylinder contains our battle plan for capturing the entire northern Galilee. I will not give you details, of course, but have you observed that day by day, we receive small shipments of arms and explosives?" I nodded. "The same has been taking place in every town sympathetic to our cause throughout the region, small distributions from our brothers in Lebanon, Syria, and Iraq, transported from the rear by routes to which the Jews have no access. By the end of the month, we will possess a huge arsenal. We will hide our strength until the last possible moment. When the ceasefire breaks, as it certainly will, we will unleash our fighters and demolish the enemy in a single blow. The battle plan relies on tight coordination among the militias from each village, without which the imam is convinced there can be no victory. Do you understand?"

"Yes. I understand."

"The scroll inside the cylinder describes the planned movements for every major and minor force under our control, and the target of each force. Once the sheikh of Sarrach receives it, he will distribute the plan to allies throughout the Galilee, villages we cannot reach from Al-Hamdan without being intercepted by the Jews.

"Is the importance of what I have said clear to you? Do you understand why delivery of the scroll to Sarrach is so vital?"

I nodded.

"But we have a problem," Abu Musa continued, "and this is why the imam asks for your assistance. Though Sarrach is only five kilometers away by road, we have no reliable way of getting there. The Jews have cut our communication wires and set up a roadblock between the villages." Muhammad rose and again sauntered toward the map, sticking a blue pin along the road connecting Al-Hamdan and Sarrach, and I rotated in my seat to observe. After a brief moment, I nodded and turned to face Abu Musa while Muhammad remained standing by the map. Abu Musa scowled. "In addition, the enemy conducts patrols throughout the area that make it too dangerous for our men to pass without risking capture."

I nodded again.

"The imam has determined that only a boy acting in the open and seeming to have nothing to hide"—Abu Musa grimaced as though he had smelled something unpleasant—"can risk the transit. You will pose as a shepherd taking his small flock of sheep to graze. If you make it to Sarrach unimpeded, you will hand over the cylinder to the sheikh and return the way you came. If the Jews stop you, you will find an opportunity to discard the cylinder and pretend you are completely innocent of any wrongdoing."

I nodded.

"You accept this task?"

"Yes. When do I leave?"

All three men erupted in laughter. "As soon as we can teach you how to herd sheep!" Abu Musa roared, striking the table with the palms of both massive hands.

And so, shepherding was added to my repertoire. It turned out that herding sheep is a simple task. A child can do it, which is why the Arabs often entrust their flocks to the youngest of children. I was ready in two days.

At dawn on the day of the mission, Abu Musa gave me a final briefing, reviewing all the particulars he had gone over in detail after our meeting in the command center. We stood on the western edge of the village. A pair of binoculars hung from a strap around Abu Musa's neck. He pointed down and to the southwest, where a hilltop village nestled on the other side of the valley. "That is Sarrach," he said. "You will walk down the hill, and when you reach the low point, head left on the path. After five hundred meters, a man named Mustafa will be waiting for you with a flock of about fifteen sheep."

I nodded.

"Repeat what I have said so far."

I pointed. "I head down toward the valley, turn left at the bottom, and after five hundred meters meet Mustafa with the flock."

"Good. He will say, '*Ahlan wasahlan, ya ibni.*' And you will answer, 'I bring you greetings from the holy imam.' That is his signal to hand over the sheep to you."

"'I bring you greetings from the holy imam,'" I repeated.

"Good. Mustafa will give you his staff, which has on its shaft a unique inscription, by which the sheikh will recognize you as the imam's messenger. You will continue in the direction of Sarrach, a fifteen-hundred-meter walk up a gentle incline to the town. But pay close attention: After three hundred meters, you will come upon a fork, with a path heading left. You must stay to the right at that fork. If you take the path on the left, it will lead you directly to the Zionist roadblock."

I nodded. "Take the staff and the sheep, walk three hundred meters, and head right, not left, at the fork. From there, it is about twelve hundred meters up the hill to Sarrach."

"Correct. And what will happen if you go left at the fork?"

"I will walk right into the Zionist roadblock."

"Excellent!" Abu Musa smiled, again without warmth. "Perhaps the imam was right to place his trust in you after all. And what do you do if the Jewish patrols stop you?"

"I hide the cylinder and tell them I am a shepherd named Ismail from Sarrach."

"Correct, and try to act as stupid as possible."

I stared at him. This was a directive he had not previously issued.

"That won't be difficult, will it? To act stupid?"

"Act stupid?"

Abu Musa laughed heartily and clapped me on the shoulder. "There you go! That's how you do it! But remember: It is vital that if anyone at all approaches, you hide the cylinder. You must remember where it is so we can recover it later. And do not forget what we discussed about the Jews—those demons have learned to pose as Arabs. They may not look like Jewish soldiers at all. You must trust no one you meet along the way. You will not be able to tell the difference between friend and enemy. Until you are alone with the sheikh, you must reveal nothing about your mission. I don't care who it is or what he says. Even if he claims to know your mission, even if he knows your real name, even if he says that I sent him, you must assume he is the enemy. You are only a shepherd boy returning home with your flock. Is that clear?"

"Yes," I answered.

He handed me a canteen and wide-brimmed hat. Then, grabbing me by the shoulders, he turned me toward the descent out of Al-Hamdan. "*Yallah*, Khalil! Off you go."

"Wait!"

"No more questions! It's time to leave!"

"But what about the cylinder?"

"Ah!" Abu Musa grinned. "The cylinder! I almost forgot." He fished it out of his pocket. "Here it is." He tossed it in my direction. In a panic, I caught it with two hands, and carefully, as though it might fracture, inserted it into my right front pocket.

And so, the hot September sun rising behind me, Abu Musa dispatched me alone down the hill.

When I was about a third of the way down, I turned to look back. Abu Musa stood at the crest, eyeing me through his binoculars. He lowered the glasses with his left hand and waved with his right. I turned and continued on.

I reached the bottom and followed the path to my left. After about four hundred meters, I spied a thin man leaning against a Galilean oak, smoking a cigarette and gazing in my direction. In his right hand, he held a staff, and his head was wrapped in a black-and-white-checkered keffiyeh. A small flock of sheep grazed about him. One of the sheep bleated as I approached, but the man did not speak.

I stopped in front of him.

He eyed me up and down and seemed to find me wanting. "You are the messenger?" he asked.

I gave no answer.

He spoke again, derision dripping from his voice: "*You* are the person entrusted with this task?"

Again, I was silent.

He curled his lips and spat on the ground at my feet. "*Ahlan wasahlan, ya ibni*," he said with a sneer.

"I bring you greetings from the holy imam." I waited for him to hand over the staff, which had an intricate knot of wood at its head.

"I think perhaps I prefer not to give you the staff."

Without answering, I turned and began to retrace my steps.

"Hey!" he called out. "Where are you going?"

I continued to walk away without turning around. "Back to where I came from."

"Where? To Al-Hamdan? To inform on me to Abu Musa?"

I stopped and faced him. "I don't know what you are talking about, but if you do not give me the staff and hand over the flock, there is nothing for me to do here."

"You are an insolent son of a whore for someone so young."

"I am a shepherd from Sarrach."

The man snickered. "I think you are a bastard from Lydda."

I did not answer.

He stared at me with loathing, as though he were considering whether it was worth the trouble of striking me with the staff. "Come here," he snapped. "Take the stick."

I approached and, when I was close enough, wrapped my hand around the staff just above his fist. He held on to it for a moment, glaring at me. I met his gaze, and he relinquished his grasp. "*Ma'a salaame,* Khalil," he hissed.

"My name is Ismail." I clicked my tongue on the roof of my mouth and prodded two of the sheep in the rear with the staff. The flock started moving down the trail. I followed them and did not look back.

After about two hundred meters, I spotted ahead of me the divergence in the path, its right arm leading to Sarrach, its left arm up toward the highway where I had been told Israeli soldiers manned a roadblock four hundred meters away. I could run that distance in less than two minutes, even uphill. I hurried forward to reach the fork and, while waiting for the sheep, examined the inscription carved along the length of the staff: *I seek Your guidance through Your knowledge, and I seek Your assistance through Your might.* I recognized the words as taken from Salat al-Istikhara, the Muslim prayer of seeking counsel.

The animals behind me shuffled toward the junction, milling about and grazing on scrub brush. I planted the foot of the staff on the ground and pondered the paths ahead, passing my gaze from right to left, left to right. My heart pounded in my chest, but I had no doubt which way I was headed.

"Gaaaaa!" I cried, and goaded the sheep down the right-hand path.

We began the ascent toward Sarrach, and I had to restrain my eagerness to make more rapid progress. The sheep stopped every few meters to nibble on grass and shrubs. I allowed the animals to dawdle. Shepherding is not a task for impatient people, and I knew that a shepherd with a full day of grazing ahead of him would not rush his flock homeward. After about an hour, I decided to rest. I placed the staff on the ground, leaned against a tree, removed my hat, and wiped my brow with my sleeve. I uncorked the canteen, threw my head back, closed my eyes, and gulped some water.

When I lowered my head, I found myself surrounded by five armed men. Each carried a rifle and a backpack, and the face of each was concealed behind a keffiyeh wrapped completely about his head. Only their eyes were visible behind narrow gaps in the fabric. They trained their guns on me, and one shouted in a Palestinian Arabic accent.

"Who are you?" he barked.

My lips trembled, but no sound issued.

"Who are you?" he repeated.

"I am Ismail . . ."

"Ismail? Ismail what?"

My voice shook. "Ismail from Sarrach."

"That is your name? Ismail from Sarrach?"

"Yes," I said, as though I was confused by the questioner's accusing tone, as though my name were a thing that ought not to be disputed.

The man snickered. "Are you an imbecile?"

I stared at him, attempting to convey the impression that I was struggling to find words to respond.

"Answer me!" He leaned in and shouted directly into my face, his voice muffled by his keffiyeh, his eyes boring into mine. "Are. You. An imbecile?"

"No."

"No, what?"

"No. I am not an imbecile."

The man laughed heartily. "Hah! Do you hear, boys?" he called to the men surrounding him. "We have the sworn testimony of this idiot that he is not an imbecile." He turned toward one of the men. "Search him!" he commanded.

The second man approached, grabbed my arms, and extended them to the sides. He passed his hands all over my body, feeling every inch of my frame through the thin fabric of my clothes, paying special attention to my pockets, and squeezing my genitals roughly. "Turn around!" he ordered. He shoved his hands between my buttocks and ran them all over my backside and down my legs. He stood back and announced, "Nothing."

"*What?*" said the first man. "Do it again."

He subjected me to the same rough search, and this time he turned my pockets inside out. Again, the second man issued his verdict: "He carries nothing."

"Search his hat, his canteen." The second man did as he was directed, scrutinizing the hat and staff and casting them aside. He drained the canteen and shook it to demonstrate that it was empty.

"Take your clothes off!" the leader commanded.

Slowly, embarrassed, I removed all my clothes except my underwear, and stood quavering before the men.

"Those also," I was instructed.

I pulled down my underwear and dropped them to my ankles.

"Turn around."

I turned around.

"Bend over."

I bent over.

"Turn and face me."

I did as I was told and raised my underwear.

The leader stepped forward and positioned his face centimeters from mine. "Where is the cylinder?" he whispered fiercely.

I stared at him.

"The cylinder!" he shouted.

I winced at the sudden outburst. "What is a cylinder?" I answered.

Without warning, he slammed his fist into the side of my face. "The cylinder!"

I stumbled from the blow and fell to the ground, stars circling about my head. I began to cry. "I don't know what you are talking about . . ."

"Get dressed," he hissed at me. "Search the area!" he commanded his men. With trembling hands, I donned my clothes. The men spent the next twenty minutes going about in concentric circles, searching under every bush, examining the fleece of each sheep, while the leader eyed me silently, picking his teeth with a twig.

The men returned empty-handed. The leader, who to this point had seemed in control of his emotions despite his angry words, rose and approached me. "If you do not tell me this instant where the cylinder is," he snarled, shaking with rage, "I will shoot you where you stand." He clicked the safety on his rifle, pointing it at my chest.

I began to cry again, tears and mucus streaming down my face. "Please, sir, I don't know what you are talking about."

"Whore." He grabbed his rifle by the forestock and struck me in the belly with the butt. I crumpled and fell on my knees, gasping for breath.

"Put a sack on him. Let's go," he commanded.

A hood was placed over my head. Rough hands raised me to my feet, turned me around several times, and pushed me forward. I stumbled up an incline, and after a few hundred meters was lifted by two men and tossed into the cargo bay of a pickup, landing with a thud on its surface. They clambered up behind me and shut the tailgate. One of the men poked me in the ribs with the barrel of his rifle. "Be careful not to make any sudden moves," he growled.

"My sheep!" I called out.

"Fuck your sheep."

The pickup began to move over uneven terrain and thereafter, a paved road.

"Where are you taking me?" I asked.

"Shut your mouth."

The rocking of the vehicle, the closeness of the hood over my head, and the blow I had received to the belly soon combined to generate a hopeless bout of nausea. "Can you remove this hood?" I called out.

No answer.

"I need to vomit!"

"Go right ahead," came the reply.

And so I did, filling the hood with sick, the vomit running down my shirt and onto my chest. The ride lasted only ten minutes more. I retched and heaved the whole time.

The vehicle came to a stop, and rough hands pulled me out of the cargo bed and propelled me up some steps and into a building, then down winding corridors and into a room. Finally, I was thrust into a chair.

"Don't move! Don't touch the hood!" a voice commanded.

A door behind me closed, then opened a moment later. Several sets of bootsteps entered the room and paced around me. I heard the scraping of chair legs and the sound of bodies seating themselves. A heavy object was lowered onto a surface in front of me, and I realized I was seated in front of a table.

"Take it off," a familiar voice ordered.

A man standing behind me ripped off the hood, and I found myself sitting directly opposite Abu Musa.

I was back in the command center. I blinked and shook my head. "Abu Musa?" My tone was that of someone who could not believe the evidence of his own eyes.

"Here is a basin of water and a towel, Khalil. Rinse your face, and dry yourself off."

I did as I was told.

When I finished, Abu Musa spoke again, softly this time. "I would have scarcely believed it, Khalil, but I see the imam's wisdom is demonstrated again."

"What . . . what is happening . . . ?"

"It was a test."

"A test?"

"There was no master attack plan, no sheikh awaiting your arrival in Sarrach. The men who detained you were mine." He pointed to Abu Jibril and Muhammad, who once again sat on either side of him, and to three men standing in the back of the room. "All of it was to prove to the imam that for the first time, his instincts were mistaken and that you were a Jewish spy."

I sat in silence, then began to sob. I wiped my face with the towel and recovered myself. "What will happen now?"

"You have proven yourself, Khalil, and I must go and debase myself to the imam." He placed his hand on Muhammad's shoulder. "Muhammad will help you move into new quarters in this section of the mosque. You may bathe and change your clothes. Then await further word."

"Thank you, Abu Musa," I said, looking down at my lap. "I am sorry to have caused you trouble."

"You are sorry? I am the one who doubted the judgment of the imam."

I wiped my eyes and stood, making to back away from the table.

One of the men standing behind me arrested me with a hand on my back. "Before you go, Khalil," Abu Musa continued, "tell me this: Where is the cylinder? I watched you myself through the binoculars until you met Mustafa with the flock, and the men insist they had you under constant surveillance from that moment. They never saw you discard it."

"Ah, the cylinder!" I smiled. "I almost forgot." I reached into my right pocket, withdrew the cylinder, and balanced it on the table, its seal of wax and rice paper unbroken.

"What . . . ? How . . . ?" Abu Musa sputtered, and in a matter of seconds, I witnessed the fearsome transformation of shame to anger, and the rekindling of the fire in his eyes. Too late, I regretted the arrogance that led me to jeopardize my mission by pricking him with sarcasm. With a single remark and a single action, I had rendered him even more dangerous than before.

Abu Musa turned on Abu Jibril and roared, "The cylinder was in the boy's pocket the entire time? How could you have failed to find it?"

"Abu Musa!" Abu Jibril protested. "I swear to you, we searched him thoroughly! We turned his pockets inside out. We undressed him completely. We examined every centimeter of his clothing and body. We even emptied his canteen. He could not have had this on his person!"

"He has it now!"

"I cannot explain it, but I swear no one could have searched him more thoroughly!"

Abu Musa turned to face me. "Where was the cylinder?" he hissed.

I gulped and sputtered. "J-j-just as my captor began to search me, I slipped the cylinder into the side compartment of his backpack, and I-I-I took it back after the second time he patted me down. It was back in my pocket by the time I was ordered to remove my clothes."

One of the men in the back of the room whistled quietly. The muscles in Abu Musa's neck tightened. He snatched the cylinder off the table, and with a twist ruptured the seal. He unscrewed the cap and decanted the scroll onto the table. Untying the thread, he opened the scroll to reveal that it was a blank sheet of paper.

He restored his gaze to me. "You may go to your room, Khalil," he whispered, menace in his voice.

I turned and followed Muhammad to my new quarters.

Chapter Twenty-Two

The day after my loyalty test was a Friday. I made my way to the back of the mosque, as usual. The left side of my face was swollen from the blow I had received from Abu Jibril, and my left eye, its white now stained crimson, was ringed in purple. The worshipers said their prayers, alternately prostrating themselves and rising from their prayer mats, and as they did so, many cast fleeting looks in my direction. Everyone, it seemed, had heard rumor of "The Test of the Cylinder," and I had become a minor celebrity. This newfound and undesired fame heightened my fears of incurring Abu Musa's wrath.

The imam's sermon was particularly inflammatory, and by its end, we were chanting, "Death to the Jews!" and pumping our fists in response to his cadences. My angry roar was among the loudest.

After the concluding prayers, a lad of about ten, whom I recognized as the imam's errand boy, approached me. He glanced at the left side of my face and quickly averted his gaze. Addressing the floor, he squeaked, "Abu Khadr wants to see you in his office!"

"Thank you," I replied, and the boy ran off. I waited until the imam finished greeting his well-wishers and watched him disappear behind the side door in the prayer hall. Meanwhile, the faithful filed past me, each slowing to stare, some squeezing my shoulder or shaking my hand, and others grasping me by the upper arms and kissing me on both cheeks. When I was alone, I made my way across the empty hall and into the corridor that led to the imam's office. I knocked on the door.

"Enter!"

I poked my head through the doorway, and a hesitant smile greeted me from behind the desk. The corners of the imam's green eyes were creased with worry. "Ah, Khalil! Come, let me look at you."

I passed over the threshold, turned to close the door behind me, and stepped forward. The imam hastened to rise from his chair, circled the desk, and grasped me by the shoulders. He kissed me three times on the cheeks in alternation, careful to only graze the left side of my face with his beard. "Please, Khalil," he said. "Come join me."

He led me toward a sitting area with sofas arranged in an open square around a table, on which were a teapot, two cups, and an arrangement of sweet cakes. He lowered himself into the corner of one couch and beckoned me to sit next to him on the adjacent one. I sat down, and he reached out his left hand to cup the uninjured right side of my face. "I am sorry, Khalil," he said, his eyes moist, his lips closed, almost smiling. "My advisors counseled me that you could not be trusted until you were tested. I agreed with that advice. I take full responsibility for asking Abu Musa to try you. The decision was mine and no one else's. I am sorry to have doubted you."

"No, Imam. You were right to doubt me."

"Thank you, Khalil. But I am asking you to forgive me, not to give an opinion on whether I acted rightly or wrongly."

I looked down into my lap. "I . . . I apologize for answering a question you did not ask. And I do not presume to know better than the learned imam. But there is nothing to forgive."

"Perhaps, Khalil. But the test did not require bringing you such pain." He examined my swollen face and clicked his tongue on the roof of his mouth. "Perhaps you will forgive me, then, not for the test, but for its extremity?"

I raised my eyes. "I forgive you," I whispered.

"Thank you, Khalil."

We sat in silence for a while, and then he spoke: "You have demonstrated your loyalty and commitment to our cause . . . but not faultlessly. Do you know to what I refer?"

"I know, Imam. I am ashamed."

"You should not have boasted to Abu Musa."

"Yes, Imam. I dishonored myself by being immodest."

The imam pursed his lips and nodded. "The Prophet, peace be upon him, teaches us, *No one with an atom's weight of arrogance in his heart will enter paradise.*"

"Yes. My father many times told me the same thing using a different verse: *God opposes the proud and gives grace to the humble.* He knew my weaknesses."

"Ah," answered the imam, "you honor your father by remembering his teaching . . ." His voice trailed off, and then he spoke again: "It is a puzzling truth that character flaws are sometimes necessary to achieve extraordinary things. I do not consider Abu Musa a humble man. Yet were he entirely humble, he could not lead men into battle. And as for me, I believe it takes a certain degree of arrogance to presume to tell five hundred people every week what they ought to think."

I was silent.

"But there is this also, Khalil: It is one thing to think, and another to act. Allah may accept your repentance for the pride in your heart, but when you boast, you embarrass others and weaken yourself."

"Yes, Imam. I should have learned this lesson many times already, but I have not learned."

"Ah, well. Praise be to Allah." He sighed, an ironical smile on his lips. "There remain some ways by which each of us may improve himself. Speaking of learning, have you glanced at the book I gave you?"

"Yes, Imam."

"What parts did you read?"

"I . . . all of it."

"*What?* You read the entire book?"

"Yes."

"But when did you have time? I gave it to you only three days ago!"

"I read most of it in the evenings after training for my mission, and then last night in my room, I finished it."

He raised his eyebrows, jutted out his lower lip, and shook his head from side to side.

"I did not understand all of it," I hastened to add.

"Indeed," he replied. "Tell me what you learned."

"Palestine was the ancient homeland of the Jews, from which almost all left nearly two thousand years ago. The Zionists came here beginning at the end of the last century to escape persecution. Many Jews believe the land was promised to them by God. But—and this is one of the things I didn't understand—those who believe God gave them the land don't want to return to it, and those who come to settle here don't believe in God."

"Ah! A paradox, yes?"

"A what?"

"Something and its opposite are both true."

I nodded. "A paradox," I repeated.

"The Jews," the imam murmured, nodding as if to confirm something to himself, "are not the only ones who live by paradoxes." Stirring, he asked, "What else did you learn?"

I cleared my throat. "According to the book, the Zionists have been successful because they are educated and use new . . . I think the word is *technologies*, instead of relying on the old methods."

"And what do you think of that, Khalil?"

I paused.

"Yes?"

"Imam, you told me I should read and then think for myself."

"Yes. That is precisely what I said."

"I think the author gives only part of the explanation. He leaves out how they enslave us and steal our land. He ignores the fact that their millionaires send money, without which they could never have succeeded here. He does not discuss how, two thousand years after abandoning this place, the Jews no longer have a right to call it their home. It is *our* home now, and we owe them nothing." As I spoke, my voice rose in vehemence. I silenced myself, panting.

"You feel these things strongly, I see." The imam interlaced his digits and placed his index fingers over his lips. "Is it accurate to say that the Jews *abandoned* this place?"

I hesitated. "They claim they were exiled."

The imam nodded. "A good point to keep in mind, Khalil. It explains why they are not likely to ever relinquish the land once they secure it. And that, in turn, is the reason we must never allow them to feel secure here." He paused. "But back to your other objections: Why do you think the author of the book omitted these facts? Do you think he is unaware of them? Do you think he is a secret Jewish sympathizer and a traitor?"

I looked down at my lap. "No. I do not think so."

"So, why did he fail to mention them in the book?"

I was silent.

"Khalil?"

"He may think we have something to learn from them."

"Ah." He nodded. "Yes. I agree with you." He rose, and I stood with him. "Khalil, that is all the time I have today. But I have enjoyed our conversation and look forward to resuming it next week. Here," he said, turning toward his bookshelf, "is another reading assignment." He drew out a volume and handed it to me: *Islam, Christianity, and Judaism: Similarities in Conflict.* "Until next week, Khalil. There is no need for you to return the other book, nor this one, when you are done with them. I am honored to help plant the first seeds of your own library. *Ma'a salaame.*"

I felt an ache behind my eyes and blinked a few times to clear the tears that formed in their corners. "Thank you, Imam. *Ma'a salaame.*" I turned on my heels and left the office.

As Abu Musa had promised, I moved into new quarters: a small room in the mosque with a young fighter named Yakub. I was taken off kitchen duty and given to the tutelage of Yakub for basic training in militia work and riflery, using his forty-year-old hunting rifle. We were not allowed to waste ammunition, so we shouted, "Bang! Bang!" when pulling the trigger while practicing urban warfare. Yakub's skills were rudimentary, and I played the novice as best I could, thanking him profusely for instructing me.

Most importantly, I was admitted to the innermost circle of the militia. Abu Musa's hostility toward me was palpable, but at the imam's behest, I was present at the weekly strategy sessions held in the command center. This gave me plenty of opportunity to memorize the locations of the pins on the area map. The number and distribution of these pins grew day by day.

I attended two such strategy sessions in silence at the back of the room. During the third, Abu Musa and the chief operations officer of the ALA—the Arab Liberation Army, established by the Arab League to fight in the north region—led a discussion on the positioning of ordinance and men throughout the Galilee. I began to fidget and pace.

Abu Musa noticed. "Khalil!" he cried. "Would you please stop hopping about like a caged rabbit? You are distracting us."

"I am sorry, Abu Musa."

I stood still for a few minutes more and then resumed my pacing. Abu Musa, standing by the map with a pointer in his hand, directed an embarrassed eye roll at the ALA commander and sighed. The imam rotated in his chair in the front row to look in my direction.

"Is something troubling you, Khalil?"

"I-I apologize, Imam," I stammered.

"Yes? What is the matter?"

"Forgive me, Imam, but I heard the Commander say the Jews have gathered their units opposite our main concentrations, and that they have shifted from defensive tactics to offensive ones . . ."

"Yes." Abu Musa growled. "What is your point?"

"I was wondering why, instead of defending ourselves against the Jews, we are not the attackers."

"Really?" Abu Musa inquired, his voice laden with exaggerated curiosity. "How, when, and with what do you propose to attack them?"

At this objection, the ALA operations chief reached out his arm to stay Abu Musa. "Let him speak," he commanded.

I cleared my throat and raised a quavering voice. "By concentrating our forces directly opposite theirs, we give them the advantage. They choose the place and time of the battle. If, instead, we lined up between their units, we might break through their lines and take them from the rear."

The imam rose slowly from his chair and turned to face the assembly, a smile rising to his lips. "Go on," he said.

"We could make a lot of noise and movement using a small number of our soldiers and vehicles directly in front of them. That will draw their attention and make them think we are preparing to meet them in the field. They will rush forward, thinking that if they act quickly and take us before we can get fully organized, they will have the advantage. Meanwhile, the larger part of our army, stationed in small units in each of the surrounding communities, can emerge to gather behind their lines and attack them from the rear."

The ALA commander stood with his mouth open. The imam smiled. A murmur rustled through the seated assembly. The men nodded and pointed, whispering affirmations that once again the imam's instincts had proved unerring: With the most meager of evidence, he had plucked a gem (me) from a pile of refuse.

"How did you come up with such a plan, Khalil?" the imam asked.

"When I was young, I used to watch my uncle play chess in the town square. He would often win when he seemed to be facing certain defeat. I remember one game when he was two moves away from checkmate. His opponent, who thought the game was already won, made a foolish attack when my uncle gave him an opening, and my uncle pounced on him from the rear. He won three moves later."

Abu Musa grasped his pointer with two hands and brought it down across his knee, snapping it in two. He glared at the imam. "Are we now consulting a peasant boy on strategy? An ignoramus who came out of nowhere less than three months ago, who once witnessed a game of chess and suddenly is a military genius?" He flung the fragments of the pointer into a corner of the room.

The ALA chief loved it.

But Abu Musa was right. It was a terrible plan. It had the virtues of boldness and creativity, but relied upon something the Arab irregulars and the ALA had repeatedly proven themselves incapable of executing—a coordinated, complex, and disciplined military action. It also ignored the fact, known to me but not fully appreciated by the ALA, that during the recent ceasefire, the Israelis had greatly improved their position, acquiring heavy guns, armored troop carriers, bomber aircraft, and tens of thousands of new, trained recruits.

Over the next few days, Abu Musa's temper continued to smolder. Nonetheless, the offensive plan was adopted, and as Arab resources were repositioned, the colored pins began to migrate over the map. I knew where all the Arab forces and their ordinance in the Galilee were stationed.

Three weeks after the "Test of the Cylinder," the time had come to write a letter to "Uncle Aboud."

20 September, 1948
Dear Uncle Aboud:

I hope this letter reaches you. I hope you and my aunt and cousins are well and safe. You probably know that the Jews captured Lydda and murdered Aziz, may his soul live forever in peace. They killed dozens of others and sent everyone else into exile. My mother and sisters crossed into Jordan. My mother was hoping to find a way to get to Beirut and stay with you there. I hope she succeeded. I escaped. I cannot tell you where I am or what I am doing, but if you know where my mother is, please tell her that I am safe and will avenge my brother and the others massacred in Lydda a thousandfold.

And how is the newsstand? Mother told me your business is going from strength to strength, thank God! I wish you and your family all good fortune. I hope to see you soon. After God grants us victory over the enemy and our family returns to Lydda, we will invite you to stay with us. Uncle, kiss my mother and sisters, and tell them I will come for them and bring them home.

Please accept an abundance of my appreciation and respect.
Khalil

I reread the letter, making sure the errors of Arabic spelling and grammar I scattered throughout seemed authentic for a poorly educated teen. I wrote an address on the front of an envelope with no return address. The destination was a newsstand and tobacconist shop on a street corner in downtown Beirut, which in reality was the front for The Dawn's espionage station in Lebanon. Before going undercover, Colonel Mizrahi and I had established the means by which I would communicate with The Dawn. A letter written to "Uncle Aboud" and sent to the kiosk would establish the terms of a meeting with agents, to whom I would transfer any useful information I had managed to procure.

We assumed that all written communications were opened and read. The purpose of the first paragraph of my letter was to bolster my cover story. The remainder contained a code indicating the date and location of the proposed meeting. The date was designated by the number of Arabic words in the first and second sentences of the second paragraph. The first sentence began with the Arabic letter representing the word *and*, indicating that the first digit was zero, and the five subsequent words meant the meeting would take place on the fifth of the month. The next sentence contained ten Arabic words, signifying the month of October. The third sentence contained the phrase *you and your family*, confirming the meeting place in one of four possible predetermined locations just across the armistice lines in Jewish territory, a distance of about four kilometers from Al-Hamdan. The time had been set between midnight and 2:00 a.m. If I did not show up on the designated date, the team would wait for me two consecutive nights more. After that, the rendezvous would be abandoned, and I would have to send another missive.

Mail delivery between the Arab villages of the northern Galilee and Lebanon was fairly good but not wholly reliable. To increase the odds of my message being received, I penned a copy, a common practice at the time, and one not likely to raise suspicion. If, when I came to the meeting place, no one was there, I was to interpret it as a sign the letters had not been received, and I would return to Al-Hamdan to write a new one.

I walked to the local post office, paid for stamps with a few coins from the weekly allowance given to me by Abu Musa, and dropped the letters in the box.

Chapter Twenty-Three

At a quarter to eleven on the night of October 5, I descended the steps of the mosque. My roommate Yakub and I had gone to bed as usual at ten o'clock. He was a sound sleeper and prodigious snorer. Over the course of our cohabitation, I had established a pattern of getting up to roam the village nightly to escape the din, frequently several times a night. This habit and its cause were well-known sources of amusement among the militia.

The guards patrolling the square changed hourly, so by the time I returned from these peregrinations, the sentries often differed from those on duty when I set out. Eventually, they ceased reporting to each other that I had left. The new sentries were usually unaware that I had gone out and how long I had been away. In establishing these routines, I was careful to walk streets and alleys that allowed me to drop out of view for long periods of time.

"Good evening," I said wearily to the militiaman pacing the square.

"Good evening," he replied. "What's the matter? Yakub 'singing' again?"

"Like a dying cow. I am surprised he doesn't wake the entire village, or at least himself."

"Have a nice walk!" the militiaman called after me. I raised an arm in reply without looking back and headed down a nearby alley, one of my usual routes. I strolled down the hill to the town's northeastern edge, which I knew would be unobserved at that hour. I passed the last house and doubled my pace. Though there was only a sliver of moon, the stars shone brightly in the cloudless sky. It was not difficult to work my way among rocks and shrubs. At one o'clock, I arrived at the rendezvous point, a lonely terebinth between enemy lines and remote from structures or fields that might house a guard dog.

Leaning against the tree, I sensed eyes that had been observing me for the previous half hour. The trudging of boots followed, and a few minutes later, four shadows emerged from the darkness.

"*Shalom*, Yosef," said Colonel Mizrahi. He extended his arm. "How have you been?"

"Very well, thank you," I answered, smiling and shaking his hand. "And you?"

"Never better."

"Oh, I think you will have a new 'never better' starting a few minutes from now."

"Really? I expected no less of you. What do you have for us?"

"A lot," I said. "Did you bring the maps?"

Over the next forty-five minutes, I pinpointed the locations and sizes of all the Arab forces in the region and shared the information I had gathered about the offensive battle plan. Among the officers in attendance was the regional commander of the northern front. His appreciation for the depth and breadth of my intelligence was exceeded only by his astonishment at the method by which I had obtained it.

When I finished, Mizrahi laid a warm hand on my shoulder. "Yosef, you must know this information not only will win the battle for us but will save hundreds of lives, both ours and the Arabs.'" His gaze fixed on me. "The people of Israel owe you a great debt."

My eyes must have been glistening in the crescent moonlight. He threw his arms about me and squeezed. "I am proud of you," he whispered.

I squeezed him back. "I had better get moving."

"Yes, Yosef. You must go. I don't know when the attack will come, but it will be unmistakable when it does. Keep yourself safe, and stay away from the line of fire. Come out into the open unarmed and with your hands up only after the fighting has ceased. The unit assigned to take Al-Hamdan will know to look for you. Make sure to wear your cross on the outside of your clothes."

⸻ ❦ ⸻

Three weeks later, the battle for the Galilee began. The Arab Liberation Army violated the truce by attacking an Israeli position near Kibbutz Manara. This attack provided the pretext for which Israel had been waiting. After a few days of escalation, Israel launched an offensive. First, Arab positions were heavily shelled and bombed, attacks that devastated morale and provoked a mass flight of villagers toward Lebanon. Then Israeli ground troops moved in, systematically defeating both the ALA and the local militias. The Arab forces never had a chance to execute the consolidation maneuver called for in the offensive battle plan. Many of them fled, abandoning the remaining citizenry.

By the will of the imam and Abu Musa, the residents and fighters of Al-Hamdan stayed in position, vowing to defend the village to the last man. Despite their valor, the militia were no match for the disciplined, well-trained, and well-equipped Israeli soldiers.

As the attack on Al-Hamdan developed, the imam took a position at the top of the minaret and broadcast continuous messages using the loudspeaker with which the muezzin called the faithful to prayer five times daily: "Citizens of Al-Hamdan! This is your day of glory! Bring us victory, or bring us martyrdom! Do not fear! Allah will use you as His sword. He will wreak punishment on the Zionists, those demons bent on stealing what is yours. Save your village from shame and looting! Save your women from rape! Fight! Fight to the last!"

Yakub and I, having both exhibited skill in marksmanship, were stationed on the second floor of the mosque. We were given single-shot French rifles with instructions to hold our fire until the enemy was in the square, then to take them out one by one. We propped the barrels of our guns on adjacent windowsills and waited as the *pop-pop-pop* of Israeli gunfire neared the town center.

The rest of the village's defenders, initially stationed on the periphery, contracted their positions as the Israelis pushed forward. Soon the town was nearly completely taken, other than the small area surrounding the mosque and its square. The militia spread themselves out in the shelter of the buildings and prepared for the assault. No Israeli soldier could yet be seen, but the Arab defenders' anxiety punctured the silence every few seconds with gunshots and bursts of automatic fire aimed at any movement, whether of birds or debris blowing in the wind. Every pillar, every darkened doorway, and every upper-floor window hid an Arab with a gun. If the courage of the defenders held, the Israeli force preparing to storm the square would be cut to pieces.

"Stay here," I said to Yakub. "I am going to find Abu Musa. The battle is lost. We must surrender."

"Khalil, wait! You heard the imam. We stay and fight! It is either victory or paradise."

"Stay here!" I repeated.

I picked up my rifle and ran to the command post on the third floor. I found Abu Musa standing alone by the room's only window, peering through the sights of his automatic rifle into the center of the square, his finger hovering over the trigger. He had returned to headquarters after directing the defense from the field and had dispersed the entire command staff to take up positions around the square with the fighting men.

"Abu Musa," I said. When he did not respond, I shouted: "Abu Musa!"

He started at the sound of my voice and whirled around, the rifle now dangling in his right hand. He was covered in grime. Clotted blood caked the side of his face from a gash by his left eye, and the left shoulder of his fatigues was soaked in dark red.

"The battle is lost, Abu Musa! We must surrender!"

"You . . ." He growled, his eyes blazing. "You and your ridiculous battle plan are the cause of this defeat." He spat on the ground. "And now you advise us to surrender. The truth about you is at last revealed, Khalil. You have always been an ignorant peasant, and now you are also shown to be a coward." He shook his head and muttered, as if to himself, "The only error I have ever known the imam to make."

Without warning, Abu Musa jerked his rifle upward. I tumbled to my left and rolled onto one knee. A burst of gunfire from Abu Musa's weapon shattered pieces of the wall behind where I had stood. The volley triggered shooting from the defenders positioned all around the square, drowning out the sound of the shot I fired into Abu Musa's upper left chest. The force of my bullet heaved him off his feet, and he staggered backward, falling into a seated position against the wall beneath the window, facing me. His arms were flung to the sides from the impact, but the rifle was still in his right hand.

"Khalil," he said with a groan. "Who are you?"

I drew a cartridge from my belt and loaded it into the chamber. Abu Musa struggled to raise his rifle with his right hand and trained it, quavering, in my direction.

"I owe you no explanations." I growled, cocking my gun. My second shot caught him below the first. The rifle was thrown from his grasp, and he collapsed sideways, blood beginning to pool beneath him. I cast aside my old French firearm, picked up his automatic and ammunition belt, and ran.

I raced up the spiral staircase toward the chamber at the top of the minaret. As I ascended, the imam continued using the loudspeaker to exhort the men to fight to the death. Bursting into the open space from the stairwell, I found the imam standing by the balcony overlooking the square, an ammunition box at his feet, a rifle propped along the railing beside him. He held the microphone in his right hand, its coiled cord secured under the ammunition box so that it would stay near him even if he let go of it. There was no movement in the square. The firing had for the moment ceased, an eerie quiet presaging the coming storm of the assault.

He paused to take a breath and released the speaker button on the handset. I called out, "Imam!"

The imam turned to look at me, astonishment in his eyes. "Khalil," he said. "What are you doing here?"

"You must tell the people to surrender!" I pleaded.

"We shall not surrender. You know this."

"But we cannot win this battle!"

"You are correct, my son. Martyrdom is the only path left to us." His lips formed a grim smile. "But we will try to make as many martyrs among the enemy as we can."

"Imam, please! Think of the women and children! There is time to save them!"

"Khalil, you must understand that we go to a place where time does not exist. We will die, and we will live again." He quoted a sura: "*And say not to those who have been slain in the Path of Allah that they are dead. Nay, they are alive and receive sustenance from their Master.*"

I began to weep. "Please . . . Abu Musa is dead. There is no one to lead."

He nodded, a pained look in his eyes. "Khalil, I grant you permission to surrender. Your faith does not obligate you to do as the Muslims must. I am not a military man, but I will do my best to direct the battle from here. When we are gone, I ask you to rejoin the fight. And if you become a man of letters, perhaps you will tell the world the story of our forsaken homeland. The Arab nations have abandoned us." He turned toward the balcony and picked up his rifle.

"I am sorry, Imam . . ."

"It is all right, Khalil," he replied without looking back. "You will find your purpose. Go now."

"I am sorry, Imam," I repeated. "I have already found my purpose." Striding up to where he stood facing the square, I shot him in the right calf. The shot echoed around the square and was followed immediately by bursts of fire from all quarters, obscuring the imam's cry of pain. He dropped his rifle, which clattered onto the stone floor. I quickly shot him in the other calf, and he collapsed, grabbing at his legs with his hands.

I reached down and drew the curved dagger that hung in a scabbard from his waistband, casting it aside. Gathering the neck of his *thawb* in my fist, I dragged him away from the balcony and propped him in a seated position against a side wall. He grimaced and groaned in pain.

"Khalil, what are you doing?" he grunted.

I did not answer. Kneeling beside him, I raised the hem of his *thawb* to ascertain that he was bleeding only minimally. The bones were shattered on both sides, but the arteries and veins were intact. I rose to my feet, retrieved the dagger from the corner of the room, and strode toward him with the hilt in my right hand.

Resolve crept into the imam's eyes. "If you are going to kill me, at least allow me to recite the *Shahadah*." He inhaled deeply and closed his eyes.

"I am not going to kill you," I said. "Save the *Shahadah* for a different time." I raised the dagger, and the imam flinched at the motion. I cut a wide ring from the hem of his garment. The action reminded me of David, the usurper and future king, who cut the hem of King Saul's robe as he slept to signal that he might have slain him. Sadness joined urgency in my consciousness, for I perceived that what David had done to demonstrate his loyalty, I was doing for the opposite reason. With quick efficiency, I sliced the ring of fabric in two, leaned the imam forward from the wall, and used one of the strips to bind his hands behind his back. He grunted as I brought down the knot. When I was done, I eased him back against the wall.

"I apologize, Imam," I said. "I need to gag you. It is only for a short while. You will not be a *shahid* today. Do you understand?"

"Who are you?" he rasped.

"I will tell you in a moment." I passed the remaining cloth strip through the angles of his mouth and tied a tight knot at the nape of his neck. Returning to the window, I knelt to pick up the microphone, easing the cord out from under the ammunition box and pressing the broadcast button.

Endeavoring to mimic the imam's timbre and cadence, and hoping the distortion of the amplifier would do the rest, I called out, "This is Amr Abu Khadr al Hamdani! Brave soldiers of Allah, hear me! You have done your duty. You have defended your village against the enemy and have fought valiantly. But Allah desires not your martyrdom today. I command you to lay down your weapons where you stand and gather in the square. Rest on your knees with your hands behind your heads. When the Jews come, do as they command without resisting. You will do this not out of fear, for you are prepared to die. You do this to protect your women and children, for who can say what crimes the Zionists might commit in their wickedness? Allah will reward you with victory a different day. This is the will of your imam. This is the will of Allah!"

I continued speaking, and after a while, the first of the militia emerged from their hiding places. Looking warily about themselves with their hands in the air, they made their way to the center of the square. There they knelt, their fingers interlaced behind their heads as I had instructed them. Within a few minutes, fifty fighters had joined them, the full complement of surviving warriors in Al-Hamdan.

Then I began to broadcast in Hebrew: "Israeli soldiers! The town has surrendered! The men have abandoned their weapons and have gathered in the square to await you. They are no threat to you. There is no need for force."

After a few repetitions of this message, an Israeli armored car lumbered up the hill and rolled into the open area. Soldiers poured from its hold and spread out, training their weapons on the kneeling men. Other soldiers began to filter into the square through streets and alleyways. Their cries of amazement at finding the defending force of an entire village on their knees in surrender reached my ears at the top of the minaret.

Before laying down the microphone, I made another announcement in Hebrew: "I am an Israeli soldier. I will be exiting the mosque unarmed in a few minutes. You will recognize me by the cross about my neck. It is my strong preference that you not shoot me when I come out. I will be carrying a wounded man. He poses no danger and will need to be evacuated. Do you understand?"

The Israeli soldiers shouted their acknowledgment. I dropped the microphone and returned to the imam, kneeling beside him to untie his gag. I left his hands bound with the strip of fabric.

"Who I really am is an Israeli spy," I said. "I came here to infiltrate your organization and do what I could to allow our army to capture this town."

"The men who sent you must be very proud," he hissed. "You have done more than they asked. In your treachery, you have delivered to them the entire Galilee."

"It is not treason to serve my country."

He spat on the ground. "Then you are no different from your so-called countrymen. They are traitors and deceivers to the last man! You think nothing of robbing us of our homeland, whether by the slow creep of the last fifty years or the sudden violence of the last few months."

I hoisted him across my shoulders. He groaned. "Imam, I read the books you gave me, and I listened carefully to the words you spoke in private. The Arab leaders have squandered every opportunity they had to thrive in this land. Had they cherished the well-being of their people as much as their hatred of the Jews, we would already be living together in peace and prosperity."

I walked toward the exit to begin our slow descent down the spiral staircase. He grunted with each movement.

"You turn my own words . . . my generosity . . . against me. What is . . . your name?"

"Yusouf," I replied.

"Of course . . . I should have . . . known." He exhaled the words sharply, his agony timed with my steps down the stairs. "You infiltrated the leadership . . . gained false trust . . . just like your . . . biblical ancestor."

I continued the descent. "You are correct about me, Imam, but not about my biblical ancestor. Joseph deserved the trust of Pharaoh. He saved Egypt. And though I have dealt falsely with you, I saved your life and the lives of your men."

"What good is . . . this salvation of yours? We have lost . . . more than our lives are worth . . . and we survive . . . only to despise you. There is nothing for you . . . in this victory . . . but endless jihad."

"I hope you are wrong, learned Imam. I hope both sides will have the wisdom to make peace. Until then, we have no choice but to fight." We passed the second floor, where Abu Musa lay dead. I shifted the imam on my back so he would not see the body.

"How . . ." the imam grunted as I continued down the stairs, "did you . . . deceive us with . . . the cylinder?"

"It was obviously a test from the start, Imam. There were so many signs. Abu Musa would never have trusted me with the real battle plan. I knew there was no roadblock where he said there would be one. I recognized all the men I encountered along the way—the shepherd, my captors. There were other clues also."

"I am shamed . . . by my error in judging you . . . but in one respect . . . I was not mistaken." We descended the final steps to the ground floor. "You are . . . extraordinary . . . Yusouf."

"Thank you, Imam. As are you."

We emerged from the mosque into the afternoon light. Four Israeli soldiers held the men of fighting age under guard in the center of the square. Two additional soldiers passed among them, blindfolding them with strips of cloth ripped from a pile of sheets someone had brought out from the houses. Others wielding loudspeakers roamed the streets beyond, broadcasting an appeal in Arabic for the citizens to emerge, along with promises that they would be reunited with their families and not harmed.

I unloaded the imam from my shoulders and lowered him onto the stones at the top of the stairs, propping him along the external wall of the mosque. At the sight of him, a wave passed among the captives. The word *jihad* was uttered aloud, and the group grew restless.

The imam raised his voice. "The time for martyrdom has passed!" he cried. "We are prepared to die in battle, but we do not commit suicide. You will cooperate!"

Hearing him speak, a soldier in his early twenties detached himself from the Israeli platoon and strutted toward us. He wore a sergeant's insignia on his sleeve and a scowl on his lips. "You are The Canaanite?" he asked gruffly in Hebrew.

"Yes."

"This is al Hamdani?"

"Yes."

The sergeant smirked at the imam, taking in his wounds and anguish, then stepped forward. Without warning, he kicked the imam savagely in the left lower leg. The imam howled in pain. Some of the men kneeling in the square made to rise but were quelled by their guards.

I rushed to interpose myself between the sergeant and the imam. "Stop!" I shouted. "This man has surrendered. You will take him for medical care immediately."

"Oh, I will take him. I promise you." The sergeant motioned to two of his men, who pulled a stretcher out of the armored car and raced up the steps with it. They laid the imam atop the stretcher and prepared to bear him out of the square.

I lifted my hand to stay them, and they halted, stooping to lay the stretcher on the earth.

"Where is your commanding officer?" I demanded of the sergeant.

"He has gone to headquarters. He left me in charge."

"My orders are to report immediately to the regional command," I told the sergeant. "Bring your radio man."

The sergeant extracted a pack of cigarettes from his breast pocket, tapped its bottom, and pulled out a gasper with his lips. "He is unavailable."

"You will make him available immediately, or I will report you to the regional commander."

The sergeant glared at me. "It looks like we have here a righteous man!" he called out. "A true zealot!" The soldiers in the square shifted their feet. Some stared at us; others looked away.

"You are the zealot," I whispered. "I am a soldier who was taught to treat prisoners with respect. You will bring me your radio man, or I will report you."

The sergeant withdrew a matchbox from his left pants pocket and lit a match, cupping the flame to ignite the end of his cigarette. He breathed in deep and then exhaled the smoke into my face. "Bring Shlomo here!" he called without taking his eyes off me.

In a few seconds, a jeep laden with communications equipment pulled into the square. I strode down the steps to the side of the jeep. "Give me the handpiece," I instructed the driver.

"Yes, sir," he answered, not realizing that, as a corporal, he outranked me. In the Palmach, I had no rank at all, and I had never been promoted.

I set the dials to the command frequency. "Apex, come in," I announced. "This is Canaanite." No answer. I repeated the call.

After a few minutes, the set came to life. "This is Apex."

"Canaanite here. Over."

"Good work, Canaanite. We have had success in every sector. I am glad to hear your voice. Anything we can do for you? Over."

"Yes. I have handed the imam to our forces. He is wounded in both legs but is otherwise well. Please see that he arrives safely and receives medical care. Over."

"It will be done. Make your way to headquarters. Out."

I gave the handpiece back to the driver. He issued an admiring whistle. I nodded at the two soldiers standing by the imam's stretcher. They picked it up and bore the imam out of the square.

I turned toward the sergeant. "What is your name?" I asked.

"Why do you want to know?"

"Because I want to know what I should call you."

"Avi," he answered.

I was about to say something but stopped myself. The contrast between this Avi and the noble Avi from my Palmach unit had momentarily incapacitated me. "Avi," I said. "I am going into the mosque to gather a few things. When I return, I will need a ride to headquarters. Can you arrange it?"

"So, you think you can give orders to everyone?" he sneered. "The regional commander as well as me?"

"Listen to me, you piece of shit! If the regional commander is taking orders from me, don't you think you should also? I will be back in fifteen minutes. I would appreciate a ride." I turned and reentered the mosque.

I came out ten minutes later carrying a duffel bag filled with maps and documents. Abu Musa's automatic was slung over my back. The imam's dagger was in its scabbard on my waistband. A satchel on my shoulder contained a toothbrush, an extra shirt, a pair of underwear, and the two books the imam had given me. A driver waited in a jeep. When he saw me emerge from the mosque, he started the engine. He seemed anxious to get moving.

I swung the duffel and satchel into the rear, laid the rifle atop them, and got into the front passenger seat. "Where is Avi?" I inquired.

The driver stared straight ahead.

"Where is Avi?" I repeated. The driver's eyes and mouth drooped in apology, and he glanced in the direction of one of the alleys leading away from the square. I dismounted and reached into the back to retrieve the rifle. Slinging it by the strap onto my shoulder, I marched in the direction he indicated. A few meters ahead, a couple of soldiers stood guard outside a one-story dwelling.

"What are you doing here?" I demanded.

They did not answer, and looked away.

"Is Avi in there?"

Still no answer.

"Step aside." They did not move. I switched the safety of the rifle to the active position, producing a recognizable click. "Step aside," I repeated, raising the barrel. They parted, and I entered the house. Passing through a narrow entryway, I emerged into a large sitting room of the type Arab families use to welcome guests. A girl lay on her back on a divan, weeping quietly, one fist clutching the skirt of her dress at the thighs, the other pressed against her mouth. Her eyes were screwed shut, and her face was averted. Avi stood in front of her, his trousers pooled at his ankles.

"You bastard," I hissed. "I didn't risk my life for the last three months so you could commit rape. Put your pants on."

He turned his head and growled at me. "Take your fucking Arab ass out of here." He wrestled the girl's hand away from her thighs, threw the hem of her skirt onto her chest, and reached for her underwear.

"It's your fucking ass I am going to take," I said, and shot him in the right buttock.

Avi howled and, because his pants were gathered around his ankles, fell sideways onto the floor. The girl was shrieking, one fist still pressing the skirt between her thighs. Hardly aware of what I was doing, I cast Abu Musa's rifle aside and threw myself upon Avi, stooping to raise his upper body by the neck of his shirt with my right fist and pummeling him with my left. "Bastard! Rapist! Son of a whore!" I yelled in rhythm with the blows I administered to his face. My spittle sprayed into the blood that began pouring from his nose.

Eventually, I became aware of two pairs of hands pulling me away. "Stop! You'll kill him!" one of the soldiers yelled. I continued to flail my arms, but the two soldiers were able to subdue me, and finally, I came to my senses.

They released me. I backed away and bent over, hands on my knees, breathless. "You will . . . place Avi . . . under arrest for attempted rape," I panted. "If you fail to do so . . . or if any other man in this unit . . . behaves in a manner that brings shame to the Israel Defense Forces . . . he will be arrested . . . on the orders of the regional commander . . . Is that clear?"

"Yes, sir!" both men answered.

"You whore!" Avi screamed into his shirt, balling it against his face to stop the bleeding. "You fucking Arab whore!"

I continued to bend over my knees while addressing the two soldiers. "You will find the next-highest ranking soldier here . . . and inform him . . . that he is in charge until an officer arrives. You will deliver this girl . . . to her family in the square . . . Is all that clear?"

"Yes, sir!"

I straightened, retrieved the rifle, and staggered through the hallway, emerging from the open door into the alley, gasping for air. What had come over me? I had acted rightly in disabling Avi, even in shooting him. But my rage had unleashed a craving to inflict pain entirely beyond my capacity to control it. I had wanted to kill Avi with my bare hands. Whence had this savagery come to me? How long had it resided within me?

I leaned against the wall of the building across the alleyway, my arm shielding my eyes, and breathed. After a few minutes, I regained myself and was able to return to the square.

I climbed into the jeep. "Drive," I commanded.

Chapter Twenty-Four

The capture of the Galilee was the last major event of Israel's War of Independence in the northern region. At the behest of Northern Command, I remained at an army base in Haifa through December 1948, when the official inquiry into my mission in Al-Hamdan was concluded. The military brass praised my efforts, noting that I had saved dozens of Israeli and Arab lives and made an incalculable contribution to our victory in the Galilee. I was lauded for my resourcefulness and praised for killing Abu Musa, for disabling the imam, and even for shooting the Israeli sergeant. The prime minister awarded me a medal, which eventually joined its predecessor from the battle of Nabi Idris at the bottom of the chest stored under my cot at the kibbutz. Everyone treated me as a hero. No one but Colonel Mizrahi recognized my need to cleanse the stains of deceit and violence from my person.

Yet even Mizrahi, in the end, had no better suggestion than to allow time to heal me. "Keep this in mind, Yosef," he said, his hand on my shoulder. "You did what was necessary. More than that, you did something extraordinary. When faced with a tactical impasse, you found a solution."

"My solution was to deceive and then cripple a good man. An honorable man."

"I believe the imam is indeed a good man, but he is also a man who, once per week, every week, exhorted hundreds of his people to kill as many of us as possible. In the real world, there are imperatives, and sometimes one imperative is incompatible with another. The Jews and the Arabs cannot occupy the same land at the same time unless they share it. Since one or both sides are unwilling to share the land, we must fight over it. And now that we have won it, we need to defend it.

"That is how it goes in life." Mizrahi sighed. "Each of us must make choices. The imam made his, and you made yours, even though it cost you. Without people like you, willing to sacrifice not only their bodies but part of their souls, our young nation will not survive its infancy."

"If I continue sacrificing parts of my soul in this fashion, soon enough there will be nothing left. I am tired, Shmuel. I have not yet lived eighteen years, yet I feel like an old man."

His lips formed a sad smile. "Give it some time. Go back to your kibbutz. A day will dawn when you arise young again."

I longed to go back to Gan Miriam. I was certain my path to redemption depended upon honest labor. There were plenty of job openings. Most of the young men and women had returned to the kibbutz after the fighting. Others had not, either because they had perished or their lives had veered elsewhere.

I hitchhiked to Gan Miriam's gate and strolled into the settlement, the familiar sounds and aromas of the kibbutz warming my chill. Yoram, the foreman, was busying himself with a hoe in his garden. He spotted me and rushed forward to envelop me in an embrace. "Come," he said. "Let's get some fruit compote." He wrapped his arm around my shoulder and directed me to the dining hall. In response to his query about what I had done during my absence, I reported that I "participated in the Galilee campaign." He asked me for the number of the unit in which I had fought and nodded knowingly when I answered, "No particular unit."

"I see from your bearing," he said, "that though you are sound in body, you have been wounded somehow."

I nodded and bowed my head.

He smiled sadly. "I am sorry, Yosef. May you find healing among us, here in your home." Yoram's prescription for all human ailments was to engage in agricultural work. "Why don't you tell me what work assignment you prefer? Your wish is my command, unto half my kingdom."

"The dairy."

Kibbutz Gan Miriam had acquired a herd of twenty Holstein-Friesian cows, and their delivery was scheduled for the following week. The Hebrew Dairy Farmers' Association of Michigan donated the bovines along with a set of state-of-the-art milking machines. These gifts were delivered in person by representatives of the Hebrew Farmers with a blend of Jewish and American Midwestern pride. Our own satisfaction was expressed in a "cow welcoming ceremony," complete with a performance by the kibbutz folk dance ensemble, an oration from the head of the regional agricultural council, and the singing of "Hatikvah," the anthem of the new State of Israel. The American farmers gave a few lessons on herd maintenance and use of the equipment, and I was assigned to run the dairy. Thus, my latest contribution to the stream of Zionist redemption consisted of flowing milk.

Yoram had raised an eyebrow when I requested assignment to the dairy. Cowsheds were unpopular workplaces. The odor never left their workers, no matter how frequently or long they showered. And the daylong stooping, shoveling, and lugging in confined spaces did not bring fulfilment to most kibbutzniks, who preferred to be in motion in the open air. But Yoram seemed to sense the new burden of sorrow and weariness layered atop the old. Perhaps he understood that bovines were as likely as any of the inanimate or living things in the settlement to satisfy my simultaneous need for solitude and companionship.

The job entailed herding cows in and out of the milking shed, giving them their feed and water, inspecting and brushing their hides, and other tasks. I shoveled a lot of excrement. But what I loved most was milking. The rich liquid drained from the udders through rubber tubes into metal containers, which I wheeled across the floor and emptied into a large vat. From there, the milk was separated, pasteurized, and processed for the production of about two dozen different dairy products.

I enjoyed the company of the cows, who maintained a dignified reserve despite my repeated invasions of their privacy. I found them easy to talk to and was gratified that, for the most part, they felt no obligation to respond to conversation.

So revitalizing was my time in the dairy that, after a while, I was able to rejoin the vibrant, idealistic, and purposeful existence that was kibbutz life. I relished the opportunity to restore an original article of my faith, the belief that through farming, I was playing a role in altering the course of Jewish history. I began to heal but did not attempt to conceal the veins of sadness that coursed through me, a fact that somehow only enhanced my popularity. Everyone wanted to be near me. There was widespread curiosity regarding what I had done during the war, but it died away when it became clear that, like my childhood, I was not going to discuss it.

I continued to enjoy the company of women. Lovemaking was a frequent diversion in those heady days of idealism and sacrifice. I set aside my recollections of Isabella and regarded these encounters for what they seemed to be: physical expressions of exhilaration. And in truth, they buoyed my sunken spirits. The women with whom I shared the hay shed or tractor cart accepted both my enthusiasm and my sincerity. But kibbutz society at the time was focused on the realization of dreams, not the baring of souls. When I declined to share the sources of melancholy they sensed within me, these women moved on without envy or resentment. Even the daughter of one of the Michigan farmers, who proposed a "transoceanic alliance," as she put it, accepted my polite refusal. She stayed at the kibbutz and married one of the other members, eventually raising four blond and blue-eyed children.

I tried to persuade myself that each of these experiences was a small step in a journey whose destination was wholeness. I now realize that they both filled and drained my soul in equal measure. The many gratifications resulting from my return to the kibbutz were insufficient to fill the voids. I yearned for more. I began to worry I would spend the rest of my life in pursuit of something I lacked but could not bring myself to name.

It was in this state of mind that I perched on my stool beneath a bovine underbelly on a Friday afternoon in July 1949. There remained about an hour and a half of work before the coming of the Sabbath. When Colonel Mizrahi limped into the dairy, I recognized his gait on the gravel. "*Ahlan wasahlan*, Shmuel," I announced in Arabic without turning around.

"*Ahlan bik*," he replied.

"Have you come to spend the Sabbath at our humble kibbutz?"

"I think you know why I have come."

"Perhaps I do. But nothing happens in the dairy before the cows are milked." I turned to face him and smiled. Mizrahi was dressed not in uniform but in blue pants and a white, short-sleeved, open-collar shirt. "Did not God Himself pledge to us 'a land flowing with milk and honey'?" I asked. "Take a respite, at least for a short while, from your spy-mongering and do your part to fulfill that promise."

I demonstrated the application of a milking cup to one of the teats. "See?" I said. "Try it, and feel the pride of a simple laborer."

"I was a simple laborer before you were nursing at your mother's teats," he snapped, a smile playing on his lips.

I rose and bowed, gesturing toward the stool. Colonel Mizrahi opened his mouth to say something, but I lifted my hand to silence him. "Rules of the dairy shed. Please seat yourself." I helped him apply the cups and flipped the switch to start the extraction. We moved on to the next cow, making our way through the herd to return to the first animal. I demonstrated how to remove the equipment, clean the udders, and transfer the cups to the sterilizer. We finished the rest of the work over the next hour, leading the herd back to their enclosure and putting everything in its place before trudging back to the central area of the settlement.

"You have now been back at the kibbutz for over half a year. Are you happy here?" Mizrahi asked.

"Yes."

"For a deceiver of the first order, you are a terrible liar."

"I am not lying. I am happy here."

He stopped walking and turned to face me, waiting.

"I am happier here than I can imagine being anywhere else."

"Ah. Now we are getting somewhere."

"My point, Shmuel, is that whatever mission you have come to ask me to fulfill, it is not likely to make me any happier than I currently am."

He shrugged. "Anyway, this is not about happiness. It is about the work you, and only you, can do."

"You are the one who introduced the topic of happiness."

We walked back to the cafeteria. I filled a thermos with coffee and set it on the little table in the corner, an empty cup in front of each of us. We sat. He poured.

Mizrahi took a sip and scowled. "Yech," he muttered in Arabic. "You call this coffee? How I long for a good Turkish by the campfire!"

"Hmmm," I agreed.

"Yusouf..." Mizrahi began.

"Yosef," I corrected him.

"Yosef." He sighed, continuing in Arabic. "When I came to you the first time, I had waited as long as I could for you to recover from Nabi Idris. And now, I have waited as long as I can for you to recover from Al-Hamdan."

"I had not recovered then, and I am not recovered now."

"I know. Our need is great."

"How is Abu Khadr?" I asked. The imam, now using crutches and a wheelchair, had been allowed to return to Al-Hamdan. The village resided in the Israeli-controlled Galilee, and its residents were Arab citizens of Israel. I could not visit, as I would be reviled there forever. I corresponded with the imam by letter.

The imam had resigned himself to the village's fate and concluded that the best way forward for his flock was to accept their status in the State of Israel. He foresaw prosperity and peace for his people, which might otherwise never have been their lot. Other Arab towns, left behind the armistice lines in Lebanon and Syria, faced decades of upheaval, homelessness, poverty, and lack of modernization.

"Abu Khadr is doing well," Colonel Mizrahi replied. "We speak frequently, and he sends his regards."

I sighed.

"He understands why you must keep your distance," Mizrahi added.

"I know. He has written to me."

"He believes that in taking his legs, you granted him life. He thinks it was a fair exchange. He forgives you."

I sighed again. "I know."

We sat in silence for a while.

"All right," I said. "I am ready to hear it."

Mizrahi lowered his voice. "Yosef, without your actions in Al-Hamdan, our conquest of the Galilee would have cost so much more in blood, both our own and the Arabs'. We—"

"Yes, yes, Shmuel," I interjected. "I have heard this before, and it is written on the scroll I received from the prime minister, which he required me to hand back to him about thirty seconds after he gave it to me because it is classified."

"And—please don't interrupt—once our forces breached the town's outer defenses, we were able to take its center with only four casualties. All thanks to you."

He opened his mouth to continue, but I interrupted again. "What do you mean *four* casualties? Which four casualties?"

Mizrahi ticked off on his fingers as he spoke. "The imam, of whom we have already spoken. And Abu Musa, of course. You remember killing him?"

"Yes, I remember Abu Musa, Shmuel. I had no choice, as the Commission of Inquiry confirmed."

"Correct. And then there was our sergeant, whom you shot in the ass."

"Also necessary. The commission exonerated me."

"One hundred percent, no argument there. The sergeant's ass needed shooting. I am not sure his nose also needed breaking, but the commission was wise to ignore his face and focus on his ass. I don't mind informing you that I had a role in persuading them to adopt that focused view."

"Thank you. Sincerely. And those are all the casualties of which I am aware."

"Come, come, Yosef. You are forgetting the fourth casualty."

"*Ya, Allah!*" I cried aloud, and when all the heads in the dining hall turned in our direction, added in hushed Arabic, "Who is the fourth casualty?"

Mizrahi smiled. "Khalil Haddad."

"Who?"

"Khalil. Haddad."

"But . . . I am Khalil Haddad."

"Wrong. Khalil is gone."

"What are you talking about?"

Mizrahi grimaced. "When we created Khalil's cover story and sent you into Al-Hamdan, we imagined that after giving him a trial run, you would take Khalil on to your next assignment. But you were so successful, and Khalil is so well known throughout the Middle East as the betrayer of Al-Hamdan, that we can never use him again. He must cease to exist. He is the fourth casualty."

"So," I replied, "one scholar crippled, one villain dead, one aspiring rapist punished, and one fictional traitor eliminated."

"Yes, Yosef, an excellent summary." Mizrahi looked about him to verify that no one else was in earshot. "And now: our new needs."

"All right. Tell me about it."

"Not here, Yosef. All I will say for the moment is that the armistice agreements we signed with the Arab states are not peace treaties. There will be no peace for us. The battles will continue, some using bullets and cannons, others in which the weapons will be intelligence and subterfuge. I would like to brief you at the camp. Can you make your way there Sunday afternoon?"

I nodded.

Shmuel Mizrahi rose, placed his palm on my shoulder, squeezed it, and limped out. I remained on the bench facing the wall, and after a couple of minutes, Yoram slid into the vacant seat.

"Leaving again?" Yoram asked.

"Yes. You will have to find a new cow master."

"When?"

"Day after tomorrow."

Yoram smiled. "I have the perfect person in mind. She was inattentive to her duties in the cannery. A stretch in the cowshed is exactly what can fix her. She will show up tomorrow morning at five o'clock with boots on. Train her, and on Sunday morning, I will drive you where you need to go."

"No need for the drive, Yoram. I can hitchhike."

"The matter is not under discussion, Yosef. We will leave together in the kibbutz's pickup at six o'clock Sunday morning."

"All right, Yoram." I sighed. "If you insist. The central bus station in Haifa will be great."

"Really? You don't want me to take you all the way to your destination?"

The truth was that it was against policy to reveal the location of The Dawn's training camp, but I did not wish for Yoram to feel he could not be trusted. "I have something to do in Haifa first," I said.

Yoram smiled, possibly imagining that I would be visiting a girl. "Anything you want to tell me about?" he asked.

I smiled back. "No, thank you."

Chapter Twenty-Five

Even at six o'clock in the morning, the July heat was oppressive, the harbinger of another blistering day in the Hula Valley. It was a weather pattern Israelis call *khamsin*, appropriating the Arabic term for the spring sandstorms of Egypt. I threw my bag into the bay of the pickup and climbed in.

Yoram shifted into gear, and we rolled out of the settlement. At the gate, I got out to raise the red-and-white-striped barrier, lowering it again after the vehicle drove through. The gate had been unmanned for months, its guard reassigned to the pomegranate grove long before. We exited the gravel road onto the asphalt heading west. A haze hovered over the fields, through which the hills of south Lebanon, though less than six kilometers away, were barely visible.

The State of Israel was just over one year old and had turned its focus to building the frameworks of governance and economy. Hundreds of thousands of immigrants were streaming in from around the globe to join the six hundred thousand Jews present when independence was declared. An uneasy peace had settled over the land. Infiltrations by gangs of saboteurs and murderers from neighboring Arab states were frequent, and a renewal of major warfare seemed only a matter of time. *Fear them not*, I whispered to myself, quoting from God's message to Joshua as he faced the northern Canaanite alliance at this very spot. *For tomorrow at this time I shall deliver them all slain before Israel.*

We turned south for about thirty kilometers and then west again to begin our climb into the Galilean hills. A dry wind streamed through the open window, bringing little relief. I gazed northward, knowing that Nabi Idris was there, out of my line of sight, and beyond that Al-Hamdan, and the border, and Marj 'Ayoun, and the Litani River, and the castle of Beaufort, and the hills of Lebanon, and the village of Bhamdoun. Again, I sensed that in casting my eyes over the terrain, I might cause my life to unspool as though from a reel.

Yoram dispelled the silence with commentary on the new crops and industry planned for Gan Miriam. The air cooled as we rose into the mountains, and I dozed off. I awoke as we came out of the hills and began our descent toward the five-thousand-year-old town of Acre. Its Ottoman fort, hulking over the ruins of a Crusader citadel at the edge of the Mediterranean, had been used by the British as a prison until they departed in 1948. The leaders of the Yishuv were incarcerated there after the Night of the Bridges, the night I entered Palestine in 1946, a little over three years earlier.

We entered Haifa from the north and passed the port, where two passenger vessels, several container ships, and cranes were visible from the road. The smokestacks of the oil refinery, idle since the Iraqis sealed the pipeline from Kirkuk at the onset of hostilities, stood silent sentry on our right. I wondered when the furnaces of the refinery might be fired again, and whether the flames of violence in the Middle East might ever be quenched. The former seemed likely, but not the latter, to judge by Colonel Mizrahi's impatience to impart my new assignment.

Yoram drove past the Ottoman clock tower of the Great Mosque of Haifa and let me out at the central bus station. "*Shalom*, Yosef," he called. "And *lehitra'ot*!" It was the Hebrew equivalent of *au revoir*. I waved as he turned the vehicle around and made his way through traffic. Shouldering my pack, I waded across the street through belching exhaust and blaring horns.

Haifa is known as a mixed city. Despite the violence of Israel's War of Independence, and though many of Haifa's Arab residents fled during the fighting, others remained as Israeli citizens, engendering a mostly peaceful coexistence. A short walk down the grimy street took me past peddlers hawking everything from brooms to jewelry, restaurants whose waiters shouted at both cooks and customers, and storefronts where radios wailed Arabic music. Beggars bestowed blessings or curses in measure with the reward they received. I chose a table on the sidewalk of an Arab café and nursed a Turkish coffee and a sweet roll, contemplating the new direction I sensed would follow my upcoming meeting with Colonel Mizrahi. The coffee's aroma conjured the unexpected memory of the sitting room in my father's house in Beirut, where my mother would serve coffee and cakes to my father's business associates while I eavesdropped from behind the curtains.

An instant later, my memory transported me to the bridge at Marj 'Ayoun, where my feet came into contact with the Land of Israel for the first time at the age of fifteen. I felt again the novel sensation of belonging that coursed through my legs and into my soul that night. From that moment onward, hiking the land had never failed to sustain my pledge to defend it. I needed to renew that closeness, like a lover committing the body of his cherished one to memory before setting out on a journey. I needed to walk.

Haifa rests at the foot of the Carmel mountain range, and by mid-1949, the city's expansion up the hills was well underway. A short incline took me to the hospital where I had recovered from my wounds after Nabi Idris. It was midmorning, and many of the staff were on break, some strolling and others eating or smoking along the square facing the waterfront. I scanned the nurses in their white frocks and caps, and before long glimpsed Yael standing with her back to me. Her braid swung from side to side as she conversed with a young male doctor, the mountain towering above them. A verse from the Song of Songs came to me: *Thy head crowns thee like Mount Carmel, the locks of thy hair like precious fabric . . . How fair and how pleasant thou art!*

The look on the face of the young doctor told all: He had come under Yael's spell. He pointed to something over her shoulder, and she turned to face the water, her closed-lip smile sending ripples of regret through me. My letter to Yael was never delivered. Colonel Mizrahi had pulled it out of his shoulder bag after I returned from Al-Hamdan and thrust it toward me. "Keep it," I instructed. "For next time."

After a few minutes, the medical staff began returning to their posts. A few people remained scattered in the square, mostly families gathered around loved ones in wheelchairs. Some of these patients were old and ill; others young and wounded. Yael and the young doctor walked shoulder to shoulder toward the entrance to the hospital, and I lost them in the crowd.

"*Shalom,* Yael," I whispered. But I did not add *lehitra'ot.* I had made my choices.

I hiked eastward, passing the Technion, the oldest university in Palestine. Students, having traded their rifles for book bags, crisscrossed the campus grounds. I felt anew the pulsing of a phantom wound: the barricading of the door to the convent's library on the whim of the new abbess, the amputation of my link to its stores of literature and knowledge. *Never mind*, I reassured myself. *There will be time.*

Leaving the campus, I continued my ascent past the Bahá'í World Centre, its elaborate gardens under construction. I came upon a small convent, the plaque at its gate identifying it as belonging to the Carmelite Order of nuns. I peered through a wrought-iron fence and spied two novices tending the garden. One averted her eyes when she noticed me staring. But the other, bending over the flowers, returned my gaze, her brow glistening with perspiration, wisps of auburn escaping from beneath her coif, her gray eyes smiling, her lips shimmering. I felt a sudden, intense aching behind my eyes. Suddenly, I was the one who averted his gaze, for I could bear for no more than an instant the memories she awakened.

I turned and aimed for the summit of Mount Carmel, forsaking the winding asphalt to follow more direct dirt paths, a steep climb of about sixteen kilometers. At the top, I turned to gaze at the blue waters of the Mediterranean Sea, its shoreline curving around the bay to the north and fading through the haze toward the ancient Lebanese towns of Tyre and Sidon. Beyond them lay Beirut. To the south, the coast bent toward the Israeli cities of Hadera, Netanya, and Tel Aviv.

A Carmelite monastery squatted on the eastern slope of the mountain, the site where Elijah defeated the 450 prophets of Baal in a test of God's powers. I sat on a boulder and ate a cheese and cucumber sandwich I had prepared before departing the kibbutz. By then, the sun had begun its descent toward the horizon. I set my path to the southwest, planning to hit the coastal road in the late afternoon, where I would hitchhike to a spot a kilometer past The Dawn's hidden training camp. From there, I would double back on foot and make it into the base before dusk.

I arrived just in time for dinner and received a hearty welcome from the watchman. "*Ahlan wasahlan!*" he exclaimed, opening the gate. And then, raising his voice toward the camp, he cried in Arabic, "Yusouf returns in triumph!" I crossed into the compound and within seconds was surrounded by members of the unit, each awaiting their turn to hug me or shake my hand or clap me on the shoulder.

I was led to the front of the food line by shouts of "Let the Ashkenazi through!" "He is hungry!" and "Watch your plates, boys! He will steal your food and convince you that *you* ate it!" I spied some faces I did not recognize, their countenances questioning, until eyebrows were raised, mouths opened, and heads nodded in response to whispered information from their fellows.

Colonel Mizrahi exited the hut that served as his office and limped forward. "Enough, boys, enough!" he called out. "What a commotion! You would think the King of England wandered into our camp. Leave Yosef alone, and let him eat. And no questions about his recent assignment, please. We will have time for that on another occasion."

Arriving at the picnic tables with my plate loaded with hummus, *ful medames,* chopped salad, and pita, I sat down and was soon surrounded by men eager to both listen and share. I learned of the whereabouts of members of the unit: who was in the field, who would soon set out, who had been captured, who was dead. After dinner, we went to the firepit, where once again the *finjanim* were filled with Turkish coffee and the men sang, told tales, and danced in slow revolutions around the campfire until it was time for bed.

The following morning after breakfast, I knocked on Colonel Mizrahi's office door and peeked inside. "Come in, Yosef," he called. "As you can tell, the men have learned something of your recent activities. My order to not speak of Al-Hamdan remains in effect outside this base. But within our little family, and to prevent the spread of rumors—after all, the truth is amazing enough—I would like you to speak to the group today about your experience. It would be a useful lesson."

We spent the next thirty minutes reviewing how I would tell my story: which particulars to emphasize and which to leave out. At noon, the men gathered under the large dining tent. They were joined by several high-ranking officers and about a dozen other civilians and military men. For nearly an hour, I relayed an account of the mission, beginning with my recruitment at the refugee camp just beyond the ceasefire lines and ending with my shooting of the Israeli Army sergeant. Mizrahi was particularly keen on including the latter episode, to demonstrate that even in the midst of crisis, we were expected to adhere to a code of conduct.

Applause and whistles interrupted my tale several times. When I was done, a few men asked questions. Mizrahi rose to thank me and exhorted the men to remember that the details I had communicated were not to be discussed outside of The Dawn. Then we ate a lunchtime meal of beef stew and carrots. The traditional complaint about being served day-old bread was issued, followed by the traditional rejoinder that if we wanted today's bread, we should come back tomorrow. The customary peals of laughter ensued.

＊

"And now, Yosef," Mizrahi said, back in his office, massaging his right thigh and lowering himself into his chair. "Ach, this damned injury. The pain never leaves me, even after four years. It grants only brief reprieves before showing me again who is master. How are your wounds?" He gestured with his chin at the right side of my face and my abdomen.

"They give me no trouble," I answered apologetically, before adding, "Is there nothing you can do to control your pain?"

"Nothing that will not make me an addict. The minister calls it my 'badge of honor,' but believe me," he grumbled, "there is no honor in sitting behind a desk while my men risk everything to do the work."

"Well, I must disagree with you on that point. Someone has to command, and no person is more qualified for command than you."

"Did Napoleon command from his desk? Did Caesar?"

"No, but Churchill did. And so does Ben-Gurion. Besides, you have agents spread all over the Middle East. You cannot run them if you yourself are in the field."

Mizrahi smiled. "Thank you, Yosef, if only for bringing the conversation round to its true focus: my agents in the Middle East. Are you ready to hear how you might be of some little assistance?"

"Yes."

He began scrutinizing my visage.

"What are you looking at?" I asked.

"I am wondering if our scientists can get that boyish face of yours to sprout a beard."

I raised my eyebrows, but Mizrahi moved on.

"We need a man in Beirut and Damascus," Colonel Mizrahi continued. "As you know, the Lebanese for the most part stayed out of the war, and we expect them to continue to keep their noses clean for now. They know their interests align with ours and that we can help them achieve economic prosperity and political stability. Were they permitted to do so by their allies and their own citizens, they might even be inclined to pursue a formal peace with us.

"But in the coming years, the uneasy truce between the various Lebanese factions will be increasingly difficult to control. Shiites, Sunnis, Christians, and Palestinian refugees will compete with each other for influence, not to mention Greeks, Armenians, Druze, capitalists, communists, hedonists, and a host of others. And through it all, the city of Beirut will remain a focal point for Middle Eastern financial interests and the international elite. The port will continue as a crucial entry and exit point for people and goods. And both the city and the countryside will crawl with zealots whose new raison d'être is our destruction. The emigration of hundreds of thousands of Palestinian Arabs has made things convenient for us here in Israel. It has delayed, for a while at least, some of the problems associated with having a sizeable Arab minority within the borders of our Jewish state. But those refugees are gathering in camps in Lebanon and elsewhere, and the time will come when they will be a formidable force arrayed against us."

"So I understand," I said. "Over Shabbat, I studied the political assessments you gave me."

"Syria is a different matter," Mizrahi continued, as though I had not interrupted him. "They do not have the liberal and Christian influences of Lebanon and are unlikely to ever relinquish their hatred of us. They will continue to seek unification with Egypt and Iraq, and when the moment is right, they will strike. We desperately need information on their capabilities and plans."

"Understood. What is the assignment?"

"To begin with, there is a related matter . . ." Shmuel Mizrahi's voice trailed off as he looked me in the eye.

"Yes?"

Mizrahi sighed. "Yosef . . ." he began, and then seemed to gather himself. "Yosef, you will have to come clean about Lebanon."

"Come clean? What are you talking about?"

"We cannot send you on this mission before we know who you are and where you came from."

"You know who I am and where I came from."

"This is what I know about you," Mizrahi answered. "You were born to Jewish parents and spent your early childhood in Beirut. Your father and mother divorced, and at the age of eight, you were sent to be raised in a Maronite nunnery, the only Jew and only male in residence. You stayed in that institution until the age of fifteen, at which time you left after first burning it down. You arrived by foot at Marj 'Ayoun during the Night of the Bridges one minute before the bridge exploded. The rest, I acknowledge, is an open book."

"So, there you are. A nice summary. The only inaccuracy is that I did not burn down the convent. I set fire to the abbess's office."

"Come, come, Yosef. At our very first meeting, we discussed the resemblance of this tale to *One Thousand and One Nights*."

"Well, it is all true."

Mizrahi continued to stare at me.

"Do you think I fabricated my past?" I asked.

"No. I do not think that."

"So what is the problem?" And when he didn't answer: "Shmuel, you cannot possibly think I am a double agent?"

"A double agent? Heaven forbid, no! The Arab intelligence services are inept, but even they are not sufficiently inept to concoct a story like that and expect anyone to believe it." He smiled, having amused himself with this observation. "I know it is all true. But I also know it is not the entire truth." He reached over to clasp my forearm. "Yosef, there are a thousand ways in which a spy's past can betray him. We need to know everything about you."

I wrenched my arm from his grasp. "First," I snapped, "I suspect you already know more about me than you let on, probably more than I do." Mizrahi raised an eyebrow. "My parents, for example: I presume you know everything that has transpired since I last saw them. I do not even know my mother's last name."

Mizrahi shifted in his chair. "Of course we have done research, Yosef. You know very well that we do not require your permission to investigate your past. I will be happy to tell you what we have learned about your parents, if you wish to hear it."

"Maybe later. But if you are satisfied on that account, what more do you need?"

"Yosef, we are contemplating a mission of the highest importance. It will entail physical risks and psychological exertions most people could not withstand. You will be alone among the enemy. Your relationships will all be false. You will be under constant threat of discovery. If you are captured, we ask you to allow yourself to be tortured and killed rather than reveal what you know."

I nodded.

"But you are not the only one at risk," Mizrahi continued. "There will be dozens of people and large networks supporting your mission. We have an obligation to you, to the nation, and to all the people investing in you. A single weakness left unattended might bring the whole structure crashing down."

"I have already proven myself. You know I will find a way to perform any task that is not impossible."

Mizrahi nodded. "I do know that. And I will add that there are things which might be possible for you that are impossible for others. But the factors on which you have relied thus far, the things you can control—preparation, calculation, daring, ingenuity—those factors are not always sufficient for success, nor is their absence necessary for catastrophe."

"That is obvious, Shmuel. What are you talking about?"

"I will tell you a story. We had an agent in Buenos Aires—"

"Why Buenos Aires?"

"He was part of a team gathering intelligence on Nazis, many of whom have gone underground in South America. But don't interrupt; what he was doing in Argentina is beside the point. The agent was solid—a combat soldier, top one percent on intelligence assessments, field-tested. We had an impregnable cover story and plenty of infrastructure supporting him. And yet, we lost him."

"What happened?"

"After fifteen months in the field, he longed to see his wife and child, and arranged to meet them in Bern. He sent letters through the regular post, providing just enough information to censors from the Argentinian Secretariat of Intelligence to expose him as an Israeli agent. They were able to figure out the rest, including the plan to abduct a major target and bring him to Israel for trial. Our man is now serving a ten-year sentence for espionage. His capture set the mission back by at least five years. And the diplomatic fallout was huge—Ben-Gurion himself was forced to promise the Argentinian president we would not betray their trust again. Naturally, we are already planning a new operation," he added, an ironic smile on his lips, "but it will take years to execute."

"How could the agent have risked the mission so recklessly?" I exclaimed.

"I told you: These jobs involve stressors most people cannot withstand. Here is another story to illustrate the point: We had a man in Jordan who identified an opportunity to gather documents from a safe in the home office of a high-ranking official in the Ministry of Defense. While developing the means of penetrating the target, he began 'penetrating' the beautiful and frustrated wife of the official, if you understand my meaning. He actually fell in love with her. In the end, she was forced to expose him. His whereabouts are unknown, as are hers, but it is almost certain both are dead. We have no choice but to assume that under torture, our man revealed everything he knew. We have folded almost all the active operations with which this agent had any connection, not only in Jordan but throughout the Middle East."

"I perceive a pattern here. I am not susceptible to such risks."

"Really? You consider yourself invulnerable to love? Your file suggests quite the opposite."

"I enjoy making love, but I have not been in love." Isabella's face flashed in my mind's eye as I had last seen it—anguished and pleading from the rear seat of the taxicab that carried her and her child—my child—away from my life. I suppressed the memory nearly as soon as it surfaced.

His eyes bored into mine. "On that last point, I am not sure I believe you. But even if it were true, that does not mean it will remain so in the future. And there are hazards other than love that can be deadly for someone in our line of work: loneliness, fatigue, resentment, regret, even compassion. Not to mention"—he eyed me narrowly—"revenge."

"What about revenge?"

"Why did you burn down the convent?" he demanded.

I glared at him. "Revenge."

Colonel Mizrahi nodded.

I added quickly, "And I did not burn down the convent. I burned only the abbess's office."

"Yes, yes. So you have informed me. What were you avenging?"

"Two years of hatred and abuse."

"Tell me about that hatred and abuse."

I ground my teeth. "She was an anti-Semite of the worst kind. She banished me from school and forced me to perform the most degrading tasks. She took away my access to the library. She did everything in her power to make my life intolerable. And then, she . . ." I swallowed my words. My thoughts had grazed a corner of my subconscious where a labyrinth lay, its dark passageways concealing a monster I dared not awaken. I shut my eyes a moment and then glowered at Mizrahi. "It doesn't matter. But the abbess deserved worse than having her office destroyed."

Mizrahi grimaced and shook his head. "And after you return to Lebanon, do you intend to mete out the remainder of what she deserves?"

I was silent.

"Do you intend to administer the rest of her punishment?"

"No. I intend to not think of her."

We sat without speaking.

"And what of the sergeant in Al-Hamdan?" Mizrahi asked.

"What of him?"

"You disabled him with a bullet to the rear end, Yosef. Why did you also nearly beat him to death?"

I looked down at my hands.

"What caused you to unleash such violence upon him?"

"I . . . I don't know."

"Look at me and repeat that."

I raised my head and looked into the warmth of his eyes. "I honestly don't know, Shmuel. Something about what he intended to do to that girl . . . it made me want to kill him with my bare hands." I closed my eyes and massaged my scalp. "For the first time in my life, I lost myself. I acted without thinking—without even the capacity for thought. I never want to feel that way again. Never."

"Are you beginning to understand why the mission, our agency, and you are placed at such risk by putting you, specifically you, back into the very environment from which you came?" Mizrahi's tone was softer now.

I nodded.

"And it is not only that, Yosef. Our background investigation is complete, but there are holes in your story. Something else happened to cause you to leave the convent so abruptly and violently. What was it?"

I chewed my lower lip. "Shmuel," I whispered, "there are some things I need to keep private. If the cost of the mission is revealing this one secret, I may have to return to the kibbutz, and you may have to find someone else for this job."

"What about your parents?"

"What about my parents?" I shifted in my chair.

"Your father abandoned you, and then your mother abandoned you. How does that make you feel?"

"It makes me feel abandoned. But I have no sentiments for my parents."

"Bullshit!" he cried, slamming his fist on the table. "You are not an automaton!"

I spoke quietly to quell the tremor in my voice. "My feelings are a private matter."

"Ah. So it turns out there is more than one secret! Your 'private feelings,'" Mizrahi shouted, "can jeopardize the lives of people, people who have no relationship with your feelings, who are risking everything for this country!"

"Shmuel," I insisted, "my parents abandoned me, and I have abandoned them. I rarely think of them anymore. They are no more part of my life than fictional characters."

Mizrahi sighed. "I believe you, Yosef. It makes me sad to say it. A report was recently compiled at my request based on information that is in the record, your psychometric testing, and your interviews with the psychologist after returning from Al-Hamdan. The file concludes that you have extraordinary empathy, but only for others, and none for yourself. Our psychologists suspect that your ability to feel others' pain is surpassed only by your capacity to suppress your own. They believe that is a defense mechanism, without which you would not have survived the traumas of your youth. And there are deep traumas there, including something that—and they cannot explain this—you are either unable or unwilling to admit even to yourself."

I looked at him squarely. "Your psychologists are right. I make no apology for it." I shook my head. "I am damaged, Shmuel. I know that. But perhaps that is what makes me so suited to serve in your unit."

"You should also know that our analysts believe the likelihood of your cracking under the strain is too high to justify the risks. They recommend against giving you the assignment."

I paused to consider this statement. "I understand, Shmuel. You know me as well as anyone. You will have to rely on your intuition and my promise that whatever my emotions respecting the abbess and my parents, I will not allow them to interfere with the mission."

"I have no doubt you make the promise with full intention to keep it. What is in question is your ability to do so." He sighed again. "At any rate, I require a more specific assurance than the one you have given."

"What do you mean?"

"I require you to promise that as long as you are in the field, under no circumstance will you investigate or contact anyone from your past in Lebanon, be they your parents, any half siblings you may have, the abbess or"—he narrowed his eyes—"anyone else."

I did not hesitate. "I promise."

He sighed and rose from his chair. "I will notify you of our decision. Tomorrow."

Chapter Twenty-Six

The following morning I entered Colonel Mizrahi's office and sat in the chair opposite his desk.

"Yosef, I am sorry," he said, his eyes brimming and his face mournful.

I was shocked. I had been certain Mizrahi would give me the assignment. I nodded and made to stand. "It's all right, Shmuel. You know best what you need. I shall return to the kibbutz."

"One moment, sit down," he instructed, reaching out to grasp my arm. "I am sorry," he began again, "that we must ask you to make a very great sacrifice for the nation. The team met about you last evening and accepted my recommendation to send you on the mission."

I smiled. "Good. It is the correct decision and exactly what I want. Do not worry about it anymore."

"Oh, I shall worry. I guarantee you that."

"Very well, go ahead and worry if you must. Now tell me about the mission."

Mizrahi heaved a deep sigh. "Yosef, this is a long-term posting. We intend to place you in Beirut as a Lebanese émigré returned to his homeland to establish a business. Over the years, this enterprise will expand to become several businesses, which will spread not only through the Levant but to Europe and East Asia. You will become a valuable connection for people in high places and have many opportunities to travel. During your trips abroad, you will meet with your handlers, sharing what you know and receiving instructions in return."

I nodded.

"But you are young. You know nothing about commerce or finances. You have never been abroad. It will take years to position you where you can have the most impact. That is part of the plan. We will give you basic instruction, and with time, you will gain a worldly education—organically, as everyone must."

Mizrahi smiled, sadly. "We will assist you financially. You'll have an unfair advantage over other businessmen, who don't have access to cash they do not have to earn or repay. But we must not overplay our hand in supporting your commercial interests, or you will be discovered. In addition to being an excellent spy, you will need to become an excellent entrepreneur. There is no telling how far you may go in the end. And as you advance in knowledge, wealth, and prominence, you may find opportunities to gather crucial information."

"Information?"

"Yes, primarily information."

I raised an eyebrow.

"All right. If you create opportunities to influence events in our favor, it would be an added benefit." Mizrahi examined my face. "But that is not an expectation."

He pulled a three-page document from a folder on his desk. "We have concocted a cover story for you based on the life of a real, though deceased, person," he said. "It's a good one."

He perused the document while relaying its contents. "Your new identity is that of Charles Choucair, the only child of Georges Choucair, a Maronite shipping clerk, and his wife, Laila. Charles was born in Beirut in 1931, the year of your own birth, by happy coincidence. He emigrated to Paris in 1933 with his parents, who were seeking a better life. Georges and Laila were killed in a traffic accident in October 1938, leaving their seven-year-old son to be reared by the French welfare system. Charles spent the next two years drifting among orphanages and foster homes."

Mizrahi related the rest of the cover story: Agents from The Dawn had contacted a Jewish merchant who lived in a one-room flat on the same floor of the apartment block where Charles Choucair was being fostered by a middle-aged couple. At 1:18 p.m. on June 3, 1940, air-raid sirens sounded over Paris. Two minutes later, before most of the occupants could escape to their designated shelters, the building was struck by a German bomb. When the Jewish merchant emerged into the hallway, covered in plaster dust, he went from apartment to apartment in search of survivors. He found nothing but dead bodies, including those of the French couple and their young charge. The merchant staggered out of the building seconds before it collapsed, burying everything inside. Eleven days later, Paris fell to the Nazis.

The merchant, anticipating the roundup and persecution of French Jews, went into hiding behind a false panel in the warehouse of one of his Catholic suppliers. He reported to no one the deaths he had witnessed. In the desperate chaos of the period, the authorities were unable to ascertain the fate of Charles or his foster parents.

That was the point in history when Charles Choucair would rise from the dead. His lack of relations, school records, permanent residence, and social network provided a perfect background for me to emerge with his identity from the confusion left in the wake of World War II.

According to the cover story fabricated by The Dawn, I escaped from the rubble of the bombing to spend the next four years as a Parisian guttersnipe. I supported myself through soup kitchens, petty theft, and the scraps Nazi soldiers threw in my direction when there were no dogs in the vicinity. Paris was liberated in August 1944, when I was thirteen years old. I participated in the economic renaissance of the city through employment as a grocery delivery boy, a baker's errand runner, a garbage collector, and other menial jobs. And though I resolved to reenter legitimate society eventually, I shunned social agencies and schools, preferring to raise myself among vagabonds in the catacombs and other dark places to which I had become accustomed.

"So there you are, 'Charles,'" Mizrahi said, placing the document back into the folder. "You will spend the next three months in training, and in September will move to Paris to become apprentice to the owner-operator of a Middle Eastern food cart in the 14th arrondissement. Your benefactor is a sixty-five-year-old Moroccan widower named Muhammad Siddiq. Six months after your arrival, he will bequeath the stand to you. We have financed a generous buyout and monthly pension for Muhammad, contingent upon his return to Morocco without leaving a forwarding address and not speaking of the arrangement to anyone."

Mizrahi finished outlining the plan. "You will run the cart on your own for a year and a half, saving as much money as you can—supplemented as needed from the coffers of The Dawn. In the spring of 1951, at the age of twenty, Charles Choucair will return to Lebanon, his homeland, to seek his fortune."

Again, specialists were brought in to round out my education: experts in small business, French history, and underground culture. I needed to learn to speak the French dialect of an impoverished immigrant raised in the streets, and the Arabic dialect of an orphan who had left Lebanon at the age of two and lost his native-speaking parents at age seven. I needed to appear to know the things, and only those things, that a young man would know who, though intelligent, had no formal schooling past his ninth year.

After nearly three months, I was ready and made one final trip to the kibbutz. "I am leaving again," I told Yoram, the foreman, when I knocked on the door to his hut carrying the chest I had removed from its storage under my cot. "Will you keep this for me?"

"Of course, Yosef." His use of my name stirred me. I suspected it would be a long time before I was addressed as anything other than *Charles* or my code name: *Samson*.

"I don't know if I shall ever be back. Should I resign my membership in the kibbutz?"

"Shh!" Yoram retorted. "You will be back, and when you return, I shall find a job for you."

We hugged, and I hitchhiked back to the base.

"There are plenty of things about this plan that make me nervous," Colonel Mizrahi confided during our final briefing before my departure. "But one worry rises above the rest, even though you might think it laughable." The colonel's concern sprouted where my chin hairs did not. Mizrahi had not been joking when he wondered aloud whether Israeli scientists could grow me a beard. Though I was known only to a small number of Lebanese citizens and Palestinian Arabs and would be returning to Lebanon as a man of twenty, there was a possibility someone from my past would identify me. I might be spotted in a photo, particularly were I to gain prominence in society. My appearance needed to differ sufficiently from that of the past to prevent recognition. Disguises in common use, such as hair dye, glasses, and fake beards and moustaches, were not practical over the long term. Natural facial hair would be a big help.

"But perhaps not sufficient," Mizrahi fretted aloud. "Beard or no beard, your appearance is so striking and your je ne sais quoi so . . . uh . . . je ne sais quoi, I will be uneasy until we bring you home permanently." He sighed.

I smiled. "I hope you are uneasy for a very long time."

At last, the day of my departure arrived. Colonel Mizrahi drove me to the terminal in Haifa, a ride of less than half an hour. Along the way, he fussed over matters we had covered a dozen times before. "Don't worry too much about making the business a success . . . but try to be a successful businessman. You must be careful to restrain your natural tendency toward intellectualism. Charles Choucair is no intellectual. In an emergency, you may escape at any time to one of the three Parisian safe houses. Do you remember their addresses?" I nodded indulgently at each utterance.

We got out of the car and rounded the vehicle. Mizrahi opened the trunk. I reached in, extracted my bag, and set it on the pavement beside me. When I extended my hand toward him, he swept it aside and enveloped me in his arms. Tears dropped onto my shoulder. His body quaked against mine.

"I'm sorry, Yosef," he wept. "I am so sorry."

"It's all right, Shmuel. We will meet according to schedule. And during those meetings, I expect to tell you tales of adventure that make the *One Thousand and One Nights* as unexciting as a grocery shopping list."

"You came to Israel to find a normal life among your own kind. Instead of helping you discover that life, I am sending you back."

"You are not doing anything to me," I whispered. "I am following my own path."

He pulled away from me. "Just make sure your path leads you back to us. I will be waiting."

We hugged again. I shouldered the bag and boarded the gangway of a ship bound for Marseilles as a third-class passenger named Avraham Cohen. A uniformed officer verified my passport against the manifest, a process that was repeated upon docking in France.

Disembarking at Marseilles, I strolled to a waiting Citroën, which drove me to a safe house in Paris. Final preparations were made over the next two weeks, and I set out into the streets to assume my new cover. At about the same time, an Israeli agent whose appearance was sufficiently similar to mine was smuggled over the Alps from Switzerland. He presented Mr. Cohen's passport in Marseilles for the return voyage to Haifa.

I began to work at the food cart. Muhammad, the Moroccan widower, was an honorable man who shared his knowledge of the business eagerly. He hosted me in his flat for three weeks until I secured an apartment of my own, a studio in Montparnasse. The neighborhood's free-fall from its former bohemian heights was on full display. Ruined buildings remained as piles of rubble for years after the war. Homeless people were nearly as numerous as feral cats. Trash was everywhere, and parks lay neglected. Nonetheless, the residents were honest, and optimism resurged after a decade of hopelessness. I reveled in the Parisian experience. The work of running the business occupied nearly all my waking hours, yet I found time to explore the city. I visited the museums and attended the theater in the standing-room-only, obstructed-view section.

I loved strolling among the tombs in Montparnasse Cemetery. I discovered the grave of Charles Baudelaire, whose collected poems were among the books concealed in a crate under my bed so that visitors would not discover my love of reading. I visited the modest tombstone of Alfred Dreyfus, the Jewish army officer whose espionage trial on false charges in the 1890s nearly cleaved French society in two and was the inspiration for modern Zionism.

After six months, my apprenticeship was over. "*Ma'a salaame*, Charles," Muhammad whispered into my ear as we embraced at the Paris bus station.

"*Ma'a salaame, ya Muhammad*," I answered. "May Allah bless you with happiness and good health." He kissed me on both cheeks and boarded the bus headed south.

The food stand thrived after Muhammad departed. I replaced the old cart with a modern version equipped with a deep fryer and interior electricity, powered via an extension cord connected to a nearby shop in exchange for hummus and kebabs. I launched an advertising campaign using street urchins who, fueled by free meals, fanned out into the neighborhood with signs, flyers, and word of mouth. I offered a discount menu on Fridays. I expanded my offerings to include sweets and Lebanese pastries prepared in a nearby bakery. Within six months, I had opened up three satellites and employed eight people. The business was so successful, there was no need to spend the budget allocated by The Dawn. I opened an account at the Société Générale bank and was able to stockpile a seed fund for Lebanon.

Charles Choucair's acquaintances in Paris, mostly Palestinian and Lebanese expats, supported his quest to reestablish himself in his native Lebanon. A week before my departure for Beirut, my friends hosted a farewell party in my honor at a Lebanese restaurant I had opened near the catacombs. Speeches and blessings were offered. Toasts were shared even by the observant Muslim members of the group. I sold most of my belongings but maintained ownership of the food stands and restaurant. I entrusted the management of these establishments to a thirty-year-old Maronite friend named Nadim, to whom I gave a generous salary.

As it turned out, Colonel Mizrahi needn't have worried about the beard. It grew in densely during my first year in France, and along with it came a learned street swagger and gregariousness that were so foreign to my true nature, they were as effective as any physical disguise. By the time I was ready to return to Lebanon, Charles Choucair could barely recognize Yosef Friedmann in the mirror. Yosef's consciousness was consigned to the depths, imperceptible in the way one's heartbeat goes unnoticed until exertion unmasks it.

I fretted over this unnatural arrangement. Any stratum of deceit, no matter how thick, is susceptible to fracture. I feared that some unavoidable disturbance might cause Yosef to erupt, like magma bursting through a crack in the Earth's crust. I worried that the unrelenting disavowal of true memories and acceptance of false ones might jeopardize my sanity—that I might awaken one day and no longer know what was real.

Chapter Twenty-Seven

I squeezed between a clean-shaven priest and a Muslim family of four behind the gunwale of the *Metropolis*, a Greek vessel bearing us toward Beirut. The youngest of these fellow passengers insisted that his father hold him up high so he could see both the city sprawled before us and the spray of the hull slicing through water. I shared his enthusiasm. I had never viewed Beirut from the sea. The sun setting behind us cast the city in orange, and the green mountains of Lebanon descended like the train of an evening gown, darkening as they crept toward the coast.

The ship approached the dock. Lights began flickering on the shoreline, igniting a glimmering progression up the foothills. Teams of sailors and port workers nestled the ship into its berth, securing it with heavy ropes, and the deck shuddered beneath our feet. I was one of the first to descend the gangway, a valise in one hand and my fedora secured against the westerly breeze by the other. I passed through immigration and customs and emerged onto a crowded street.

Streams of people were leaving the port in all directions. I joined one of these streams for a short distance to the east, past a line of taxis and limousines stretched around the block, their drivers leaning against hoods, cigarettes dangling from mouths. Vendors eager to make their final sales of the day voiced urgent calls to shoppers. Spices, sizzling meats, and fish from the morning catch lifted their aromas from stalls lining the rubbish-strewn street, awakening memories of accompanying my father to this very spot, my hand engulfed in his, to inspect his shipments or to purchase goods for the Sabbath. A crier offered discounts and free rides to the Casino Méditerranée. Prostitutes postured with voluptuous gazes.

I made my way toward the boarding house where I had reserved a one-month sojourn. Arriving at a low fence before the three-story hostelry, I experienced a strange, yet strangely comforting, memory of awaiting admittance to the convent in Bhamdoun for the first time as a boy of eight. I unlatched the gate and stepped inside. A weary attendant extinguished his cigarette in an ashtray overflowing with spent butts and copied the information from my passport into a ledger. He gave me instructions and the key to a room shared with three other young men. He rotated the register toward me. I signed the name *Charles Choucair* with the fountain pen he proffered and ascended the stairs toward an uncertain future.

⟶⬤⟵

Ten years passed. I turned thirty years old in the spring of 1961 and was the owner of Cedars Trading International, an import-export business with offices in Beirut, Paris, London, Zurich, Cairo, Damascus, Istanbul, and most recently, Bombay. The company shipped foodstuffs, kitchen supplies, luxury furnishings, gems, household appliances, crafts, and a host of other products across the eastern hemisphere. This vast enterprise had sprouted from the seedling of the food cart in Paris, of which I retained ownership out of nostalgia and a sense of obligation to my employees.

I purchased a large flat in the Kantari quarter, the prime location for a member of the nouveau riche to flaunt his success. From my wraparound balcony on the fifth floor, I had views of the mountains and sea. The presidential palace was directly outside my building. To the east, the Al-Omari Grand Mosque rose above the foundations of a Crusader church, and to its south rested the Bachoura graveyard, whose origins dated to the first century. To the west were the narrow streets of the old Jewish quarter of Wadi Abou Jamil, in which a remnant of the city's depleted Jewish community still resided. I never entered those alleyways, abiding by my promise to Colonel Mizrahi to leave the past unmolested.

My growing wealth and influence brought me access to many of the elite, both in Lebanon and in Syria. I hosted generous parties, where alcohol was served even to Muslims, and midlevel government officials could safely consort with beautiful women (and occasionally men), confident in my discretion. I entertained guests at the casino and cabarets. Beirut was one of the few cities in the Levant where such establishments existed openly. Corruption was rampant in both Lebanon and Syria, and I was often called upon to perform favors for dishonest officials. I gave lavish gifts to influential people. But my personal business dealings were beyond reproach. I was seen as incorruptible. I treated my employees fairly, befitting a man who had not forgotten his good fortune at having ascended from the Parisian gutter.

Unmarried men and those uninterested in women raise suspicion in Arab society. I had no choice but to either marry or act the playboy. I chose the latter. I was careful never to become involved with the wives or daughters of prominent men, confining my dalliances to young women looking for a good time and access to a social echelon to which they might not otherwise gain admittance. And when these relationships ended, it always seemed that the women tired of me rather than the other way around. In this way, I avoided entanglements, but at the cost of a lonely heart.

I traveled overseas frequently to manage the business and meet with my Israeli case officers, now brought under the umbrella of the Mossad. The first-class airline accommodations and hired limousines required by my new station were a welcome contrast to the berth in steerage and pair of legs that had conveyed me to Beirut.

And I did all this without spending a lira of the Mossad's budget, a fact I highlighted in a London tea shop to Shmuel Mizrahi during one of our periodic meetings.

"On behalf of the bookkeeper in the prime minister's office, I thank you," Mizrahi said, grinning.

"You are welcome," I responded, saluting him with a cup of Earl Grey.

"Speaking of your finances," Mizrahi added, "you might find this amusing: One of our analysts in Tel Aviv wrote a report about you."

"Me? What did he say?"

"That you were an up-and-coming star in Lebanese and Syrian circles, and that we might recruit you for the right price."

"Hah!" I cried, and when heads turned all over the tea shop, I lowered my voice. "You couldn't possibly afford to pay me enough!"

"I know . . . but getting our analyst to back off without explaining why was challenging. We considered transferring him to the Egyptian desk, but you would have only popped up there also. So in the end, we told him you rejected our advances."

"Of course I rejected your advances. What need have I of your ill-gotten riches? I have already amassed the single greatest stockpile of one of the rarest treasures in the Middle East: integrity."

⸺⸺●⸺⸺

Over the years, my mission began to bear fruit. I provided information about influential people in government and society. I shared assessments of political and social trends. I identified people who might be converted into assets for the Mossad: individuals with ideological differences with the regime, or with expensive tastes, or with debts they were struggling to repay, or who feared exposure for taking bribes or committing adultery. Such people were turned by Mossad operatives in painstaking operations, usually in Europe.

Through my contacts in shipping offices, I could produce information about the movement of almost any vessel in the world. Some of these ships carried arms and other matériel bound for Israel's enemies, and several disappeared mysteriously or blew up in freak accidents. As I acquired friends in the Arab military, I was taken on weekend tours of infantry, artillery, armored corps, and air bases throughout Syria and Lebanon. I reported my observations of the number, size, locations, and equipping of these forces to the Mossad.

On one of my visits to Damascus, I was invited by an acquaintance who worked as a midlevel official in the Syrian Ministry of Defense to a gathering of "friends of the State." I inquired whether the meeting was social or business. "A little of both," he replied.

Arriving at the ministry building, I was ushered into a room where five other men stood in a circle, smoking, the stench of their Turkish cigarettes curling through the room. Uniformed male servants circulated with tea and coffee. My acquaintance broke from the group to greet me, kissing me on both cheeks in the Arab fashion.

"Charles Choucair!" he exclaimed. "Allow me to introduce you to our dear friends." He presented each of the men in turn. Two were businessmen I knew by reputation but had never met, one in his sixties and the other in his forties. Both were substantially more established than I. A third was Herr Wilhelm, a German interpreter. The last member of the group was introduced as Professor Köhler.

The professor stood nearly a head taller than any other man in the room. His bearing was rigid and he was dressed in Teutonic chic: a dark suit with gleaming black shoes, crisp white shirt, and gray-and-blue-striped tie. His face, freshly shaved, was lean, with vertical furrows excavating a line through each cheek from his eyes to his jawline. He extended a manicured hand, and as I took it and looked into his pale blue eyes, apprehension, like an electric shock, ran up my arm.

"Welcome to Syria," I murmured. Herr Wilhelm translated my words from Arabic to German in an undertone.

Professor Köhler answered loudly, and Wilhelm delivered the translation: "I have now been residing here since over six months. And from what I have learned about you, you are not a frequent visitor. It is *I*, perhaps, who should welcome *you* to Syria."

"Ah," I answered. "In that case, thank you for welcoming me."

We made small talk for a few minutes more. Herr Wilhelm translated from Arabic to German in low tones into Köhler's ear, or from German to Arabic in a commanding voice, mimicking Köhler's clipped words and condescending tone, whenever the professor spoke. The interpreter never uttered a word that was not a translation of someone else's speech.

My friend from the ministry strode to the front of the room and asked us to take seats in front of a projection screen positioned alongside a lectern. "Professor Köhler is leading a new initiative conducted in collaboration with colleagues in Egypt. We are developing a new weapon to correct the injustices of the *Nakba*," he announced, using the Arabic word for *catastrophe*, referring to the loss of Palestinian land and displacement of its people in Israel's War of Independence. "The Zionist incursion into the Sinai in 1956 demonstrates more than ever the need to wipe the Jewish colonialist entity off the map."

The professor rose to stand at the lectern. His interpreter stood by a slide projector and translated while advancing the images. "At the Technische Hochschule Berlin I started my academic career," Köhler began, "and my doctorate I received in physics at the Friedrich-Wilhelm University." Kodachrome slides projected images of his alma maters. "During the War, I was lead engineer on our V-2 missile project." The next slide displayed a rocket painted in checkerboard black and white. "And this," the professor proclaimed, as the ruins of a London city block in Whitechapel appeared on the screen, "is the result of a single V-2 striking an urban target. The V-2 program could have turned the tide of war in our favor in 1944. Alas, cowardice and failure of vision on the part of the political echelons—not the Führer, of course, but his advisors—prevented expansion of the project in time to save the Reich."

The following slide showed a missile so enormous that it dwarfed a man kneeling on a platform near its nose cone. "More than tenfold has missile technology advanced in the fifteen years since the end of the war," the professor continued. "Larger, faster, more destructive, and more accurate than even we had imagined are the projectiles we can produce today. The Americans and Russians, aided by German scientists, are developing rockets that can fly across oceans and destroy entire cities.

"Next slide," the professor ordered in his harsh tenor. The same huge rocket was shown lifting off, fire and smoke erupting from its base. "Within a decade," the professor continued, "a rocket like this will carry men to the moon."

An appreciative murmur passed through the seated assembly.

Köhler smiled as he observed the impact the interpreter's translation of his words was having on the audience. "Easily you can imagine what effect this weapon will have on your enemies. And what if it were equipped with a radioactive or chemical warhead? I am not speaking of an atom bomb—that technology is not possible here—but of the dispersing upon impact of radioactive material or toxic gas. Between launch locations in Egypt and Syria, there is not a square meter of land in Palestine that is not within range. We can help you create an arsenal of thousands. One or two live demonstrations on civilian targets, followed by a threat to send more, will be sufficient to spread terror. Such a display of force might accomplish your political objectives without further military expenditures."

The professor was correct. Word had leaked about the existence of this program, and the Israeli leadership was beginning to panic. At my most recent meeting with Colonel Mizrahi, he had requested that I try to gather information about the initiative.

The lights came on, and I clapped my hands to simulate the excitement of the other members of the audience.

"How can we help with this?" the elder of the other two businessmen exclaimed.

The official from the Ministry of Defense rose, extending his hand to invite the professor and his interpreter to take chairs in the seating area. He stood at the podium. "As you can guess," he said, speaking in Arabic while Herr Wilhelm translated for Professor Köhler, "this initiative requires complete secrecy. Very specific supplies must be gathered discreetly from all over the world and assembled without our enemies learning of it. Teams of technicians and line workers must have facilities for work and housing, and they must be fed and transported. Finished product must be moved from assembly sites to deployment locations.

"What we need from you is assistance through your import and export operations, your shipping resources, your warehouses, your contacts. This will be a unique business opportunity for you. Participation will be rewarded handsomely. But more important, you will play a role in an Arab victory that will go down in history alongside Saladin. You will be the heroes of our generation."

"My resources are at your disposal!" the elder businessmen exclaimed, adding that a mutually beneficial price point should not be difficult to determine.

"Tell me how I can be of service," I added, glancing in Professor Köhler's direction. He smiled.

At the conclusion of the official portion of the meeting, we assembled in the outer chamber, and servers returned with tea and coffee, piling sweets onto a low table surrounded by six chairs.

I was seated to the left of the professor, the interpreter on his right. I leaned forward to look at both men simultaneously. "How did you come to be involved in the V-2 missile program?" I inquired. The professor waited for the interpreter to finish the translation, He seemed pleased by the question.

The others inclined their heads to listen to the response. "Professor Wernher von Braun, the Director, recruited me from university. Always he was inquiring with the department chairman for names of the best students, and I was very eager to participate. My graduation was accelerated to allow me to join the scientific group as soon as possible. I was a member already of the Nazi party since a young man, so no obstacles stood in my way.

"An expert in rocket science I was already from my studies, and I learned much more from Professor von Braun, who currently is leading the American missile program. But during the development of our project, I also became an expert in methods for mass manufacturing. After the enemy invaded Normandy in June of 1944, the Director wished to accelerate production of the V-2 to save the Reich. He entrusted me with the task. I transferred myself to the Mittelwerk underground factory site in Thuringia. And so, I became an expert in behavior and psychology."

"Fascinating," I murmured. "What do you mean?"

"You must understand." His grin was ivory and ice. "All the good workers were off fighting the war. We had to use prisoners from the Mittelbau-Dora camp. The Jews are not like normal people. Though they resemble us in form, they are as unlike us as we are from apes. When one cannot motivate them with money, as of course was both impossible and morally objectionable in those desperate times, one must find other ways."

The elder of the other two businessmen spoke up: "They did not want to participate in building missiles?" The professor nodded. The businessman added, "I also have trouble motivating my workers. What was your solution?"

"Laborers must know who is in charge. If you treat a person like you are his herdsman and he is your sheep, he will behave as a sheep. I was surprised to learn how small an investment, when properly applied, is required to extract a maximum amount of effort from a worker. But you must use psychological methods to help the worker understand his position in the order of things and the consequences of lax discipline."

"How did you accomplish it?" the businessman asked.

The professor opened his mouth to respond, but the translator shifted in his seat, brushing his shoulder against the professor's, and pointing to his watch. "*Ach*," Professor Köhler exclaimed, "it is getting late! Perhaps we stop here." He stood, and the rest of us followed his example. Köhler turned to me first and extended his arm. We shook hands, and in his grasp I again felt the strange surge of energy up my arm. This time, it carried with it an element of dread.

⸎

My next trip abroad was not scheduled for three months. In the interim, I began providing logistical assistance for the missile project. I arranged for dismantled production-line equipment to be packed in the bottom of my shipping containers. After unloading at the port in Latakia, these parts were transported to assembly sites concealed behind new walls erected in my warehouses. I imported huge vats of liquid fuel labeled *isopropyl alcohol, medical grade* from Saudi Arabia. I supplied Scotch whisky and American cigarettes to customs inspectors as encouragement to not examine these shipments too closely. I accepted as much business as possible for the project, knowing that in doing so I would ingratiate myself with the Syrian Ministry of Defense. I also knew that the more resources were concentrated under my control, the easier it would be for the Mossad to sabotage operations.

At last, my planned visit to Europe arrived. I met Colonel Mizrahi at a corner table in a café on the Löwenstrasse in Zurich, arriving on foot after engaging in the standard maneuvers to ensure I was not being followed.

Mizrahi was already seated. Over the years his hair had turned completely gray, and his face had become creased with worry. I sat opposite him, facing the back wall. A waiter approached to take our orders, a cappuccino for him and an espresso for me. I was eager to share my news, but he began with some news of his own. He reached under the table to massage his right thigh. "Oof, this old injury," he muttered in the hushed tones we always used for such meetings. "It never leaves me."

"I am sorry, Shmuel."

"Do you have pain from your wounds?"

I looked at the sadness in his eyes but decided to tell him the truth: "I am fortunate that the pain is only in my memory."

"That is good. Do not think for a moment that I prefer to hear otherwise. My discomfort would not be diminished even slightly by yours. Besides"—he sighed—"I am not persuaded that the memory of your wounds is less painful than the physical experience of mine."

We sat in silence a while longer.

"I am retiring, Yosef," he said. "I have lived in the shadows long enough. I wish to come into the sunshine for just a little bit toward the end."

"*The end?* That is a long way off, *inshallah*." I sipped my espresso. "But do you think you will be happy away from the action?"

"My eldest is expecting a baby next month. The second will marry in August. My wife has suffered in silence long enough. I tell you frankly that after all these years, it seems to me now that being a husband, father, and grandfather is just the right amount of excitement for me."

"Well, then, I wish you all the excitement you can endure."

He smiled. We never touched during these encounters, other than businesslike handshakes at the beginning and end, but a warm embrace emanated from his eyes. He dabbed at them with his napkin.

"All right, Yosef, enough of the tearful *adieux*. When we next meet, I hope it will be for a grateful *salut* when you are ready to take yourself out of the field. Don't look so skeptical," he added, observing my reaction. "A day will come when you, too, will have had enough. We will meet daily for coffee at a sidewalk café on Rothschild Boulevard in Tel Aviv."

"If I ever take myself out of the field, I expect to head toward a different field—the cucumber patch at Gan Miriam where you found me."

"Gan Miriam? Is there still a kibbutznik inside the capitalist sitting before me?"

"For sure. I dream of produce the way you dream of grandchildren."

"Ah, I understand. Very well. I shall come visit you at Gan Miriam, even though I suspect that instead of cucumbers, they will be cultivating computer chips by then." He laced his fingers behind his head and stretched. "All right. What do you have for me?"

I could see Mizrahi tense up as I confirmed specific plans for a missile program that would sow panic and destruction throughout Israel. I described what I had done to insinuate myself into the process.

"We have had corroborating reports of this initiative from all across the Middle East and Europe," he said. "You have done very well to position yourself to our advantage. We will begin making plans to disrupt these operations in ways that will not expose you."

"There is more," I said.

Mizrahi waited.

"The scientific director is a German rocket engineer." I told him about Professor Köhler. Mizrahi's jaw clenched and his countenance hardened as I repeated the professor's self-reported qualifications to lead the project, particularly his expertise in "mass production" using Jewish concentration camp prisoners. Mizrahi's dark eyes seemed to have caught fire by the time I was done.

"Yosef, the cabinet has determined that disruption of logistics and facilities will not be sufficient. At most, such actions would delay but not scuttle the project. In addition to sabotage, the prime minister has ordered us to eliminate some of the key players. I intend to submit your Nazi at the top of the list."

I sipped my espresso. "How is this elimination done?"

"We have experimented with different methods. Letter bombs are inaccurate. There is too much risk that a wife, secretary, or child will open the package. Besides, they often do not finish off the target, though it must be said that even if they fail to kill, such letters still function as a deterrent. I think the professor merits a coordinated hit by one of our teams on a future trip to Europe."

"I want to do it."

He laid down his cup. "What?"

"I want to pull the trigger that finishes him."

"No."

"Shmuel."

"Have you lost your mind?" he hissed. "You are an intelligence asset, not an assassin. We have people trained for these jobs. Such operations require coordination among up to a dozen agents. The target is precisely tracked, sometimes for weeks. His identity must be verified by two independent observers immediately before the hit. A separate team is dedicated to assuring that only he, and no innocent bystander, is harmed. Afterward, everyone needs to be extracted safely. It is incredibly complex."

"Shmuel, you did not see this man. You did not hear him call Jews apes and boast about exploiting them for slave labor. You know as well as I what his methods must have consisted of for 'motivating' workers. I have looked it up. Twenty thousand Jews were murdered at the Mittelbau-Dora camp while he presided there."

"The Angel of Death will come for this monster, Yosef, I assure you. The prime minister will approve the action. Professor Köhler has earned his elimination, for both his past acts and his future plans. But you are too valuable an asset for a job like this. In addition, you are untrained for the work."

"I have killed before."

"Yes, in battle. There is a world of difference between that and taking a man's life in cold blood, no matter how much he deserves it."

"I cannot stand by without avenging the lives he has taken. I cannot pass that responsibility to someone else."

"You will avenge the lives. The information you provide will be the instrument of Köhler's death. But you will pull no triggers, Yosef. That is final."

Chapter Twenty-Eight

Over the next few months, my anxiety increased. Professor Köhler had a mesmerizing effect on everyone around him, a phenomenon to which I was not immune. All did his bidding without question, from the Syrian defense minister to the lowliest worker. Köhler took personal control of nearly every aspect of the work, visiting frequently to inspect my warehouses and verify the security of my shipments. I had never met a person whose effect on me was so chilling. Whenever the ghostly blue eyes fixed on me, they seemed to pierce Charles Choucair's veneer and peer directly into the substratum of deceit that lay beneath.

I was summoned to periodic briefings in Damascus, where the professor gave astonishing progress reports while exhorting each member of the chain to pull harder and work faster. Before long, a prototype towered on a launchpad in a remote plain in north-central Syria. I attended the test-firing of this missile, which roared into the sky atop a pillar of fire on a cloudless day in March. Cheers erupted when a report crackled over the loudspeaker that the warhead had splashed into the Mediterranean Sea within seventy-five meters of a buoy bobbing off the Syrian coast 160 kilometers away.

After the demonstration, a reception was held in a hangar near the launch site. The minister of defense was present, as were dozens of other medal-festooned military brass. I was introduced as one of the "heroes" providing material support for the missile program. But Professor Köhler was the focus of everyone's attention. He stood ramrod straight in the center of the room, his interpreter, Herr Wilhelm, at his side. The professor acknowledged each accolade with a brisk bow of the head or click of the heels.

My acquaintance from the Ministry of Defense had invited me to "a small gathering of the original planning group." When the reception began to wind down, he led me to a meeting room. In its center was a round table set for an elaborate meal and surrounded by half a dozen chairs clothed in white linen.

My friend from the ministry, the two other businessmen I had originally met in Damascus, and I were making small talk when the Minister of Defense entered with Köhler and Herr Wilhelm. The minister motioned for us to take our seats while he remained standing. "The six of you," he began, his voice gravelly and the ribbons on his chest rising and falling with the cadence of his words, "had the vision, the means, and the resolve to develop this new weapon. On behalf of the Syrian people and Arabs everywhere, I congratulate and thank you! This rocket will be a critical instrument, perhaps the most important instrument, to correct the injustices of the last decade and a half in the Middle East!" He cast his gaze about the room and was acknowledged with polite clapping.

"I intend to ask the cabinet to fund two hundred units, with a target completion date one year from today," he continued. "Our friends in Egypt will order an even larger consignment." There were soft whistles and murmurs. "Clearly, the project must now move into a more active phase. We will no longer rely on this small group, concealing their work behind false-bottom shipping containers and makeshift walls. We will need to increase production facilities severalfold. Professor Köhler will continue to lead our effort."

Throughout this oration, Wilhelm translated the general's remarks into German in an undertone and Köhler nodded repeatedly, his features impassive.

The minister shifted his focus to the three entrepreneurs, the other two and me. "Your services will no longer be required, but believe me when I say that the government will never forget your patriotism. There will be future opportunities for each of you, and I predict they will be very profitable. You may take the evening to celebrate your achievement," he added, smiling. "As a parting gift to you, I have authorized Professor Köhler's request for a special . . . celebration." He nodded once more, and we stood when he turned and strode toward the exit.

As soon as the minister departed, a platoon of white-gloved servants entered wheeling trolleys covered in ivory tablecloths and laden with a sumptuous Syrian feast. Plates filled with tabbouleh, *yalanji*, hummus, *ful medames*, *fattoush* salad, and stacks of pita and *manakish* were followed by steaming platters of kebabs, kibbe, *maqluba*, and mounds of yellow rice. In addition, presumably to accommodate a preference for European dishes, there was a tray stacked high with chicken cordon bleu. A separate dessert table followed overflowing with *knafeh, barazek, mshabak,* and syrup-soaked baklava.

At the head of this procession were two tables comprising a full bar: French wines, Scotch whisky, American bourbon, Russian vodka, Syrian arak, and a wide assortment of other libations, along with boxes of Cuban cigars. I was no stranger to clandestine violations by Syrian elites of the Islamic prohibition of alcohol. Yet even I was taken aback by the extravagance of this display. The professor was the first to approach the bar, demanding "Whisky!" even before the trolley rolled to a stop.

The bartender extended a crystal glass containing a generous helping of liquor. "*Mehr!*" the professor ordered with a summoning motion of the fingers of his right hand, as though he were commanding a dog. The bartender obeyed by doubling the portion in the glass. Köhler held the glass high, examining it in the light of the ceiling fixture. Apparently deeming it satisfactory, he downed most of it in one swallow. "*Meine Herren!*" he declared, turning toward us. He raised his glass with his right hand and indicated the bar with his left. "*Bitte!*"

We each sidled up to the bartender and collected a drink. Professor Köhler raised his glass once more. He roared in German, and Herr Wilhelm provided the translation, delivering it, as always, while mimicking the professor's tone and inflections: "Congratulations, colleagues! You have done well!" He then led us to the table. Köhler finished off the rest of his whiskey and handed the glass to Wilhelm, indicating with a sideways jerk of his head toward the bar that he desired a refill.

The servants whirled and scurried about us, refilling empty plates and glasses. I never liked drinking, but over the years had developed a tolerance for alcohol. I had also cultivated the skill of pretending to drink more than I did and feigning drunkenness when it suited me.

The professor, continuing in his role as overseer, directed the feast, the conversation, the drinks, and the toasts. His cheeks acquired a rosy hue, and he smiled broadly, a divergence from the baring of clenched teeth with which he usually affected congeniality. He delivered his pronouncements with increasing gusto, pausing after every sentence or two to allow Herr Wilhelm to translate his words into Arabic. The interpreter's habitually stony facial expression increased in severity as the evening wore on.

"An amusing tale I wish to relate," the professor announced. "By 1930, Hitler was showing already signs of greatness, but polite society took him not seriously. He was disrespected as a vulgar upstart. A fancy dinner he attended one time, where everyone treated him as though he was the most repulsive being in the world. Finally, he asked the hostess, the heiress to an aristocratic family, in a loud voice that silenced all conversation: 'If ten million marks I gave you, would you go to bed with me?' 'For ten million marks,' she replied with a smirk, 'yes, I would consider going to bed even with you, Herr Hitler.' The Führer answered, 'What about one hundred marks?' *'One hundred marks!'* she exclaimed in shock. 'What kind of a woman do you think I am?' And Hitler answered, 'Madam, we have already established that you are a whore. At the moment, we are merely haggling over the price!'"

Köhler roared and slammed the table repeatedly with his open palm, causing the silverware to rattle and the water glasses to spill their contents. The rest of us joined in the amusement.

"A good one!" I cried, clapping Köhler on the shoulder.

"Speaking of whores," Köhler shouted, laughing, "the minister assures me that once we are done with the sweets, the real dessert will become available to us!"

Eager grins passed among the men at the table.

Köhler leaned toward me and whispered hoarsely, his breath sour with liquor. I looked beyond him toward the interpreter and raised my eyebrows.

"Professor Köhler wishes to inform you that he has only two weaknesses," Herr Wilhelm said, scowling. "Alcohol and women."

"Alkohol und Frauen!" the professor cried, thrusting his glass skyward and spilling half its contents. Suddenly, he stood.

"Let us go to those other chairs," he announced in a loud voice, waving his arm toward a sitting area with comfortable loungers arrayed around a coffee table. He lurched toward the largest of the armchairs, prompting a surge of activity among the servers, who hastened to transfer the coffee, sweets, and port wine. "Ah." Köhler sighed before sitting down. "I am afraid I have overindulged. Forgive me, please." He waited for Herr Wilhelm to complete the translation, then loosened the pants button at his waist, lifted his right leg, and broke wind noisily. He howled with laughter and dropped into his seat, beckoning the rest of us with both arms to gather around.

We took positions around the low table, the interpreter to Köhler's right and I to his left.

"Herr Professor," I said, "I must tell you that I have been amazed to see your work on the missile project. I would not have believed it possible to achieve so much in so short a time. It certainly could not have happened without your personal leadership."

"Yes, true." He chuckled. "I am forced to agree with you. A true leader"—he wagged his finger at me—"must not indulge in false modesty."

"What would you say are the principal components of your method?"

"My young friend," he exclaimed, "extraordinary training in project management I had during the war. When I was responsible for V-2 manufacturing, it was a mission tenfold more complicated than this one, and I did it with tenfold fewer resources! The British have a saying: 'Necessity is the mother of invention.' No choice had I but to become an expert in motivating people to achieve what they themselves believed was impossible."

"What do you mean?"

"*Ach!*" the professor cried. "You must understand. As I said when we first met, the good workers were all off at the front. It was necessary to use prisoners for labor. The Jews, they were interested only in avoiding work and stuffing their bellies. The importance of the project and the extremity of our need meant nothing to them. Other incentives they required, just as do beasts of the field. When your donkey refuses to budge, you do not attempt to reason with it."

"You took harsh measures?" the elder of the other two businessmen in the group asked.

Köhler gave a response in German. We waited while Herr Wilhelm glowered in his chair. When the professor realized his words were not being translated, a heated exchange between the two followed. Köhler shouted in German and repeatedly slammed his fist into the palm of his hand, while the interpreter responded in low tones through clenched teeth.

Finally, Wilhelm relented. "We had no other options," he translated. "If a laborer complained that he could not work on one bowl of soup and two hundred grams of bread a day, I had him shot in front of the others. If there was even the slightest defect in workmanship, I had the responsible prisoner shot."

The professor continued: "Sometimes I did the shooting myself. Although this was unpleasant for me, it was necessary to demonstrate who was in charge.

The others soon discovered they could do the work on rations after all. But over time, many of the prisoners became so diseased—I believe it was moral decay that led to their physical infirmity—they had to be eliminated. The cost of keeping them alive was greater than the value of their labor."

The professor suddenly looked in my direction, and the others' gazes followed. I realized that I had been gnashing my teeth. I exerted myself to loosen the tension in my jaw and shoulders, managing a look of concentration. But I was seized by the fear that in my fury I might be radiating heat. "A common problem," I said, trying to cool myself. "It is difficult to run a profitable business when one's costs exceed one's gains."

Köhler reached out across the table and, with a shaking hand, poured a full measure of port into his own glass and then mine. His words were slurred. "A personal appeal I made to Obersturmbannführer Eichmann to divert fresh prisoners from other facilities to our plant. Each new shipment of workers we received with great happiness, for it allowed us to recover from our production delays. The old laborers we made to perform one final act: to dig a trench outside the camp, which they did with appalling incompetence. It put a regrettable delay in the work schedule, but we had no choice—we had not the more efficient tools available in other camps."

"What was the purpose of the trench?" asked the younger of the two other entrepreneurs. I listened intently, knowing the answer, but wanting to hear the professor say it, as though by doing so, he might become his own prosecutor.

"When the trench was deep enough, the prisoners lined up along the edge, and we shot them so they fell backward into it. Most died immediately, and those who remained alive made a terrible wailing. You would not believe people could make such a noise, like animals in a slaughterhouse. But the new workers we brought in to cover everything up, and the clamor soon stopped. This task, a few hours after their arrival at the camp, helped the new Jews find the motivation to put in an honest day's work in the factory beginning the very next day—until they began to fail at their jobs, and we were forced to repeat the cycle."

There was a hush in the room.

"I was proud to report to my superiors that over the summer, we exceeded our production goals while staying under budget." The professor stretched his neck this way and that like a peacock. "I received a letter of commendation signed in the Führer's own hand. It is one of my most prized possessions."

I had not yet heard enough, though I feared I might lack the strength to hear more. Quelling the tremor in my voice, I asked, "Did any of the prisoners escape or attempt a rebellion?"

"Rebellion?" he replied, downing the port and pouring out a fresh serving. "It was out of the question. We had them under constant surveillance. They were so busy worrying about where the next blow would come from, they could hardly focus on anything else. I learned a valuable lesson in human psychology: This preoccupation with survival prevented them from organizing. It was an amazing thing to see: A Jew might betray his own mother for a scrap of bread. You would scarcely believe it, but I saw this with my own eyes, many times."

"What about escape?" asked the ministry official.

Köhler grinned, and I imagined I saw flames reflected in his pupils. "An ingenious method I discovered to discourage escapes: Every once in a while, I persuaded a prisoner that he was free to leave if he could run fast enough toward the fence and climb over it to the other side. You would think it impossible, but they allowed themselves to believe it every time—another demonstration of the mental frailty of the Jewish race. When he made a run for it, I would give the Jew a head start, and then take one of the soldiers' rifles and shoot at him. Alas, I am not a very good marksman. It usually took me several shots—but I always got him. One such demonstration, once or twice a week, convinced the others not to attempt an escape."

One last question. Just one last question, I whispered to myself. "How many Jews did you kill in this fashion?" I noticed Herr Wilhelm press the back of his hand against Köhler's leg, an apparent attempt to restrain him, but the professor brushed the hand away.

He fixed me with his pale eyes. "A strange query," he answered, scowling. "Why does it matter? This is not the point of the story. But to satisfy your curiosity: no more than one hundred or one hundred twenty."

The younger of the two other businessmen, who had begun sweating halfway through this account, took out a handkerchief and wiped his brow. He was ashen. "I am ashamed," he whispered. "I am ashamed to have worked with you on this project." He rose to his feet. "I wish to defeat the Zionists no less than any other patriot, but not by burying people alive or shooting them for sport or because they complain of being hungry when they are starved." He staggered toward the exit.

The Ministry of Defense official rose to detain him.

"Let him go!" barked Professor Köhler. "He demonstrates all too clearly that he lacks the will to defeat your enemy."

The younger businessman turned by the exit and supported himself on the doorjamb. "I wonder, by the way," he snapped, "whether you consider your new Semitic friend, the Arab, any more elevated than his cousin, the Jew." He left the room, slamming the door behind him.

We sat in silence.

"In case you are curious," the professor said with a sigh, "after the war, I was exonerated in absentia by an American war crimes tribunal." He looked around the room, his gaze lingering on each of us. "But come, my friends, why do we dwell on the past? This is a celebration! And a very pleasant future is before us. *Alkohol und Frauen!*" he roared, raising his glass once more, and several attractive young women glided into the room in harem pants, their midriffs bare and their breasts swelling over meager tops.

I was sick to my stomach, but allowed myself to be led away by two of the prostitutes. During the course of a life finding solutions when it seemed I had run out of options, never had I felt so trapped by circumstance. I found the strength to do what was required of me that night. But never before or since has the act of taking a woman to bed seemed such a defilement of my humanity.

Early the following morning, I dictated a letter from my office in Damascus to the manager of my warehouse in Zurich. The manager was my main conduit for information exchange with the Mossad and my only employee who was, in fact, an Israeli agent. The letter was disguised as routine business correspondence regarding shipments and inventory. It concealed an encoded message composed with a cipher whose sophistication was an order of magnitude more complex than the one I had used for the letter from Al-Hamdan to "Uncle Aboud." I requested an urgent meeting with my handlers two weeks hence in London, at which I would be prepared to share all the information in my possession and to make specific recommendations for targeted action. I instructed my secretary to book air travel and hotel accommodations for London and, in order to maintain my cover, arrange meetings with Cedar Trading's distributors and agents.

Two days later, my secretary knocked on the door to my office. "Professor Köhler is here," she whispered.

I cleared some papers off my desk and deposited them in one of my drawers. "Show him in, please."

Köhler strode into the office twenty seconds later, his gray suit pressed, his tie knotted tightly, his posture erect. He displayed no aftereffects of our "celebration." So overbearing was his presence that one hardly noticed the interpreter, who, as usual, stood at his elbow. It occurred to me that I had not seen Wilhelm take even a sip of alcohol at the gathering, and that he had been observing everything keenly all the while.

I rose from my chair, preparing to extend my hand. "Good morning, Herr Professor."

Köhler did not wait for me to round the desk. He lowered himself into one of my guest chairs and indicated that I should take the one opposite. "Herr Wilhelm informs me that I overindulged, perhaps, in celebrating our success. If I offended you, I offer my apology."

I nodded and smiled. "I was not offended. I was pleased to learn that you have a more . . . human . . . side."

"Thank you," he answered, casting a sidelong glance at his interpreter, seemingly gratified at having dispensed with his confession so easily. "What thought you of the missile demonstration?"

"Extremely impressive."

His eyes sparkled. "Yes. I observed your . . . appreciation of the launch, and of the accuracy of the landing also."

"As I say, it was extraordinary. An inspiring demonstration of your principles at work."

"Thank you. It has been challenging, I acknowledge, to overcome the inertia of your Arab brethren. To get them to imagine that, if only they would work in the correct way, they might accomplish things that seem to them initially impossible. But when we are fully committed to something, as am I to this initiative, we let nothing stand in our way. All obstacles are mere challenges to overcome, like a game or puzzle, you see."

As always in his presence, something recoiled within me at the heat and chill of his gaze.

"Is everything well with you?" he inquired.

"Oh, yes. It is only that at the moment I am dealing with several problems with my suppliers, as well as the aftereffects of last year's labor unrest in India. But I shall endeavor to follow your example and overcome."

"Good. I wish you to accompany me."

"Where are you going?"

"To the Turkish bathhouse."

"The *hammam*? When?"

"Now."

"I am sorry, Herr Professor, but at the moment I am otherwise occupied. I am expecting a call from Bombay this morning."

"That is interesting. Your secretary informed me that you have nothing on your schedule until the afternoon."

"Ah . . . er . . . well, she must be unaware that we had to reschedule this conversation because of the interruption of a prior call. International telephone service is even worse than local services here in Syria, as no doubt you are aware."

"Ah, yes, the Syrian telephone service. A notorious example, among many, of the backwardness of this society. Do you know what is holding the Levant back from joining advanced civilizations?" He did not await a response once Wilhelm concluded his translation. "A mule-like adherence to the past, and failure to embrace the latest technology."

"I hope, Professor, that the benefits of your work here extend beyond the missile program. It will help transform us into a modern nation."

We sat a while in silence. He seemed to be waiting for something. Finally, he cleared his throat. "I have instructed your secretary to clear your schedule for a few hours. You will not resolve the aftereffects of last year's labor crisis with a telephone call this morning."

"Well . . ." I sighed. "Perhaps you are right." I gathered my things, and we exited the building. A Mercedes stood idling on the street. Herr Wilhelm opened the right rear passenger door, and the professor got in. I rounded the car and slid into the left passenger seat while Wilhelm slipped behind the wheel. We drove through sparse traffic.

"I am struck by how different you are from your colleagues, Charles," said the professor, staring at the road ahead. Wilhelm translated as he drove.

"Different? What do you mean?"

"You do not seem to be cut from the same cloth as they. Lazy are your colleagues, and they require external inducements to exert themselves. You are motivated apparently on your own. The others always are striving to prove their superiority. More intelligent and knowledgeable are you than any of them, yet you seem eager to disguise that fact. They are greedy and corrupt. You are wealthy but seem not to care for money. You treat your employees with a respect I am not certain they have earned—and which I am certain is not healthy for them. Your colleagues only grant their workers what is necessary in order to continue exploiting them. You are the only one among them with whom a man of the world can imagine doing business beyond this narrow project in the Middle East."

"I do not have the same background as my colleagues. I was raised in Paris."

Professor Köhler waited for Herr Wilhelm to complete the translation, but interrupted when I opened my mouth to continue my response. "Yes, yes" he interjected. "I am familiar with your story. Your friend from the Ministry of Defense, who first introduced us, related it to me. It is remarkable. One can hardly believe it is not fiction."

"I have heard the English say that truth is stranger than fiction."

"Indeed. And this moderation of yours, and freedom from vice, were acquired in the Parisian gutter, to which you were driven by a German bomb, I am told?"

"I am not free from vice, but neither have I forgotten where I came from."

"Really? From where did you come?"

I stuttered. "Er . . . from Paris . . . as you just acknowledged. And before that, from Lebanon."

"A fascinating history. One might think you emerged directly out of the pages of the *One Thousand and One Nights*. Or that you are a modern Count of Monte Cristo. You are familiar with Monte Cristo?"

"No, Herr Professor. Who is he?" I immediately regretted not acknowledging that I was aware of Alexandre Dumas's novel, a major influence on me ever since I had read it for the first time as a boy in the convent's library. Köhler's interrogation had shaken me. I harbored the irrational fear that a confession of having read the book was the thread that, if tugged, might unravel the fabric of my cover story.

"Can this be? Not familiar with *The Count of Monte Cristo*? It is, perhaps, the greatest of all French books!"

"My education was, er, patchy. I was never in school after the age of nine."

"And yet, obvious it is that since that time you have educated yourself in nearly every intellectual domain. How could there remain such a void in your knowledge? I shall inform you of the plot, yes?"

I nodded.

"The book tells the story of an honest and hardworking sailorman named Edmond Dantès. A group of his acquaintances falsely accuses Dantès of treason, out of jealousy for his good name and to steal from him the woman he loves, a beautiful girl named Mercédès Mondego. After many years in prison, Dantès escapes and acquires a vast fortune. And then, like you, the Count of Monte Cristo seems to materialize out of thin air as a very wealthy man." He suddenly shook his head. "*Ach*, but there the analogy ends, for Monte Cristo took terrible revenge against all those who wronged him, whereas you are a willing partner in our joint project."

Professor Köhler turned to impale me with his eyes at the very moment Wilhelm pulled up in front of the entrance to the hammam. "Ah!" he cried. "Here we are." He addressed the translator in German. I understood only the appellation *Herr Wilhelm* and my name: *Monsieur Choucair*.

I was not fond of the hammam, but I visited it frequently with colleagues and guests, an obligation of my station. It was evident that the professor was a regular patron, for we were both greeted by name with the customary obsequiousness and ushered toward the changing room. We stood at the bench before a bank of cedar cabinets. The professor hung his jacket on a hook and loosened his tie.

I turned my back to Köhler, removed my pants and underwear, and hung them in my locker. I reached for the thick towel that hung on the door and was about to wrap it around my waist, as is the custom in Turkish bathhouses, when the professor laid a hand on my upper arm. He turned me round and looked down at my genitals. The interpreter was now at his side, fully clothed.

"Ah. You are circumcised, I see. That is strange, is it not?"

"No."

"You are a Christian?"

"Yes."

"I am also a Christian." The professor stepped out of his underwear, exhibiting his penis, which was unusually large. Its hooded head awakened within me a primitive apprehension, as though it were a cobra.

I hoped Köhler would interpret my consternation as embarrassment. Arab men are unaccustomed to displaying their private parts, even in the locker room. I swallowed. "It is common for Christians in Arab lands to circumcise their boys."

"Ah. I have learned from you something new. I have not known this before. I see also that scars you have on your back and abdomen."

"Yes, I was injured in the bombing to which you referred earlier."

He reached out a forefinger and ran it along my wound. "A miracle that you survived such an injury," he murmured. He clicked his tongue on the roof of his mouth. "Ah, well. Everything is now explained." Turning to his interpreter, he added some words in German.

"Professor Köhler requests me to return to the locker room in ninety minutes," Wilhelm informed me.

We spent an hour and a half cycling through the various stations of the hammam. Köhler did not speak, grunting as his body was kneaded by the masseuse, wincing and sighing with pleasure as he was beaten with palm fronds. The visit culminated in an exfoliation treatment in the steam room. Finally, Köhler rose from his couch and headed toward the locker room, a signal that our visit was at an end. I followed.

Later, in the Mercedes, Professor Köhler spoke up again: "You travel frequently to Europe, yes?"

"Yes."

"Now that the missile program has ended for you, an opportunity you have to move on to other projects. I wish to invite you to a meeting with some of my . . . colleagues . . . in Geneva the week after next. We will be discussing plans for the future, including expansion of the missile project beyond the borders of the Middle East. Vast are the opportunities in Africa, South America, and East Asia. We are having a . . . convention, you might say, on the fifth and sixth of April at the Hôtel Métropole. I believe our discussions would be of interest to you. And profitable."

This was a clear invitation to infiltrate a network of former Nazi officers, an incomparable opportunity. Nonetheless, I was happy to have an excuse to decline. I had already posted the letter requesting the meeting with the Mossad in London at the same time. But even more than that, I feared Köhler had broken my cover. Charles Choucair's mask had proven impregnable for over a decade, yet every instinct within me screamed that my presence at the "convention" would spring a trap.

"Thank you for the invitation, Professor Köhler, but I must decline. I have meetings in London that week to deal with various issues in my operations which, if not attended to, may lead to serious disruptions. My plans absolutely cannot be changed at this late date."

Köhler seemed disappointed. "Ah. I now recall that your secretary mentioned this trip to me. To deal with the aftereffects of the Indian unrest, I presume, yes?"

I nodded.

"A shame. I am surprised you decline such an opportunity. You are certain you do not wish to join us?"

"Yes, unfortunately. Perhaps another time?"

"So. Another time. If there *is* another time. You may not have a second chance."

"Thank you, Herr Professor."

Chapter Twenty-Nine

Ten days later, at Heathrow, I disembarked a BOAC flight from Beirut. A middle-aged, uniformed driver awaited me bearing a sign labeled "Choucair."

"Monsieur Choucair?" he inquired as I approached him.

"Yes."

"Allow me, sir," he said, extending his arm to relieve me of my suitcase. He led me toward a limousine parked in the arrivals lane and opened the left rear passenger door. I slid in next to a man seated on the right side, behind the driver's seat. His black hair was cut short, and he sported a trim beard, as did I. His athletic frame was well fitted in a dark suit, white shirt, and gray-striped tie, similar to my own. The driver rounded the car and started the engine. He shifted into gear and pulled into traffic heading toward the M4.

"Shalom, Reggie," I said to the driver once we were underway. "Good to see you again." Reggie was a *sayan*, one of thousands of Jews scattered across the globe, almost all of them loyal citizens of their countries of residence, who volunteered services to the Mossad.

"Shalom, Samson," the driver answered, using my code name. "Always a pleasure."

"How's the family?"

"My eldest brought home a *sheigetz* the other day. Said she wanted us to meet him. 'Really?' says I. 'By all means,' says I, 'let the meetin' commence!' Top item on the agenda was yours truly grabbin' 'im by the back of the collar and belt. The second and final item was givin' 'im the heave-ho out the front door." Reggie chuckled. "So everything is fine, thank you kindly for askin.'"

"Ouch. I am glad I have simpler problems to deal with. And you, Michael? How are you?" I turned toward the man sharing the passenger compartment with me.

Michael responded with his usual briskness. "Shalom, Samson. I am fine. We don't have much time for conversation. The hotel is not far away in this light traffic."

Michael was a retired Mossad agent who worked as a jeweler in London. I had used him off the books for odd jobs over the years.

"Thank you, as always, for keeping us on track," I answered, smiling. "Any questions about the plan?"

"I don't think so," Michael replied. "The exchange should be easy. Done it a dozen times. Then I spend a couple of days in your hotel room making phone calls, ordering room service, and declining the assistance of the chambermaid. When you return, I slip out the rear service door, nice and quiet."

"Good. And you, Reggie?"

"After droppin' Michael off at the Langham, we drive directly to the dock at Portsmouth. A first-class round-trip ticket across the channel has been booked for Mousa Ilbawi." He extended his left arm to the front passenger seat and, keeping his right hand on the steering wheel, passed an envelope and haversack to the rear. "From Cherbourg, the overnight train is booked to Geneva, also first class. Flexible returns, laddie, for both the train and the ship."

"Well done. Wait for me at the dock on the return voyage in two days."

"What do I do if you don't show?"

"First, I will be there. And second, if I am not, go home and tell no one you saw me. Same for you, Michael. If I am not back in the hotel by the afternoon of the second day, leave this in an envelope on the nightstand and abscond." I reached into my breast pocket and handed him a signed check made out to the Langham for five hundred pounds on Charles Choucair's London account. "And don't volunteer information to anyone, unless our friends from the Institute come to ask in person. In that event, you may tell them everything you know."

"And what is that?" Michael asked.

"What is what?"

"What is it that I know?"

I grinned. "Very little. For the time being, at least, let's keep it that way."

"So, you won't be telling us what all this is about, Samson?"

"I will not. It is better for everyone."

We pulled into the circular drive at the Langham. A valet ran up to the car, and Reggie got out quickly to direct him to the trunk. He passed the valet a five-pound note and an instruction to deliver the suitcase directly to my room. Reggie then opened the rear door, and I exited the limousine, leaving Michael in the shadows. Reggie shut the door behind me and, saluting me with a nod, made his way back to the driver's seat.

I passed into the hotel through the revolving door. A few minutes later, the desk clerk bestowed upon me a room key and a wish for "a very pleasant stay."

I placed the key in my pocket. "May I have two keys, please?"

"Very good, sir." The clerk turned to extract a second key from the wood-paneled cabinet behind him and placed it on the countertop.

I picked up the key, strode toward the elevators, and without slowing down, delivered it into the palm of Michael's lowered hand just as he rounded the turn from the other direction. Michael proceeded toward the elevator bank. I continued in the direction from which he had come toward the rear exit, where I found Reggie in the limousine, its engine idling.

"Let's go," I said, sliding into the back.

Two and a half hours later, we arrived at the passenger terminal at Portsmouth. I entered one of the washroom stalls in the first-class lounge. I shaved off my trim dark beard, the first step in transforming myself into Mousa Ilbawi. Mr. Ilbawi was one of a small number of alter egos furnished to me by the forgers at the Mossad. Usual protocol required preapproval from HQ before a false identity could be used, except in extreme emergency. I had dispensed with this requirement, knowing that my handlers would chastise me for it. But that would come later.

Mousa Ilbawi's documents identified him as a forty-five-year-old tradesman with glasses, curly salt-and-pepper hair, and a full, gray beard. The haversack Reggie had given me contained the elements of this disguise. I donned a light business suit with a modern Moroccan cut. I packed Charles Choucair's folded clothes in the haversack.

Using a key Reggie had provided for coin locker #24F, I exchanged the haversack for a plus-size leather satchel, pocketed the locker key, and boarded the ship for Cherbourg.

The following morning, after a semi-restful night in the pajamas provided by the first-class sleeping service of the Société nationale des chemins de fer français (the French railway service), I arrived at the Gare de Genève. Mousa

Ilbawi's passport passed a quick inspection by the immigration officer. From there, I entered a bathroom stall and, using supplies Reggie had prepacked in the leather satchel, exited with yet a new disguise: a blond pompadour and moustache, long sideburns, and dark glasses. I wore the slim slacks, white shirt, dark tie, and trim overcoat that were in vogue among young professionals in Geneva's financial district. Before exiting the restroom, I examined myself in the mirror: almost no trace of Charles Choucair. I stored Mousa Ilbawi's disguise, neatly folded in a plastic bag, in the satchel.

Leaving the station, I took a leisurely stroll to the Musée Ariana to view its collection of ceramic and glass, which I had never before seen. I ate a light lunch of Salade Niçoise at a sidewalk bistro, paying no heed to the waiter's raised eyebrows at my refusal of a suitable wine. From the museum, I walked to La Cathédrale Saint-Pierre, the waters of Lake Geneva shimmering on my left, and entered one of my favorite sites, the Chapel of the Maccabees. Despite its name, the chapel had little to do with those ancient heroes of mine, the band of warriors who, against all odds, defeated the Greeks, liberated the temple in Jerusalem, and established a kingly dynasty in Judea.

The afternoon sun streamed through the stained-glass windows of the chapel, splattering color onto the high-arched eastern wall. After about half an hour sitting in a pew in the back, I rose for the brief walk to the lobby of the Hôtel Métropole, where I sat reading *Le Monde* in view of the elevators while nursing a glass of sparkling water without ice.

Thirty minutes later, I spotted him.

Professor Köhler emerged from a lift with half a dozen middle-aged and older men dressed in business suits, their loud German accents slicing through the hush that had prevailed prior to their appearance. I recognized none of them other than Köhler, but little imagination was required to label them all as Nazis. The words *Herr Professor* wafted repeatedly in my direction, jarring me each time. The group sauntered toward the front of the lobby. As they passed, I extracted a pack of cigarettes from my breast pocket and snapped some photos using a camera hidden within, courtesy of the "toy department" of the Mossad.

The group chatted by the hotel's entrance, then exited one by one, taking leave of the professor with a click of the heels or sharp bow of the head.

Köhler waited a while and left through the revolving door. I laid some Swiss francs on the table and rose. I had been taught surveillance techniques by one of the Mossad's finest agents, of whom his admirers at HQ said that he could measure the length of your penis with a ruler at the urinal without your taking notice. The professor strode toward the lake with the confidence of a man completely in his element. Few pedestrians were out, and I followed him at a distance of about a hundred meters. He entered the Jardin Anglais and slowed his pace, strolling along the paths and stopping from time to time to admire the flower displays by the rays of the setting sun. The Jet d'Eau, Geneva's famous lake fountain, rocketed skyward to his right. He bore west toward the newly renamed Quai du Général-Guisan, a street bordering the lake path on its north side and lined with elegant buildings on its south. After a short walk, he stopped outside the entrance to a nondescript three-story structure sandwiched between two taller and newer buildings, then pressed a button with his index finger. He leaned forward, mouthed a few words, opened the door, and stepped inside.

I strolled by the building without altering my pace. There was no signage and only one button atop an intercom grill adjacent to the door.

I figured I had about three hours.

Passing the building, I rounded the corner, slipped into a bookstore, and bought a thin volume of poetry by one of my favorite authors, Victor Hugo. Upon exiting, I purchased a sandwich at a local shop and walked to the lakefront, where I sat on a bench with a view of the doorway to the building Köhler had entered. I opened the book and began to leaf through the pages while keeping watch. I had trouble focusing on the poems, reading and rereading the same lines:

I will walk, eyes fixed on my thoughts,
Seeing nothing around me, hearing no sound,
Alone, unknown, back hunched, hands crossed,
Sorrowed, and the day for me will be as the night.

The streetlights buzzed and flashed on. I stowed the book in my satchel, ate the sandwich, and waited. About two hours later, Köhler emerged from the building, adjusted his tie, and reached under the sleeves of his suit jacket to extend his cuffs. I glanced at my watch: 10:15 p.m. He turned to his right, in the direction of the Hôtel Métropole.

I rose from my bench, walking briskly on a diagonal route. Our paths converged at the street corner.

"Hello, Professor." I spoke in English, knowing that he was fluent in that language.

He stopped, and stared. "Who are you?"

"You do not recognize me?"

He looked me up and down. "Charles Choucair."

"I see you do not travel with your interpreter."

"In Switzerland, one does not require an interpreter, as I am conversant in German, French, and English."

"Really?" I answered in English. "Why did you not say earlier that you speak French? We might have communicated directly without your translator."

"Yes, so we might have. But it is perhaps ironical that you never mentioned you understand more than the most basic English. It appears that neither you nor I have been completely frank with each other. At any rate, Herr Wilhelm fills my needs with more than his linguistic skills; there is also the Walther he carries in a holster near his heart. That weapon, as you might say, speaks an international language."

I clicked my tongue. "Interpreter, driver, bodyguard. I see what you mean. The man provides many useful services. I regret that I cannot converse with you in your native tongue, but I give you the choice to continue our conversation in English or French, as per your preference."

"It matters not to me," he continued in English. "And of course, I do not apologize for not knowing Hebrew."

"Hebrew? Why Hebrew?"

"Come, come, let us drop our pretenses. I have long suspected you of something, but now, finally, you have made clear what you are. There is, perhaps, a remaining question of *who* you are. What is your real name?"

"Charles Choucair."

"Charles Choucair? The orphaned Lebanese refugee, the miracle survivor of a German bombing, the gutter rat who transformed himself into an international man of business? I think not."

Throughout this exchange, my left hand was in the pocket of my overcoat. "I am pointing a pistol at your chest, Professor. Kindly turn around and walk toward the lake."

"You are left-handed? I have made a close study of you, yet have not before observed this."

"I read that, as a boy, before deciding to dedicate your life to exterminating Jews, you considered a career as a Lutheran pastor. Are you familiar with the biblical judge Ehud, son of Gera?"

"I am. A left-handed assassin. You model yourself after him?"

"No. I can kill you equally well with either hand. Please turn around and walk toward the lake."

"What will you do if I refuse? What if I cry for help?"

"In either of those instances, I shall shoot you where you stand right now. I almost prefer it that way. Honestly."

"You are not concerned about being identified by witnesses?"

"I am not. There are few of those at this hour. I am wearing a disguise. I am a fast runner. And my escape route is already plotted out. Now, if you please, turn around and start walking."

"Hmph," the professor said. "You speak as though you are reciting lines from an American gangster film. Your dialogue is not sufficient to hide your weakness, however."

"Move."

Köhler rotated on his heels and began the shallow descent toward the lakefront.

"How was your visit to the whorehouse?" I inquired as we walked.

"Very gratifying," he answered without turning around. "I had two girls there. Unless I am mistaken, one of them was your tribeswoman. I took her from the rear, and admit to rather enjoying her screams."

My hand tightened on the Beretta in my pocket. We proceeded the rest of the way in silence.

When he reached the paved walkway by the water, I instructed him to turn right. "Stop," I ordered at a point of relative darkness between two streetlamps. "Turn around." I pulled out my handgun, holding it close to my body and aiming it at his chest.

"Why did you invite me to this meeting of yours here in Geneva?"

Köhler smirked. "To exhibit you in front of my colleagues, to verify my suspicions, and then to have you—what is the word you used?—exterminated." His tone was calm and, as usual, condescending. "I congratulate you. I thought my invitation would prove irresistible, but you were one step ahead of me. That is a rare thing, I assure you. After I determined that your trip to London was previously planned, and after verifying that you arrived at Heathrow and the Langham as scheduled, I decided to leave it for another time."

"And now," I said, "you have lost your opportunity."

Köhler sucked his teeth. "One never runs out of opportunities if one's mind is agile enough."

"I agree with you, which is why I have left myself many options."

"You lack the will to kill me. I see it in your eyes. I observe it in the tremor of your hand."

Köhler's observation was correct. The Beretta was quavering in my grasp. I clenched my left arm closer to my body.

"What is your name?" he demanded.

I gave no answer.

"What . . . is . . . your . . . name?" He took a step toward me. I jerked my hand in silent threat. "Tell me your name."

"I hardly know it myself anymore," I murmured. "Yusouf. And *al Yahudi*. And *al Arabi*. And Khalil and Ismail and the Canaanite and Samson and Mousa and Charles."

"Your real name!"

"Joseph." I used the French pronunciation of the word, the one I had grown up with in my father's house. The name sounded alien to my own ears. It was mine, yet somehow not of me.

"Joseph?" he sneered. "How appropriate. Joseph, the impostor. The manipulator. The man who led his people into slavery in Egypt—the first to realize the natural state of the Jew."

"Yes. And Joseph, the interpreter of dreams. Do you remember Pharaoh's dream of the seven fat and seven lean cows? Your years of plenty are behind you, Professor Köhler."

"Give me the gun."

"I will give you only a bullet from the gun."

He bared his teeth, that grimace he employed as a smile. His eyes were a lacerating blue. "More dialogue from an American film? You lack the will to pull the trigger. See how your hand trembles! And how your face betrays you! I have seen that expression a thousand times before in your brethren: hatred, yes, but also fear and paralysis. I have witnessed one German soldier quell five hundreds of your people, who might have risen in revolt but instead lined up like sheep to be slaughtered."

Rage coursed through me, overwhelming, nearly blinding. Yet I struggled to pull the trigger. In planning this operation without the approval of my superiors, I had suppressed my indecision with certainty regarding the depravity of Köhler's past and future crimes. But now, my resolve faded into a feeble fear: that killing him in cold blood would induce a chain reaction, a mirroring blow that would slay something vital within me. A shimmering appeared in the dark lake waters behind Köhler and spread outward, unfocusing my vision. I felt faint and staggered to my left. Köhler saw an opportunity and lurched forward. With effort, I righted myself and jerked the pistol, still clenched to my side, arresting him.

"You are looking at a different kind of Jew, Professor," I panted. "I have come to avenge those human beings you slaughtered like sheep. I am so relieved to know that the last thing you see in this sadistic life of yours will be the Jew who gives you your reward."

"Do not speak to me of vengeance and reward!" Köhler thundered. "Would you take the life of an unarmed man without trial, and tell yourself you are a virtuous murderer? You would become as abhorrent to yourself as I am to you."

I shook my head to clear the fog. "How ironic," I murmured. "A mass murderer teaching morality to an assassin."

"You are no assassin."

Those words, precisely the ones Mizrahi had used, struck me like a blow. Köhler deserved to die, but what right had I to be his executioner? His pronouncement echoed in my head, adding to my disorientation. Time seemed to stand still. Was I an assassin? A catalogue of my deeds flashed before me. As a boy of eight, I had viciously broken the hand of a classmate and stabbed him with a fork. I had assisted in a castration. I had impregnated a woman I loved and stood by as she was humiliated and ostracized. I had torched the abbess's office. I had slain. I had deceived. I had spent my life cheating fate. I had erected walls between myself and those who might have loved me. And through it all, I had claimed righteousness. Would I now add murder to the ledger?

I focused on Köhler's face and breathed in deep. His eyes bored into mine. He extended his right arm, palm up. "Give me the gun, Joseph," he said, his voice almost tender, like a priest granting absolution. "You are no assassin."

"You are incorrect, Professor," I said, and shot him. The silencer emitted a muffled exhalation, and the bullet struck him in the left shoulder, my aim errant. He cried out and instinctively grasped his shoulder with his right hand. But I was already upon him and swung the Beretta with all my strength to the side of his face. His right cheekbone ruptured under the blow with a loud crack. He staggered to his left, and I grabbed his tie with my right fist, placed the barrel of the gun to his temple, and pulled the trigger a second time. His head exploded, spraying my face with gray matter, bone, and blood, and I dropped him onto the pavement.

I fell to my knees and vomited everything I had eaten and drunk since noon. A moment later I rose, still gripping the pistol in my left hand. I grasped the barrel with my shirttail, wiped the handle down, and flung the gun into the water. The weapon was untraceable, its serial number having been filed away, but searching for it would delay Swiss investigators at least for a while. I removed Köhler's wallet from his breast pocket and deposited it in the satchel. My head swimming, I ran up the incline and into the city, shouts coming from the lakefront and the wail of a siren approaching from the south.

I raced toward a back street near the Place du Molard, where I removed a key from under a garbage can. Slowing my pace after verifying that I was not being followed, I walked down the alley and unlocked the back entrance of a four-story building. An apartment on the third floor belonged to a *sayan* who Michael, the ex-Mossad agent from London, had employed in prior operations.

I let myself in and bolted the door behind me. Flicking the light switch, I strode to the washroom, pulled off my wig, fake moustache, and sideburns, and tossed them into the bathtub. I leaned over the sink and stared into the face in the mirror. The right side was splattered with blood and brain. The left eye was twitching, and the lips quivered. I ripped off the remainder of my clothes and threw them into the pile in the tub, panting. I ran cold water in the sink and splashed it on my face repeatedly, each time raising my head to examine the effect in the mirror.

"What is your name?" I muttered to the reflection.

The words of Isaiah came to me: "*For thy hands are defiled with blood, and thy fingers with iniquity; thy lips have spoken falsehoods, thy tongue murmureth perversity.*"

Yes, but what is your name?

"He told me himself that he was preparing to murder me. I acted in self-defense."

No. You acted out of vengeance.

"All right, then. Out of vengeance. For the slaughter of tens of thousands of innocent people. And because he was planning to kill thousands more."

I ran my hand through my hair. I needed to move without delay, yet I felt a greater urgency: to wash the stain of murder off me. I removed Mousa Ilbawi's disguise from the plastic bag in my satchel and laid it on the closed toilet seat. In its place, I stuffed the clothes and wig from the bathtub. I ran the water and took a cold shower, drying myself with a towel that hung on a rack. Then I transformed myself back into Mousa Ilbawi—the curly salt-and-pepper wig, the gray beard, the spectacles, and the clothes.

One final inspection in the mirror. It was Mousa Ilbawi, but something in him had changed. He flickered like a phantom. "My name is Yosef," I murmured.

I exited the building the way I had come, locking the back door. I tossed the bag with the blond disguise into a large trash bin behind a restaurant and the apartment key into one of the garbage cans that lined the alley. Stepping out onto the Rue du Marché, I searched in both directions for a cab to take me back to the Gare de Genève.

"*Monsieur!*" came a cry from across the street, but it did not penetrate my consciousness until the second, more urgent, call. It was a gendarme. He trotted over the road, and I froze. "Have you seen a young man, long blond hair, maybe with a moustache, wearing a dark or gray overcoat?"

"No," I answered. "Why?"

"If you see that person, call the cantonal police without delay!" he commanded, and sped down the street.

Chest heaving, I hailed a taxi to the Gare de Genève. A short time later, Mousa Ilbawi tossed Professor Köhler's wallet into a garbage can and boarded the overnight train to Cherbourg, and from there returned to Portsmouth on the channel transport. I retrieved the haversack from locker #24F and entered the washroom, emerging once again as Charles Choucair, his trim beard now replaced with a one-day growth of stubble. I staggered with my last vestige of strength toward the welcoming smile of Reggie, who, supporting me by the arm, led me to his car.

Chapter Thirty

It was a night of fitful dreams. I was trapped in a maze, its walls seeping blood. Desperate to escape, I found myself instead returning over and over to the point of origin, an inexorable loop of revulsion and fear.

I got out of bed before first light and staggered to the bathroom. The eyes that examined me in the mirror were swollen, dull, exhausted, bloodshot. I brushed my teeth and took a long shower. Whether the lingering smell of sulfur and blood was real or imagined, I could not tell. I splashed myself with Charles Choucair's French cologne and dressed in a suit and tie, his dress code for doing business in Europe.

Donning tinted glasses, I rode the lift to the lobby of the Langham, where I ordered a coffee and scone and a copy of *Le Monde*. A short item on page six reported the murder in Geneva, Switzerland, of the respected German rocket scientist Professor Erich Werner Köhler. The article reported that the professor, an international consultant on energy policy, was visiting Geneva for business. The motive for the killing was unclear, perhaps robbery, as Professor Köhler's wallet was missing. The police conjectured there had been a fight; in addition to two bullet wounds, the professor had suffered a facial fracture.

I downed the last sips of coffee and saluted the Mossad watcher I had spotted in the northeast corner of the lobby with a tip of my empty cup. He threw up his hands, shook his head, and smiled at the ease with which I had blown his cover. He was there not to keep tabs on me but to assure I was not being followed by someone else.

I exited the front door of the hotel lobby and nodded at a second watcher, who stood smoking by a newsstand. He ignored me, and as I turned west on Portland Place, threw his cigarette on the pavement and squashed it with his toe. I did not look back, but I could feel him following me at a distance of about thirty meters.

It was a ten-minute walk to the four-story brick building on Harley Street where my London office was situated among other small- and medium-size enterprises. I took the stairs to the third floor and entered through a ground-glass doorway emblazoned with the image of a cedar tree and the words *Cedars Trading International, Beirut*. My secretary, Fatima, greeted me with a pretty smile.

"Can I get you some coffee?" she chirruped in her British-accented English.

"Yes, please," I answered in Arabic. "What a refreshing sight to behold you, Fatima." She blushed. I knew she nursed a chaste infatuation with me. "How are your parents?" Fatima was the daughter of a Lebanese expatriate who worked as a waiter in the House of Commons.

"Very well, thanks," she answered, again in English.

"Arabic," I scolded. "I promised your father to not permit you to forget your native tongue."

Fatima scowled. "My native tongue is English."

I screwed up my face in confusion. "What?" I persisted in Arabic. "I don't understand you."

She glared at me.

"Oh, Fatima, I can hear your mother now: 'Stop pouting, or your beautiful face will get stuck in that horrible expression!'"

"*Ya, Allah!*" she exclaimed. "*El 'erd fi ein ommoh ghazal!* (A monkey in his mother's eye is a gazelle!)"

"Ha!" I laughed. "Very good! Well articulated!"

It was indeed rejuvenating to see Fatima's face, so youthful and eager. It quelled, if only for the moment, the turmoil I was struggling to subdue beneath my exterior.

I stepped into my office and sat behind my desk. Fatima brought me black coffee and sesame biscuits. For the next few hours, I engaged in the welcome distraction of conducting the legitimate business of the company. I telephoned suppliers and met with my local distributor, who occupied a second office in the flat.

At noon, I opened the door to the inner office and stepped out. "I have a lunch engagement," I informed Fatima. "You may close the office for the hour while you take a break. I expect to be back in the afternoon."

Her smile accompanied me out the door.

I set out on Harley Street, navigating a circuitous route toward the Mossad safe house in central London. One of the two surveillance men from the Langham shadowed me. Arriving at the destination, I stepped up to the intercom. The buzzer sounded before I could press the switch. I pulled open the door and stepped inside, climbing the stairs to the second floor and pausing before an unlabeled wooden door at the end of the hallway. The sound of a sliding plate was accompanied by the momentary brightening and then darkening of the peephole.

The door was opened wide by Shmuel Mizrahi.

I suppressed a cry of pleasure at seeing my old friend and recruiter, and waited until the door shut behind me before enveloping him in a hug. "What are you doing here?"

"Stop squeezing me!" He grunted. "I think you cracked one of my ribs!"

I relented and took a step back to survey him. He had gained some weight. "You look good!" I exclaimed. "Uncommonly handsome! Is this the effect of retirement?"

"Perhaps it is, or more precisely, it was, until they called me here. I am missing my granddaughter's first birthday for this meeting."

"I am sorry to have caused you trouble, Shmuel. Please buy Shoshana a nice toy and tell her it is from me, a secret uncle." I could not refrain from throwing my arms about him again and squeezing.

"All right, all right." He chuckled. "We are not alone."

I released Shmuel and surveyed the other people in the room. The London station chief was there, as were the Mossad chief of operations and Moshe Har-Nof, who had taken Mizrahi's position as my handler. And emerging behind them was the Director himself. "He just flew in from Tel Aviv," Mizrahi whispered in my ear. The director of the Mossad was a stocky, balding man whose face radiated energy and intelligence. His exploits were legendary. Most famously, he had led the team that apprehended Adolf Eichmann, the architect of the Final Solution, the Nazi program to exterminate the Jews, and smuggled him from Argentina to stand trial in Israel.

"Shalom, Samson," the Director said in his Russian-accented Hebrew—he had immigrated to Israel at the age of seventeen. "I am pleased to finally meet you." He stretched out his hand, and I shook it. It was surprisingly warm and soft, but it had heft, like a sledgehammer wrapped in cotton balls.

The Director summoned me to sit at the head of the table in the flat's dining room, on which pitchers of water and juice had been stationed with six cups and several ashtrays. All four men other than Mizrahi and me lit up cigarettes, and the room quickly filled with smoke.

The Director opened the proceedings, his tone stern: "When you arranged this meeting, Samson, we understood the topic was the Egyptian and Syrian missile programs."

"That is the topic, Director."

"We also assumed we would be discussing what to do about Professor Erich Werner Köhler, whose elimination, in case you are curious, has been approved by the prime minister."

I nodded.

"We did not anticipate that instead of reviewing options, we would be discussing the assassination of Köhler as a completed task."

I kept my face expressionless.

The Director eyed me. He was known to like men of few words. "To permit us to move forward in this discussion while avoiding unnecessary detours, let me say that we became aware Mousa Ilbawi was on the move within eight hours of his passport being stamped at Cherbourg. I presume you already deduced this."

I nodded.

"By the time we figured out what you were up to, the deed had already been done. We were watching when you boarded the train back to France, when Reginald Mason picked you up at Portsmouth, and when Michael Ben-Ami sneaked out of your room at the Langham."

I opened my mouth to say something, but he interrupted me.

"Don't worry about those two collaborators of yours, Samson. We know they were unaware of your purpose. We have already thanked them for their contributions to your operation. We trust them to keep it to themselves."

"Thank you."

"But as to this 'operation.'" His hard mouth formed the word as though it were distasteful to him. "You are one of our most valuable intelligence assets.

Intelligence asset"—he repeated the phrase pointedly—"not operative. I know you understand the distinction."

"Yes, Director."

"Assassinations are complex operations. They require meticulous preparation, usually lasting months, and always entailing teams of specialists."

"I understand."

"And yet you took it upon yourself to perform this act alone. You do not realize how lucky you are to have succeeded and to have escaped detection, assuming you have indeed escaped detection. Your success cannot be attributed to any specific decision or planning on your part. There are a dozen ways in which this might have ended in the worst imaginable failure. It is important that you understand this. Had you been exposed, it would have entailed the sacrifice of one of our most important resources—namely, you—in which we have invested years of effort and millions of pounds."

"Yes, Director."

"I will not give you the details, but we have already begun a campaign of disruption against the missile project. To demonstrate the complexity of these operations, I will share with you that many of our efforts have been unsuccessful—targets left unharmed or only lightly wounded, agents exposed, innocent people injured."

"Yes, Director."

"These efforts will be even less successful if they are uncoordinated—if individuals take matters into their own hands. Do you understand me?"

"Yes, Director."

"And now, are you prepared to say something other than 'Yes, Director'?"

"Yes, Director."

He smiled and waited.

"Köhler had broken my cover. He made active preparations to have me eliminated. Had I not acted when I did, you probably would have lost your valuable asset anyway."

"Really? How do you know he was about to have you killed?"

"He told me himself."

"You mean just before you shot him."

"Yes."

"Then you cannot claim self-defense as a motive. You did not know you were averting a trap until after you had already confronted Köhler?"

"That is partially true. I suspected he would act, but I was unaware of how close he was to doing so."

"I believe, on the whole, it is better to be meticulous than lucky," said the Director, taking a drag on his cigarette and setting it back in the ashtray in front of him. "Luck runs out."

"I may still be in jeopardy. We do not know what Köhler revealed to his associates."

"Ah, but we *do* know what he revealed to his associates, Samson." The Director smiled when he saw my expression of surprise. "We have a *shtinker* among those associates. Your professor suspected you, but he was not yet ready to lay all his cards on the table. As far as we can tell, your position is secure."

I breathed in deep and exhaled. Something uncoiled in my upper back and behind my eyes. Until that moment, I was unaware how gravely my dread over being compromised had affected me.

We sat in silence for a while. "As I say, Samson, there were certain elements of forethought in your operation, but in other respects, it was extraordinarily clumsy."

I raised an eyebrow. The Director seemed to be hinting at something of which I was unaware.

"Feldman witnessed the whole thing."

"*Feldman?*" Feldman was the legendary surveillance artist who had taught me how to shadow.

"I told you, Samson. We have a man inside Köhler's cell. A former Nazi who genuinely seems more interested in atonement than in the remuneration we provide him. To keep an eye on this asset, and to record other observations from the meeting in Geneva, we placed Feldman in the lobby of the Métropole. It took him about five seconds to spot you as an observer when you sat at a table in view of the elevators, with your blond wig and fake moustache, pretending to read an issue of *Le Monde*, a glass of sparkling water, no ice, in front of you."

I stared at him, at a loss for words.

The Director continued. "What Feldman didn't know was who you were and what you were doing there. Even he didn't recognize you under the disguise, at least initially. When you rather inelegantly snapped photos with a cigarette case clearly manufactured in one of our workshops, Feldman was baffled. We had not informed him of a parallel observation team, and he knew we were unlikely to have fielded one quite so incompetent. So he assumed you belonged to some other intelligence service, or perhaps a criminal organization that had acquired or copied the camera."

I pulled the cigarette case out of the breast pocket of my blazer and tossed it onto the table. "I suppose this will be of no use to you."

"True. To render a short story even shorter, Feldman made the correct decision to follow you instead of any of the many other targets he might have chosen. He tracked you tracking Köhler, watched you confront and kill him, and then observed in exasperation as you wasted precious time vomiting onto the pavement. Only then was he certain that the bold, amateurish, and penitent assassin could only be you."

The Director's eyes twinkled, and I observed the other men around the table suppressing smirks.

"Feldman put aside for the moment his disappointment at the ineptness of your technique, which he considers a personal failure, as he trained you himself. He then dedicated himself to your preservation. When the police arrived a few minutes later, he posed as a confused eyewitness and delayed them as long as he could, giving an account rife with inconsistencies seemingly bred of shock and panic. One thing he made certain to report accurately: your description, knowing that it would be corroborated by any other witnesses who might have seen the event from a distance. He reasoned, apparently correctly, that even you possessed the good sense to shed your disguise immediately. Whether you emerged as Charles Choucair or someone else, Feldman assumed your appearance was likely to be very different from that of the person who committed the murder."

"*Alhamdulillah*," I whispered in Arabic, thanking God.

"Better to say, *Alhamdulifeldman*." The Director winked, glancing sideways at the other men seated around the table, who quickly nodded affirmation of his cleverness.

"But is Feldman safe?" I inquired. "The police could detain him for weeks while they investigate. Eventually, they will discover who he is!"

"No, they will not. Feldman was wearing his own disguise and had false papers. Once he provided his evidence, he 'vanished as though he never existed,' according to the gendarme who was watching him with both eyes. Feldman overheard the policeman report the disappearance of the eyewitness to his superior in precisely those words. By then, Feldman had insinuated himself among the crowd of curious onlookers who had gathered at the scene."

I shook my head in disbelief.

"Make sure to buy him a nice box of bonbons next time you see him," the Director advised.

The following hour was spent debriefing me. I supplied all the details of which I was aware regarding the missile program. While much of my report confirmed what the Mossad already knew, much was new. The team was ecstatic. I had provided them with multiple fresh opportunities to scuttle the initiative.

The Director terminated the meeting, and the four other men departed one by one, leaving Shmuel Mizrahi alone with me in the apartment.

Mizrahi pulled a sheet of paper from his briefcase and some spectacles from the breast pocket of his suit jacket.

"What is this, Shmuel?" I asked, smiling at him. "Reading glasses?"

"Yes, reading glasses. It turns out time moves in one direction only—the one that makes me older with each passing day. I wish the same for you. There were occasions during the past couple of days when I feared time might cease flowing for you."

"I am sorry to have caused you concern."

"As well you should be. But even your most heartfelt apologies are insufficient to neutralize all the concern I have harbored for you over the years." His smile was sad. "Anyway, you may wonder why I am here, Yosef."

"I was hoping it is because you have un-retired."

He shook his head. "I made the right decision to leave active service. I enjoy spending time with my wife, children, and granddaughter. You will be delighted to learn that I have started a small garden. I call it my *Friedmann farm*, but only in my own head, as your name is classified. I grow a small number of cucumber vines in addition to flowers, tomatoes, peppers, dill, and a few other crops."

"That is wonderful, Shmuel. You deserve the peace and fulfilment of farming."

We sat in silence a while. He sighed.

"So, why are you here?" I prompted.

Mizrahi shifted in his seat and glanced down at the sheet of paper before him. "Yosef," he began. He reached across the table to place a callused hand on my forearm. "The Director called me back to lead the difficult parts of this meeting. He is, perhaps, one of the most physically courageous men in the world, but he does not do as well with the . . . emotional."

"Go on."

"To his credit, the Director recognizes that this episode is likely to have wounded you."

I looked down at my fingers, interlaced on the tabletop.

Mizrahi waited for me.

"Yes, Shmuel, I am wounded."

"Tell me how you feel."

"Like a murderer."

Mizrahi squeezed my arm and shook his head. He opened his mouth to say something.

"I know you warned me," I interjected. "I underestimated what this would do to me."

"And what about the fact that Köhler deserved to die, and that we would have taken him out had you not done so? What about the fact that he was preparing to kill you?"

"This is not about him. It is about me."

"That is true. Köhler is not worth half a shit. The loss of his life is meaningless but for its disruption of the missile program and deterrence of our enemies. Your action, along with the other measures we have taken, is likely to scuttle the missile project. It will have tremendous impact."

"The Director was right," I continued, barely absorbing his words. "I cannot claim to have acted in self-defense. There was an opportunity to bring Köhler to justice. I took it upon myself to condemn and then execute him." I covered my face with my hands. "What does this say about who I am?"

"Who you are is a man who was placed in a position not one in a million could withstand."

"I feel that something has shifted. If I can commit this act, what else might I do?"

"Yosef, I want you to look at me."

I raised my head and cupped my brow in my left hand. Mizrahi continued, "The world in which you reside, in which the two and a half million citizens of Israel have entrusted you with their survival, has different rules from other realities. It is challenging enough to live an ethical life in civil society. It is impossible to do so in the secret world, in which what is moral on one plane is immoral on another. Sometimes you must choose between bad options and worse ones. I am not trying to persuade you that you made the right choice. It certainly was the wrong decision in a tactical sense." He laid his palm on the fist my right hand had formed on the table. "But I acknowledge it might also have been the wrong choice in an ethical sense. You will have to come to terms with that."

I sighed. "So, what happens now?"

"One of two things. The first option is for Charles Choucair to disappear. The Director offers you the opportunity to come in, receive the thanks of a grateful nation, and return to a normal life in Israel or anywhere in the world you prefer. That is the option you can actuate by signing this sheet of paper." He pulled a pen out of his shirt pocket and unscrewed the cap, extending it in my direction.

I shook my head.

"Why not? You have contributed enough. Return to your cucumbers in peace."

"This cannot be my last act as an agent. Besides, there is much left for me to do."

He laid the pen on the table. "The second option is for Charles Choucair to return promptly to the Middle East to resume his activities as before. Naturally, he will be shocked to learn of the death of Professor Köhler. And then, after a suitable interval, and after a decade of relentless work building his business, he will go on holiday. Find a person to whom you can entrust your business operations, and book yourself a three-month retreat on a Caribbean island."

"Shmuel, I do not need a vacation."

"You do."

"I do not want a vacation."

"You should."

I sighed.

"You will arrange a three-month leave on a sparsely populated Caribbean island that has almost no phone service and patchy mail delivery. After two weeks at this retreat, we will replace you with a double and bring you home to the kibbutz for a couple of months. You will engage in the redemptive work of the cowshed or the cucumber patch or whatever else gives you 'the peace and fulfilment of farming,' as you call it. After two months, we will send you back to the Caribbean to finish up Charles Choucair's holiday, and you will return to Lebanon from there."

"Shmuel—"

"This is not open to negotiation. You must decide between these two courses of action. You will do it, Yosef, if not out of compassion for yourself, then because you are ordered to. If not because you are ordered to, then because you recognize that a man cannot function forever as you have, without genuine human contacts, without relief, without from time to time seeing with his own eyes the cherished thing he is fighting for."

I looked into his warm, sad face, and nodded.

"There is more," Mizrahi said after a pause. "We are pulling you from Syria. You will close operations there and focus on Lebanon."

"Shmuel!"

"I'm sorry, Yosef. The Director is firm on this point. But it is not just him. The grapevine says that within a few days or weeks, he will be ousted from his position. Our operations against the missile program will be successful ultimately, but there have been too many mishaps. Too many letter bombs exploding in post offices or in the hands of wives and daughters. Too many messy hits. The new guy will want to take a different direction in Syria."

I stared at my hands and nodded.

I later learned that the "different direction in Syria" was Eli Cohen, one of the most famous and, for a time, successful spies in history. The up-and-coming director had been grooming Cohen for some time and had already set in motion Cohen's infiltration into the highest echelons of the Syrian political and defense establishments.

Among other achievements, Cohen—who would ultimately be exposed and hanged in Syria in May 1965—was credited with much of the intelligence that led to Israel's astonishing victory in the Six-Day War in June 1967.

I followed the plan Mizrahi outlined. I entrusted the global business to my London distributor. After two weeks in the Caribbean sun, I flew to Israel. Shmuel Mizrahi met me at the airport outside Lydda and drove me to Gan Miriam, where Yoram greeted me with an embrace and a kiss on the cheek. He had suffered a stroke and used a cane to hobble around his garden. A new forewoman named Dafna declared that the cowshed's technological improvements would be more than I could master in a two-month residency. She assigned me to the cucumber patch, which was equipped with new drip irrigation technology developed in Israel.

I received a warm welcome from the founding members of the settlement, but two-thirds of the residents had joined since I left, and the veterans had full lives—children and grandchildren and other interests that left me on the outside looking in.

After two months, my home visit was over. I flew back to the Caribbean for the final two weeks of Charles Choucair's vacation, exchanging places with my tanned and appreciative stand-in. He was a young agent from Be'er-Sheva who couldn't believe his good fortune at landing the assignment of impersonating me on holiday.

I returned to Lebanon feeling more than ever that there was nowhere I belonged.

Chapter Thirty-One

Once back in Beirut, I continued my business and espionage operations. My commitment to protecting the State of Israel and its citizens, and my belief in the righteousness of our cause, remained strong. But something had come unmoored in Geneva. I felt as though I were standing on the deck of a ship, struggling to maintain balance while waves swelled beneath my feet. With each passing day, week, month, and year of my double life, it seemed that the small corner of Charles Choucair's consciousness occupied by Joseph Friedmann was contracting. I feared that one day I would wake up and not even recognize that Joseph was gone.

Beginning in my early twenties, I had been known by the code name Samson, the biblical hero who defended the Israelites from the Philistines. So mighty was Samson that he ripped a lion in two with his bare hands and defeated a Philistine army of a thousand men with nothing more than the jawbone of a donkey. But later, shorn of his hair and blinded by his enemies, Samson lost his divine strength. I, too, perceived the sapping of my vitality with the evolution of time.

Even the kibbutz, my own source of strength, receded from consciousness, like a shore disappearing beneath the horizon. My last visit to Gan Miriam, during my three-month Caribbean "retreat," proved it was no longer an anchor to my perception of self.

I brooded with my books. I consorted with women whose ages remained the same while mine increased, and whose physical attractions could not compensate for what they lacked in intellect. By the spring of 1973, nearly a dozen years after assassinating Professor Köhler, I had been living under a false identity for over two decades. I was forty-two years old and weary.

And there were nightmares. In one recurring dream, I was pinned beneath a weight so heavy, it seemed I might suffocate in my sleep while a high-pitched rasp whispered denunciations of criminality in my ear. I was always incapacitated by paralysis in these nightmares, unable to either free myself or answer my accuser. I would awaken drenched in sweat, often at the very moment of ejaculating into the sheets. This latter phenomenon worried me most of all. I feared that self-loathing had seeded itself deep within my soul, a perverse insanity germinating where decency once resided.

Despite my fatigue and dejection, Cedars Trading grew to become one of the ten most prominent private enterprises in Lebanon. I maintained a position among the elite. My relationships spanned the breadth of the contentious patchwork of religious and ethnic factions that constituted Lebanese society. From this vantage point, I was ideally positioned to fill the evolving intelligence needs of the State of Israel.

With its stunning Six-Day War victory, Israel suddenly had acquired a land mass more than three times its original size. On those lands dwelled more than a million Palestinian Arabs, people who were stateless before, and now were both stateless and living under occupation. Hundreds of thousands more Palestinian refugees dwelt in slums and camps within the borders of neighboring Arab countries. Those countries had little incentive to integrate Palestinian exiles into their societies.

The rise of the Palestinian National Liberation Movement was an inevitable outcome, but in its early years, it went almost unnoticed by the Mossad. By the time I issued my first report about *Fatah*, the largest faction in what would become the Palestine Liberation Organization (PLO), the group was responsible for dozens—and eventually hundreds—of acts of sabotage, terrorism, and murder. Each of these incidents was a step in a deadly dance of attack and reprisal, whose audacity and violence intensified with each cycle.

A Palestinian National Charter was composed, leaving no room for compromise. Armed struggle was the only path to liberating Palestine, and the only acceptable outcome of that struggle entailed the elimination of the State of Israel.

Over the years, multiple Palestinian militant groups moved their command apparatuses to Lebanon. A surge of international terror was the product.

Terrorists bombed buses, detonated explosives in shopping and community centers, slaughtered schoolchildren. Jews around the world were targeted. The most spectacular elements of this campaign included several airline hijackings and terminal attacks and the Black September group's murder of eleven Israeli athletes at the 1972 Munich Olympics. The struggle morphed into a shadow war between Israel's secret services and an international terror network comprised of *Fatah* and other Palestinian and some foreign groups.

I was positioned at the epicenter of this conflict.

In addition to providing political analysis, I assisted by smuggling both supplies and people for the Mossad. I provided intelligence for Israeli commando units infiltrating Lebanon. I delivered information that was used to sabotage dozens of arms depots and shipments. I identified the locations of terrorist training camps. I furnished the names and locations of leaders of Palestinian militias, some of whom turned up dead.

Over the years, Charles Choucair became a member of a network of financiers bankrolling the PLO. The precarious irony of this circumstance was not lost upon Israel's security establishment, who thus provided funding for the very organizations it worked so hard to vanquish. We considered the costs reasonable in exchange for the tactical advantages of this arrangement. Had I not funded the groups, someone else would have done so. And there was a hard-and-fast rule that no act of terror to which I contributed material assistance was permitted to succeed.

In my role as a PLO financier, I ferried arms, information, and supplies for terrorists. My deliveries were disrupted in patterns calculated by the Mossad to allay suspicions that would come my way were I the sole mediator whose shipments either always reached their destinations or always failed to do so.

From time to time I heard whispers of specific planned attacks, which I transmitted to headquarters in Tel Aviv via encrypted written communications. The Mossad's web of information was so extensive that most such plots were foiled. The Palestinian leadership became obsessed with leaks. Everyone was suspected of being a double agent, and more than once I was the recipient of "social calls" from heads of internal security, thinly veiled attempts to discover whether I was a mole. I emerged free of suspicion each time.

At a social function in Beirut, the wife of the operations chief of a Marxist Palestinian terror group told me that ever since her husband had survived an

Israeli car bombing in rural Lebanon, he had been plagued by chronic backaches. She had heard from a friend that I had access to top-of-the-line executive desk chairs. Would I be willing to procure one for her husband?

"Certainly," I replied. "It would be my honor to furnish your husband with the finest chair at no cost. I shall order one tomorrow from Sweden. *Inshallah*, he will find relief from his pain. I pray this small gift will aid him in leading the jihad against our enemies."

The chair arrived in a crate three weeks later. State-of-the-art ergonomic features were accompanied by a single clandestine element: a bug installed by Mossad engineers. For two years, while the battery lasted, the listening post beneath the sand dunes south of Tel Aviv had ears on every conversation occurring in the functionary's office.

Yasser Arafat himself tried to recruit me as an operative: "My brother," declared the leader of the PLO in his distinctive singsong, "you can do more for the struggle. Do you not wish to contribute to our jihad with your own two hands? Think of what someone with your impeccable reputation and access could accomplish!"

"I am honored by your confidence, Abu Ammar," I answered, using his nom de guerre. "It is a privilege to support the restoration of our beloved Palestine. But we must each know our limitations. I am no operative. I can do more from the sidelines than I can in the field." Having concluded this declaration, I extracted a checkbook from my breast pocket and inked a contribution of ten thousand dollars.

But despite my efforts and those of other assets the Mossad controlled all over the globe, the waves of murder and terrorism continued to swell. Finally, Israel had had enough. The prime minister tasked her intelligence services with looking for opportunities to take out Palestinian terrorists and their leaders wherever they were.

"Can you help identify some suitable targets?" inquired Moshe Har-Nof, deputy director of the Mossad and my case officer, at a debriefing in Tel Aviv. We sat at a conference table with a half dozen leaders of the intelligence and military services.

"Yes."

"What do you have in mind?"

I reached into my briefcase and threw a folder onto the table. It contained a handwritten report I had composed in my hotel room the evening before. The report provided the names and home addresses of three top officials in the PLO and Black September, who lived in adjoining apartment buildings in the heart of Beirut. Also noted was the location of a structure housing nearly one hundred militants from the Popular Front for the Liberation of Palestine (PFLP), and a few smaller targets, including a PLO arms and bomb-making workshop.

A clerk ran off copies, and when he returned, I reviewed the contents with the assembly. The details included a proposed landing site for commandos ferried ashore on small watercraft and land routes leading to the targets and back to the beach for extraction. I provided the locations of telephone junction boxes and electrical transformers that could be disabled. Police patrol schedules were listed, as were the numbers and positions of bodyguards. I specified radio frequencies for jamming, along with other information that could be used in a decisive operation.

When I finished, the assembly sat in silence.

"This is a real treasure trove of material, Samson," said the IDF's operations chief.

"Thank you."

"Each of these targets has the blood of dozens or even hundreds on their hands. I have no doubt the prime minister will approve the action."

"I hope so."

"The impact on the terrorist organizations' operations will be crippling."

I nodded. "That is the idea."

The operations chief continued to muse aloud, seeming to work out the details as he spoke. "The human objectives are residents in apartment complexes in a densely populated part of the city. Those hits will have to be close-range and elegant to avoid harming innocents. The other installations will require some real firepower. I think our people can work out the logistics. It will take some creativity, but I can see the outlines of an operation that achieves all the aims."

Moshe Har-Nof cleared his throat. "One solution I don't see at the moment is how we pull this off without blowing your cover, Samson. The risk of all this information forming an arrow that points directly at you is high."

"No need to worry about that," I answered.

He raised an eyebrow.

"I want to come in," I said.

Har-Nof plucked his cigarette from the ashtray in front of him, took a deep drag, and blew smoke from the side of his mouth, staring at me all the while. He tapped the table with his index and middle fingers, as though he were testing it for defects. Finally, he spoke: "Gentlemen, this is top-secret information. Discuss it with no one until instructed otherwise. Yuval," he said, addressing the IDF operations chief, "take this to the chief of staff. I will discuss it with the Director." Then, to the room: "May Samson and I have some privacy, please?"

One by one, the attendees rose and filed out, each one squeezing my shoulder or patting me on the back.

Har-Nof and I were left alone. He took another drag on his cigarette and exhaled.

"I have nothing left, Moshe," I sighed.

He laid down the cigarette and tapped the table again. "No problem, Samson. We anticipated this day. You have served above and beyond what was ever expected of you. A grateful nation awaits your return, though only a handful of people will know enough to acknowledge all you have done. Come home."

"Home," I muttered, wondering where that was. My thoughts returned to the biblical Samson. In the end, blinded and feeble, the once-mighty hero of Israel was brought forth from the dungeon and made to dance for his Philistine captors. Samson rested in his weariness on the pillars of the Temple of Dagon, where thousands were congregated in celebration of their victory over the Israelites. He prayed to the Lord: "*Remember me and give me strength just this once . . .*". The text in the book of Judges continues: "*. . . and he leaned against [the pillars] . . . and Samson cried out, 'May my soul perish with the Philistines!' and the temple came crashing down on the lords and on all the people therein.*"

⊸◉⊷

Over the next two months, the operation took shape. The strike would be a night action coordinated between the Israeli navy and several commando units, with teams assigned to each of the targets.

The men were to be ferried to a beach in south Beirut in motorized rubber pontoon boats launched from navy vessels anchored five kilometers offshore. I would meet them with one of my large-capacity lorries and conduct the first group to the apartment complex housing the leaders targeted for assassination. On the way, I would drop the remote squads off at my garage, where each would take one of my other vehicles to their destinations. A synchronized assault on the targets was planned, with all units regrouping at the beach. The vehicles would be abandoned, and the pontoons would transport everyone back to the missile boats. The ships would then proceed at full speed to their base in Israel, a voyage of under four hours. The Mossad was unwilling to risk having me anywhere but safely in Israeli hands at the conclusion of the operation. I was to be extracted with everyone else on the pontoons.

Finally, the morning of the raid dawned. I was careful to not alter any of my routines. I conducted my usual meetings and phone calls and lunched alone at one of my favorite seaside restaurants, reading a book of poetry by the Palestinian Mahmoud Darwish. I returned to the warehouse where my office was located and dismissed the staff as usual at 7:00 p.m., informing them that I intended to stay late at work. I tuned the radio to the classic Arabic music channel, where at 8:18 p.m., a birthday greeting from Leilah to Maryam was aired during the *Messages from Friends and Family* broadcast. The birthday announcement was the "go" signal from the Mossad, who had received notice from surveillance teams that "all the birds are in their nests." At 9:50 p.m., I selected the keys for four of my lorries from the rack by the door, went into the parking garage, and drove. Sixteen minutes later, I was at the rendezvous point south of the city, lights doused and engine off, eyes scanning the Mediterranean.

At 10:30 p.m., a light flashed twice from about one hundred fifty meters offshore, and I returned the signal with a small torch. Six minutes later, four rubber dinghies carrying about forty men in wetsuits rowed ashore, their engines silenced to avoid detection. Passwords were exchanged, heavy bags were loaded into the back of the lorry, and the men boarded silently. Within four minutes, the soldiers had changed into civilian disguises, some as women, and armed themselves with weapons they concealed either under clothes or in side bags. The unit commander, now wearing a dark green dress and a brown shoulder-length wig, signaled me to get behind the wheel, and he climbed into the passenger seat.

We drove to my warehouse and entered the garage. I distributed the keys of the remaining three trucks to the team leaders. Five minutes later, all four groups were underway.

I drove the assassination team to an alley around the block from the adjacent seven-story apartment buildings where the terrorist leaders lived. The soldiers filed out and took up their positions, some on the perimeter to block potential attackers, and others posing as couples out for an evening stroll. I killed the engine and waited.

Fifteen minutes later, several flashes of light appeared through upper-floor windows, as the silenced pistols of the assassins did their work. Six minutes after that, the teams emerged from the buildings, racing back to the lorry. At that moment, two sirens sounded from the northeast, followed by machine-gun fire. The perimeter team had been engaged.

"Stay by the truck," the unit commander ordered, reaching for an assault rifle he had stowed in the lorry's cab. He and four of his men ran toward the fire. At the same moment, two separate bursts of light came from the city's south, followed four seconds later by a deep rumble. The other facilities had been blown up by the remote squads. The *pop-pop-pop* of distant gunfire reached our position.

A few minutes later, all was quiet, and I discerned the shadows of soldiers racing back, two of the men carrying a wounded comrade between them. "Let's go, let's go!" the commander called. "Back to the beach!"

I held out the ignition key. "You are driving," I said.

"What? Why?"

The time had come to break my promises. "Because I am not coming back with you."

Chapter Thirty-Two

"What?" the commando chief again demanded. His brown wig was askew.

"You heard me, Madam. I am not coming back with you."

He tore the wig from his head and tossed it aside. "I'm not joking, Samson. I have a wounded soldier here. I was just informed that two of our men were killed in the assault on the PFLP facility. We have about ten minutes for all the teams to meet at the extraction point before the entire city turns into a shooting gallery, with us as the targets. Get in the truck."

"Everything is set for you to move," I answered. "Go."

He levelled his Uzi at me. "I have never left a man in the field. You will not be the first."

"We both know you are not going to shoot me, Ehud. I am staying here. There are things I need to finish."

Neither his eyes nor his weapon wavered. "I have my orders. I'm saying this for the last time: Get in the truck."

I moved steadily forward and nudged the barrel of the gun to his right with my left hand, extending the lorry key with my right. Fresh sirens sounded in the distance. "Come on, Ehud. Take your wounded man and get out of here."

"And when I return without you, what am I supposed to report?"

"The truth. That I refused to come with you and would not tell you why. That I assured you I will be OK. That I vowed I would die before jeopardizing anyone on our side."

Ehud stared at me. The sirens multiplied and grew louder. He snatched the key from my fingertips. "Let's go!" he barked at the soldiers who had clustered around us. "Everyone in the truck! Move, move, move!"

The men raced to the back of the lorry and began loading themselves into it. I ran with Ehud and helped him climb into the cab in his ladies' shoes. "I'm coming with you partway," I called as he started the engine.

"Why?"

"I need you to drop me off somewhere. It is on the way."

"Get in."

I ran around to the passenger seat and climbed up. A thump sounded on the back of the cab from the rear, the signal that everyone had loaded. Ehud put the lorry in gear and tore off toward the south, past groups of citizens who had emerged from their buildings at the commotion. Dozens more watched from their balconies. We sped down city streets, taking the turns at breakneck speed. The soldiers and equipment in the compartment clattered from side to side.

"Three blocks ahead," I said, "thirty meters before the corner, slow down just enough for me to jump out."

He pulled a pistol out of the holster fastened into the waistband of his skirt and extended it to me, grip first.

"No, thank you, my brother," I said. "It would be a liability."

"OK. Good luck, Samson."

"One more thing. Find my old commander. His name is Shmuel Mizrahi. Tell him I have decided to redeem myself at last. Tell him I need our people not to search for me. I will find them before the end."

Ehud nodded. "Got it. Shmuel Mizrahi. Redemption. Don't search for you." He sped toward the intersection.

He slowed near the corner, and I tumbled out. I rolled onto my feet and ran into the labyrinth of alleys and shop stalls that were the local outdoor market, known as the souk. I had chosen the drop-off point so the vehicle would shield me from any observers who were not already on the sidewalk with a view to the narrow space between the curb and the alley. Behind me, the lorry ground its gears and roared off.

To avoid capture, I needed to come as close to disappearing as possible. I made my way to an abandoned storeroom I had stocked with supplies. I shaved my head and beard, exchanging my clothes for beggar's rags. Before pulling on a pair of stained canvas trousers and tying the drawstring, I wrapped a bandage around my left knee. This was an old trick Feldman once recommended to facilitate a limp. Donning threadbare slippers and affecting a hunched back, I hobbled out into the alley and tossed everything other than the clothes I was wearing into a half-filled trash container reeking with refuse from the souk. I selected two spent cardboard boxes from a pile strewn near the garbage bin, carried them to a storefront stoop, repurposed them as a mattress and blanket, and went to sleep.

I spent the following five days as a vagrant, initially in the souk, and afterward elsewhere in the city, feigning physical infirmity and mental illness. I subsisted on the generosity of citizens and shopkeepers. Beggars were common in Beirut, and they often migrated from place to place, propelled by the gendarmerie. Three times, investigators interrogated me about what I had seen during the night of the raid, but my apparent insanity was so prodigious they soon abandoned hope of extracting useful information from me.

The streets were full of rumors about the assault. The vagabond I was impersonating was illiterate, so I could not risk reading newspapers. I learned as much as I could from eavesdropping on conversations among shop owners and customers. Everybody had a theory of how the Israeli military had managed to conduct such an audacious operation and who was responsible for the intelligence failures that permitted it. I was able to snatch some information from headlines and billboards:

"Three Leaders From Fatah and Black September Assassinated. Hundreds of Thousands of Mourners Expected at Funeral."

"Dozens Killed in Israeli Assault on Training Facility of the Popular Front for the Liberation of Palestine."

"Weapons Depot and Armaments Manufacturing Site Destroyed."

"Palestinian Official: Assault Was 'A Disaster.' Attackers Seize Hundreds of Vital Documents."

"Israeli Defense Minister: Two Soldiers Dead and One Wounded in Beirut Attack. All Returned Home."

Meanwhile, Lebanese authorities searched for someone they could punish. Placards bearing my image were posted throughout the city: *Have you seen this man? Report him to the police immediately!* The accompanying photo of Charles Choucair came directly from the wall of my Beirut office. It had been taken at a party the previous year. A person examining the cropped picture closely would discover a uniformed sleeve draped affectionately over my shoulders. The owner of the arm in that sleeve was the Lebanese minister of national defense.

I knew the manhunt was a charade to appease the populace. The police must have assumed I had been spirited away by the Israeli commandos and would never resurface, as indeed had been the plan. The authorities searched for other accomplices as well, but these, too, would never be found. The spotters who reported that the "birds are in their nests" had departed the country on commercial flights two hours before the action began.

In the days before the operation, I had taken pains to assure that my employees around the world, most of whom were Arab nationals, would not come under suspicion through their association with me. They all received letters signed by Charles Choucair, thanking them for their long years of service and apologizing for misleading them about my true identity. I had deposited these letters in a postbox on my way to meeting the assault teams at the beach. I absolved each of my employees of any role in the attack, affirming that they were entirely unaware of my double life. Each received between two and ten thousand dollars in bank transfers, executed one hour after the banks opened the day after the operation, fulfilling instructions I had filed one day earlier. The single employee of Cedars Trading who was in fact a Mossad agent, my warehouse manager in Zurich, would never be seen in Europe again. He had departed at noon the day of the operation on a Swissair flight to Paris with a connection to Tel Aviv.

After five days, with my beard and hair starting to grow in, it was time to refresh my disguise. I made my way to the central train station in Beirut and retrieved a duffel bag I had stowed in a coin locker. The bag contained Lebanese identity papers for Fadi Amin, whose age was listed as fifty-five and occupation as *shopkeeper*. Fadi Amin was recently divorced and had relocated from Tripoli to Beirut to seek "opportunities." He was awkward and vaguely melancholy. He had a hesitating pattern of speech. I was hoping to achieve what Feldman, the master of surveillance from the Mossad, described as "the ultimate effect": that if you rode with Fadi Amin in an elevator, you were unlikely to have any recollection of it.

I shaved the dark stubble on my head and face and donned a gray wig of short, curly hair in a conservative cut and a bushy moustache. This new appearance was a sharp contrast to Charles Choucair's look for the previous decade: a stylishly trim black beard and black hair combed straight backward to below the jawline. A change of clothes packed in the duffel bag included a conservative suit and white button-down shirt with no tie. Thick-rimmed glasses and a shuffling gait completed the disguise. Also in the duffel was a small sack containing a sizeable sum of money in Lebanese pounds in various denominations, enough to last three and a half years with frugal living.

I walked out of the station, carrying the duffel by its handles at my right side. I treated myself to a plate of hummus and pita at a nearby shop—the first food I had eaten off a plate in five days—while scanning the local newspaper for apartments to rent. From there, I went to a neighborhood bank and rented a safe deposit box, into which I placed the bulk of my cash.

"Are you new to the area, Mr. Amin?" asked the pretty bank manager as she signed and witnessed the papers establishing my ownership of the safe deposit box.

"Yes. I have recently relocated to Beirut."

"Are you interested in opening an account with us?"

"No, thank you."

"Well, here is the key," she said, glancing at the clock on the wall behind my left shoulder. I had become accustomed to receiving lingering looks and subtle invitations to prolong conversations with women meeting me for the first time. The bank manager's indifference simultaneously pleased and disappointed me. The disguise was working.

A brief walk took me to a lower-middle-class neighborhood, where I rented the first apartment I had circled in the newspaper, a studio located across the hall from the owner.

"Are you new to the area, Mr. Amin?" inquired my new landlady, eyeing my bag. She seemed like the kind of person who might spend substantial time peering through the peephole in the door of her apartment.

"Yes. I have just relocated to Beirut."

Her eyebrows lifted. I had aroused her curiosity, though she feigned indifference.

"I recently divorced," I continued. "Allah did not bless me with children, so I have come from Tripoli to seek business opportunities. I expect to travel the region. You will no doubt notice that I am away much of the time, and might come and go at unusual hours."

She scowled.

"I hope that will not disturb you."

"Your comings and goings are your own affair." She sniffed. "As long as you do so quietly and are not involved in anything disreputable."

"I can assure you of that. Thank you."

"You will find a pot and pan, a teakettle, and a few dishes and utensils in the kitchenette. As you can see, I have granted you use of this small table and chair at no charge."

"You are most generous," I said with an appreciative smile.

"There is a market down the street for anything else you need."

"Thank you. Do you have a mattress I might use?"

She pretended to ponder the question. "Yes," she answered. "My son is away. But it will cost you extra. And you must provide your own bedclothes."

"Thank you," I repeated. "You are very kind." I extracted a billfold from my pocket, counted out three months' rent plus an extra amount for the mattress, and extended the cash toward her. She accepted the money warily and, with a final glance over her shoulder, left the apartment and returned to her lair.

When she was gone, I transferred most of my remaining cash to a plastic bag I taped under the kitchen sink. I left a sizeable sum in small bills in an envelope on top of my clothes in the duffel and, after buckling it, laid the bag on the floor in the middle of the room. To gauge the landlady's trustworthiness, I set tells on the duffel, the sink cabinet, and the front door, then exited the studio. The remainder of the afternoon was spent buying supplies that were needed for subsistence in the small apartment: personal items, clothes, hangers, cleaning supplies, sheets, towels, groceries. Shortly after sundown, I returned to the apartment. I checked the tells, noting that the landlady had entered my room and inspected my bag. An inquisitive but honest woman, she had taken nothing. I made my mattress, a welcome improvement from five days lying on cardboard, and slept soundly through the night.

Chapter Thirty-Three

I estimated I could sustain my sojourn in Lebanon for one more week at most. The Mossad would soon become impatient to bring me in. They had ways of finding me. And there was a chance one of the civilians who lined their balconies during the noisy retreat of the strike force had spotted me exiting the getaway truck. A determined Lebanese investigator might pursue an eyewitness account of a solitary man sneaking into the souk rather than absconding with the attackers. One way or another, the net would start closing in, and with time, I would be ensnared.

In the morning, I awoke, showered, donned my disguise, and set out. Armed soldiers continued to patrol the streets, but random stops and demands for identity cards had ceased. Almost all the posters bearing Charles Choucair's image had been pasted over or torn down to make room for new notices. Newspapers had shifted their focus from the attack to its aftermath. The headlines I scanned while drinking coffee and eating *shakshuka* at a street café read, "Calls Increase for Government to Resign Amid Security Debacle" and "Arafat: Israel Will Pay a Steep Price. We Will Emerge Stronger Than Before."

But there was sunshine and a northerly sea breeze, which cheered me during my half-hour walk to the Municipality of Beirut. The municipality building housed birth records and death certificates, marriage and divorce licenses, and a vast collection of Lebanese and international newspapers. I paused to read the ornate Arabic text etched into the stone above the lintel: *These are the traces that identify us: Seek out henceforth our traces.*

My pledge to Mizrahi to refrain from disturbing old ghosts as long as I was an active agent had at last expired. *All right.* I exhaled. *I shall seek.*

I followed the signs toward the reference section. A woman stood behind the counter, the shelves around her crammed with bound volumes and file boxes. She was about forty-five years old. Black hair wound about her head in a stylish beehive above the thick collar of a European-style business suit. She smiled as I approached.

I had accepted the reality that bland, middle-aged Fadi Amin lacked Charles Choucair's magnetism. Nevertheless, I hoped a sufficient vestige of the old magic remained to stimulate interest from this member of a more mature demographic group.

"*Sabah al-khair*," I said with a smile.

"*Sabah an-nour*," the woman behind the counter replied, examining my face with arched brows. "How may I assist you?"

"I am conducting research for a book on international businesses based in Lebanon."

"Ah. You have come to the right place. We have many relevant records."

The librarian led me to the files and tutored me in use of the microfiche reader and film catalogue. "Do not hesitate to ask for help," she instructed. She stole a glance in my direction while sashaying back to her desk, and I flashed an eager grin. The beginning of a smile flickered on her face before she spun around toward her station.

An hour's research revealed the fate of my father. The Lebanese government had seized his assets during Israel's War of Independence in 1948. Afterward, he had liquidated the remainder of his commercial interests in the Middle East. The rest of the trail was brief, and it led to an obituary published on October 12, 1967 in *The Brussels Times*, an English-language Belgian newspaper: *Albert Friedmann, an importer-exporter whose business activities stretched from London to Moscow to Tokyo, passed away this week at the age of eighty-two. He was a prominent member of the Brussels Jewish community and participated in its rebuilding after World War II. Mr. Friedmann maintained a residence in Beirut until May 1948. He is survived by his wife of twelve years, Sarah Hochberg Friedmann; two children from a previous marriage, Bernadette Peeters and Claudia De Smet; and two grandchildren.*

No mention of a first wife, Ziva, nor of a firstborn son, Joseph. "Bastard," I said with a hiss. A young man in the cubicle next to me raised his head and stole a glance out of the corner of his eye. I suppressed my resentment. I knew I had never been more than an inconvenience to my father. It was no surprise to receive this confirmation, three and a half decades later, that he'd preferred to deny the existence of my mother and me. Knowledge of his fate and of the existence of two half sisters had no power to change me. I pulled the film out of the reader and replaced it in the file.

I went to the marriage catalogue next. Marriages were documented on cards slotted into tracks and set in long wooden boxes. They were filed by religion, decade, and last name of the groom. If I ever knew the surname of my mother's second husband, Pierre, I had forgotten it. There was no record of a Friedmann marriage in Lebanon. My parents had married in Damascus. On the unlikely chance that my mother's second wedding was recorded using her maiden name, Hedaya, I searched the catalogue. There were a few Hedaya marriages in the late 1930s and early 1940s in the Jewish records, but none involved a Ziva, and there were no Hedayas in the Christian files at all.

Next, I searched the birth records. There was only one Friedmann in the catalogue, Yusouf, born April 1, 1931. I pulled the card out of the file. *Father: Albert. Mother: Ziva. Place of Birth: Infirmary of the Maronite Mission of the Sisters of Lebanon, Bhamdoun.* Hardening my heart, I replaced the card in the box. I was not searching for myself.

I returned to the reference desk. "Yes?" the librarian inquired, the smile still playing on her lips, now adorned with red lipstick.

"Thank you. You have been so helpful. I am seeking information regarding a Belgian importer-exporter active in Lebanon until 1948," I said. "I have identified him in your files. He is deceased. His first wife may still be alive, but I find nothing regarding her in the records. She remarried, and I do not know the last name of her second husband." I gazed into her eyes. "It appears I have struck an impasse."

The librarian's mouth formed a determined line. "Ah, a challenge. The records are all kept under the name of the husband." She thought for a moment. "Have you tried searching the divorce records?"

"No. I did not think of it." Of course, I had thought of it, but the divorce files, unlike birth, death, and marriage records, were not open to the public.

Her eyes twinkled as she swung open the gate to the area behind her desk and led me through a rear door to a large room with dozens of wooden card files. "What is the name of the couple you are searching for?"

"Friedmann." I spelled it for her.

"An uncommon name . . ."

"Yes. He was a European Jew."

She raised an eyebrow.

"It is possible that when his wife remarried, she took a Christian husband."

"How unusual . . ."

The librarian stopped at one of the file boxes, opened a drawer, and began to rifle through its contents with the tips of her fingers. After a few seconds, she fished an index card from the drawer. She scrutinized it for a moment and smacked her lips.

"Here it is," she said, proffering the card between her index and middle fingers.

It was a printed form, with handwritten entries in black ink on each line and a municipal stamp in the corner. The dissolution of my life, distilled to raw data:

Divorce Record
Husband: Friedmann, Albert
Wife: Friedmann (Hedaya), Ziva
Date: December 4, 1938
Location: Municipality of Beirut
Children: Yusouf

I kept my hand steady and my expression impassive as I examined the information, though my heart was galloping.

Address of husband: The entry was the well-remembered house in the old Jewish quarter of Beirut. I knew already that the building had been razed in the 1950s and an apartment complex erected on the site.

Address of wife: The same entry was listed and crossed out with a single line. A new address was added in compressed script above the first.

Here was the lead I sought. I pulled a pen and pad from my breast pocket and copied the information. In the late 1930s, the location was on the southern outskirts of Beirut, but by 1973, it had been engulfed by the growing city. It was typical of the Lebanese to remain in their original houses for generations, building extensions as their needs grew. There was a chance that, if the second address was the one to which my mother had moved with Pierre, she was still there.

The reference librarian was "more than happy" to access the deeds registry to identify the owner of the property at the address scribbled into the divorce document, but I was not allowed in that area. We returned to her desk from the back room, and she opened the swinging gate, instructing me to wait on the visitors' side. She disappeared behind the back door and returned in less than five minutes, a proud smile on her face, and a name printed in blue ink on an index card: *Pierre Darwish*. Born in 1915 in Damascus, Syria.

"You may be able to learn more about him and his wife in the public records, as you did with Mr. Friedmann," the librarian commented.

"Thank you for your help," I said and, glancing at her name tag, added, "Madame Chahine."

"It's Mademoiselle Chahine."

"Mademoiselle," I repeated, inclining my head. "I shall return to the cubicle to finish my research."

"It is my pleasure. Please find me," she added, narrowing her eyes, "if you wish to pursue anything else."

In less than an hour, I had gained all the information available on Pierre. He had established or partnered with several failed businesses over the years, and his most recent employment was with a debt collection firm. Two suits for fraud had been filed against him in small claims court, but he was not found liable in either case. The records contained no references to his wife or family.

Mademoiselle Chahine left her post for lunch, placing a small tabletop sign on the desk that read, "Away." When she had gone, I gathered my things, went into the street, and bought a bouquet of carnations from a sidewalk vendor. I returned to the reference desk and leaned over the counter to pluck an index card from the pile on the librarian's desk. *Thank you again for your help*, I wrote. I could not risk having the librarian search for Fadi Amin, so I signed the note with a new alias: *Jibril 'Ayoun*, hoping this would be the last false identity I would ever require. Leaving the flowers and card on the desk, I exited the building.

I hailed a cab and instructed the driver to let me out a few blocks from the destination. It was a typical Beiruti neighborhood, in which shops intermingled with private residences. At a sidewalk café opposite the entrance to the house,

I ordered a Turkish coffee and unfurled my newspaper, examining it while keeping one eye on the entrance to the structure.

After about half an hour, she emerged through the doorway, a broom in hand. In my mind's eye, my mother had remained as she was when I last saw her: a twenty-three-year-old beauty, all raven hair and honeyed cheeks, her trim figure gazing down at me from a second-story window. But here, I saw a woman who had aged poorly. Her face was furrowed, her hair dyed jet black, her bulk draped in a loose housedress overlaid with a flowery apron. She shuffled about the stoop, sweeping off the dust and pausing before descending each stair toward the sidewalk.

As she worked, a boy of about sixteen exited the house. He wore tight orange pants and a blue shirt with buttons open to the navel. The shadow of a moustache darkened his upper lip. She turned to face him. The youth swept by her, his swagger radiating disrespect. She detained him with a hand on his elbow. He attempted to shake his arm loose and uttered some short words, and when she leaned forward to kiss him on the forehead, he pulled away and trotted into the street.

My mother, leaning on her broom handle, watched him go. My heart constricted, empathy and scorn vying within me as I imagined how she must feel to have produced that insolent progeny—the sequel of forsaking me. I had intended to observe from a distance only, but now found I could sit still no longer. I rose, dug into my pocket, threw some bills on the table, and ran across the street.

"Madame!"

She turned at the sound and pulled the broom handle in front of herself protectively.

"One moment!" I called.

"Yes?"

"Are you . . . Ziva?"

She stared at me. "Ziva?"

"Yes. Is that your name?"

She scrutinized my face. "Who are you?"

"I . . . I . . ." I searched her eyes. Fadi Amin was reflected in her pupils.

"How do you know the name Ziva?" she whispered.

I could not speak.

"My name is Nour." She paused. "I have not been called *Ziva* in over thirty years . . . Who are you, that you know the name Ziva?"

"I am . . ." My voice trailed off.

Her eyes widened. "Joseph? Is that you?"

I nodded and bowed my head. She threw her arms about me and buried her face in my chest. My arms hung at my sides.

She pulled away and squinted up at me. Worry creased the corners of her eyes as she scanned the area about us. "Come inside. Quickly." And when I hesitated: "Please, Joseph, come inside." She placed her hand on my elbow and drew me past the threshold, shutting the door behind us. She parted the drapes to peer through the glass and turned to face me, taking me by the hand and leading me past a sitting room into a small kitchen.

"Sit, *habibi* (my darling)." She indicated the head of her kitchen table. "Let me make you some tea."

The word *tea* hurtled me backward in time. Part of my consciousness seemed to detach from my body and float to the ceiling. I watched from two vantage points as she shuffled about, filling the kettle with water and placing it on the stove. In my childhood, my mother used to mix hot water with a little milk and honey, a concoction I called *tea* because I associated that beverage with heat. She would instruct me to take a seat at the head of the table, a book propped in front of me. And then she would sit in the chair to my left and watch me, as though she required nothing more in the world.

"Tea," I murmured. "Yes, please. The grown-up kind."

She turned from the stove, and I saw again, as in my childhood, the melancholy in her eyes. "Of course, the grown-up kind," she said. "I can see you have become a man. How handsome you are, *ya rouhi, ya albi* (my soul, my heart)! And your eyes—so intelligent, so understanding!" She selected a sprig of nana mint from a jar on the countertop, placing it into a glass teacup. "I was beautiful, too, in my youth. The boys in the neighborhood couldn't take their eyes off me.

"Your father was unattractive," she continued. "Very unsightly. I was horrified when I first met him. I feared our children would be ugly. But I see you are beautiful, like me. You are more Hedaya than Friedmann, *alhamdulillah*. But your hair is completely gray! We have that in common," she added, winking at me conspiratorially. "I dye my hair."

"This is not my real hair."

"*What?* Why would you make yourself appear older than you are?"

Instead of answering, I took the chair she had indicated at the head of the kitchen table and gazed at her.

"I wish you had told me you were coming, my darling," she continued. "What a surprise to see you after all these years! I thought I might die from shock! Of course, one never knows when a surprise will happen. That is why I try to be ready for surprises at all times. The neighbors say I am very steady. They marvel at how steady I am, despite the disappointments I have suffered in life. But the neighbors are hypocrites! Not a single one of them is a true friend. They would sooner stab me in the back than lift a finger to help in my time of need. 'Talk to your husband!' they say. 'Why do you come to us with your complaints?' One of my father's favorite sayings was: *Choose the neighbor before the house.* Pierre did not choose good neighbors. He leaves the house every morning, and I am left behind to deal with these rotten neighbors until he returns for supper."

I was mystified by the seeming randomness with which she prattled on, as though we had nothing more momentous to discuss. I cleared my throat. "What has happened since you . . . since I left?"

"*Tfoo 'aleik!*" she exclaimed, using an Arabic phrase signifying spitting in disgust, and swept her arm about her. "You can see for yourself! I have become a servant in my own home. When I lived in my father's house, and also in my first husband's, I had attendants, fine clothes, all the luxuries I could imagine. And now, I sweep my own stairs. Pierre is an ungenerous man, very tightfisted."

I tried again. "Do you have regrets?"

"Of course, my sweetheart! I was foolish to leave your father. He was cold and demanding, but at least he did not begrudge every penny he spent on me. I was too young when I married Albert. I did not know how to be a wife to a man like him. But Pierre? He flits about from one business to the next. He does not provide as a husband should. He pays no attention to my needs. He sees that his son is restless—such a fine boy, my Daoud—but my husband ignores him. Pierre is happy to let the street hooligans raise Daoud." She wagged her finger at me. "Very irresponsible! He is a sweet child, so good, so respectful!"

I continued to gape at her. A brief observation had been sufficient to convince me that her son possessed little goodness and even less respect. Was she deluding herself, or putting on airs? And the expressions of affection with which she ornamented her speech—*my darling, my heart, my soul*—only increased my bewilderment. Each of these utterances echoed fraudulently in the hollows excavated by my abandonment.

She busied herself packing tea leaves into a spoon infuser, setting it into the glass in front of me. She pulled a small honey pot from one of the cabinets and set it beside the glass. The kettle whistled, and she hurried to extinguish the flame and pour the water. I watched the orange pigment swirl through the perforations of the spoon.

My mother sat in the chair to my left.

"Daoud—that is your son?" I asked.

"Yes, praise God! After many years of barrenness, heaven finally blessed us with a child. I was already in my forties when Daoud was born. *Ya hayati, ya nouri* (my life, my light)! Such a special boy! He loves me most in all the world."

I swallowed. "And what of your first son?"

My mother scowled. "Joseph, you must understand: After my husband left, my family disowned me. Without Pierre, I would have had no home, no clothes, no society. I had nowhere to turn."

"But why did marrying Pierre require sending me away?"

She tutted her tongue on the roof of her mouth. "He did not wish to raise another man's son. He considered that Albert's responsibility."

"And what of your responsibilities?"

She raised both her hands, palms facing me. "The abbess assured me she would care for you like her own child."

"The abbess? What did she know of raising a child?"

"What did I know of it? I was a child myself! And the abbess was mother to hundreds of children."

"None of them hers. None of them Jewish. None of them boys," I muttered.

"Pierre gave me no other choice. My options were to send you to be cared for by the nuns or to be utterly destitute. Marrying Pierre was the only way for me to survive. And had I not survived, or had you and I lived together in poverty, my darling, would you be better off than you are today?"

"Sending me away was not the only way for you to survive. We would have found a way together. Instead, I was an orphan with two living parents."

My mother cast an anxious glance at the wall clock behind me. "My husband will be back in half an hour."

"The abbess was indeed the closest thing I had to a mother," I continued. "In reality, however, I raised myself. And in the end, when the abbess died, I was left in the hands of a tormentor."

She drew in her breath. "No one ever tried to contact me!"

"The abbess told me she tried to find you many times. I wrote to you, but all my letters were returned with no forwarding address."

"*Ya hayati*, how unlucky we are! How distressing to learn that you, too, have experienced pain! I have suffered terrible indignities over the years!"

We sat in silence, the glass of tea dark between us.

"Did you ever try to contact the abbess?" I whispered. "Did you look for me?"

She folded her arms across her chest. "No, my sweetheart. Mother Maria Theresa and I agreed I would never do that."

I nodded. "The agreement. She told me about that agreement. It was carried out on your terms, not hers."

My mother reached out and covered my clenched fists with both hands. "Not mine. My husband's."

"What is the distinction?"

Her eyes darted again toward the wall clock. "Pierre will be back soon."

"After all these years, and after everything I have been through," I hissed, "do you believe your husband retains the power to banish me from this house? Instead of leaving, it would be simple enough for me to stay and take his life in payment for all that was taken from me."

She shook her head. "A man has the right to determine who may live in his own house, Joseph."

"Do his preferences outweigh his wife's obligations toward her child?"

"My soul! Do not disparage your mother so! I placed you in good hands—a bed to sleep in, food on the table, an education! Better conditions than you would ever find under Pierre's roof, believe me. I persuaded Albert to make a generous donation to the convent. I hoped that with this foundation, you would become a successful, even a happy man, despite the inconveniences."

"*Inconveniences . . . ?*"

She furrowed her brow and wagged her finger again. "I would be very angry to learn that the sisters betrayed the trust I placed in them!"

The word *trust* pierced me like a blade.

She returned to squeezing my fists, her knuckles whitening over mine. "But what else, my beloved! Have you prospered? Will you tell me what you have done all these years?"

"No, Madame. Because I cannot. And because I am unwilling."

"'Madame?'" She frowned. "Will you not call me *Maman?*"

I shook my head.

"I know you, Joseph. You were so devoted to me! The son I raised—"

"You did not raise me."

She glanced once more at the clock and seemed to come to a decision. She looked me up and down, appraising me. As Fadi Amin, there was nothing about my appearance that implied more than a modest income. My mother spoke again, this time more urgently. "For years, I have prayed for an opportunity to start a new life in a different place. God has answered my prayers by sending you to us precisely at this moment." She caressed my hands. "You must find a way to help us. Daoud and I need funds only for two tickets abroad and an additional small amount to establish ourselves there. Pierre mustn't find out. He is a jealous man, but you needn't worry about him. Once we are gone, he will find another woman to cook his meals and mend his clothes. We need nothing extravagant, my sweetheart, my darling, just enough for an apartment in Paris. I know you will not forsake your mother and brother. There is compassion within you."

I glared at her. I felt no compassion at all. When I set out to observe her, I was not sure which of my many emotions would predominate. And now that I had confronted her, I discovered that everything but a core of bitterness had been stripped away. "I have to go," I muttered. "I cannot stay here any longer."

"Yes, my sweetest, you must go. Pierre will be home soon."

"What? No, this is not about Pierre . . ."

"When will I see you again?"

I felt weak. "Never."

"No, Joseph. Tell me when you will return."

"In three days' time, I will leave Lebanon and never return," I murmured.

"Joseph!"

"If you have any sense at all, you will never mention to anyone that I was here. You risk your life to do otherwise." I pulled my hands out from under hers and stood.

"Very well!" she spat. "I see that you are more like your father than I imagined! Go! Abandon me a second time!"

Anger welled within me. Hoping to calm myself, I raised the tea glass, now cooled to room temperature, and with a quaking hand, drained it in a single swallow. I brought the empty cup down on the table, not realizing until I heard the sound of shattering glass that I did so with enough force to crack it. I stared at my hands. My left palm was bleeding. I raised my eyes and scrutinized hers, searching one last time for a vestige of selflessness. Finding none, I turned to go.

"That's right! Leave us, if you refuse to help us!" she shouted. And when I hesitated, she added: "What are you waiting for? More ghosts to rise up out of your past?"

I turned to face her. "Ghosts?"

She nodded, a triumphant smile on her face. "I know something."

"What? What do you know?"

"I know there is at least one other you have deserted in your life."

"Wh-what?"

"About sixteen years ago, a young woman knocked on our door. I remember because Daoud was a newborn and sleeping in his crib. She asked if I was your mother, and—"

Suddenly, I was completely alert. "What was her name?" I demanded.

My mother recoiled in fear. "I decline to tell you. Get out!"

"Her name!" I barked.

"If I tell you, will you leave?"

"Yes! Her name!"

"It sounded foreign. Miranda? Mirabella?"

"Isabella?"

"No . . ."

"Not Isabella? Are you sure?"

"It was not Isabella. It began with an *M*. Marlena? Madeline?"

"Was it . . ." I whispered, "Mercédès?"

"Yes! That was it! Mercédès . . . Mercédès . . ."

My voice quavered. "Mercédès Mondego."

"Yes!"

"What did she look like?" And when my mother didn't answer, I gripped her right forearm in my left hand and squeezed with a menace that frightened even me. A trickle of my blood dripped down her forearm. "What did she look like?" I growled.

My mother spoke rapidly. "She was petite, pretty, about your age. She had ginger hair covered by a headscarf, but her curls were bursting out all over the sides of it."

"What did she say?"

"Joseph, you are hurting me!"

"Answer my question," I whispered, bending her arm back toward her shoulder.

"She asked if I knew where you were." My mother winced and began to rotate her body away from me to relieve the pain in her shoulder. "I said I had heard no word of you for almost twenty years, and she whispered something . . . something like, 'Now I know at last that I have lost everything.' Joseph, stop, you are hurting me! The woman ran away. I never saw her again!"

"Is that all?"

"Yes!"

"Did she say where she lives?"

"No. She said nothing more than what I told you!"

"No matter," I murmured. "I will find her." I released my mother's arm. It was smeared with the blood from my palm.

She reached for a dish towel with her left hand and began to wipe the blood from her forearm, stealing another glance at the kitchen clock. "Who is she?"

"Mercédès Mondego is a character in the book *The Count of Monte Cristo*. The lost love of Edmond Dantès." I turned toward the door.

"Joseph!" She attempted to grasp my elbow.

I shook my arm loose and exited the house.

Chapter Thirty-Four

The next day, I made another visit to the Beirut municipality building. The reference librarian's face lit up when she spotted me entering the records hall. "Mister 'Ayoun!" she exclaimed. "How nice to see you again!"

"The pleasure is all mine."

She blushed. "And thank you for the flowers. Carnations are my favorite."

"Something about you made me think so. I am happy you liked them."

"What brings you back to the library? More research?"

"Yes."

She rubbed her hands together. "Good! What can I help you with this time?"

"There is a woman who at one point resided in Sidon. She is about forty-five years old."

"Where does she live now?"

"I do not know; perhaps she is still in Sidon."

"When did she last live there?"

"The latest information I have is that she resided there with her family in 1946."

"*1946?* Twenty-seven years ago? What other information do you have?"

"Her name is . . ." I gulped. "Isabella."

"Isabella what?"

I smiled. "Isabella I-don't-know. She had red hair."

"Ah. So it is a simple matter of finding a red-haired woman whose first name is common, whose last name is unknown, and whose trail went cold twenty-seven years ago." The librarian grinned. "I believe you have overestimated my powers, Mr. 'Ayoun, and those of the reference library. This is not a wishing well." She squinted at me. "Is this related to your prior search for the European Jewish businessman and his family?"

"In truth, it is not, mademoiselle. It is . . . a side project."

"Ah. Perhaps something of personal interest?"

I looked into her eyes and found sympathy there. "Yes."

"Well, if that is the case, you must know something more about her."

"She resided in a nunnery in Bhamdoun until her return to Sidon in 1946."

"She is a Maronite? That narrows it down. The Maronites have become a small minority in Sidon in recent decades. You say she is now forty-five years old? So, she was born between 1927 and 1929?"

I nodded.

The librarian pursed her lips. "Anything else?"

"Not that I can think of."

"Birth records from Sidon are housed in the local repository, not here in Beirut."

"I know."

"Unlike our files, there is no public access to the Sidonese records."

"I know."

"Would you like me to inquire for you?"

"Yes, if you please."

Her eyes glinted. "What's in it for me?"

I smiled. "Another bouquet of carnations?"

"Hmph."

"Roses?"

"You are making some progress."

"But a moment ago, you said carnations are your favorites."

"Only when roses are not an option." She slapped her hands onto the desktop. "I will contact my colleague in Sidon. Please return the day after tomorrow, and we will see what I am able to learn."

"Thank you very kindly, mademoiselle."

At ten the following morning, I rose from my seat near the back of a bus and tugged the cord that ran atop the windows. A bell sounded near the driver, and he pulled over near the main square in Bhamdoun. I had passed through the village at least fifty times traveling to and from Damascus before closing the Cedars Trading office in Syria. Though it is located only twenty kilometers east of Beirut along the Beirut-Damascus road, I had never stopped there since returning to Lebanon. My promise to Shmuel Mizrahi forbade me from visiting the town where I had spent half my childhood.

Alighting onto Bhamdoun's pavement for the first time in nearly three decades, a sensation, like a mournful whisper, passed through me. I looked down. Arising from the grass at the edge of the sidewalk by my feet was a cluster of white wildflowers.

I closed my eyes.

Twenty-eight years earlier, Dr. al-Moualem had taken me on an excursion to collect herbs for his apothecary. We passed this very spot on our way to the open fields outside town. He noticed something and moved forward a few paces to kneel by a group of white blossoms near the road, summoning me with his index finger. A large yellow-and-black-striped butterfly flaunted its wings on the flowers. "The plant is called *Saxifraga*," he whispered. "It is used to treat kidney stones. And the butterfly is the *Papilio alexanor maccabaeus*, known to the English as the tiger swallowtail. It is very rare. The mountains of Lebanon are among the richest in the world for butterfly migration, as we are a land bridge between Africa, Asia, and Europe. This butterfly has returned from a very great distance to lay her eggs. Shortly after doing so, she will die." I held my breath alongside the doctor until the creature fluttered off.

Back in the present, I opened my eyes, shouldered my bag, and walked toward the convent. Familiar buildings lined the street, but much had changed. Automobiles, a rare sight in former days, were parked outside many of the structures, though they lagged behind the latest models by about a decade. Illuminated signs glowered above storefronts, and television antennas sprouted on rooftops. Yet Arabic music still wailed through the open doors of shops. Children still ran in the alleys, playing football. Clothes and sheets still hung to dry on lines suspended between balconies.

I climbed the incline on newly laid asphalt and paused at a spot a few hundred meters before the last curve in the road. The convent lay unseen beyond. I faced south, easily spotting the goat path that had carried me into the backcountry all those years before, the night I made my escape. Unfocusing my eyes, I imagined the shadow of a boy rushing along the trail, a red glow behind him, his future winding north and east and south and west, then east again.

I rounded the curve, approached the gate, and stopped. The wrought-iron fence was just as it had been the day I had arrived at the compound at the age of eight, when the old abbess shuffled down the ancient stone steps and ushered me inside. A shiny plaque identified the site as the Maronite Mission of the Sisters of Lebanon. But there was no lock on the gate, and the three-story edifice of hewn limestone that had been my home for more than seven years . . . was gone. In its stead was a squat, gray building made of poured concrete. It was a structure that seemed incapable of sustaining memories.

A sign above the entryway read, "Administration–Chapel." Like a queen bee surrounded by attendants, this building stood at the head of a semicircle of barracks, which I presumed were dormitories for the sisters. To the left was a one-story structure labeled, simply, *School*. The insane asylum and its surrounding wall were no more.

I pushed on the gate, and it swung open, whispering on its hinges. Walking through the open door of the administration building, I followed signs pointing toward the office.

A pretty woman of approximately twenty-five years raised her head from the desk and smiled when I peeked in at the open threshold. A beige scarf covered most of her dark hair. She had striking blue eyes, deep-set in porcelain cheeks. Directly behind her was a closed door, which a plaque identified as the office of the Mother Superior.

"*Salaam aleikum*," she said. "I am Magdalena."

I stared.

She cocked her head, and her smile broadened. "*Salaam aleikum*," she repeated.

"*Aleikum salaam.*"

"Ah. So you speak after all."

Echoes and murmurs of the past.

Finally, I found words. "Excuse me. Where is the convent that used to stand here?"

"It *is* standing here. Where *you* are standing and I am sitting."

"No, no. The former facility. An older structure."

"Oh, you must mean the building that was destroyed in 1946." She passed her arm in an arc around her. "As you can see, we have rebuilt."

"Destroyed . . . ?"

"Yes. The building was irreparably damaged. It had to be torn down."

"What happened?"

"A fire." She gazed at me. "And who are you?"

"I . . . In my childhood, I spent time in Bhamdoun and am now revisiting some of the old places."

"Your name?"

"Oh! Forgive me. Amin. Fadi Amin."

"Hmm. I know no family here by that name."

"Our family moved away long ago. Before you were born." I cleared my throat. "Is anybody left here from former times?"

"Only one. All the rest have moved on."

"Was anybody . . . injured . . . in the fire?"

Magdalena frowned. "The former doctor of the facility is buried in our cemetery. His tombstone tells that he perished trying to save the books in the library."

The room began to shimmer around me. "The doctor . . . the library?"

Magdalena leaped from her chair. "You look pale, sir." She grasped my elbow and led me to an armchair. "Sit down. I will have someone bring you water." She picked up a bell from her desk and rang. I closed my eyes and leaned my head back.

Within seconds, a youthful female voice sounded by the door. "Is something needed?"

"Please bring a glass of water," the secretary ordered. "Make haste."

A few minutes later, a novice returned with the water and a wet washcloth, which she prepared to place on my forehead. I was concerned she might dislodge my wig, so I took the rag from her and wiped my cheeks and brow, and sipping the water, recovered quickly.

"Thank you," I said to Magdalena. "I am well."

She gave a bright smile and nodded at the novice, who curtsied and departed.

"How long have you lived here at the convent?" I inquired.

"As long as I can remember."

I raised an eyebrow.

"I was deposited here as a newborn a few months after the fire, while the facility was being reconstructed. My parents have never been identified. The Mother Superior took me in."

"That is an interesting coincidence, mademoiselle: Your life began at the same moment the convent was reborn."

She nodded. "I have often reflected on that fact myself. If one were inclined toward symbolism, one might find a message of hope in it."

"Yes," I mused. "And a cynic might search for a more practical link between the two events." Magdalena's smile faded. I shook my head. "I apologize, Magdalena. You are not a cynic. And my experiences over the years have tarnished my idealism. Please forgive me."

"Of course you are forgiven, though you have done nothing wrong."

I paused before speaking again. "Who gave you the name *Magdalena*?"

"My benefactress, the Mother Superior."

"You have been here your whole life?"

Magdalena nodded. "The abbess has been most generous in providing me a home, an education, and now, employment."

"Do you not wish to see the world?"

Magdalena's eyes appeared unfocused for an instant, and then she smiled at me. "The Mother Superior prefers to have me nearby." She shrugged. "She tells me I am indispensable."

"You provide unique services to the convent?" I asked.

"I do not think so. Anyone could do my job, sir."

"I see."

Suddenly, a voice issued from an intercom positioned on the secretary's desk. It hissed, like water thrown on embers, and it was unmistakable. "Magdalena! What is happening? Who is there?" An almost-painful thrill ran through me at the memory of hearing that voice for the first time, when I had been summoned to the new abbess's office the morning after her arrival at the convent. I recalled my astonishment that such a rasp might issue from so flawless a visage, and I was struck again, just as I had been all those years ago, by my recollection of the contrast with the craggy complexion and melodious voice of the old abbess.

"It's the Mother Superior," the secretary whispered, a troubled look on her face. "Please wait here."

She hurried toward the inner office, cracked the door open, and slipped through.

A short time later, the secretary emerged, shutting the door behind her. "The Reverend Mother wishes to meet with you," she whispered.

"There is no need to disturb her," I answered. "I am quite well now. I was shocked to hear of the terrible history of the institution, of which I was previously unaware."

"Nonetheless, she requests to meet you. She always wants to greet those who step through our gate. Besides, she is curious to learn more about you. She, too, does not recognize your family name." When she saw me hesitate, Magdalena frowned. "To be honest, Monsieur Amin, it will be more difficult for me if I fail to persuade you to come into the office."

"Very well." I sighed, rising. "Lead on."

"Thank you. One thing for you to know . . ."

"Yes?" I prompted, when she paused before opening the door.

She whispered, and I leaned in to hear her. "The Mother Superior is blind."

Magdalena knocked twice and pushed open the door to the inner chamber. "Mister Fadi Amin," she announced. "And this," she declared, stepping aside, "is our Mother Superior, the Reverend Abbess Maria Constanta." Magdalena exited the room and shut the door.

Hesitatingly, like the schoolboy I once was, I crept into the office. How often had I been summoned to the old abbess's chambers, an orphan in need of gentle chastisement or guidance? It had been a refuge to me until the arrival of the new abbess, when it became the place from which my life careened off course.

The office preserved none of its predecessor's warmth. Shades were pulled over the single window behind the desk, casting the space into gloom. Two straight-backed visitor's chairs were set opposite the abbess's table. No children's artwork was arrayed on the desk and walls. The sole ornament was a crucifix affixed to the wall on the abbess's right. To her left stood a single bookcase with four sparsely populated shelves.

Behind the large cedar desk, shrouded by a black habit and headdress, sat the abbess. I inhaled sharply.

Her once-alabaster complexion was wrinkled and worn on the right side of her face; the other shone with the cicatrix of scalded flesh. A band of contracted skin along her cheek pulled the left side of her face into an unnatural scowl, her brow drawn downward and the corner of her mouth angled up. Her irises, once a piercing blue, now peered through filmy corneas, like faded reproductions of an original. She glowered, unblinking, in my direction. Just as in the old days, I felt as though I were being examined and had been found wanting.

"*Sabah al-khair* (good morning)," she said without warmth, her voice even harsher than it had been in my youth, the effects of age and conflagration.

After a pause, I was able to issue a response. "*Ya'atik al 'afiya* (may God give you health)."

"Hah!" she scoffed. "It is too late for that, as you perceive with your own eyes. But God gives what He sees fit to give."

I knew not what to say, so I simply nodded, which, of course, she did not observe.

"You are speechless." She exhaled. "Many a time, sitting at this desk, I have heard that gasp that escaped you a moment ago."

"I apologize if I offended you, madame. Your secretary told me that you are blind. But she did not inform me that you were burned in the fire that destroyed the former facility. I was unprepared." I could not detach my gaze from the unnatural sheen of her left cheek.

"Perhaps I should be grateful that I cannot look upon myself in the mirror and suffer the same shock every day as you did a moment ago." She shifted in her chair. "When our Lord returns, I may learn more about the sin for which I have paid this price."

"I was taught in my school days that we are birthed into sin. Before a newborn baby acquires its first breath, it is already tainted with sin."

"Very true. It appears you have had a Catholic education."

"I did. As a child. But I left all that behind. May I sit down?"

She gestured toward one of the two chairs opposite her desk. "You do not believe in sin?" she inquired. The right side of her face rose, while the scarred left remained fixed.

"On the contrary, I have learned that iniquity is ever-present in life."

"Ah. You and I are of one mind on this topic."

"I doubt it. I suspect we have very different views on sin and repentance."

She dabbed with a lace handkerchief at a pool of spittle that formed at the left corner of her mouth. "We have just met each other," her voice chafed, "and yet you presume to know my views on sin and repentance."

"A moment ago, you presumed to know mine."

After sitting in silence a while, I spoke. "I see you have some books here."

"You are fond of books, Mr. Amin?"

"Very much."

"*Marhaban*," she said, sweeping her left arm in the direction of the bookcase.

I got up and walked toward the modest collection. It comprised mostly bibles, theological texts, collected letters of the Maronite Patriarch of Antioch and similar works. One volume in particular interested me. I removed it from its perch and settled back into my chair, the book nestled in my lap. "Where do your books come from?" I asked.

"We use our meager funds to stock the library, which is housed in a separate room near our chapel. Here, in my office, I keep only a few essential texts. By necessity, our collection is limited to practical works in support of our mission. The tender minds of our residents are better off without the more . . . advanced . . . material that formerly resided on our shelves. We used to have a vast library, but our books were destroyed in the fire twenty-seven years ago."

I ran my finger along the spine of the volume I held in my lap, its title stirring the embers of memory. My breath quickened as I felt a small area of unevenness in the binding, the size and shape of a key. I had a strange sensation, as though the key were vibrating beneath my touch. And then, a bolt of energy seemed to leap from the book and course through me, dislodging my consciousness and sending it hurtling on a torrent of wind and fire through dim labyrinths in my mind. Scenes from my past, fractured images and disembodied voices, shadows and patches of light, raced past too rapidly to discern what and who they were.

I closed my eyes, forcing my breath into a slow rhythm. The cataract in my mind began to decelerate, and by degrees the milestones passing by took form: nightmares shedding their veils, memories shimmering through a mist before coalescing into almost-recognizable shapes. Then, suddenly, all movement stopped, and the unknowns of my life snapped into focus. I understood everything with a near-blinding clarity.

I realized the abbess had been speaking, and with a shudder recovered myself sufficiently to ask a question. "All your books were destroyed in the fire?"

She glared at me through her clouded eyes, perhaps offended that I had drifted off. "Yes," she said with irritation in her voice. "As I have told you. Not a single one remains. The entire library, the hymnals and prayer books in our chapel, and the volumes that were housed in my office."

"A shame."

"It is worse than that. Aside from my own injuries, the fire took the life of our doctor, who died trying to save the library from the flames."

"Yes, your . . . secretary . . . informed me. Truly a tragedy. What caused the fire?"

"A wicked child was housed here, a Jew, abandoned by his parents and left to the charity of the church. A troubled boy from birth, he repaid our generosity one night by setting fire to my office, the library, and the chapel before running away."

"Why did he do that?"

She scowled. "Evil does for evil's sake, monsieur. It requires no other reason."

"Yes." I sighed. "So it seems. Did you lose your sight in the fire?"

The abbess caught her breath, no doubt deeming my question impertinent, yet she answered. "My eyesight began to fade on that day, but I lost my vision completely over the course of the next two or three years."

"How do you read your books if you are blind?"

"Magdalena reads to me when the workday is done."

"She is a devoted assistant, clearly. She tells me you raised her from infancy."

"Yes. I have no doubt she was born into disgrace and sin. But the church does not judge. We only serve."

I could not shift my eyes from the ruined left side of the abbess's face. "Do you not think that perhaps the sin into which Magdalena was born has stained her soul? That she cannot be redeemed?"

The abbess's mouth hardened. "As I said, the church does not judge."

"But are not some people wicked to the core? Are they not beyond salvation?"

"I do believe such people exist, but they are rare. And Magdalena certainly is not among them."

"No doubt," I murmured. "She radiates goodness. Do you not find it strange that such virtue might be born of wickedness?"

She dabbed with the cloth at the left corner of her mouth. "What makes you think that Magdalena was born of wickedness?"

"Oh, pardon me, Reverend Abbess. I must have misinterpreted your statement that she was born of sin." After a pause, I spoke again: "Can you see anything at all?"

I shifted quietly to my right, and she tracked my movement, squinting. "I see shadows," she rasped. "But when one loses one's eyes, one acquires the ability to see in other ways."

"I suspect you do not yet see me in my entirety," I murmured. "Perhaps you will before I leave the room." I shifted back to the center of my seat, and she followed the motion.

The abbess scowled. "We were speaking earlier of sin and redemption. Do you have something you wish to confess?"

"Yes."

Her right cheek rose, baring the teeth on that side. "I commend you. Many people cannot identify their own needs, even as their souls cry out for forgiveness."

"Very true." I cleared my throat. "If I tell you of my transgressions, will you receive my confession?"

"Normally, that is the role of a priest. Would you like me to find a priest for you?"

"No. I wish to confess to you. Do you consider yourself sufficiently free from sin to receive my confession?"

"Do you not consider it disrespectful to ask a nun and leader of a convent such a question?" she scolded, her croak rising in pitch. "Most people come to me for help examining their own consciences, not to probe mine." I did not answer, and she leaned back in her chair. "At any rate, freedom from sin is not a requirement to receive confession. If it were, no one could receive confession."

"I see. But does the nature of one's sin matter? May a thief receive confession from an impostor?"

She scowled again. "The answer is yes, if the receiver of confession has repented their crimes. But why do you raise that example?"

"I am an impostor."

"You may be, but I am not a thief."

"But if you *were* a thief, might you receive my confession?"

"Again, monsieur, I am no thief. I have tried to live a blameless life. No doubt, I have failed from time to time."

"I have failed many times," I retorted. "As recently as fifteen minutes ago, I learned of four things that were taken as a result of my actions."

"What are the four items you took?"

"I did not take them."

"What do you mean? Did you not just say you took four things?"

"Ah. I am speaking incoherently. Four things were taken. I was unaware of these losses until a few minutes ago. When I first learned of them, I thought I was responsible and was nearly incapacitated with guilt. But then, almost immediately, I discovered that the blame belongs to another."

Her breath quickened. "What are the four things that were taken?"

"A life. An institution. A library. And the eyesight of a wicked person."

"You dare call me wicked, Monsieur"—she spat out the name—"Friedmann!"

"Ah. So, you see me after all. How did you recognize me? By my voice?"

She shook her head. "By your insolence. By your insincerity. By the evil that emanates from you."

"I perceive that not even the passage of decades has softened your opinion of me."

"Softened? Every day solidifies it! And now, after twenty-seven years, you return to mock me, unremorseful for the pain and destruction you have wrought."

"I mock no one. But it is strange how understanding can turn in a moment, is it not? After a lifetime of uncertainty, of self-recrimination, of seeking to redeem myself, I find the key is right here, in the most unexpected of places. At last, I see everything. I know who bears the guilt for the devastation that occurred in this place and in my life."

"Who bears the guilt, you evil man?"

"You, of course," I snapped. "Through your zealotry. Your selfishness. Your hypocrisy. Your baseless hatred."

"I will suffer no more of this! Leave my office at once!" Her hand reached out for the intercom on her desk.

"It is better if you do not summon Magdalena," I interjected. "I know who she is."

The abbess hesitated, her finger above the button.

"I will leave," I said calmly. "But first, I wish to have a few more words with you."

"Say what you like. The moment you depart this office, I will call the police."

"You will not."

"Why not? Do you intend to take my life in addition to my sight?"

"No. I wish I had the certainty in my own merit to take your life. I once killed a man who was even more despicable than you. I have never recovered from it. God will need to find a different instrument if that is His plan for you."

"So, why would I not call the police?"

"Because of your crimes."

"*Crimes?*" She scoffed, and again dabbed at the left corner of her mouth with the lace handkerchief. "What crimes?"

"The crime of castrating dozens of men."

"Castration of murderers and rapists? That was no crime. Wickedness was diminished in the world by having those men castrated."

"The crime of castrating a fifteen-year-old boy."

"Another rapist. Besides, I did not perform those procedures. The doctor did. And there is no record of any of it. All was lost in the fire."

"Ah. The fire. The doctor. Let us then add the crimes of arson and murder."

She sputtered. "What . . . what . . . are you talking about?"

"I am holding one of your books in my lap, Reverend Abbess. Can you guess which one it is? I shall give you a hint: One page is missing, and that page has confessed all your sins to me."

Her eyes narrowed.

"Ah. I perceive you know the answer. *The Count of Monte Cristo.* A strange exception to your rule of permitting only works of religious orthodoxy to reside on your shelves. The only artifact still in existence from the small number of items I kept in my room here at the convent."

The right side of the abbess's face contorted in anger, exposing her teeth. A stream of spittle ran from the left corner of her mouth.

"For the first time in my life, I see the truth in its entirety," I continued. "What did you do with the missing page? The page in which Edmond Dantès names himself an avenger of the wicked? The page I tore from the book and tied to a rock I threw through your window the night of the fire. Where is it?"

The abbess clenched her fists and writhed in her chair.

"No matter," I continued. "It is the absence of the page that condemns you. Let us move on to the topic of fire. The fire I set in your office—in your office and nowhere else, as both you and I know—was the lesser of the two for which I was responsible. That blaze was nothing compared to the conflagration in your soul, the loathing that ignited your anger beyond reason.

"In your rage at being bested by a child, a Jew, you determined to quench the fire within you by burning everything to the ground. You took the leftover kerosene I had placed a safe distance from the convent. You set fire to the library, the thing you knew was most precious to me in the world after Isabella. And for good measure, you set fire to your own chapel. Then you roused the doctor, drunk and confused, and sent him to his death by telling him I was in the library trying to save the books."

"You are mad."

"You are a murderer." I rose to stand opposite her at the desk. "You murdered a good man to conceal your own crimes. You were the only person with the key. How do you explain that the library was unlocked—that anyone other than yourself could enter it, whether to set it on fire or to save it?"

"I need not explain anything to you!" she spat.

"But where is the key? Where is the key that proves you are an arsonist and a murderer?"

"Get out of my office!" the abbess screeched.

I opened the book at its midpoint and, grasping one half in either hand, ripped it in two along its spine. A key fell out of the space in which it had been secreted, clattering onto the desk.

The abbess's hand shot out toward the sound.

"Too late. It is already in my grasp," I said. Angling the key toward the faint light from the window, I murmured, "Even in the darkness into which you have cast both this room and the past, the etching is visible: *Library*."

A howl escaped her, like that of a baying hound. Magdalena entered hurriedly from the outer office.

"Mother Superior—"

"Leave us!" the abbess screamed. The secretary retreated and shut the door.

"And finally, though it is not the worst of what you have done, there is the crime of rape."

"*Rape?*" She shrieked the word.

I pressed on, leaning across the desk and speaking centimeters from the abbess's face. "God took your eyes, not I, for a sin you were unable to resist and unwilling to acknowledge. Memory has returned to me, and with it, understanding. I was always mystified by the vehemence of your animosity toward me. It seemed impossible to attribute only to Jew-hatred. I now see it for what it really was: retribution for awakening your lust. Your loathing was ignited not because I was a Jew, but because I was the source of a poison you discovered within yourself: physical attraction to a child. Isabella had succumbed to the same desire, but with a full and generous heart. That heart, beating with innocence, the unpolluted echo of your perversion, drove you mad for vengeance."

The right side of the abbess's face rose, a beastly snarl. The left retained its glossy impassivity.

"But finding that your lust still blazed after banishing Isabella, you tried to purge your guilt by inflicting corporal punishment on me. If I were emasculated, you said to yourself, perhaps your desire would be quenched.

"Yet even that would not satisfy you. The night you sent Isabella away in disgrace, just before you ordered the doctor to castrate me, you drugged me in my sleep. You allowed me to emerge partially from anesthesia, just enough to have a dim awareness, sufficient for a lifetime of shame, of what you were doing. Just enough for me to respond while you . . . stimulated me with your hands. Until a few moments ago, I thought my nightmares were the result of my own depravity, the delirium of a traumatized mind. You mounted"—I swallowed—"and raped me. You then summoned the doctor to take me to the infirmary for the operation. And you carried away from my room an incriminating souvenir, the copy of *The Count of Monte Cristo* Isabella had taken from the library and given to me. The book from which I had already torn out a single page. You took the book, and later, after setting fire to the library, hid the key in its spine, where you believed no one would ever find it."

The abbess spat in my face.

I slapped her across her mutilated cheek.

"Satan incarnate!" she screeched. "Thus do you come back from the depths of time to haunt me!"

"One more thing before I leave," I said, straightening. "You will free your daughter, Magdalena, from her servitude to you."

She emitted an inarticulate scream.

"Yes, your daughter. You concealed your pregnancy and used the opportunity, while the convent was being razed and rebuilt, to have your baby in secret elsewhere. You returned here, claiming in your cowardice and selfishness that the sin into which she was born was someone else's and not yours. You then kept her captive for the last twenty-seven years."

"How dare you accuse me—me! The leader of a religious institution!—of concealing a pregnancy! How could I possibly achieve such a deception?"

"Let us stop pretending. My own mother concealed her pregnancy, even from herself, not to mention all the people around her. A person of your malice and cunning could do it easily."

Apprehension took the place of defiance on the abbess's features. I saw the fear and hatred in her eyes, and was struck by the irony that those orbs, now useless to her as instruments of vision, gave me such a clear view into her thoughts.

"You will set your daughter free. I do not intend to correct Magdalena's misunderstanding of her origins. She has already suffered enough. I presume you will continue to do the same. I will fund Magdalena's education at the American University of Beirut. If I do not see her name in the university student roster by October of this year, or if I perceive even the slightest indication of you reporting me to the authorities, a letter detailing your crimes will be delivered to the office of the Patriarch of Antioch, with copies to the police station in Bhamdoun and the *Al Akhbar* newspaper."

The abbess ground her eyes shut and slapped the table repeatedly with her hands. The right side of her mouth writhed.

"My connections in Lebanon are very wide and deep," I lied. I had lost all my influence since going underground. "The allegations alone, even without a full investigation, would be sufficient to lay ruin to your life."

"Devil!" she screamed as I walked toward the door.

"Whore," I hissed, without turning around.

I exited the office and shut the door behind me. Magdalena sat at the desk wringing her hands. "Magdalena," I said softly, "the abbess requires some time to herself. I have upset her, but I assure you she is otherwise just the same as always. Please do not disturb her for half an hour. At the end of that period, you may enter with a glass of water."

Magdalena raised her brows. "What—"

"I can tell you no more, and I expect the abbess not to reveal what she and I discussed. It is a private matter."

"But—"

"I am sorry, Magdalena. I can say no more."

She sighed. "Will we be seeing you again, Monsieur Amin?"

"No. But you may receive a letter from me. It will be addressed to you, and it is for you alone to open."

Magdalena nodded.

"Thank you for your kindness to me when I was feeling unwell. I will see myself out."

I exited the building and walked to the cemetery. Graves dotted the hillside. I found the doctor's flat tombstone. Stooping to wipe off the dirt with the palm of my hand, I unveiled the inscription: *Doctor Ismail al-Moualem, December 5, 1898–June 10, 1946. He served our community faithfully and perished trying to save our library from fire.* "I am sorry, Dr. al-Moualem," I whispered. "Neither of us escaped our past."

I gathered three pebbles from the ground and put them on his stone in the Jewish fashion. "*Ma'a salaame* (go in peace)," I muttered.

From the doctor's grave I walked the short distance to the top of the hillock, where the old abbess's marker stood. A stone statue of the Virgin Mary knelt at its base. A Maronite cross rose above the tomb, its single vertical stem intersected by three horizontal bars, a representation of both the Trinity and the cedar tree of Lebanon. The marble surface of the tomb bore an inscription: *Sister Maria*

Theresa, January 8, 1862–April 15, 1944, Beloved Mother Superior, Daughter of Lebanon, Lover of Creation. "He leadeth me in the path of righteousness for His name's sake."

I knelt and lowered my forehead onto the palm of my right hand. "The mother who cared for me when my real mother would not," I whispered. "You gave me everything you had to give. If I have betrayed your faith, please forgive me. My life has been extraordinary, just as you anticipated. I hope that does not sound too arrogant. But I am broken. Even you cannot heal me." I kissed my fingers and touched them to the name etched in stone.

I stood and brushed the dust off my pants. "One more task before leaving Lebanon for the last time," I muttered.

Chapter Thirty-Five

I was waiting at the entrance to the municipality building in Beirut the following morning when a security guard unlocked the door. Cradling a vase crowded with two dozen roses, I approached the reference librarian's desk.

Mademoiselle Chahine smiled. "I see you are impatient to get the information you requested, Mr. 'Ayoun."

I nodded.

"For whom are the flowers?"

I was perplexed. "For you, of course."

"And yet I perceive that in your heart, they are intended for another. Is that not the case?"

"They are intended exactly for you, and I give them to you with genuine admiration." Her face brightened. "And yet, if you mean to suggest that my heart belongs to someone else, you are correct."

Her countenance darkened. "Always the same story. Or worse."

"If it helps, I will tell you that my heart has been hers for almost thirty-five years. There has never been another."

"That is very nice for her. It helps me not at all."

"Perhaps in a different world, Mademoiselle Chahine."

She gave a sad smile. "But I live only in this world, Mister 'Ayoun." She took the vase from me and set it down in a corner of her desk. "Would you like to know what I have learned?"

I nodded.

She sighed. "I left a message for my colleague in Sidon shortly after I saw you two days ago and received her return call yesterday afternoon. She had no difficulty identifying the person you seek despite the scant particulars I provided. In fact, she knows the family personally. My information comes from my colleague's direct familiarity with the events."

I waited.

"Her name is Isabella Elias. She has never been married." Mademoiselle Chahine paused. "It appears that Isabella has had an unfortunate life."

The space behind my eyes began to throb.

"She is the eldest of seven children, and at a young age was sent to the convent in Bhamdoun to serve as a *bride of Christ*, as I believe is the phrase. She returned under a cloud of disgrace just before she was to be accepted into the order of nuns. A child was born about six months later. Name of…" The librarian scanned the notes on the index card she held in her left hand, and I trembled. "Yusouf."

The ache in back of my eyes gave way, like a dam bursting, and tears flooded out. Mademoiselle Chahine plucked a tissue from the pack on her desk and handed it to me. "Please come into the back room," she said. "We have a small kitchen there. I will make some tea." She reached into her drawer and withdrew the "Away" tabletop sign, propping it on the counter.

I passed through the swinging gate and followed Mademoiselle Chahine through the rear door, finding myself in a kitchenette with a sink, a small stove, and a round table surrounded by three plastic chairs. I sat. She boiled some water, packed tea into an infuser, and poured. I stared through the glass as the tea bled into the water.

She took the chair opposite me.

"Isabella refused to conceal her pregnancy or give the baby up for adoption. The birth of this child was certain to cast the family into disrepute. Her parents disowned her, and when that proved insufficient to salvage their reputation, they moved away."

I ground my teeth.

"Mister 'Ayoun," the librarian scolded, "surely you know that in that time and place, they had no other option. The futures of their other daughters were at stake. They would have been tainted for life by their association with Isabella. The family relocated initially to Beirut, and my colleague heard they may have emigrated from there to France."

Mademoiselle Chahine scrutinized me. She seemed to anticipate my questions and, mercifully, shortened the interval to delivering answers. "Isabella stayed behind in Sidon." I exhaled, not realizing until that moment that I had been holding my breath. "She secured a small shack on the edge of town, where she subsisted by cleaning houses and doing laundry for several of the wealthier Muslim families in the area. But poverty was ever her lot.

"The child Yusouf was, by all accounts, the delight of his mother's life. He was a bright boy, extraordinarily good-looking and clever, and popular among his peers, despite his parentage. They say the smile never left his lips."

"How like his mother and unlike his father," I murmured. I am not sure Mademoiselle Chahine heard me.

"And here, Mr. 'Ayoun, I have some sad news to report."

I pleaded in silence, my fists clenching and unclenching on the tabletop.

"One day, when he was eleven years old, Yusouf and his friends went to swim in the Mediterranean after school. One of the other boys ran first into the water and was swept away by a riptide. The children watched in horror as the boy struggled and was drawn beneath the waves. Before any of the other children knew what was happening, Yusouf, a strong swimmer, ran into the surf to save the drowning boy. They reported that within seconds, the current had drawn Yusouf a hundred meters out from shore. He dove, emerged a short time later supporting the other child with a hand across his chest, and a few seconds after that, both boys disappeared beneath the surface."

"Please," I whispered. "Please . . ."

"Neither was ever seen alive again."

I covered my face in my hands and, resting my elbows on the table, shook with agony.

Mademoiselle Chahine placed a hand on my upper arm and gave a light squeeze. She waited a few minutes, then added, "The bodies floated to the surface the following day, two kilometers south of where they were lost. They were picked up by local fishermen and returned to their parents. The second boy's family paid for Yusouf's funeral, as Isabella had neither the funds, nor the connections, nor the emotional strength to arrange for his burial.

"So beloved had she and her son become over the years that the whole community, both Muslim and Christian, came out to support Isabella. The neighbor women took turns staying in her shack. She neither spoke nor moved unless someone led her by the hand, and she did not eat unless someone fed her like a baby. A collection was begun, sufficient funds for her to live for six months without working. My Sidonian colleague's mother was a member of this group of supporters.

"Isabella was undone by the tragedy. Although she took the money, it was discovered later that she donated all of it to the convent in Bhamdoun. About a week afterward, she disappeared, and the neighbors feared she had done away with herself. To their surprise, she returned a few days later. She resumed her life, but was forever melancholy and alone. She continues to clean houses and wash laundry, and still lives in the shack on the edge of town. My associate describes her as nature's saddest and loveliest creation."

Tears filled Mademoiselle Chahine's eyes, and she dabbed at them with a handkerchief she withdrew from her sleeve. She grasped the index card she still held in her left hand with the fingertips of her right and laid it aside, revealing a second card beneath the first. She set the second card onto the surface of the table and slid it forward with one finger. "Here," she said, "is the address."

I clasped both her hands in mine and held them to my lips for a long while. "Thank you for your kindness."

Chapter Thirty-Six

Stepping out into the street, I glanced at my watch. I had about an hour before the 11:05 a.m. bus departed from Beirut to Sidon. I rushed to the local post office and made an international call to Geneva, paying in cash. From there, I ran to the station, purchased a ticket and a local map of Sidon, and boarded the bus just as the doors were closing.

We traveled the coastal route south, a trip of only forty-five kilometers. After what seemed like hours, the city came into view, the ruins of its Crusader sea castle jutting into the Mediterranean. I had passed through Sidon several times during my sojourn in Lebanon and had always appreciated the town's quiet repose. Now, it seemed to me that the earth beneath the city heaved as though it were aboil.

Sidon was once a great metropolis of ancient Phoenicia. It had endured the usual procession of conquerors. Assyrians, Babylonians, Egyptians, Persians, Greeks, Romans, Byzantines, Arabs, Crusaders, Ayyubids, Mongols, French, and British all occupied Sidon before Lebanon gained its independence in 1943. And in 1973, as I traveled south toward Isabella, the region once again stood on the verge of chaos. Palestinian militias were amassing in south Lebanon, and a battle for supremacy against Christian forces—the Lebanese Civil War—was about to begin. But for the time being, a middle-aged man might journey alone with a reasonable expectation of staying out of trouble.

As we entered the northern outskirts of the city, I rose to pull the cord. The driver veered to the side of the road and stopped. I descended the steps.

The April sun beat down from a cloudless sky. I ran the four hundred meters toward Isabella's hovel, which was set about eighty meters from the nearest other structure. "Isabella!" I began to call under my breath as I approached.

And suddenly, I stood before a small yard planted with spring flowers and vegetables. I strode toward the shack, its trim doorframe painted green, and pounded. After a few seconds, I could wait no longer and tried the latch. The door was unlocked, and I entered the one-room dwelling.

A cot, neatly made, stood in one corner. On a nightstand next to the bed was a half-used candle, wax droplets congealed along its side, and beside it a closed book. A plywood cabinet stood along a wall, its doors shut. There was a small food preparation area, with an icebox standing next to a stainless-steel sink, and a plastic vat with a spigot perched on a shelf above it. Large, round aluminum bins were stacked on the floor in another corner, adjacent to a stove with several burners and shelves stocked with cleaning and laundering supplies. A tiny writing desk was positioned against the only available wall space, adjacent to the laundry area. About fifteen thin volumes stood sentry on the rear edge of the desk, supported on either side by makeshift bookends—lacquered conches. I extracted one of the volumes. It was a diary, written in a cramped yet flowing Arabic script. I closed the book without examining it further and repositioned it among its mates.

Returning to the entryway, I stepped outside.

And then, I saw her. She was approaching from the south, a large sack slung over her right shoulder. She wore a peasant's blouse and a dark ankle-length skirt. Her head was covered with a blue scarf. Ginger curls erupted at both temples.

She was the most beautiful thing I had ever seen.

I ran toward her, arresting myself when I was three meters away. She stared at me, a quizzical look on her face. There was no fear in her eyes, only curiosity at encountering what must have seemed to her a madman.

Tears began streaming down my face.

The gray of Isabella's irises deepened.

I nodded.

"You cannot be . . ." she murmured.

"Oh, never mind my gray hair." I sobbed. "It is Joseph."

"But . . . I thought you were dead."

"I was." I strode forward, took the sack from her, and laid it on the ground. And then I threw my arms about her and buried my face in her neck. "Until this very moment."

She returned my embrace, at first tentatively, then with increasing pressure. I felt her quaking under my grasp. *Isabella is weeping*, I said to myself. But then she started to giggle. "Joseph, you must stop now, your moustache is tickling me!"

"*What?*" I exclaimed and leaned back to look at her. Tears brimmed over her lower lids, and she was laughing. "I don't care," I said, and thrust my chin back into her neck.

She gave a little scream, then shrieked, "Joseph, the neighbors! Someone will see us!"

"I do not care."

She pulled herself away. "Nor do I." She hurled herself into my arms and smothered my face with kisses.

We embraced in the sun a few minutes more. "Let's go back to the house," she said. I picked up the sack, and we walked side by side to her hut. I held her hand, small and callused in mine, and felt a strange sensation: I was happy.

We sat in her room for hours, talking all the while. She told me of her son, whom she acknowledged was also my son. When he drowned, it was as though the light had been extinguished from her world. She recounted her continued devotion to the church that had cast her away. She confessed to years of regret for compelling me to not seek her out.

"About a week after Yusouf died, I went in search of you. It wasn't difficult to find your mother. My plan was to throw myself upon you, beg your forgiveness for lying about Yusouf, and implore you to take me back. When your mother told me she had not heard from you in almost twenty years, I assumed you were either dead or as good as dead, at least to me. *He must have found some other woman*, I told myself, *one with more sense than to throw away the best thing that ever happened to her.*"

"Never," I protested, taking her hands in mine. "There was only you."

"I contacted my friends at the mission," she continued. "There were rumors that something . . . terrible . . . was done to you the day I was banished. And there was a fire the following night, which they blamed on you. They said you burned down the entire compound and that the doctor died trying to save the books. That you vanished into thin air, despite a search all over the countryside."

"Isabella, did you believe it? That I set fire to the compound? That I was responsible for Dr. al-Moualem's death?"

"There was no other explanation, and yet I could not accept that you intended to cause such harm."

"I did no such harm, nor did I intend to. The abbess is responsible." I told her everything that happened that day: how, after falling asleep in my room, the abbess anesthetized me with a rag soaked in methylbenzene. That after raping me, she ordered the doctor to castrate me. That he performed a vasectomy and arranged for me to be spirited away in a taxi to the southern border. That I escaped on foot instead, first heading north to elude capture. That, before departing the convent, I set fire to the abbess's office, taking care to spare the rest of the compound. And that the abbess, in her rage, destroyed her own chapel and library and sent the doctor to his death.

Tears streamed down Isabella's cheeks as I related these details. She looked into my eyes, and I knew she saw the truth there: "I believe you."

Together we prepared a meal of rye bread, olives, and hard cheese with onions, olive oil, salt, and pepper.

"What have you been doing for twenty-seven years?" Isabella asked.

"I walked across the border to Palestine. After spending a few years in Israel, I returned to Lebanon, where I became a wealthy and influential man."

"*What?* Have you been in Lebanon all these years? And you did not contact your mother? Or me?"

"To be with you is the only thing I have ever wanted. But I was bound by two promises, the first to you, and the second to . . . another."

Her countenance clouded. "Oh? Who is this *other*?"

I smiled. "He is an Iraqi Jew."

"*He?*"

"He."

She grinned. "And who is this Iraqi Jewish man who has such a hold on you?"

"I will tell you about him and everything else that transpired after I left the convent. But not now. Isabella, you must believe me when I say it is for your own safety."

She examined my face. "Why have you come back to me now?"

"The promise to the Iraqi Jew expired last week. And when my mother informed me, two days ago, of your visit to her, I interpreted it as a voiding of my pledge to you."

"You saw your mother? How is she? Is she well?"

I shook my head. "My childish recollections deceived me all these years. She is a selfish and petty woman. I see now that she has always been so."

Isabella reached out to clasp my hand. "Now that I know the pain of losing a child, I understand how terrible one's agony must be to give a child away."

"Your goodness leads you astray, Isabella. There was no agony in my mother's abandonment of me, only self-interest."

She frowned and shook her head. "Can that be? I have difficulty imagining it. And yet . . . when I met her, she asked for money in exchange for trying to locate you."

"I am sorry. I wish I had been there when you were alone."

"No matter." She sighed. "You are here now." Her smile eclipsed the sorrow in her eyes, a vestige of the once-irrepressible joy that so enthralled me when I saw her for the first time as a child of eight.

We rose to clear the dishes. She washed. I dried.

After putting the last plate away, I turned to face her. "I must leave Lebanon. Immediately."

"What? No! Stay here! With me."

I paused. "I cannot."

She clutched my forearm with her damp hand. "Joseph, you mustn't go."

I wrapped her hands in the dish towel and dried them. "I hope to never leave your side. But I must depart this place."

"Why?"

"I am being hunted." I searched her eyes. "If you choose to do so . . . you might come with me."

The corners of her eyes creased in worry. "Joseph, what is happening?"

"The only thing I have ever wanted is to spend the rest of my life with you. But now that I have seen you again, I am prepared to exchange my future for this one afternoon. What I am unwilling to do is put *your* life in jeopardy. If I stay here and am discovered, or if I reveal to you what I have done, you will be swept up in my affairs. You will be accused as an accomplice."

She inhaled sharply. "What did you do?"

"I cannot tell you." And in response to the confusion that clouded her countenance, I hurried to add, "I acted honorably, but that is not how others see it. They will want revenge."

"Then I shall hide you here. No one will know."

"I am sorry, Isabella. The risk is too great. I may already have been seen. And you cannot conceal me forever. When I am discovered in your house, it will be seen as proof of your guilt."

Isabella looked down and wrung her hands. "My heart has been ripped from me twice," she murmured. "I could not survive it a third time."

"Will you come with me?"

"It sounds risky."

"It is."

Her gaze was at once trusting, concerned, and unwavering. "I perceive that now you have arrived at my doorstep, I am in danger regardless of what I do."

"Yes," I acknowledged. "I lacked the strength to stay away, yet I dared hope you wished for me to come. And whatever you decide to do, I promise to keep you safe."

"Not everything can be under your control, Joseph, regardless of your intent. Or your promises." She sighed. "Nevertheless, you are correct; I would have wished for you to come, whatever the risks. It is the only thing I have prayed for on my own behalf."

We sat in silence. Isabella closed her eyes and clasped her hands together while her lips moved. After a while, I whispered, "Will you come with me?"

She opened her eyes. Her mouth formed the beginning of a smile. Sweeping her arm about the room, she said, "What, and leave all this?"

I grinned. "Yes."

"But I committed to wash this load of laundry." She indicated the sack I had laid in the corner by the aluminum basin.

"And after that?"

"I have few specific plans. More laundry, perhaps. If I leave, I will need to inform the families that they must find someone else to do the work."

"You will have to do that by mail after we are gone."

"Why?"

"I will tell you later."

"More secrets to keep me safe?"

"Yes. What do you need to bring with you?"

"The clothes I am wearing. And a small box with some memories of . . ." Her eyes flooded, and she swallowed. "Yusouf."

"Do you have a passport?"

"No."

"An identification card?"

"Of course."

"Is there anyone to whom you wish to say goodbye?"

"Only to my employers."

"Will you follow where I lead?"

"Yes."

"Anywhere? Your life will never be the same."

"I am glad to hear it. I love you."

"My heart is yours," I whispered, "my sweet Mercédès."

She smiled sadly at the name. "Poor Mercédès," she whispered. "She forsook her love for Edmond, and fate never gave her a second chance. If the Lord now grants me another opportunity, I shall cherish it forever."

We held each other's hands, and I allowed myself to imagine her goodness flowing into me, diluting my guilt and anger. "We cannot risk staying here until morning," I said. "Isabella . . ."

"Joseph?"

"Do you wish to know where we are going?"

"I think I know where we are going."

"I need to leave for a short while to confirm some arrangements. If someone observed me and comes to inquire, you must tell them that I am Fadi Amin, your cousin on your mother's side. Repeat the name."

"Joseph, is this really necessary?" When I continued to stare at her, she sighed. "Fadi Amin."

"Good. We have not seen each other in over twenty years, and that is why we greeted each other so warmly when we first met outside."

She nodded.

"I will be back in ninety minutes. If I fail to return in two hours, you must forget about me."

The smile fled from Isabella's face. "What is this errand you must leave me for?"

"I need to make a phone call."

"Can making a phone call be so dangerous?"

"Yes," I answered.

She shook her head. "If you don't come back in two hours, I will set out to look for you."

"No," I protested. "I have special resources at my disposal. If I do not return, you can be certain it is because I am gone forever. There will be no way for you to help me."

"Nonetheless, that is what I will do. I have resources also. Until this afternoon, I often wished to be free from the world's burdens. I can be hurt no more, except by losing you."

I sighed. "All right, Isabella. Soon enough, people would come for you either way. Tell them the truth: that you knew me when we were young, and that you have neither seen nor heard of me for nearly thirty years. That I revealed nothing to you of my recent activities."

I kissed her on the cheek and left the shack to walk toward town.

⟷ ◉ ⟷

The call I had placed before leaving Beirut went to the Mossad field office in Geneva, a low-risk communication, given the bustle of the big city. Using a simple code, I conveyed coordinates for a helicopter pickup by the Israeli Air Force twelve kilometers east of Sidon at 2 a.m. I now needed to confirm that arrangement. The task seemed simple: Ask the local operator in Sidon to place a collect call from *Fadi* to *Moustafa* in the office in Geneva, the pair of names being the prearranged signal for *Go*. The recipient would decline the call. If she said Moustafa was away and would be back tomorrow, the rendezvous was confirmed. If she said Moustafa would return on Tuesday, the pickup had been called off.

The risk of making this telephone call from Sidon was substantial. A hypervigilance reigned throughout south Lebanon, the outcome of sectarian divisions among Shiites, Sunnis, Christians, Druze, and Palestinians and amplified by fears that Israeli spies and collaborators were everywhere. Armed PLO militiamen roamed the streets. Informants were quick to relay suspicions up a reporting chain, and rapid-response teams were activated to confront potential threats. Standing orders were to not await the results of investigation prior to eliminating perceived dangers.

Fadi Amin, a stranger to the area, would have to confirm his identity at a checkpoint at the entrance to the town center, an event likely to be included in the daily report to the regional PLO security chief. An eyewitness account of that same stranger materializing at the doorstep of Isabella Elias, a woman with almost no outside contacts for the past decade and a half, might trigger an investigation. In addition, many telephone operators were sympathizers of militant organizations. They tapped into conversations and reported suspicious interactions to the regional command, particularly for international calls. There was a possibility that the telephone number in Geneva had already been placed on a watch list. The seemingly innocuous collect call to Moustafa might bring down disaster in a dozen different ways.

I walked toward the town center, encountering a roadblock along the way. The sidewalk and street were obstructed with concrete barriers and tire spikes, forcing all vehicles and pedestrians through a passageway in the center of the road. Three unshaven young men draped in keffiyehs and shouldering Soviet-manufactured Kalashnikov assault rifles stood in the gap. I approached the checkpoint.

"Identification card," demanded one of the men.

I patted my pockets, located my wallet, and pulled out Fadi Amin's identification card.

The young man scrutinized it, holding it up to my face. "From Tripoli, eh? What are you doing in Sidon?" He handed back the card.

"Visiting my cousin."

"Where does your cousin live?"

"On the north side of town."

"What do you need in the town center?"

"To make a phone call."

He stared me in the eye, a study in intimidation. I lowered my gaze submissively. "Do you wish to make a donation to the Fund for Freedom in South Lebanon?" he drawled.

I gulped. "Of course." I pulled all the bills from my wallet, the equivalent of about four days' wages for a laborer. Fanning the money out for display, I selected half to hand over. "I wish I could afford to contribute more to your worthy cause."

"I think you can indeed afford more," the militiaman said, making a summoning motion with the fingers of his right hand. I handed over a few more bills. The militiaman spat on the ground and stepped aside.

"*Ma'a salaame*," I murmured toward the pavement, and slipped by.

I entered the post office and walked to the far side, where three pay phones were attached to the wall. I waited in line ten minutes for my turn, lifted the receiver, and dialed the operator.

"*Marhaban.*"

"I would like to make a collect call overseas."

"Number."

I provided the number.

"Who is calling?"

"Fadi calling for Moustafa."

I waited for the last clicks of the operator's rotary phone.

"*Bonjour.* Geneva Home Design. How may I help you?" asked a female voice in French.

The operator answered in French: "Collect call from Fadi to Moustafa."

There was a moment of silence on the other end. I chewed my lower lip. "Moustafa is away. He will return tomorrow."

The operator spoke to me: "The person you are calling is away and will return tomorrow. Would you like to leave a message?"

"No. No message. Thank you."

"*Ma'a salaame.*" The operator disconnected.

On my return from the post office, the guards let me through the checkpoint without comment. In my mind, a clock began to tick. I estimated it would take at least twelve hours for any intelligence received at PLO headquarters to trigger an investigation. More than enough time for Isabella and me to disappear.

I returned to Isabella's hut with dusk. "Did anyone come while I was gone?" I inquired.

"No. My laundry and I were here alone the whole time." She was nearly done with the load, and I folded as she ironed. Afterward, we laid out a light supper of bread and cheese, and drank tea. When darkness descended, I rose. "We leave in ten minutes. Put on some black clothes, a coat, and comfortable shoes, and bring your mementos."

"The dishes first."

"Dishes? We will never be back here."

"Exactly."

I grinned. "What a wonderful example of domesticity! I wish for thousands more like it. I will take care of tidying up while you get ready."

"We must make a brief stop on the way," Isabella said. "It is nearby." When she saw the concerned look on my face, she added, "Don't worry. Just the two of us. And one other to bless us on our journey."

I nodded.

Ten minutes later, we emerged from the hut. The moon, nearly full, had risen, producing more light than I wished for. Isabella took my hand and led me east. After four hundred meters, we arrived at a small cemetery and proceeded to its northern edge. In the moonlight, I made out the etching in limestone:

Yusouf Elias
December 20, 1946–June 1, 1958
Return now, child, to the embrace of angels.

Isabella got down on her knees in front of the grave, and I knelt by her side. She bowed her head and prayed, her lips moving without sound. When she lifted her eyes, I reached over to clasp her hand.

I whispered, "I hoped that, despite my absence from his life, I might prove myself worthier of this child than my own father was of me. I sent spirit messages of love to both of you every night."

"He must have received those messages. In so many ways, Yusouf was your son."

I squeezed her hand. "I am sorry, Isabella. I wish I had been able to protect him."

She kissed her fingers and touched the inscription on the tombstone. Then she rose and brushed the dust off her skirt. "There was nothing you could do,

Joseph. I learned to stop blaming myself long ago. And now, he will protect us. Lead on."

I took Isabella's hand, and we ventured into open country. We walked along goat paths at a deliberate pace, navigating by the North Star on a course due east into the foothills. Our destination was an isolated hilltop on the south bank of the Awali River, known as Roûs al Franj. The peak was situated at the south end of a bend in the west-flowing Awali. I had hiked there three years earlier on a weekend excursion in the company of some Lebanese military officers. At the time, I had noted that the site was perfect for a pickup such as the one I contemplated. The nearest settlement, a tiny cluster of houses, was over one kilometer away. There were no army or militia installations nearby. It was the kind of place where the most exciting thing that ever happened was the annual shearing of sheep.

I held Isabella's hand as we climbed, two middle-aged trekkers stumbling their way up rocky inclines in the moonlight, the river gorge on our left. We spoke softly. I refused to tell Isabella anything more about myself, promising to do so later. This left her no choice but to report to me everything that had transpired since she had left the convent. I seethed anew at the recollection of her humiliation by the abbess. I wept at her abandonment by her family, and at her years of loneliness. About forty-five minutes into our journey, when we had progressed about two kilometers, the faint rumble of engines rose from the west. I looked back and pulled field glasses out of my satchel, training them on Isabella's hut at the north edge of the populated area.

Four pickup trucks circled Isabella's shack, their headlamps shining harsh light on the entrance and windows. Men armed with rifles stood by the trucks, aiming at the building.

"What do you see?" Isabella asked.

"Trouble," I muttered. "I underestimated our time."

I handed her the binoculars and showed her how to adjust the focus. She spent some time gazing through the glasses, her mouth agape. Suddenly, she gasped, and I saw flashes of gunfire in the distance.

"What is that?" she cried out.

Several seconds later, staccato bursts reached our ears.

"Heavens!" Isabella shouted. "They will soil the laundry!"

I turned and hugged her tightly, lifting her off the ground. "What a woman!" I exclaimed. "Joking at a time like this!"

"Who is joking? They are leaving a mess in my house! What will people say?"

"Believe me, people will talk about more than the disorder in your house. Come, Isabella, we must move on." I retrieved the field glasses and replaced them in the satchel. Taking her hand, I led us forward at a brisker pace.

"Will they find us?"

"No. They have no idea where to look. They will search the beach, as they are aware that night landings occur from time to time. And they will raid every house within five hundred meters of yours. At daybreak, they will scour every inch of land in a twenty-kilometer radius, but by then, we will be far away. In the meantime, we must move more quickly. And silently. Let's go," I said, pointing east. "The future is that way."

The air chilled as we ascended. After about five hours of walking, we halted near the peak of Roûs al Franj. I looked at my watch. It was one o'clock in the morning.

"What now?" she whispered.

"We wait. One hour."

"How will we get out of this place?"

"You will see. Don't be frightened when it happens."

After a few minutes, Isabella spoke up: "What would you have done had I not agreed to come with you?"

"I would have reminded you of the many years neither of us has been at peace."

"But had I insisted on staying behind, what would have become of me?"

I chewed my lip. "You would have been safe."

"How would you have kept me safe?"

I was silent for a while, then answered, "I would have presented myself to the local PLO commander, confessed to everything, and sworn that you knew nothing of me from 1946 until today. Then, I would have broken this between my teeth." I reached into my pocket and withdrew a capsule. "Cyanide. It kills in seconds."

"Oh, Lord Jesus, help us!" she cried. But as she continued to gaze at me, her alarm gave way to a tentative smile. "A satisfactory answer." Then she grinned and her eyes glinted in the moonlight, and I saw again that unrestrainable substratum of enthusiasm. "I consent to leaving with you," she said.

"*Alhamdulillah*," I breathed.

About an hour later, we heard the thumping of helicopter rotors in the south. I led Isabella to the edge of a clearing near the top of the hill. I removed a flashlight from my bag, pointed it toward the south, and flashed it on and off four times. Thirty seconds later, the shadow of a Bell UH-1 helicopter descended from the sky and roared onto the hilltop, whipping up a ferocious wind as it landed. Soldiers jumped out of the open doors and took positions on either side, aiming their rifles into the void. I turned on the flashlight, pointed it toward the ground, seized Isabella's hand, and ran toward them. She screamed all the way.

Epilogue

We flew to an air force base in northern Israel, where a waiting sedan transported us to Tel Aviv. A male Mossad officer sat in front, next to the driver. Isabella slumped against me in the back seat, clasping my hand in her sleep. At six thirty in the morning, the car halted in front of an apartment building on Rothschild Boulevard. The Mossad officer escorted us up three flights to a furnished unit, handed me a set of keys, and instructed me to be ready at two thirty in the afternoon.

Isabella and I showered and slept, and awoke at noon to the rumble of traffic. I dressed in a fresh set of clothes in my size that had been laid out on the armoire. Isabella, a surprise guest, donned the clothes in which she had arrived. The apartment was stocked with the basics of a typical Israeli kitchen. Over a light lunch of pickled fish and crackers with chopped salad, I delivered a synopsis of my life since the day I had escaped the convent. Isabella punctuated my narrative with cries of *mon Dieu!* and *alhamdullilah*, and caressed my cheek and wept when I described the battle at Nabi Idris and my assassination of Professor Köhler. We were drinking coffee when the doorbell rang.

I opened the door to find the Mossad agent from the night before. A female companion stood at his side. I accompanied the man to HQ, while the second agent, a French-speaking officer, took Isabella shopping.

Arriving at the office, I was greeted by the Director, his deputy, and a handful of other officials. They debriefed me, and the chief handed me two letters. One was a reprimand listing my recent offenses: disobeying orders to leave Lebanon with the commando unit, forcing a risky cross-border helicopter mission, and bringing an unauthorized immigrant into the country. The other, time-stamped one hour after the first, was a commendation for extraordinary service. Both letters were taken from me as soon as I had read them, for they were classified.

Over the next three days, I attended several additional debriefings and a reception in my honor. Isabella was given free rein to explore Tel Aviv. It took approximately seventy-two hours for everyone around us to move on to the next assignment, the next threat, the next crisis. Isabella and I discussed our plans. I would receive a state-funded pension, sufficient for us to live in comfort anywhere in Israel. I called Kibbutz Gan Miriam and, finding that I was still a member in good standing, arranged to return the following afternoon.

Isabella and I were assigned a small shack in the residential section of the settlement, next door to Yoram, now fully retired. Yoram stood in the roundabout as the car carrying us from Tel Aviv pulled onto the grounds. His hair was gray and his face creased with age and a lifetime of labor in the outdoors, but he retained his wiry energy. He seized me and shuddered in my arms, soaking my shoulder with his tears. He escorted us to our one-bedroom dwelling and gave us a tour of our new home. Then he exited, returning a few minutes later with the chest I had given him for safekeeping all those years before. Isabella and I examined its contents—artifacts that defined the only part of me that seemed real: a couple of work shirts and pants, a few favorite books, a photo of me with Gidi, my hero from the Palmach, and at the bottom of the trunk, my medals and commendations.

"*Mon Dieu*," Isabella whispered. "Looking at this collection, one might conclude that your life began when you were sixteen and ended three years later. The sum of your belongings fills less than half a crate."

I nodded. "And yours fits into a small box." I was referring to the collection of mementos she had brought with her from Lebanon. It contained a pocket-size prayer book, a lock of Yusouf's hair, some drawings and poems, and cards Yusouf had written to his mother.

She scowled, then brightened. "One of the nice things about memory is that it occupies no space at all, and all the space in the world." Her kiss lingered on my lips. "My life ended at thirty and only now has begun again," she said. "Thank the Lord, we have been granted the opportunity to build our lives anew, you and I."

"What is the foundation for this new life of mine you wish to build?" I muttered. "A boyhood marred by abandonment, an adulthood tainted with deception . . . and three years of belonging?"

"No. That is not the foundation."

I felt myself falling into the gray of her eyes.

Isabella found work as a French and Arabic teacher in the regional high school, and I rotated among the various agricultural posts in Gan Miriam. I volunteered as the kibbutz librarian, securing a budget to assemble what would become the largest book collection in the Galilee outside of government and academia. My monthly pension was deposited into the kibbutz's community fund. We subsisted on love and the fulfilment of basic needs, and never spent more than a few hours parted from each other's company.

We learned that the abbess resigned her position two days after I confronted her at the mission. It was not difficult for my contacts at the Mossad to track her down. She relocated to a nunnery in France and was found dead in her bed a few months later. The words *I am not a thief* were scrawled in charcoal all over the walls of her room.

Within a week of arriving at Gan Miriam, I wrote Magdalena a letter into which I secreted the key to my safe deposit box in Beirut, with instructions to withdraw all the cash. She was to take as much as was needed to support her education and living expenses, and the remainder was used to establish the Yusouf Elias Foundation for the education of Lebanese orphans at the convent in Bhamdoun. Magdalena became the foundation's director after obtaining her degree in social work from the American University of Beirut.

About a decade after leaving Lebanon, the Mossad considered it safe enough to allow Isabella and me to take a holiday in Europe. We met Magdalena in Amsterdam, and I revealed to her the truth about her origins.

I never again contacted my mother or inquired about her fate.

A few months after Isabella and I settled into kibbutz life, in October 1973, the Yom Kippur War erupted. The surprise attack by Egypt and Syria in the Sinai and Golan stunned the Israeli security establishment, which had retained only skeleton crews at the front for the holiday. Were it not for the valor of a small number of tank crews and infantry units, who repelled the onslaught of hundreds of Syrian tanks and thousands of enemy foot soldiers, the Galilee, including Kibbutz Gan Miriam, would have fallen. The intelligence failure was a national trauma that persisted for decades after the war. The finding of the commission of inquiry that no actionable information might have been collected in Lebanon only partially assuaged my feelings of guilt at not having done more to anticipate the assault.

I fulfilled a promise to myself and obtained a PhD in Middle Eastern history from the University of Haifa. I am the author of three scholarly books, including one on relations between the region's religious factions since the time of Jesus, coauthored with Imam Amr Abu Khadr al Hamdani and a Christian theologian from the University of Haifa. The imam and I taught classes on coexistence to the Jewish and Arab children of the Galilee until his death in 1995.

Every year, on the anniversary of that calamitous day at Nabi Idris, Isabella and I joined a group of veterans and their families, now swelled to hundreds, for a commemorative service at the battleground. As a minor celebrity in security circles, I was asked one year to give a memorial lecture, which I entitled "By Their Deaths They Commanded Us to Live: Some Thoughts on a Pathway to Peace with our Arab Neighbors."

Wars between Israel and its neighboring countries came to a practical end with the peace agreement with Egypt in 1979 and with Jordan in 1994. The conflict with Palestinian Arabs continues to this day, with no foreseeable end to the cycle of violence. I have no regrets and no solutions. I fought and killed and was prepared to die to defend a homeland for the Jewish people, a tiny nation resurrected from the ashes of history and assailed by hostile states and terrorist organizations. It was my remarkable fate to participate in the return of the Jews to Zion, foretold over twenty-five hundred years ago by the prophet Isaiah: *And it shall come to pass on that day, the Lord shall set His hand to recover the remnant of His people.*

Yet my dreams for the State of Israel cannot be satisfied until the remainder of the prophecy is fulfilled: *And the wolf shall dwell with the lamb, and the leopard shall lie down with the kid ... None shall hurt or destroy in all My holy mountain.* When peace finally comes, it will provide Israel with security and Palestinian Arabs with the things all people need: opportunity, self-determination, and expansive rights. I only wish I might have witnessed it during my lifetime.

As I write these sentences, I am dying, having reached almost ninety years, the age the Talmud refers to as *the bent body*. I am ready. My alternate selves all departed many years ago: Khalil Haddad, Charles Choucair, Mousa Ilbawi, Fadi Amin, and others. I was relieved to discover, a few years after returning to Gan Miriam, that only Joseph Friedmann resided in my consciousness. But now, each word that leaves my pen seems to take with it a small measure of my life force. Soon, nothing will be left to me but my pain. Where will Joseph Friedmann go after the electrical impulses that generate my thoughts cease to flow, my heart stops beating, and my lungs no longer pump air? Perhaps I will rejoin my Isabella, who died from breast cancer in 1998 at the age of seventy. Perhaps I shall meet the child I never saw in life.

During one of his final visits to Gan Miriam, Shmuel Mizrahi observed that a human life resembles a bank account whose balance is determined by the deposits and withdrawals made over the course of time. Now that my account is nearly drained, I resist the inclination to return to an old grievance. I have told you all. Search through the ledger and tell me: When and where were the deposits made upon which I might have drawn for the first half of my life? Was there more than abandonment, sacrifice, and loss until Isabella returned to replenish the account? How did I survive so long with my balance in deficit?

One morning, as Isabella's life was ebbing away, I entered the bedroom in our little shack and parted the blinds. The sun streamed through the eastern window. I checked her IV bag and sat in a chair beside her bed. Isabella laid her hand on mine, the veins coursing through skin creased and thin as parchment. Her cheeks were hollow, her face ashen, her flesh little more than veneer over bones. Her hair had turned gray years before, yet the curls still peeked out from the sides of the kerchief with which she covered her head. "I love this life you have gifted me," she whispered through cracked lips, her eyes sparkling. "I love this place." She was at that moment, as she has always been for me, the most beautiful creature in the world.

"I am tired, Yosef. It is time for you to send me on my way."

I shook my head. "I cannot." I sobbed, an ache welling behind my eyes and constricting my throat.

"You must find the strength. We have talked about it. You can do this."

I nodded. A lifetime of dammed emotion streamed from my eyes. Tears blurred my vision and my hands shook, but after several attempts, I was able to draw morphine from a vial into a syringe. I sat beside her and prepared to inject the solution into her IV port.

"Are you happy?" she whispered.

"Yes."

"When I am gone, I leave you with a single task, the one thing an extraordinary person living an extraordinary life has not yet mastered. Send your negativity away with me. You know the truth. There were people. People who made deposits on your behalf. A mother who recognized her incapacity and found someone else to raise you. The abbess of blessed memory, who created a safe haven for you. The authors of the books who sustained you in your loneliness. The doctor, who inspired you until the moment when, enfeebled by his own flaws, he failed you, and who later redeemed himself by sacrificing his own life in the belief he might save yours. A nation that welcomed orphans into its midst, raised them as its own, and cared for them when they were wounded. The people who merited your love—Gidi, Yoram, Shmuel Mizrahi. And, of course . . ."

And with these words, my Isabella said no more. She gazed into my eyes and nodded. I pushed the barrel of the syringe through, and bent over to kiss her cheek. I sat in the chair at her side, rested my head upon her chest, and wept, remaining in that position for almost an hour as her breathing subsided and her heart beat ever more faintly, until it stopped.

All flesh is grass, Isaiah tells us, *and all its goodness is like the flower of the field*. I have always been aware of my impermanence. There were times during my life when I felt almost translucent. Perhaps that is what gave me the ability to blend in anywhere. I tried to contribute to the survival of a people who, throughout most of history, has had one foot on the threshold of annihilation. In the process, I lied. I was vengeful. I begrudged people who wronged me. And now, as my horizons contract upon me, wisdom, memory, identity, love, and truth converge to the point where I can no longer distinguish among them.

No matter. The work is not mine to finish. As I wither away like grass, I find satisfaction in believing I made a difference.

Gan Miriam, Israel
January 2021

Author's Note

The Wolf Shall Dwell with the Lamb is a work of fiction. The characters, places, and events portrayed in the novel are products of the author's imagination or have been used fictitiously. Nonetheless, I have attempted to place Joseph Friedmann's story within a credible version of the history of the Middle East in the twentieth century. I am well aware that the facts of this history, not to mention their interpretation and contextualization, are the subjects of fierce dispute.

As omnipotent sovereign of the parallel universe Joseph inhabits, I have arranged for him to participate in several historical events resembling ones that occurred in our world. There really were Jewish children raised in Lebanese Maronite convents. My wife's mother was one of them. There really was a Night of the Bridges during which the span over Nahal 'Ayoun was blown up by the *Palmach*, the "Strike Companies" of the nascent Jewish army in Palestine. There really was a three-stage assault on a former British police station in the Galilee, in which twenty-eight *Palmachniks* fell. There really was an Arab missile program led by German rocket scientists. There really was an assault by Israeli forces against Palestinian terrorist organizations in the heart of Beirut in the spring of 1973.

In each of these instances and in others that appear throughout the novel, I have used my imagination to embellish kernels of truth to varying and, in some cases, great extents in service of the narrative. Any inaccuracies, omissions, or inventions out of whole cloth are mine. I caution readers not to extrapolate injudiciously from Joseph's world to our own. Those who wish to enhance their knowledge regarding the history of the Middle East should seek out researched and referenced works on the topic.

A partial list of my own sources (among dozens of references) includes the following:

My research on Syria and Lebanon was greatly enhanced by the book *Syria and Lebanon* by N. A. Ziadeh (edition published in 1968).

Much of the information about the Palmach is taken from their official website, available in Hebrew or English at https://www.palmach.org.il/.

Benny Morris's excellent book *1948: A History of the First Arab-Israeli War* provides a thoroughly referenced account of the events surrounding the establishment of the State of Israel. The book takes a hard look at the mythology that has arisen around Israel's War of Independence, referred to by Palestinians as the *Nakba* (catastrophe). Among other topics, Morris documents instances of war crimes committed by the Jewish side, which, though rare, are lasting stains on Israel's military. The book also addresses the displacement of large swaths of the Palestinian Arab population. For many years, this displacement was explained away in Israeli accounts of the conflict by a convenient simplification, in some cases true and in others fictional: that these Palestinians either left their homes and lands voluntarily or were instructed by their leaders to do so, in order to give Arab armies free rein to execute the war.

Two invaluable references for the history and tactics of Israel's secret services are *Spies of No Country: Secret Lives at the Birth of Israel* by Matti Friedman, which details the origins of Israel's *mista'arabin* ("those who become as Arabs"); and *Rise and Kill First: The Secret History of Israel's Targeted Assassinations* by Ronen Bergman. These two well-researched books tell the incredible-yet-true chronicle of Israel's Mossad and Shin Bet and their predecessors, the Arab Section and The Dawn unit.

My work colleague, toxicologist Jerrold B. Leikin, MD, helped me identify a serviceable "knockout drug" that was physiologically, historically, geographically, and literarily appropriate. I was also aided by an article entitled "History of Anesthesia in Lebanon & at the American University of Beirut" by Fouad Salim Haddad and Musa K. Muallem, published in 2004 in the *Middle East Journal of Anesthesiology*.

Certain facts regarding the border between Lebanon and Palestine were extracted from a paper entitled "The Israel-Lebanon Border Enigma" by David

Eshel, published in IBRU's quarterly *Boundary and Security Bulletin* in the Winter 2000–2001 issue.

I owe an incalculable debt to the members of my writers' critique group, who provided unflinching feedback on every word of this novel, and without whom I would never have had the confidence to carry it to its conclusion: Adrianne Hayward, Anna DaSilva, Fred Fitzsimmons, Judy Panko-Reis, Peter Hoppock, and Roberta Liebler.

Too many readers to list previewed this work, providing suggestions and encouragement. Thank you.

Thanks and love to my children: Rachel, Alec, Yoni, Abby, Aviva, and Shira, and one grandchild (so far), Asher. What a joy and inspiration they are to me!

My wife, Arica, is the most beautiful and intelligent person in the world. I don't think I am revealing any secrets when I acknowledge that, despite many differences between the two women, she is the inspiration for Isabella, Joseph's one and only true love, and his North Star.

The title *The Wolf Shall Dwell with the Lamb* is taken from the prophecy of Isaiah, depicting an era of such pervasive tranquility that predator and prey live side by side in peace. Millions of people in the Middle East and around the world yearn for the arrival of that age. Yet the region continues to know bloodshed and destruction, displacement and alienation. This heartbreaking reality continues at the time of this writing, September 2025, on a scale that seems more traumatic than ever before during the long history of the conflict between Jews and Arabs in the Holy Land. Both the author and the protagonist of *The Wolf Shall Dwell with the Lamb* long for a day when, as improbable as it seems at the moment, peace and prosperity will come to all decent people in the Middle East. May we see it in our lifetimes.